GIRLS OF PAPER AND FIRE

GIRLS
OF
PAPER
AND
FIRE

NATASHA NGAN

FOREWORD BY JAMES PATTERSON

JIMMY Patterson Books
Little, Brown and Company
New York Boston London

JIMMY Patterson Books / Little, Brown and Company
Hachette Book Group
1290 Avenue of the Americas, New York, NY 10104
JimmyPatterson.org

First Paperback Edition: October 2019
Originally published in hardcover by JIMMY Patterson Books, / Little, Brown and Company, November 2018.

JIMMY Patterson Books is an imprint of Little, Brown and Company, a division of Hachette Book Group, Inc. The Little, Brown name and logo are trademarks of Hachette Book Group, Inc. The JIMMY Patterson Books® name and logo are trademarks of JBP Business, LLC.

The publisher is not responsible for websites (or their content) that are not owned by the publisher.

The Hachette Speakers Bureau provides a wide range of authors for speaking events. To find out more, go to hachettespeakersbureau.com or call (866) 376-6591.

Library of Congress Cataloging-in-Publication Data
Names: Ngan, Natasha, author.
Title: Girls of paper and fire / Natasha Ngan; foreword by James Patterson.
Description: First edition. | New York; Boston: JIMMY Patterson Books, Little, Brown and Company, 2018. | Summary: When Lei, seventeen, is stolen from her home to become one of nine Paper Girls, the Demon King's concubines, she proves to be more fire than paper.
Identifiers: LCCN 2018024788| ISBN 9780316561365 (hc) | ISBN 9780316530408 (Barnes & Noble Exclusive Edition) | ISBN 978031645352-3 (Barnes & Noble Signed Edition | ISBN 9780316452205 (international tpb) | ISBN 9780316561358 (tpb)
Subjects: | CYAC: Courtesans—Fiction. | Social classes—Fiction. | Kings, queens, rulers, etc.—Fiction. | Revolutions—Fiction. | Imaginary creatures—Fiction. | Fantasy.
Classification: LCC PZ7.N48845 Gir 2018 | DDC [Fic]—dc23
LC record available at https://lccn.loc.gov/2018024788

Printing 6, 2021

LSC-C

Printed in the United States of America

To Alex,
This book is about brave, brilliant girls,
and you are one of the bravest,
most brilliant there is. Thank you, always.

Please be aware that this book contains
scenes of violence and sexual assault.

FOREWORD

O N OCCASION, I COME UPON THE literary equivalent of a priceless hidden treasure—and it's *exhilarating*. Even as a writer myself, I can't begin to describe how terrific it makes me feel.

I started JIMMY Patterson Books with the mission to give young readers the kinds of books they really want, but the exceptional ones are hard to find. One of the joys of being a publisher is that I get to read many stories, and then bring the best ones to life as books. When I first read *Girls of Paper and Fire*, I knew I had stumbled upon something special.

With her lyrical voice and epic imagination, Natasha Ngan has created a vivid world where the line between people and animals is blurred, but the consequences of love, power, and revenge are clear. *Girls of Paper and Fire* is many stories in one—a portrait of an oppressed girl finding her strength, a forbidden romance in the unlikeliest circumstances, a tale of injustice that must be made right, an homage to the author's multicultural upbringing. Somehow, Natasha brilliantly weaves together these different threads into a single literary work of art.

I believe *Girls of Paper and Fire* is one of the most important novels that we have published at JIMMY Patterson Books. With its heartfelt inclusivity and emotionally-charged yet sensitively handled scenes, Natasha's spellbinding own-voices story offers illumination to all who read it.

I'm fortunate to have played a small part in bringing this book to life for you.

—James Patterson

THE HIDDEN PALACE

Shadow Passage

GHOST COURT

Royal Palace

ROYAL COURT

Gardens

Paper House

MILITARY COURT

River of Infinity

WOMEN'S COURT

INNER

MORTAL COURT

COURTS

Night Houses

Floating Hall

INDUSTRY COURT

CEREMONY COURT

CITY COURT

TEMPLE COURT

Gates

PLASSE

The Great Bamboo Forest of Han

CASTES

At night, the heavenly rulers dreamed of colors, and into the day those colors bled onto the earth, raining down onto the paper people and blessing them with the gifts of the gods. But in their fear, some of the paper people hid from the rain and so were left untouched. And some basked in the storm, and so were blessed above all others with the strength and wisdom of the heavens.

—The Ikharan Mae Scripts

Paper caste—*Fully human, unadorned with any animal-demon features, and incapable of demon abilities such as flight.*

Steel caste—*Humans endowed with partial animal-demon qualities, both in physicality and abilities.*

Moon caste—*Fully demon, with whole animal-demon features such as horns, wings, or fur on a humanoid form, and complete demon capabilities.*

—the Demon King's postwar *Treaty on the Castes*

GIRLS
OF
PAPER
AND
FIRE

THERE IS A TRADITION IN OUR kingdom, one all castes of demon and human follow. We call it the Birth-blessing. It is such an old, deep-rooted custom that it's said even our gods themselves practiced it when they bore our race onto the earth. When babies die before their first year, there are whispers like leaves fluttering darkly on the wind: the ceremony was performed too late; the parents must have spoken during it; the shaman who executed the blessing was unskilled, a fake.

Coming from the lowest caste—Paper caste, fully human—my parents had to save for the full nine months after the news of my mother's pregnancy. Though I've never seen a Birth-blessing cere-mony, I've imagined my own so many times that it feels almost like a memory, or some half remembered dream.

Picture smoke-cut night and darkness like a heavy black hand cupped round the world. Crackling fire. Standing before the flames—a shaman, his leathery skin webbed with tattoos, teeth sharpened to wolflike points. He's bent over the naked form of a newborn, just hours old. She's crying. On the other side of the fire, her parents watch in silence, hands clasped so tightly their knuckles are white. The shaman's eyes roll as he chants a dao, painting its characters in the air with his fingers, where they hang above the baby, glowing softly before fading away.

As he comes to the crest of the prayer, a wind picks up. The grass stirs in a feathery rustle. Faster and faster the shaman chants, and louder and louder the rustle and the wind, until the fire whips upward, a whorl of orange-red flame dancing high into the sky before flashing suddenly out.

Blackness.

The starlit night.

Then the shaman reaches into the air where the fire had been for the object floating in its wake: a small, egglike golden pendant. But the pendant isn't what's important. What's important is what the pendant hides within.

The baby's fate. *My* fate.

Our kingdom believes words have power. That the characters of our language can bless or curse a life. Inside the pendant is a single character. One word that we believe will reveal a person's true destiny—and if my life will be blessed, as my parents hoped when they saved for my ceremony, or whether my fate is something far darker. Cursed years to be played out in fire and shadow.

In six months, when I turn eighteen, the pendant will open and its answer will finally be revealed.

ONE

OUR SHOP IS BUSY THIS MORNING. Not even noon yet and it's already packed with customers, the room bright with chatter, Tien's brusque voice cutting through the thick summer air. Sunlight streams in through the slatted windows, drowsy with cicada song. Sandals slap on the floorboards. Beneath it all, like the shop's familiar heartbeat, comes the bubble of the mixing barrels where we brew our herbal medicines. The six tubs are lined along the back of the store, so big they reach my shoulders. Five are full of pungent mixtures. The sixth is empty, filled instead with me—admittedly *also* pungent after an hour's hard work scrubbing dried residue from the buckled wood.

"Almost done, little nuisance?"

I'm working at a particularly stubborn stain when Tien's face appears over the edge of the barrel. Feline eyes rimmed with black; graying hair flowing softly over pointed cat ears. She regards me with her head cocked.

I swipe the back of my hand over my forehead. *Little nuisance.* She's been calling me that for as long as I can recall.

"I'm seventeen, Tien," I point out. "Not little anymore."

"Well," she says with a click of her tongue. "Still a nuisance."

"I wonder where I get it from."

A smirk rises up to challenge my own. "I'll pretend you're talking about your father. *Aiyah*, where is that lazy man? He was meant to refill our stock of monsoon berries an hour ago!" She waves a hand. "Go fetch him. Mistress Zembi is waiting for her consultation."

"Only if you say please," I retort, and her ears twitch.

"Demanding for a Paper caste, aren't you?"

"You're the Steel with a Paper boss."

She sighs. "And I regret it every day."

As she bustles off to deal with a customer, I smile despite myself at the proud flick of her neat lynx ears. Tien has worked for us for as long as I can remember, more family now than shop hand despite our caste differences. Because of that, sometimes it's easy to forget that there *are* differences between us. But while my father and I are Paper caste, Tien belongs to the middle caste, Steel. Somewhere between my plain human body and the animal-like strength of Moon castes, Steel castes have elements of both, making them a strange meeting point between human and demon, like a drawing only halfway finished. As with most Steels, Tien has just touches of demon: a tapered feline maw; the graying amber cat's fur wrapped around her neck and shoulders, like a shawl.

As she greets the customer, Tien's hands automatically pat down that messy ruff of fur where it pokes from the collar of her samfoo shirt. But it just sticks straight back up.

My lips quirk. It must have been a prank by the gods to give someone as fussy as her such unruly hair.

I climb over the side of the tub and catch a better look at the woman Tien is talking to. Her long black hair is pulled back, twining past a pair of elegant deer antlers as slender as vine. Another Steel demon. My eyes travel over her elegant kebaya glittering with silver embroidery. It's clear that she belongs to an affluent family. The jewels dangling from her earlobes alone would keep our shop running for a year.

As I'm wondering why someone like her has come to our shop—she must be from out of town; no one here has that kind of money—her gaze glides past Tien and catches mine.

Her eyes grow wide. "So it's true."

I just make out her murmur over the noise of the shop. My face flushes.

Of course. She heard the rumors.

I turn away, ducking through the bead-curtained doorway to the back rooms of our old shop building. The deer-woman's elegance has made me extra aware of the state I'm in. Clumps of dirt cling to my clothes—a pair of loose sand-colored trousers and a wrap shirt knotted at the waist with a frayed sash—and my ankles are soaked with the camphor liquid I was using to clean the mixing barrel. Stray hairs stick to my cheeks with sweat. Sweeping them back, I retie my ponytail, and my mind slips for a moment, remembering.

Other fingers looping a red ribbon through my hair.

A smile like sunshine. Laughter even brighter.

Strange, how grief works. Seven years on and some days I struggle to remember her face, while other times my mother seems so real to me that I almost expect her to amble in through the front door, smelling like peony petals in the rain, a laugh on her lips and a kiss for Baba and me.

"She's gone," I tell myself roughly. "And she's not coming back."

With a shake of my head, I continue down the corridor and out onto the sunlit veranda. Our garden is narrow and long, bordered by a mossy wall. An old fig tree dapples the grass with shade. The summer warmth heightens the fragrances of our herb plot, the tangled patchwork of plants running down the center of the garden, familiar scents rising from it to tease my nose: chrysanthemum, sage, ginger. Charms threaded along wire to keep the birds away chime in the breeze.

A cheerful-sounding bark draws my attention. My father is crouched in the grass a few feet away. Bao wriggles happily at his toes as my father scratches the little dog's belly and feeds him scraps of dried mango, his favorite treat.

At my footsteps, my father quickly hides the fruit behind his back. Bao lets out an indignant bark. Bouncing up, he snatches the last piece of mango from my father's fingers before running to me, stubbed tail wagging victoriously.

I squat down, fingers finding the sensitive spot behind his ear to tickle. "Hello, greedy," I laugh.

"About what you just saw…" my father starts as he comes over.

I shoot him a sideways look. "Don't worry, Baba. I won't tell Tien."

"Good," he says. "Because then I'd have to tell her how you over-slept this morning and forgot to pick up that batch of galangal Master Ohsa is keeping for us."

Gods. I completely forgot.

I spring to my feet. "I'll go and get it now," I say, but my father shakes his head.

"It's not urgent, dear. Go tomorrow."

"Well," I reply with a knowing smile, "Mistress Zembi is here for her consultation, and that *is* urgent. So unless you want Tien to threaten to skin you alive…"

He shudders. "Don't remind me. The things that woman can do with a fish-gutting knife."

Laughing, we head back into the house, our steps falling in line. For a moment, it's almost like before—when our family was still whole, and our hearts. When it didn't hurt to think of my mother, to whisper her name in the middle of the night and know she can't answer.

But despite his joking, Baba's smile doesn't quite reach his eyes, and it reminds me that I'm not the only one haunted by their memories.

I was born on the first day of the New Year, under the watchful gaze of the full moon. My parents named me Lei, with a soft rising tone. They told me they chose it because the word makes your mouth form a smile, and they wanted to smile every time they thought of me. Even when I'd accidentally knocked over a tray of herbs or let Bao in to paw muddy footprints across the floor, the corners of their mouths couldn't help but tuck up, no matter how loudly they shouted.

But these past seven years, even my name hasn't been able to make my father smile often enough.

I look a lot like her, my mother. I catch Baba startling some mornings when I come down, my raven hair long and loose, my short frame silhouetted in the doorway. Though neither of my parents knew where I inherited my eyes.

How did they react when they first saw them? What did they say when baby-me opened her eyes to reveal luminous, liquid gold?

For most, my eye color is a sign of luck—a gift from the Heavenly Kingdom. Customers request for me to make their herbal mixtures, hoping my involvement will make them more potent. Even demons visit our shop occasionally, like the deer-woman today, lured by the rumor of the human girl with golden eyes.

Tien always laughs about that. "They don't believe you're pure Paper," she tells me conspiratorially. "They say you must be part demon to have eyes the color of the new year's moon."

What I don't tell her is that sometimes I wish I *were* part demon.

On my rare days off, I head into the valleys surrounding our village to watch the bird-form clan that lives in the mountains to the north. Though they're too far to be anything more than silhouetted shapes, dark cutouts of wings spread in motion, in my mind's eye I make out every detail. I paint their feathers in silvers and pearls, sketch the light of the sun on their wing tips. The demons soar through the sky over the valley, riding the wind in effortless movements as graceful as dance, and they look so free it aches some part deep in me.

Even though it isn't fair, I can't help but wonder whether, if Mama had been born with wings, she'd have escaped from wherever she was taken to and flown back to us by now.

Sometimes I watch the sky, just waiting, and hoping.

Over the next few hours, the bubble of the mixing pots and Bao's little barks play a familiar soundtrack while we work. As usual, my father takes consultations with new clients and meets with farmers and rare-plant traders from out of town, Tien deals with the general running of the store, and all the odd jobs nobody wants to do are handed to me. Tien frequently bustles over to chide me on the roughness of my chopped herbs and could I *be* any slower when picking up a customer's package from the storeroom? Or do I need reminding that she's a distant descendant of the legendary Xia warriors, so if I don't work any harder she'll be forced to practice her deadly martial arts skills on me?

"Still sounds a lot more fun than this," I grumble as I swelter in the storeroom sorting out deliveries—though I wait until she's out of earshot before saying it.

My last task of the day is refilling the herb boxes lining the walls of the store that contain ingredients for our medicines. Hundreds of them are stacked from floor to ceiling. Behind the countertop that rings the room, a ladder on metal rollers runs along the walls to access the boxes. I slide the ladder to the back wall and climb halfway up, arms aching from the day's work. I'm just reaching for a box marked GINSENG ROOTS, my thoughts drifting to what Tien will be cooking for dinner, when a noise sounds in the distance.

A low, carrying horn blow.

At once, everything falls quiet. Conversations, the slap of sandals, even the simmer of the mixing barrels seems to drop. All thoughts of food are whipped away as I freeze where I am, arm still outstretched. Only my mind moves, lurching back, returning to that day.

To fire.

To claws, and screaming, and the feel of my mother's fingers being torn from mine.

For a few moments, nothing happens. It's just long enough to hesitate. For a flutter of doubt to lift a hopeful wing. Then the horn sounds again, closer this time—and with it comes the pound of hooves.

Horses, moving fast. They draw nearer, their heavy hoof-fall growing louder and louder, until the noise of it is almost deafening, and all of a sudden hulking shadows in the street block the windows at the front of the shop, casting the room into darkness.

Distorted shadows, like the nightmare version of what a human should be.

Stillness, and the dark pulse of terror. A baby wails in a house nearby. From further away comes a dog bark—Bao. A shiver runs down my back. He went off a while ago, probably to the food stalls to beg for treats or play with the children who ruffle his hair and giggle when he licks their faces.

"Lei."

My father has moved to the bottom of the ladder. His voice is low, a rough whisper. He holds out his hand. Despite the hard set of his jaw, his face has drained.

I step down from the ladder and weave my fingers through his, the quick trip of his pulse at his wrist a mirror to mine. Because the last time we heard the call of this horn was the night my mother was taken. And if that's what the Demon King's men stole from us then, what might they possibly take from us *this* time?

TWO

THE THUD OF HOOF-FALL OUTSIDE IS loud in the silence. Every detail carries: the crunch of dirt, the creak of leather armor as the riders dismount. The horses snort and stamp, but it's easy to tell the sound of their hooves apart from that of their owners. Though lighter, their riders' steps are deliberate. Measured. They prowl slowly up and down the street, clearly searching for something.

Not us, I think, cupping the thought like a prayer.

After just a few minutes, the figures come to a stop right outside the shop. Voices sound—deep, male.

Demon.

Even without the warning of the horn, I'd be certain of it. There is strength, a power in their voices.

These are voices that *bite.*

"This is it?"

"Yes, General."

"It doesn't look like much. The sign is broken."

"The usual Paper negligence. I assure you, General, it's the right place."

A pause, fierce as a growl. "It had better be."

There's movement, and then our front door slams open, the entrance bells crying.

The effect is instant. As the soldiers shoulder their way inside, panic floods the shop, customers dropping to the floor in deep bows, knocking things over in their rush, the air filled with whimpers and whispered prayers. Something ceramic shatters nearby. I flinch at the sound, then again as my father throws an arm out to push me behind him.

"Bow!" he urges.

The demons advance. Yet despite the weight in my chest, despite the whoosh of blood in my ears, I don't budge. The fear might be strong.

But my hatred is stronger.

Soldiers took my mother. Moon caste soldiers like these.

It's only when my father says my name under his breath, more plea than command, that I finally lower. Most of my hair has loosened from its ponytail after the day's work, and it falls forward past my ears as I fold stiffly at the waist, exposing the pale arch of the back of my neck, almost like an arrowmark. I dig my fingernails into my hands to stop from covering it.

When I straighten, my father is still blocking me from view. I shift carefully to peer past his shoulder, my heart clamoring as I get a proper look at the soldiers.

There are three of them, so big they seem to take up the whole shop. All three are Moon caste, alien to me with their beastlike forms—still recognizably human in shape and proportion, but more bizarre for it, the melding of human and animal creating something that seems even more foreign. Because of our shop's popularity, I've had some exposure to demons, but it's mostly been Steel castes, their bodies for the most part human, touches here and there of demon details woven into the fabric of their skin like adornments. A spark of jackal eyes; rounded bear ears; the smooth curve of wolf incisors. Tien's familiar lynx features. Any Moon castes I did meet were simply not like...*this*.

These demons have stepped right out of my worst memories, nightmares made solid.

The bull-form in the middle is largest and evidently the highest ranking—the General. The bulk of him, the sheer weight in those boulderlike muscles, sends a pulse of something chilled down my veins. He wears a plum-colored tunic and wide trousers, a leather belt slung round his hips. His short bull horns are roped with charms and talismans. Snaking all the way from his left ear to the opposite jaw, a scar twists the leathery skin of his face out of shape, pulling his smile into a sneer.

I get a sudden surge of gratitude toward whoever made that mark.

Flanking him are an emerald-eyed tiger-form demon and an ugly reptilian soldier. Moss-colored scales wrap the lizard-man's long humanoid limbs like armor. His head cocks from side to side, eyes darting all around. A serpent tongue flicks out in a flash of pink.

Slowly, the General raises his hands, and as one the room braces. "Please, please," he says in a lazy drawl. "There's no need to be fearful, friends."

Friends. He speaks the word with a smile, but it tastes like poison.

"We know what happened here some years ago," he continues, "But I assure you, friends, we do not come with violent intent. I am General Yu of the Seventh Royal Battalion, the Demon King's finest and most honorable soldiers. Perhaps you've heard of us?" Silence stretches out, and his smile tightens. He settles one hand on the ivory hilt of the sword at his belt. "No matter. You will remember our name after today."

He steps closer, moving in a heavy bovine sway. I resist the urge to shrink back. Only the wooden counter separates him from Baba and me, and it barely reaches the General's waist. Slanting light catches on the charms dangling from his horns as he turns his head, sweeping his gaze over the shop. Then it lands on me.

General Yu freezes. Somehow this is scarier than if he'd shouted or made some move toward me; beneath his stillness, I sense something coiling in him. I jut my chin, staring back as defiantly as I can. But my cheeks are burning, my heart stuttering like hummingbird wings, and when he turns back to the room, his smile is satisfied. Gloating.

Something slithers in my belly. Why does he seem so pleased to see… *me?*

"W-welcome, General Yu." My father's voice sounds so small in the wake of the General's, its human timbre thin in comparison with the rich bass of bull. "It's a privilege to serve you and your men. If you tell us what errand has brought you here, we'll do our best to help you. Then we will let you on your way."

There's a quiet defiance in his wording. I want to throw my arms around him, kiss his cheeks, cheer him on.

Either ignoring or oblivious to my father's tone, the General throws his arms open. "Why, of course! We wouldn't wish to disrupt your busy day. It must be hard, running such a popular place like this without the help of your wife. I heard she was one of the women taken that day?" he adds casually.

Both Baba and I stiffen. On the far side of the room, Tien's fur bristles, a murderous look entering her eyes. For the first time I wish what she told me about her being a descendant of legendary warriors were true.

The General's fingers flex on the hilt of his sword. "Yet," he continues to the sniggers of his two soldiers, "you've at least had the help of your daughter. And she is a particularly… *lucky* girl from what the rumors say." His voice drops, just a whisper now but dangerous and bone-deep, every word clear in the hush. "Well, old man? May I see if the rumors are true? Will you show us this daughter of yours with paper skin and the stolen eyes of a demon?"

"The—the errand," my father starts in a desperate tone, but the soldiers are already moving forward.

"The girl *is* the errand," the General growls.

And lunges for me.

Everything happens at once—Tien's cry, Baba throwing me back, shouting, "Run!"

I spin on my heel as the General bounds onto the counter, shattering it beneath his weight.

There's a scream. Sounds of customers scrambling to get away. A tiger's deep-throated snarl. I lurch forward, making for the archway at the back of the shop, and dive through just as the General tears aside the beaded curtain.

Beads scatter everywhere. My feet skid, one sandal coming loose. But it's the sandal the General has grabbed for, and I crawl back to my feet, dashing down the corridor, hands flying out to brace myself as I take the turns flying.

The back of our house is narrow. The General's crashes and grunts fall behind me as he struggles to navigate the tight corners. Breathless, I race out into the golden blare of the lowering sun, leaping blindly down the steps of the porch.

A flock of birds scatter in a flurry of startled wing-flaps. I make it to the wall at the end of the garden just as a roar behind me tells me the General has made it out of the house. Using the web of leaves that cover the wall, I climb up, messily but fast. Vines slash my hands. Puffing, my palms crisscrossed red, I reach the top, hook an arm over, and hiss through my teeth as I pull, pull, *pull*—

Hands, on my legs.

I cling to the wall, but General Yu is too strong. I drop back, a hiss of air escaping my lips as I smash onto the ground.

In a second, the General is upon me.

"No!" I yell. I thrash against his ironlike grip, but he swipes me up easily, throwing me over his shoulder, and strides back to the house.

My head cracks against a wall as he squeezes through the narrow corridors. The world turns fuzzy. I catch a glimpse of the main shop room as we pass through: the broken counter, herbs strewn across the floor, pale faces peering from corners. Then we're outside.

I twist round to see where the General is taking me. A little way down the street is a large carriage, two horses strapped to its front. They're enormous, bigger than any breed I have seen, with wild eyes and foaming mouths, heads enclosed in metal muzzles. Two more are roped to the carriage on either side, I assume for the General's men.

"Lei!" comes a shout.

I crane my head round to see my father and Tien by the front of the shop. The lizard and tiger soldiers are holding them back.

"Baba!" I cry. There's blood on his brow.

His neck is strained, face flushed as he struggles to get free. "General Yu!" he calls after us. "Please, tell us what you want with my daughter!"

The lizard-man spits in his face. "What do you *think* he wants, old man?"

"Now, now, Sith," General Yu says. "You know it's not like that." Slowly, he turns and lowers me to the ground, clutching me to his side so tightly his fingers pinch my flesh through my clothes. "I am merely collecting your daughter for delivery," he tells my father. "I heard rumors of her pretty eyes and thought she would make the perfect gift for our Heavenly Master."

Baba's face falls. "You—you can't mean..."

"You should be smiling, old man. The girl is to become what so many in our kingdom dream for their own daughters. She'll live in the Hidden Palace of Han. Lead a privileged life of service to our gracious leader...outside of *and* in the royal bed."

Tien goes still.

"No," my father breathes.

The General gives my hair a ruffle. "Your own daughter, a Paper Girl. I bet you never dreamed you'd be so fortunate."

Paper Girl.

The phrase hangs in the air. It feels wrong, all angular and edges that don't fit together, because surely it can't be. Not a Paper Girl. Not me.

Before I can say anything, the sound of barking makes us all look round. A tiny figure sprints down the street toward us on stubby legs—white fur, gray spots.

My stomach drops. "Bao," I croak. Then, louder, "*Bao!* Inside, now!"

As usual, he ignores my orders. He skitters to a stop in front of us and sinks down on his front legs, baring his teeth.

The General smiles back, revealing his own.

"Hello, little one," he murmurs. He peers down his muzzled nose at Bao, who is skittering on his paws at the General's hooved feet, which are almost bigger than Bao himself and mounted with thick copper plates that look as though they could crush even a human skull in one stamp. "Have you come to say good-bye to your friend?"

He reaches out. Growling, Bao snaps at his hand.

The General's eyes cut to the lizard-form soldier as he withdraws. "Sith. Help him, would you?"

The reptile smirks. "Of course, General."

He reaches for the sword at his belt. There's the cry of steel, the flash of a blade through the air. In one fluid movement, Sith lunges forward and drives the point of his sword into Bao's belly. Then he raises the blade toward me, and my dog with it.

It's as though the world had suddenly tilted off-kilter. The ground, shifted. My heartbeat goes jagged, and it's as if I were floating, rising up and away from everything as, at the same time, everything spiraled closer toward me.

Bile lurches up my throat.

Bao.

Bao—who hasn't yet made a sound. For one desperate moment I convince myself that he's all right. That somehow his belly is hollow and the sword has lanced nothing but empty air, and in a minute he'll hop to the floor and wag his tail, run to Baba for treats, dance circles around Tien's legs. Life will be normal again, and this awful nightmare will be just that: a nightmare.

Something to wake from. To escape.

But then Bao begins to twitch and whimper. Blood wells at his wound. It runs down the blade, thick and dark, pooling around Sith's scaled fingers, where they grip the lacquered bone hilt.

"Better say good-bye, girl," the lizard hisses to me. A forked tongue skates over his lips. "This is the last you'll see of your family. And if you don't come quietly, this'll be how your father will end up, too, and that ugly old lynx-woman. Is that what you want?"

I wrench my gaze to where Baba and Tien are struggling against the tiger soldier's hold. My eyes meet my father's. I give him a half smile, and he stills, face slackening with something like hope.

"I love you," I whisper. Just as understanding sparks in his gaze, I turn to General Yu. I force out a deep exhale, blinking back tears. "I'll come quietly," I tell him.

"That's a good girl."

He pushes me into the carriage, so roughly I trip. Baba and Tien erupt with cries, pulling a ragged sob from me, and it takes everything I have not to look back as I climb onto the padded bench. The carriage heaves under the General's weight as he gets in beside me. Moments later the horses start to move, breaking into a loping canter that carries us quickly out of the village, my world once again crumbling around me to the sharp stench of bull demon and the sound of trampling hooves.

THREE

EVERYONE IN IKHARA KNOWS OF THE Paper Girls.

The tradition began two hundred years ago after the Night War, when the Bull King of Han, the central-most province in Ikhara, won control of the other seven, from desert-like Jana in the South to my home, Xienzo, in the North. Before, each province had its own sets of governing systems, its own laws and customs specific to their cultures. Some provinces were ruled by a dominant clan, while others were unstable landscapes of ever-shifting power plays between ambitious clan lords. And while Paper castes had always been viewed as lesser than demons, there was respect for the positions we held in society, the services and skills we offered. But after the Night War, the King imposed his rule on every province—and along with them, his prejudices. Royal soldiers patrolled the flatlands and plains, scoured villages and cities to dispense the new regulations. Demon-run businesses flourished; Paper caste families were pushed to the dirt. Within the centralized system, the larger cities grew ever richer and more powerful, while smaller settlements faded into servitude.

The years following the Night War were almost as dark as the ones they left behind. In the absence of the duels and political deliberations that would have once sorted temporary peace in a way all parties could respect, old resentments between clans grew. Long-standing rivalries continued to simmer unchallenged. And now there were additional uprisings and plays for power between the royal emissaries and the clans.

Order was restored the only way the King knew how.

Bloodshed.

To encourage union among the diverse clans and cultures, the court established a new custom. Each year, the King would select eight Paper caste girls as his courtesans. The court said that choosing girls of the lowest caste proved what a just ruler the King was, and the families of chosen girls were showered with gifts and wealth, ensuring they never had to work another day in their lives.

Tien told me once how families in provinces close to the royal heart of the kingdom, such as Rain and Ang-Khen, prepare their most beautiful daughters for the role from youth, even making underhanded deals to ensure the girls are remembered when the annual selection time comes.

In my village, the story of the Paper Girls is told in whispers behind closed doors. We lost too much in the raid seven years ago to want to share anything more with the court.

But perhaps the gods have forgotten us, or grown bored with our small corner of the kingdom. Because here I am, about to share the last thing I'd ever want to offer the King.

Myself.

For a long time, the General and I ride in silence. The carriage is luxuriously decorated, the bench adorned with perfumed cushions and silks, intricate carvings detailing the wooden walls. Scatters of light feel their way in through the shuttered windows. There's a slight charge in the air, an electric quiver that, even with my limited experience of it, I recognize as magic. That must be what's guiding the horses, what lends them their unnatural speed.

Another time and I would have been fascinated by it all—the mysticism of shaman work, the beauty of the carriage. But my vision is red-tinted, filtered through recent events, an unrelenting bombardment of one nightmarish image after another. Bao, speared through. Blood on my father's brow. Tien's scream when the General came for me. My home, *our* home, our lovely little shop-house shattered and broken, and farther from my reach with every sway and bump of the carriage.

And instead, drawing ever closer—the King's palace.

A Paper Girl.

Me.

"Don't look so sad, girl."

General Yu's rumbling voice makes me start. I press further against the side of the bench, but there's no way to ignore the reek of him, the wet heat of his breath.

Is this what the King is like? The thought of touching—of *being* touched—by a demon like this sends a fresh wave of nausea into my throat.

"You have just been handed a fate girls across the kingdom can only dream of," the General says. "Surely it would not pain you to smile?"

I swipe my tears away. "I dream of a different fate," I reply with a sniff.

He laughs, smug. "What better life could a daughter of an herb-shop owner wish for?"

"*Anything* than being the concubine of the King."

The words have barely left my lips when the General seizes my face with his brown-haired hand, pinching my cheeks so hard my jaw pops open. "You think you are special?" he growls. "That you're above being a Paper Girl? You have no idea what the rest of the kingdom is like, foolish girl. All you country folk hiding here in your nowhere corner of your nowhere province, thinking only of your small, closed lives…" His nostrils flare, hot air hitting my face. "You think you are beyond the reach of the court. But you are wrong. The Demon King's rule is all-powerful. You felt that power once seven years ago, and you feel it again today. How easy it was for me to take you from your home—like plucking a flower from a bed of weeds. Just as it happened with your whore of a mother."

With a throaty rumble, he casts me aside. My cheekbone dashes into the wall. I can't help but cry out, and I stuff my hand quickly over my mouth to smother it.

General Yu smirks. "That's it, girl. From what I hear, the King enjoys it when his whores scream."

Glowering, I sit back up, rubbing my cheek. "You know what happened to my mother," I say through gritted teeth. "What those soldiers did to our village."

"I might have heard something," he replies with a shrug. "But I can't be sure. Those kinds of things all merge into one another."

My hands bunch into fists. "They destroyed our village. My *family.*"

The General's voice is cool. "You'd best forget you ever had a family, girl. Because you won't be coming back."

"Yes, I will," I whisper as he turns away, and the words feel like a promise on my lips.

A new thought comes to me then, so brittle I'm scared to let it take hold: Did Mama make a similar promise, too, once? Seven years ago, did she travel this same route that I'm on now, whispering a wish for the wind to carry to the kinder gods? Burumi perhaps, God of Lost Lovers? Or sweet, patient Ling-yi with her wings and blind eyes, Goddess of Impossible Dreams? Mama always held the gods closer than Baba and me. They might have listened to her. And if, and if…

I always imagined the soldiers would have taken Mama and the other women they captured to the royal palace—the very place General Yu his soldiers are bringing me.

I gaze out the window through glazed eyes, a warm kernel of hope working through me. Because as much as I don't want to leave my home, this might be my chance to finally find out the truth about my mother.

And, just maybe, find *her*.

The horses ride on for hours, showing no sign of slowing. We sweep through the Xienzo countryside, a green-brown blur of fields and low mountains, flowering meadowland, and forests. I've never been this far from my village—not even more than a few hours' walk home—but the scenery is recognizable so far, similar to the landscape around our village.

Until, suddenly, it isn't.

We're looping past a patch of scorched land. The horses keep their distance, but we ride close enough to smell ash in the air. The charred area is vast, a wound on the earth. Stumps of what must have once been buildings poke from the ground like broken teeth. Scarlet flags snap in the wind, stamped in obsidian with the silhouette of a bull skull.

The King's symbol.

It takes me a few moments to recognize the ruins for what they are. "This…this was a village," I murmur. I lick my lips, then say louder "What happened?"

"A rebel group was found hiding in the village," The General answers in a flat, impassionate voice. "It was burned, along with every keeda in it."

Keeda: worm. It's an old insult for Paper castes. I've heard the word just once before, from a wolf-form demon who had come to our village by accident, half dead and delirious from an infected wound. He'd spat the word like a stone from his mouth, and it had felt sharp to me even then, when I didn't understand what it meant.

The wolf had refused to let our doctor near him. Some of the men found his body on the road that winds from our village a few days later.

"Are there other places like this?" I ask.

The General cuts me a smirk. "Of course. We're taking the scenic route. Just for you."

I turn away from the window, my stomach knotted. Our village is so isolated that I've never given much thought to what the King's rule has done to the rest of Ikhara. To my fellow Paper castes. But here is the evidence before me, in ugly brushstrokes of destruction and scarred earth.

We ride on into the falling night. Somehow, despite everything, tiredness eventually overtakes me. Rocked by the steady sway of the carriage, I drift off into an uneasy sleep. The next thing I know, I am opening my eyes to stillness and lantern-lit dark.

General Yu is gone.

I sit up so quickly I bang my head on the side of the carriage. Rubbing my temple, I perch on the edge of the bench, breathing hard and listening harder. There's activity outside. Beyond the carriage comes the muffled noise of footsteps and shouted orders, the thud of boxes being dropped. And there's something else, underneath it all. It takes me a few moments more to recognize the sound for what it is.

Water. The rhythmic slap of waves.

I've never been to the sea before. I take a deep inhale and taste salt in the wind.

Salt, sea. With those two words comes another one.

Escape.

Blowing the mussed hair from my eyes, I spring up and scramble to the front of the carriage. Light spills across my face as I loosen one corner of the fabric covering to look out. We're on a backstreet of what seems to be a seaside town. The road is lined with two-tiered buildings with roof-covered porches, paper lanterns hanging from the eaves. Someone has tethered our horses to a wooden column at the base of one of the houses. With the covering open, the noises of the town are louder, and the hairs on my arms prickle. The General and his soldiers could return any minute.

Before I lose my nerve, I suck in a deep breath and launch out of the carriage.

I land heavily, knees buckling. The drop was bigger than I'd expected. It startles the two horses still tethered to the carriage, and they rear up on their hind legs, whinnying and kicking out. Rolling out from under their hooves, I clamber to my feet.

And run.

The packed earth of the road is hard under my bare soles, but I bite down the discomfort. I run fast. Everything around me is a blur of nighttime hues, the disorienting newness of an unfamiliar place. Colored lights glaze the edges of my vision. Faces turn as I pass—human skin, demon eyes.

A crazy image comes to me of what I must look like to them, my clothes scuffed, feet bare. I let out a mad laugh, knowing what Tien would say—*Aiyah, look at you! What a mess!*—choking off as I come to the end of the street.

Doubling over, I gulp down air. I spin left. Right. Neither looks much different, so I swerve left, away from the sound of water. Swimming would be impossible, but maybe I can find somewhere to hide in the town, some stable-horse to steal. I can lead the General and his soldiers away from my home. Get word to Baba and Tien. We'll be able to be together again once this is all over.

The General will give up on me, and it will be safe for me to go home.

I dash down one unfamiliar street after another. There are shouts now, cries at my back. I drive myself faster. Panting, my calves screaming for respite, I reach the end of the street. Just as I turn the corner, I risk a glance over my shoulder.

And barrel straight into someone.

The impact makes my teeth jam down on my tongue. We crash to the ground in a tangle of limbs. All the air rushes out of me as I land painfully on my back. I roll over, groaning. Spitting out a wad of blood, I dig my hands into the earth, trying to push myself to my feet. But before I can stand back up, a scaled arm loops round my neck.

"Stupid girl," a serpentine voice taunts. "You run on my watch?" The point of a dagger presses against my throat. "I'm going to make you pay for that."

Sith.

The lizard soldier drags me back down the street, ignoring my screams and thrashing. People are watching from the shadows of porches and walkways. I shout at them for help. But they shrink back, silent. They must have noticed Sith's uniform, the King's crest stitched on his shirt.

When we get back to the carriage, Sith tosses me inside. I skid across the paneled floor. There's the click of clawed feet as he climbs in after me, and I start to push myself to my knees, but a second later his foot crushes down on the small of my back. My jawbone cracks on the floor. I cry out, more in surprise than pain, and he digs his heels in harder, grinding my hips against the wood.

He leans over me. Turning his ugly, scaled face to the side, he fixes me with a cold stare. His glassy eyes are reptilian, a vertical strip of black slicing through the blue-gray. There's a streak of pink as his tongue darts out to taste my skin.

He spits. "Disgusting. The stink of the herb shop is all over you." His leer rolls down my body, slow, creeping. "Perhaps you need a good *licking* to clean it off."

Panic flares inside me like a firecracker: bright and burning, a sudden flare.

"You—you wouldn't," I stammer. "I'm a Paper Girl—"

"So you'll admit it now?" Sith laughs, cutting me off. "Well, you know exactly what is expected of you, then. Better start practicing."

He runs a hand along my shoulder and tugs my shirt back. Rough fingers brush down my arm, sending a wave of nausea into my throat. I squirm away, buck my hips, trying to throw him off. But my struggling barely moves him.

So I scream.

Sith clamps a hand over my mouth. "Quiet!" he hisses. "Not a sound, or—"

"Get off her."

The command is delivered quietly yet firm as a fist. At once, Sith lurches off me. General Yu stands framed in the doorway, one hand resting on the hilt of the sword at his belt.

Sith points at me. "The girl tried to escape, General," he starts, and I'm glad to see a tremor in his outstretched finger. "She's fast, but I caught her and brought her straight back. I was just—just keeping her here until your return."

"Liar!" I snarl.

The General regards us in silence, his face impassive. "The boat is ready to set sail," he says, turning. "Follow me."

I sense Sith relax. "Yes, General."

"But, Sith?" The General pauses, continuing over his shoulder, "If I ever catch you touching the girl inappropriately again, it will be your job to explain to the King how you soiled one of his concubines. Do you understand?"

Sith flinches. "Yes, General."

This time when he grabs me, Sith takes care to keep to where my shoulders are covered. But he marches me forward with the same aggression and shoots me a sideways look, slatted eyes narrowed in disgust.

I scowl openly back, but I don't struggle. His grip is tight, and ahead of us the General's fist is still around the hilt of his sword, reminding me how easily he would be able to turn it against me.

We follow General Yu in the opposite direction to which I ran, out to the oceanfront. There's a port, busy even at this hour. Lights glint from the wooden gantries, rippling the water with color. A wide, star-speckled sky stretches out to an invisible horizon. Despite everything that's going on, my eyes go wide at the sight.

I've always dreamed about seeing the sea.

Behind us, restaurants and hookah cafés line the street, the night filled with raucous laughter, the jeers and yells of an argument bursting into life. Wherever we are, it doesn't seem like a rich town. There are only a few demon figures amid the crowds and all of them are Steel. Outside one of the shops, a salt-stained banner snaps in the wind. I make out the faded pattern of two rearing canines back-to-back painted in sweeping brushstrokes across the fabric—the famous dog clan of Noei, the Black Jackals.

I do a double take. "Noei?" Louder, I call ahead to General Yu, "We're in Noei?"

He doesn't turn, but his head tilts, which I take as a yes.

My mouth goes dry. Noei is the province to the east of Xienzo. We've traveled farther than I hoped.

As the General leads us to the far side of the port, we pass young ship hands dressed in grubby sarongs and fishermen deftly picking squid from clouds of tangled nets. We come to a stop at a large boat moored at the end of a dock. A crowd of cream, fin-shaped sails, unfurled, flutter in the wind.

The tiger soldier is waiting at the top of the gangplank. "The captain is ready to set sail, General," he says with a tuck of his chin.

"Good. Sith—take the girl to her room."

"Yes, General."

"And remember what I said."

As soon as he turns away, Sith scowls. He lowers his mouth close to my cheek, and I stare ahead with my lips pressed, holding down a shiver as his words unspool silkily in my ear. "You're welcome to try to escape again, pretty girl, but this time it will be the sea's arms waiting to catch you. And I think you'll find them an even crueler embrace than mine."

FOUR

No one tells me how long we'll be sailing. I watch for differences in the ocean, scan the horizon for signs of land, any opportunity for escape. But after three days, the rolling slate-blue of the sea still looks identical. And besides, most of the time I'm crouched with my head over a bucket, watching another kind of liquid slop back and forth. I'm so seasick I barely have the energy to worry about what will happen when we arrive at our destination. Resignation is beginning to settle in my bones like a poison, black and slow.

There's no going back now. I'm ready for whatever is coming my way, I tell myself, so many times that I wonder who I'm trying to convince.

Two times a day the General sends a ship hand to bring me food. After I throw up the steamed taro dumplings he serves me one night, the boy sneaks back with a second helping. He's a Moon caste fox-form, probably just a couple of years younger than me. Maybe it's because of his age, or how he can barely look me in the eye, but for whatever reason it's the first time I haven't been completely intimidated by a Moon demon. Over the days I've come to appreciate the lovely umber hue of his fur. How there's something beautiful about the way his jaw is molded, a hard curve tapering to a sharp chin.

"Wait," I say now as he hurries to leave. I don't dare touch the bamboo basket, even though the smell of the dumplings inside makes my mouth water.

The fox-boy stops in the doorway. The white tip of his tail flicks.

"It's just…they'll notice," I continue. "That some food is missing."

He hesitates. Then he says jerkily, "It's my portion."

This simple act, the kindness of it, surprises me so much—especially coming from a Moon caste, willowy vulpine haunches showing beneath his worker's sarong—that I just blurt straight out, "Why?"

Looking over his shoulder, he doesn't quite meet my eyes. "Why what?"

"Why help me? I'm…I'm Paper."

The fox-boy turns back to the door. "So?" he answers. "You need the help more than anyone."

I blink, glad that he's gone before he can see how much his comment has stung. I consider not eating the dumplings out of principle—who needs pity dumplings, anyway? But I'm too weary to hold out for long. Still, his words stay with me. It makes me recall something Mama once told me, when I'd come back from a trip with my father to a neighboring town to collect a batch of rare herbs.

"A fat man threw his banana skin at us!" I told her when we arrived home, indignant, my eyes puffy from crying.

My mother had shared a look with my father before crouching

down in front of me, hands cupping my wet cheeks. "Oh, darling," she said, before asking me calmly, "Do you know why?"

I sniffed, my little fists bunched. "He told us we shouldn't be in the same shop as Steels or Moons."

"He was a demon?"

I pouted. "A fat, ugly dog one."

Behind me, Baba snorted—falling quiet quickly at the look my mother gave him.

"Would you like to know a secret?" she said, pulling me closer and tucking a stray lock of hair behind my ears. "A secret *so* secret not even those who know it are always aware?"

I nodded.

Mama smiled. "Well, despite what they look like, all demons have the same blood as us. Yes, even fat, ugly dog ones. If the gods gave birth to us, why *should* we be any different? We are all the same really, little one. Deep down. So don't you worry about what the silly man said."

And six-year-old me had nodded, believing her. Trusting in the certainty of her words even if the world was trying to prove me otherwise.

Then—a year later. The claws and fire, the crush and cries.

We might be the same deep down, Paper, Steel, and Moon, but it didn't matter then.

I rub my arms over my pale leaf-thin skin.

And it doesn't matter now.

On the morning of the fifth day at sea, shouts ring out from the deck. Though the words are muffled, stolen by the wind, one reaches me. It flies into my heart on wings both shadowed with fear and bright with relief.

Han. The royal province.

We've arrived.

I scramble to the window. At first I can't see anything, but after a minute the shape of the coast reveals itself, the city nestled in the bay growing clearer as we approach.

The Black Port, Han's famous port city. The dark rock of the surrounding cliffs are what gave it its name, and under the glare of the sun the stone has a sheen to it, making it look almost wet. But what strikes me more is the size of the city. It's bigger than I could possibly have imagined, dense and sprawling, carving a deep line along the coast and backing into the mountainous terrain. Tiers of wooden houses stretch for miles. Their dark walls are stained from the salt-rich air, and their roofs curl upward at the edges like paper that has started to burn.

Mirroring the city, the harbor in front is just as crowded. Thousands of boats cluster in the water, from small fishing tugs with multicolored sails to papaya-shaped boats laden with fruits to round, barrel-like water taxis all in a line, waiting to ferry passengers along the bay, and elegant ships decorated with silk ribbons. We weave through them, drawing close enough to some to make out the individual patterns of their sails, the names scrawled on their sides. There are good-fortune characters, clan insignias, coal-black bull skulls stamped on the scarlet sails of towering military ships.

"You're alive, then. We thought you were so sick you might vomit up your own soul."

I pivot round to see General Yu in the doorway.

I give him a scowl. At least I *have* a soul.

Before I can speak, he waves a hand, already turning. "Come."

When we emerge onto the deck half a minute later, my hand

flies to shade my eyes. After so long inside, the openness of the sky and sea all around stuns me. Everything is luminous. Sun-glazed. As my eyes adjust, I make out our surroundings, from the gaudy-colored sails of the ship docked beside us to the spotted bellies of gulls swooping overhead. The dock is alive with movement. Every gangway, air-walk, bridge, and boat deck swarms with hurrying figures. Unlike at the port in Noei, there are far more demons here—more so than humans—an indication of the province's affluence and power.

I swallow. The sight of so many Steel and Moon castes is an unwelcome reminder of where I am. *Who* I am.

I hug my arms around myself, feeling exposed in my tatty clothes.

"General," Sith announces, appearing at the top of the gang-plank. "The carriage is ready." As he bows, his eyes lift and find me. A smirk plays across his thin lips.

Something hot sparks in my chest as I remember his scaled fingers on me. Glaring, I jut my chin.

"Hurry up, girl," General Yu growls, shoving me forward.

As we make our way down toward the waiting carriage, the fierce sun pricking sweat under my arms, I scan the teeming dock for escape routes. But it's broad daylight in the middle of the busiest port in Ikhara—if I run, I won't get far. And besides, the General's heavy hoof-fall beside me is reminder enough that I have to be obedient.

Sith comes up behind me to my other side, a fraction too close. "Need a hand, pretty girl?"

I jerk away before he can touch me. "Never from you."

Well, obedient doesn't have to mean cowering.

Tien's proud face flashes into my mind. *Wah, little nuisance! Look at you, standing up to a demon like your skin is Moon and not Paper.*

The thought brings a sad, defiant smile to my lips. I blow out a breath. Then, rolling my shoulders back, I take the last few steps to the carriage, my chin high. Because if this is to be my fate, I'm going to walk boldly into it on my own two feet.

Without any demon claws dragging me forward.

Outside the port city, our carriage joins a long road winding through the flat land behind the mountains. It's filled with strange rock formations, scraggly pines, and tiny white wildflowers clinging to their faces. The dry ground is covered in red dust. The air is thick with it, too, coppery clouds kicked up by the horses. Even though the shutters are pulled down and the covering is drawn tightly across the entranceway, the dust still finds its way inside the carriage, coating my skin in a light layer.

I lick my lips. The dust tastes like how it looks—of rust, and dirt, and endings.

All around us, the thoroughfare is a chaotic whirl of activity. There are men on bear- and horseback. Carts pulled by tusked boars. Huge ground-ships with their sails spread wide. While the busyness makes me shrink farther back from the window, General Yu seems buoyed by the energy and noise, and he leans over to my side, pointing out the crests of notable clans.

"See there? The green-and-white flag? That's Kitori's reptilian clan, the Czo. Exquisite clothes-makers. Even the King has their fabrics imported. And there—that chain of ground-boats belongs to the Feng-shi. Very powerful family from Shomu province." An ornate, silver carriage pulls into place alongside us, and the General notes the insignia. "Ah. The White Wing clan. One of the most powerful bird families in Ikhara. Surely even *you* must have heard of them?"

I don't give him the satisfaction of admitting I haven't. Velvet curtains are draped across the carriage windows. I'm just turning away when one of the curtains twitches aside, and my gaze locks with the glossy eyes of a swan-form girl. The white feathers covering her skin are so lustrous it's as though they were powdered in pearl dust.

She's so beautiful that I instinctively smile. But the girl doesn't return it. A feather-clad hand touches her shoulder and she releases the curtain, disappearing behind the smooth gold.

"Filthy felines," comes a growl from the General.

I glance round, confused. But he's staring in the opposite direction, his lip furled.

Beyond the other window, a sleek ground-ship is passing by. Marigold sails billow in a presumably magic-enhanced wind. Craning my head to look out, I track the figures stalking the deck. The way they move reminds me of Tien's feline slink, and beneath the cloths wrapped over their mouths I make out the jut of their maws. Cat-forms. My eyes flick to the sails. Each is stamped with three claw-tipped paw prints.

Our carriage gives a kick, hitting a pothole in the road, just as I place the crest.

The Amala, or the Cat Clan, as they're more affectionately known. My father has told me stories about them, not even trying to hide the note of admiration in his voice. Out of all demon clans, the Cat Clan is the one Paper castes feel the most affinity for. They're known for their rebellious nature, uprising and causing trouble wherever they can, especially if it involves annoying the King. *I heard they intercepted a wagon carrying crates of the King's pastries from a specialist bakery in Ang-Khen,* Baba told me just a few weeks ago, a glimmer in his eyes. *When it arrived at the Hidden Palace, they found that a single bite had been taken out of each of the pastries. Every one.*

I push down a snigger at the memory. Now, *these* are demons I can get behind.

As we watch, two men on horseback ride up beside the Amala's ground-ship. Wind billows their long peacock-blue capes, so I can't make out the white brushstrokes that would reveal their clan, but there's something about the elegant manner in which the men ride that invokes royalty. Even though, of course, they can't be. They're human.

One of the Amala's members leans over the edge of the ship, shouting something to the two men, gesturing wildly. They shout back—or at least they seem to from the movement of their heads—before pulling their horses away.

"Who were they?" I ask as the men disappear into the lines of traffic.

General Yu doesn't look round. "The Hannos," he answers distractedly. Something flickers across his face, gone too quickly for me to interpret.

I've heard of the Hannos from my father and Tien, though with none of the warmth in their voices as when they'd spoken of the Cat Clan. The largest Paper caste clan in Ikhara, the Hannos are one of the Demon King's most prominent supporters. When it comes to Paper clans, one of his *only* supporters.

So why were two of their men talking with one of the King's main opponents?

We ride on, day slipping into night as a steady rain claims the land. Hour after hour, the number of travelers drops away. I stare out the window. A moonless sky hangs vast and heavy over the plains. The air is cool, and with the rain the darkness is complete, viscous, like I could dive right into it. An image comes to me of one of the sky gods: Zhokka, Harbinger of Night. How he'd extend his hand to catch me as I fell toward him, a grin of swallowed starlight widening across his face.

"Eat," commands General Yu suddenly, snapping me from my dark imagining. He hands me a leather flask and a package wrapped in a pandan leaf. "I don't want you fainting from hunger during your inspection at the palace."

I take a grateful bite of the fragrant sticky rice inside, the spices warming my belly. "The magic on this carriage," I begin between chews. I risk a glance at the General. "Was it cast by the royal shamans?"

"Our little village girl has heard of them, huh?"

"*Everyone* in Ikhara has heard of them."

He grunts. "I suppose. But the way some in the royal palace revere them, as if they are gods...even the Demon King himself acts as though their powers are holy," he adds with a snort.

My brow furrows at the General's dismissal. The royal shamans hold legendary status across Ikhara. Like the Paper Girls, they're a feature of the Hidden Palace whose mystery has been cloaked with layers of gossip and superstition. The story goes that when the Demon King created the Hidden Palace, he ordered his architects to design an impenetrable fortress. His architects told him there could be no such thing—and so the King had them executed. Their replacements were more careful. After many discussions, they suggested a constant dao to be woven into the perimeter wall. No single shaman could do this, but a group of them, constantly at work, might be capable.

Shamans combining power isn't unheard of, but it's usually only a small group working on behalf of a clan or an army, a temporary arrangement. What the King's advisers suggested was a permanent one. A large group taking turns to craft the magic that would live within the palace walls.

"Is it true there're over a thousand shamans in the royal guard?" I ask.

"A thousand? That is nothing, girl. There are *many* thousand. Which is why I didn't understand—"

The General stops abruptly.

"Didn't understand what?" I prompt.

With a jerky movement, he gestures to the scar splitting his face. It would be an ugly face even without the scar: the wide, flat bull's nose, too large between narrow cheekbones; the heavy-set lower jaw. But the scar twists it into a macabre mask, less demon than monster.

"I received *this* recently in a battle in Jana," the General scowls, glaring stonily ahead. "I asked the King's permission for one of the royal shamans to heal it, but…he refused. He told me that battle scars are a badge of honor. Of power. That to want to rid myself of one is a sign of weakness. You can imagine the King's reaction when I pointed out that he himself has often used magic on his own scars." A muscle twitches in his neck. "It's not often I am so foolish. I was lucky he only demoted me."

I get a sudden flare of empathy for General Yu—which disappears in an instant as he traces a calloused finger along my cheek.

"That's where you come in."

I draw back. "What do you mean?"

"It's true you are no classic beauty," he muses, looking over me. "You lack the elegance of girls who have grown up in the affluent societal circles. And yet…those *eyes*. It might just be enough to stir the King's interest." He pauses, expression darkening. "At least, let us hope so. The chosen girls will be arriving at the palace tonight. We'll have to be careful about how we approach Mistress Eira and Madam Himura about you."

I blink. "The selection process is already over?"

"Weeks ago."

"Then, what am *I* here for?" My voice rises. "What happens if they don't want me?" I grip the edge of the bench, pitching forward. "If they don't, can I go back home—"

"Of course not," the General cuts in. "And you will make sure they want you. I need to get back into the King's favor after the incident with my scar. Sith heard rumors of a human girl with eyes the color of gold, but I didn't quite believe it until I saw you." There's a challenge in his gaze. "Tell me, girl, do you have what it takes to win over the court?"

Anger hardens inside me. So that's what he's bringing me to the palace for? A bargaining chip?

"I don't *want* to win over the court," I retort.

Nostrils flaring, General Yu seizes my throat. "You are going to try," he snarls, "and you are going to succeed! Or else your family— what pitiful part that's left of it—will be punished. Make no mistake, keeda." He grasps my wrists and yanks them up to my face, fingers digging into my skin. "Their blood will be here. Do you understand me? On *your* hands."

His words chill me. I wrench away from him, shaking, as horror slinks in an ice-cold flood down my veins.

The General laughs. "You think you're above this. I can see that. But believe me, girl, you are not. Because once you find out what happens to paper gone rotten—when you see what they do to whores who won't play along—you will beg the palace to keep you." His eyes glide past me, to the window. "We're here."

I whip round. Outside, willowy stalks of bamboo trees are flashing past, an ivory-green blur. Eerie sounds fill the forest—the song of owls, rain dripping on leaves, distant calls from animals hidden in the dark. The air is loamy with the smell of wet earth. After hours of empty plains, the closeness of the trees startles me. We're passing through them impossibly fast, and even though there's the snap and sweep of leaves on the carriage's exterior, the noise is muffled. More magic.

"The great Bamboo Forest of Han," the General announces, pride in his voice. "Part of the palace's defenses. Too dense to enter on animal-back, too difficult for an army to traverse. It would take days to tear down a path. Visitors and traders must obtain the correct permits to be granted the daos from the royal shamans that open up this hidden road."

I watch the trees whip past, my eyes wide. After a few minutes, the carriage slows. The horses drop to a canter, then a trot, as the forest opens, and I reel back, eyes even wider than before.

The Hidden Palace of Han.

Fortress of the Demon King.

Black rock as dark as night; walls so high they eclipse the moon. The perimeter of the palace rears up from the earth like some kind of giant stone monster. Far above, the tiny figures of guards pace the parapet. The walls have an unearthly shimmer about them, and as we draw closer, I notice millions of glowing characters ingrained in the marbled stone, swirling and spinning off one another beneath the rain-slicked surface. The low hum of chanting vibrates through the air.

The royal shamans.

Goose bumps prick across my skin. I've never felt magic like this.

"Shut your mouth," General Yu commands. "It's not womanly to stare."

I do as he says, too awed even to be insulted by his comment. The carriage slows to a stop. There's the squelch of footsteps in the mud. Moments later, a rap on the wood makes me start.

A round-faced bear-form guard pulls aside the cover, drops of rain nestling in the tufts of his brown fur. "General Yu! Back from Xienzo already!" He bows. "I hope the heavens smiled upon your journey." When he lifts his head, he blinks at me, ears twitching. "If I may ask, General, who is your guest?"

"Lei-zhi is here to join the court as a Paper Girl," the General replies with an impatient click of his tongue. "I sent two of my men ahead earlier to inform you. I assume you got the message? Or are we to be kept here waiting outside the palace like a couple of lowly street peddlers?"

The guard dips his head. "Of course not, General. One moment. Let me confirm with Gate Master Zhar."

I watch out the window as the soldier, hunched against the rain, crosses to an outpost stationed beside a set of towering doors. The gates are set deep into the wall. To each side stand giant pecalang, the statues sometimes placed outside buildings as protection from evil spirits. Most of the pecalang in my village are small, just tokens, really, hand-sized and easily torn from their plinths in a storm. These ones are enormous. They stand imposing at over twenty feet tall, carved in the likeness of bulls, their faces contorted into snarls that seem so real they snatch my breath away. Stone hands grip flame-lit braziers. As my eyes adjust to the light, I notice more statues lined along the wall. Then I start.

Because *these* guards are alive.

The hairs on my arms stand up at the sight of hundreds of demons standing flank-to-flank along the perimeter of the palace. They stare fixedly ahead, swords crossed at their chests. The wet flicker of flames reflects in their eyes—demon eyes. Gazelle, snow leopard, lion, boar. So many forms I've never seen before, and each one Moon caste. Buffalo, wildcat, ibex, ape. Cobra, jackal, tiger, rhinoceros. So many forms I've never even *dreamed*, and the thrum of barely contained strength in each glint of tapered incisor and horn and claw.

I draw back, swallowing.

"Impressive, yes?" the General states, but I don't give him the satisfaction of a reply. Or rather, I don't speak because I *can't*. It's as though there were hands wrapped over my throat. As though the press of the demons were everywhere.

At a wave from the bear guard, a smaller set of doors beside the main gate draw open. The horses pull us through into a long tunnel. Its ceiling curves low, forming a cocoon of darkness. The chanting of the royal shamans echoes all around, a heavy hum in the air, the unsettling noise vibrating right down to my bones. Then everything goes silent.

There's a flash, like lightning.

A fiery shiver explodes across my skin.

I bite back a cry. The heat is just on the edge of bearable. I spin around but can't see anything that might be causing it. "What's— what's happening?" I stammer, rubbing my hands over my goose-pricked arms.

"We're passing through the shamans' protection," General Yu answers. "If we are not who we say we are, this dao will reveal us to the guards inside. Only the most powerful shaman could weave magic to evade an enchantment like this. I would tell you that you get used to it, but it's not as if you'll ever be leaving." The corners of his lips curve into sharp points. "Welcome to the palace, Paper Girl."

FIVE

As we clear the tunnel, the sensation lifts, along with the uneasy silence.

My first impression of the world within the palace grounds is a smell, so sweet it makes my mouth water: night-blooming jasmine. The flowers burst in a fiery-green tangle along the walls. The familiarity of the scent shocks me, and I take in my first look at the palace, gripping the edge of the bench as I lean forward to stare out, half holding my breath.

We're in an enormous square. Braziers illuminate the vast space, shadows deep at its edges, empty except for a guards' pavilion and a row of stables. A couple of guards hurry over as our carriage comes to a stop. The General seems to know them well, and greets them warmly—or at least what constitutes as warmth coming from him—before we continue on.

Now that we're actually here, a strange sense of calm starts to take over me, like a blanket laid gently over something smoldering. I angle myself at the window, trying to get a better view, but the horses pick up the pace. Everything flies by in a blur. I catch only quick glimpses of my new home. Rain-slicked cobbles. The dark rush of gardens at night. Elegant temples with furled roofs, their ornate architectural styles unfamiliar to me. We pass through small courtyards and wide, open spaces; linked squares with bridges arching over water; grand, imposing structures crafted from marble. It stuns me how vast the palace is. Not just a palace really, but a city—a labyrinth of streets, courtyards, and gardens, like the veins and arteries flowing through a giant creature with the King nestled at its core, its own living, beating heart.

I wonder if that heart is as black as I've been told.

After twenty minutes, the horses slow. "This is it," General Yu announces as they draw to a halt. He leans forward to tug aside the curtain at the front of the carriage. "Women's Court."

Massaging the numbness in my legs, I get to my feet and step out into rain and lantern-lit darkness. We're in what looks to be some kind of residential area. Tall walls enclose a web of streets comprised of interlocking houses and covered walkways set on raised platforms. The buildings are ornate, with dark walls of what looks like mahogany and rosewood, glossy under the downpour. Sliding bamboo screens—so delicate compared to the thick doors we have in Xienzo—reveal the backlit silhouettes of figures inside. Porches ring every house, lined with vases of white-petaled orchids and peonies.

My feet slip in the muddy earth as the General leads me down one of the unlit paths at the base of the buildings. He keeps one hand on my shoulder to stop me from bolting. Though even if I knew where to run to, I'm not sure I could. My body seems bound to some unseen current as we move through the unfamiliar space, everything cast in a dreamlike ruby haze from the red lanterns dangling from the curved eaves of buildings, like ripe fruit. Rain-dampened sounds drift out from open windows and doorways above—female voices raised in laughter, plucked zither music, lilting and beautiful.

We stop beside a servants' entrance built into the side of a grand-looking house. The General pulls a rope, sounding a bell.

A few seconds later the door flies open. Light spills into the alley. A young girl of ten or eleven blinks out at us. She has a gentle, moonlike face and round doe eyes, her hair pulled messily back into a lopsided bun. Loose strands unwind around her long, fluted ears. They are the only part of her that suggests she's not Paper; she's a deer-form—Steel, but barely. Lantern light glides across her smooth human skin, a mirror of mine, and an immediate sense of kinship rushes through me. After days in the sole company of demons, I want to hug her, press her soft, bare cheek to mine.

"Oh!" she cries, dropping to the floor in a low bow. "General Yu!"

He barely looks at her. "Fetch Mistress Eira," he commands.

The girl bounces to her feet at once, scuttling back inside the house. Her bun of hair bobs like a doe's stubbed tail, as though try-ing to help her appear more demon than she is.

I peer after her. Past the doorway, a flight of stairs leads up to a lantern-lit corridor. Voices float down from the rooms beyond, and the air is warm, tea-scented. There's something so welcoming about the house that for a second it's easy to imagine myself walk-ing inside to find Tien and Baba and Bao. The pain is so sharp then that I have to dig my fingernails into my palms just to feel some-thing else.

This is not my home.

Nowhere else ever will be.

We've only been waiting a few minutes before the young girl reap-pears at the top of the steps, this time with a tall woman at her side.

"Thank you, Lill," the woman says, and the girl scurries off.

The Paper woman turns to us. There's a pause as her eyes settle on me, and then she begins to make her way down the staircase.

She moves impossibly lightly, a grace even to how she holds the hem of her plum-colored silk robes—the most exquisite I have seen in my life. They drape round her slim form effortlessly, pattered with silver embroidery and held together at her waist by a wide band of fabric. It's this that jolts my memory to Tien showing me drawings one of our customers once gifted her. The illustrations reflected the styles of women's clothing favored by the central provinces. If I'm remembering correctly, these types of robes are a specific style of hanfu originally worn by the aristocracy of northeastern Shomu.

At the bottom of the stairs, she bows. "General Yu." She stays just beyond the doorway, under the shelter of the house. Her jet-black eyes shine with intelligence, and a serene smile touches her lips. Instincts tell me that this woman was once a Paper Girl herself. Though she looks in her early forties, the bronzed skin stretched over her high cheekbones is as smooth and poreless as a young girl's.

The General inclines his head. "Mistress Eira. I apologize for coming to Women's Court and disturbing you without forewarning. But this matter couldn't wait." He pushes me forward. "May I present Lei-zhi."

The woman's gaze flicks to me at his use of this suffix. She turns back to the General, a hint of something hard-edged in her smile. "How strange that you give her the Paper Girl title," she says, still smiling calmly. "The girls arrived a couple of hours ago—I was just entertaining them myself. Last time I checked, all eight were present."

"I'm aware this is unusual," the General says quickly. "But I hope you'll agree it's for a worthy cause. When I found the girl, and saw how striking her beauty was, I dropped everything to bring her to the palace."

"I assure you, General, our girls are more than striking enough for the King." Folding her palms at her waist, Mistress Eira gives a short bow. "Now, I really must return—"

A bit too roughly, the General seizes my cheeks. He wrests my face up so that light from the stairwell catches my eyes.

Gold upon gold.

She was already half turning away, but in an instant Mistress Eira freezes. Her lips part, and then she presses them firmly closed. Her eyes don't leave mine as she steps in close. Delicate perfume lifts from her skin; rosewater and the sweetly spiced scent of neroli. I blink the water from my eyelashes, trying to keep my gaze steady as she regards me properly for the first time.

"Heavens' blessings, those *eyes*..." Mistress Eira glances at General Yu. "She really is pure Paper?"

"I assure you, Mistress, her blood is human."

"Her parents?"

"Herb-shop owners from western Xienzo."

"So she has no experience with the court?"

"Unfortunately, not. But she can learn fast. The girl is used to hard work. And look at how striking she is even now, dressed so plainly. Imagine the transformation once you and Madam Himura have worked on her. Once she has been educated in the ways of women." The General's tone turns silky. "And I'm sure you don't need me to remind you of our King's superstitious nature. Imagine how appreciative he might be to receive a girl who is as much a symbol of the heavens' good fortune as one of beauty. It could be the much-needed boost of confidence he needs. Given everything we've been facing lately..." He trails off, and the two of them share a pointed look.

The idea of the Demon King lacking confidence is so opposite to how I've been imagining him. I want to ask more about what things exactly the court has been facing lately, but Mistress Eira's focus pins me in place.

"It's as if Ahla herself smiled down from the heavens as you were born," she muses. It's something I've heard before; many people believe the Moon Goddess had a hand in coloring my eyes. Mistress Eira gives me a gentle smile. "Lei," she asks, "are you sure you are ready for the life of a Paper Girl?"

Behind her, the General's eyes fix on me. I remember his words in the carriage earlier. *Their blood will be here. Do you understand me? On your hands.*

Tien's face, my father's come to my mind. The way they looked when the General thrust me into the carriage. The way they would look if I gave him reason to act out his threat. Tears prick my eyes. I force out this gruesome image and instead picture them smiling, working, laughing, *living.*

There is only one answer I can give if I want that for them. So I offer it, even though it breaks my heart, pushing the word from my tongue like a stone.

"Yes."

I knew it even earlier, at the dock in Noei and on the boat to Han, and maybe even before then, from the minute General Yu's eyes met mine in the shop. It was pointless to hope for a different outcome. And, even though it's the slimmest of chances, at least being here in the palace means I might find out what happened to my mother.

Still. The word leaves a bitter flavor in my mouth. It tastes like failure.

Like betrayal.

I swallow it down as Mistress Eira smiles, draping an arm across my back.

"Thank you, General," she tells him. "You were right to bring Lei here. I'll introduce her to Madam Himura right away. Hopefully her reaction will be as positive as mine. We'll be sure to make it known to the King that Lei comes as your personal gift." Bowing one last time, she ushers me into the house.

Before she shuts the door, I look back at the General. His smirk is wider than I've seen it, his eyes bright with triumph.

Mistress Eira leads me to a small, windowless room and asks me to wait, leaving me standing awkwardly in the middle of the floor. Water drips from my soaked clothes onto the polished teak boards. I smooth my hands over my matted hair, trying—and failing—to slow my heart. Even after the long journey here, it doesn't feel real. I'm in the royal palace.

In one of its buildings, the King is waiting.

I don't know when I'll be introduced to him—the horror hits me that it could be *tonight*—and the palace is so vast he's not likely to be close by. Still, there's something intimate about it, to be inside the palace walls. Perhaps even in a building he's been in once before.

My spine tingles. Hugging my arms, I glance over my shoulder with a ridiculous notion that he could even be standing behind me.

The next time steps sound in the corridor, hard clicks accompany the light footfall of Mistress Eira. A strange, hunched shadow appears behind the sliding door. It's not quite human, too bulky in the shoulders and neck. Instinctively, I back away, readying myself, but I can't help the curl of fear as the door opens and the woman I assume to be Madam Himura enters the room.

Only she isn't *just* a woman—she is a demon.

An eagle demon.

Eagle-forms are one of the rarest kinds of demon. Like a lot of bird forms, many lost their lives fighting in the Night War, and they've been mostly recruited since as soldiers for the King's army. I've never seen a bird-form up close before, apart from the quick glimpse of the swan-girl on the road out of the Black Port. The first thing I notice are her eyes: two hooded crescents of yellow. Their piercing gaze cuts straight through me. Pearl-white feathers flow down to a hooked beak that pulls her humanoid jaw out of place, so her face is at once familiar but extremely... *not*. Graphite robes set off the inky plumage that sheathes her body.

"So," she says, glaring at me. "*This* is what all the fuss is about."

Her voice is hoarse, a croak that seems to come from the back of her throat. She steps closer, revealing the glint of scaled claws from beneath her robes. A taloned hand at the end of one arm—human limbs melded with eagle feathers—clutches the handle of a bone walking stick, but despite the hunched-over way she moves, there's still power there, brimming energy.

"Your age, girl?" she snaps brusquely, making me jump.

I wet my lips. "S-seventeen."

"When were you born?"

"The first day of the New Year."

"An auspicious sign," she muses. "And the moon would have been golden then....Perhaps that is what lent you those eyes."

"Well," I say, my cheeks hot, "it wasn't a demon."

Madam Himura bristles at this. The sleek feathers coating her arms ruffle, seeming to blur her arms into wings as they fan out before settling back against her skin. "Anyone with half a brain can tell your skin is Paper, stupid girl. You even stand like a servant. A demon wouldn't hold themselves in such a way. Besides, the official inspection tomorrow will reveal if you are not who you say you are. You won't be able to hide anything from them, no matter how many enchantments you might have used. Turn!" she commands abruptly.

I do as she says, feeling her stare roam over me.

"Mistress Eira tells me you have no experience whatsoever with the court. No connections that you are aware of."

I shake my head.

In a flash, she jerks forward, clasping my chin in her talons. "You do not answer with crude movements, girl!" Sour breath hits my face. "If I ask you a question, you respond with 'Yes, Madam Himura' or 'No, Madam Himura.' Is that clear?"

I swallow. "*Yes*, Madam Himura."

"Do you even possess any skills aside from being insolent to your superiors?"

Glowering, I mutter, "I'm good with herbs, and cleaning—"

"Herbs?" She lets out a racking laugh. "Cleaning? We are women of the court. Those are jobs for servants and maids. As a Paper Girl, it's your nu skills—your female skills—you're to cultivate. Are you telling me you have no such talents?" She clacks her beak. "How worthless."

I grind my teeth to hold back a retort. Those are the skills my parents and Tien taught me. Skills that are surely more worthwhile than knowing how to entertain a King.

Madam Himura cocks her head, appraising me coolly. She makes a strange, almost purring sound at the back of her throat. "Ah. I see. You think you're better than this. Well, just wait until your lessons start. You'll see how hard such skills are to master." Her eyes narrow. "Despite what you think, I see the hunger in you. The desire to prove yourself. Your qi fire is strong—perhaps *too* strong. We'll have to keep careful watch, or it might end up burning all you touch." With barely a pause, she snaps, "Are you pure?"

"Pure?"

"Sex. Your nu core. Have you allowed a man to enter you?"

My face flushes. Considering what I'm here for, her frank language shouldn't be a surprise. But Tien has only ever broached the subject with me in a half joking manner, and my father certainly never mentioned it. I'd been working in the shop full time since Mama was taken, so I wasn't able to keep up with girls my own age. If things had been different, maybe I'd have already spent a few years giggling with friends about love and lust. Instead, those thoughts were secret ones. Feverish dreams in the middle of velvety nights.

I drop my eyes from the eagle-woman's fierce gaze. "No," I reply truthfully.

I sense her watching me, perhaps searching for a lie. A glimmer of hope rises in my belly—because maybe if she doesn't believe me, she'll order General Yu to take me back. But I shove the idea away, remembering his threat.

Finally, Madam Himura turns to Mistress Eira. "Fetch Lill," she orders. "Have her bring soap and clean clothes. A plain hanfu set will suffice."

We wait in silence. I want to ask what's going on, but from the eagle-woman's stance I can tell she expects me to stay quiet. Mistress Eira returns a minute later with the same doe-form maid who opened the door to the General and me. The girl gives me a grin—which disappears as soon as Madam Himura rounds on her.

"Clean and dress Lei," she commands with a jab of her cane, "then bring her to join the rest of the girls." Without a backward glance, she moves toward the door, taloned feet clicking.

"Wait!" I shout. It's out before I can help it. Madam Himura swirls round, and I recoil at the cutting glare she gives me. "I mean, Madam Himura...does this mean I'm one of the Paper Girls now?"

The eagle-woman scowls. "You'd better not be so dense in your classes," she snaps before leaving the room.

But Mistress Eira offers me a smile. "Yes, Lei-zhi. It does."

She slides the door shut behind her, but I keep staring at the place she had stood. The air is solid in my lungs, my throat filled with rocks. I run my tongue over my dry lips.

The young maid beams at me like this is the best news anyone could receive. "Congratulations, Mistress!" she sings. "You must be so happy!"

Her words pull a rough laugh from my throat. Me, a mistress. And to be congratulated for...*this*. Whatever *this* will turn out to be. And then I'm rounding my back on her, hiding my face with my hands to stifle the manic laughter that's pouring out of me even as tears arrive to accompany them, hot and wet, leaking out of me just as uncontrollably. Everything that's happened over the past few days seems to drain from my body as it finally hits me.

I'm here. In the royal palace.

And I will be staying here if I want to keep Baba and Tien safe.

If I want to keep them *alive*.

SIX

A WOODEN TUB IS BROUGHT TO the room and filled with warm, fragranced water. While she bathes me, Lill quizzes me about my life before the palace, questions tumbling from her mouth so quickly I barely finish answering one when the next comes. Which province am I from? Do I have siblings? What's it like to be Paper caste? Is my mother as beautiful as I am?

I'm not used to being naked in front of someone else, but Lill acts like it's nothing, as direct with her work as with her questions. She dunks a sponge into the water and scrubs it over me before dragging a comb through my knotted hair. Eventually, her chatter starts to put me at ease. She reminds me of Tien, albeit a younger and far less bossy version. And after my long journey to the palace, it's impossible to deny the pleasure of warm water on my skin. The bathwater is soon muddy, while my skin has done the opposite, the grime and sweat-gray sheen that has accumulated over the past few days shed with each stroke of the sponge, until I am revealed anew, baby pale and as polished as a coin.

Afterward, Lill dresses me in simple taupe-colored robes similar to Madam Himura's hanfu, though the design and material is far plainer and the sash is slimmer. "You'll only wear this type of hanfu on days you don't have to leave the house," she explains.

"The design of Mistress Eira's robes are beautiful," I say as her deft fingers adjust the cerulean sash at my waist. "Am I right that their style is originally from Shomu?"

Lill nods. "It's the traditional dress of the White Wing Clan themselves."

"So why is it worn here in Han?"

"Well, I don't know if this is true exactly, but legend has it that the original Bull King fell in love with one of the clan lord's daughters. He admired the clothing style she wore so much that he had it adopted here in Han, and Rain and Ang-Khen too."

Of course. Forced assimilation. Just another of the wonderful things to come from the Night War two hundred years ago.

Lill's doe ears quiver as she steps back to assess her work. "You'll see, Mistress. Food, architecture, art, music...all the most beautiful things in Ikhara can be found in the palace. Like you!"

I grimace at this, but she doesn't seem to notice. "Speaking of that," I say. "What are they like? The other girls?"

"Oh, beautiful, too, of course. But they're going to be so jealous when they see you. No Paper Girl has ever been blessed with eyes like yours." She picks up my dirty clothes, adding, "Wait here, Mistress. I'll just throw these away."

I nod, distracted. *Blessed.* The word rings even more hollow tonight. My eyes are the reason I've been ripped from my home. Just like the original Bull King spying something so beautiful that he claimed it for his own. They're not a blessing—they're a curse.

And then I remember.

"Wait!" I say, lurching after her. Lill blinks as I reach into my trouser pocket, drawing out the familiar egglike object inside.

She smiles up at me. "Your Birth-blessing pendant!"

Its gold casing gleams in the lantern-light. Ever since I was young I've kept it with me, worn it as a necklace, something comforting about its weight against my chest bone.

"When does it open?" Lill asks, eager, as I loop it around my neck and tuck it under my robes.

"In six months," I mutter.

Her eyes light up. "Maybe your fate is love, Mistress—with the King! What an honor that would be!"

And her look is so hopeful I have to turn away.

When Tien told me how many families see great honor in their daughters being chosen, I couldn't understand it. Honor is in family, in hard work and care and love, in a small life well lived. Yes, sometimes I've wished for more. Grumbled at Tien's bossing about, at the long, tiring days of shop life. Dreamed of starlit nights of adventures and a world outside the village and a love so bold it sets my heart alight. But always my future was framed in the safe arms of Xienzo. Of my family. Of my home.

A few minutes later, Lill leads me through the muted house, sounds of daily life muffled behind the painted doors. Dark wood corridors shine with polish. The paneled walls are draped with batik silks and delicate paintings. Every inch of the house drips with elegance. Even the air seems rich somehow, clean and perfumed.

We reach a set of sliding screen doors. Raised voices sound from within.

"Nine girls?" a thin, reedy voice declares. "*Nine?* It makes no sense! It's eight. It's always been eight. That's the tradition."

"Continue this way, Blue, and I shall gladly throw you out to return the group to its original number."

"I'd like to see you try, *Madam* Himura. You know the power my father holds in the court. I don't think he'd take kindly to you casting me out."

"Who's that?" I whisper to Lill.

"Mistress Blue," she replies. "Her father, Lord Ito, is very famous. He's one of the only Paper caste members of the court." As the voices die down, she asks, "Are you ready to go in, Mistress?"

I take a slow inhale, then nod.

Lill gives me an encouraging smile. Then, sliding the door open, she announces with a bow to the room beyond, "Presenting Mistress Lei-zhi!"

The scents hit me first: incense from joss sticks and burners; the delicate fragrance of chrysanthemum tea. Maids in pastel-colored robes drift round, pouring the tea from porcelain pots with graceful curves of their wrists, and even they would be intimidating if they had walked into my parents' shop. But compared with who they're serving, their presence fades.

The Paper Girls.

Kneeling round a low table in the center of the room, they cut striking figures draped in vivid, lustrous fabrics, like a collection of living jewels. I take them in one by one. There is a girl with the bronzed, almost russet-brown skin common in the Southern provinces, draped in vibrant orange robes that remind me of the sarongs we have in the North, her raven hair twisted into a plait threaded with beads. At her sides are a stern-looking girl with a sharp, bobbed haircut at odds with her curvaceous figure, and a petite girl in an ice-blue dress. Opposite them sits a sweet-faced girl with rust-colored hair, dense clusters of freckles adorning her nose and cheeks. She gives me a nervous smile as our eyes meet. A pair of twins kneel next to her, pale-faced and straight-backed, like identical dolls, their lips drawn in a berry color to match their modern, high-collared dresses, so figure-hugging it pulls a blush to my cheeks.

Then I notice a girl set apart from the group. Unlike the rest, she's sitting almost casually, long legs folded to the side. Her draped skirt and blouse are tailored from a velvety ink-black fabric shimmering with intricate embroidery, like a star-dusted night. Wavy hair cascades to her waist. Even the maids have been openly staring since I came in, but this girl is still facing away, gazing over her shoulder with a bored expression. A slight pout puckers her darkly glossed lips. Just when I'm about to turn away, she looks round.

Our eyes catch. At least, that's what it feels like—a physical hold. She returns my gaze with a look so intense it roots me to the spot before her curved, catlike eyes flick away.

"This is her? *This* is the irresistible Nine?"

A high voice cuts through the quiet. It's the girl we heard outside, Blue. She's tall, even standing next to Madam Himura, with narrow shoulders and glossy azure-black hair, straight and smooth. Her features match the sharpness in her voice, angled cheekbones like two blades and narrow eyes shadowed with paint glinting out from beneath blunt bangs. The front of her emerald dress dips daringly low, revealing a flat triangle of alabaster skin.

"Well," she says, wielding her voice like a scythe. "If she hadn't been announced, I'd have mistaken *her* for the maid."

Her high laugh rings out—cutting off abruptly as Madam Himura slaps her.

The room falls silent.

Blue's head is twisted to the side. She holds it stiffly, her shoulders jerking with shallow breaths, dark hair hiding her face.

Despite her hunch, Madam Himura seems to double in size as she glares down her beak at Blue, her feathers ruffled. "I know who your father is, girl. After you were chosen, he came to me to ask that I don't treat you any differently because of his status. So you'd better give me the respect I'm owed." As Blue's cheeks flush, the eagle-woman's gaze sweeps over the room. "That goes for all of you. No matter your background, whether you have grown up with all or nothing, here you are all on the same level. And that level is beneath *me*." She jabs her cane in my direction. "Now, welcome Lei-zhi in the proper manner."

The girls drop into bows, Blue a fraction slower than the rest.

"I have already explained why she's here," Madam Himura continues. "I don't expect to repeat myself. Mistress Eira will show you to your sleeping quarters and instruct the maids to attend you. Tomorrow you have your assessments. Be ready for when I come for you."

"Yes, Madam Himura," the girls recite.

I hurry to echo them. When I look round, I catch Blue watching me, her eyes shining darkly.

Mistress Eira takes us to our private quarters on the northeast side of the house. She explains that the building we're in, Paper House, is where we will live during our year as the King's concubines. Her and Madam Himura's rooms are also to be found here, along with the maids' dormitory and a variety of parlors, kitchens, and entertaining rooms. Paper House is in the center of Women's Court, flanked to the north and east by gardens and to the south and west by other buildings: suites for the women of the court, as well as bathhouses, tearooms, and shops.

Our bedrooms run off a long corridor. Though immaculately kept, the rooms aren't what I was expecting. They're bare, furnished simply with a sleeping mat and a shrine stocked with joss sticks and a charcoal fire to burn them. Not exactly rooms to host a King. Then I shudder. Because where instead will that take place?

"This isn't very private," Blue sniffs, trailing a manicured nail along the edge of a door, which is barely more than a few thin pressed sheets of rice paper. Light from the hallway shines right through them.

"It isn't meant to be," replies Mistress Eira. "Your lives belong to the court now, girls. The sooner you understand that, the better."

Her voice is kind, but Blue scowls at her.

As Mistress Eira answers a question from one of the other girls, the pretty freckled girl I noticed earlier slips in beside me, offering a hesitant smile. She looks young—too young really to be here— with a round face framed with short auburn hair and luminous opal-green irises. Their shade is the exact color of the fields outside our village, rich and vibrant after the monsoon rains, and I return her smile, fighting the stab of homesickness that shoots through me.

"It's to stop us from taking lovers, isn't it?" the girl whispers, gesturing to the doors.

"I guess so."

"Not that I'd know." Her freckled cheeks grow pink. "I haven't ever had one. A lover, I mean! Not a bedroom. Though even that I shared with my sisters. Have you—have you had one?" she adds, breathless.

I lift my brows. "A bedroom?"

"No!" she giggles. "A lover."

I shake my head, and her face relaxes.

"I'm glad I'm not the only one. Mistress Eira told me I'm the youngest here. I just turned sixteen last week. I thought I'd be the only one without any, um, experience." She leans in, earnest. "I mean, I know we're not supposed to do anything before we're married anyway, but some of my sisters have done . . . *things*. And not just kissing." She lets out another nervous laugh, hiding her mouth behind her hands. "Sorry, I forgot to introduce myself! I'm Aoki."

"I'm—"

"Lei. I know. The ninth girl." Her eyes shift to the crown of azure-black hair at the front of the group as she adds under her breath, "Though maybe not for long. I don't know how much longer *she'll* last if she continues talking to Madam Himura that way." Aoki flashes a quick grin. "Can't say I'd be sad to see her go."

I laugh, stopping quickly when the other girls look around.

Mistress Eira shows us to our rooms, instructing us to wait for our maids. My room is at the end of the corridor, opposite Aoki's. I step inside slowly while she practically dances into hers.

"I don't think I'm going to be able to sleep!" she calls from across the hall. "Isn't this so exciting?"

I make a noncommittal murmur.

She takes a few steps forward, fingers twined together at her waist. "Do you maybe want to wait with me? We can leave the doors open so your maid knows where you are, and—"

"I'm going to rest for a bit," I cut in. "Sorry, I'm just so tired."

Disappointment flickers over her face. "Oh. All right."

The instant I shut my door, my smile drops. I stand awkwardly in the center of the room, loosening a long exhale. It looks just the way I feel—bare, stripped apart. For the first time since waiting for Madam Himura's inspection, I am alone, and as I'm finally able to let go of the pretense, the forced smiles and chatter, everything else drains from me, too.

I loop the room, running my fingers along the walls. Back in our shop-house, I knew all the knots in every wood panel. Each kink and nick and stain had a history, a memory attached to it. You could read my childhood in the fabric of the building. But here, it's all blank.

Or—not quite. I lift my fingertips back to the wall. Even recently, this room must have belonged to a previous Paper Girl. And others before. The Paper Girl tradition has been going on for hundreds of years. The walls might be clear of my own memories, but they are dense with layers upon layers of other girls' memories, a whole story—a whole *saga*—of lives that came before.

I rest my forehead to the wood. There's something comforting in knowing other girls were here before me, and survived. What was she like, the previous girl to live here? What did she feel on her first night in this room? What dreams did she dream here?

My stomach gives a kick.

What dreams of hers were *lost?*

At the sound of the door opening, I spring back from the wall. Lill rushes in. She's grinning and breathless, her uniform rumpled. "Mistress Eira is making me your maid!" she exclaims. "We were one short, and I've been wanting to progress from a housemaid for the last year! I've just given my eighty thanks to the heavenly masters but I still can't believe it!"

Her smile is infectious. "Then I'd better bow to *you*," I say, my lips twitching. I kneel, a bit awkwardly in my robes, flattening my palms on the floor. "How may I be of service, Mistress Lill?"

She erupts into giggles. "Oh, please don't! Madam Himura will have a heart attack if she sees!"

I look up with a smirk. "All the more reason to do it."

As Lill gets me ready for bed, the fear and unease start to shift, the pressure on my ribs unknotting just a little. I didn't imagine making friends here, but Lill and Aoki and Mistress Eira have given me hope that things might be different.

On the way to the palace, I was prepared for sadness. For tears. For having to do things I don't want to, and many more I am terrified of. For pain. For homesickness. As the hours went by in the carriage and then during that seemingly endless boat journey, I prepared myself for all the things that I could possibly find within the palace walls.

The one thing I didn't prepare for was kindness.

And yet somehow, kindness, these light exchanges with Aoki and Lill...it still feels wrong, like the worst kind of betrayal. My father and Tien must be heartbroken that I'm gone. And here I am, able to smile. To *laugh*, even.

That night, lying under the unfamiliar coolness of silk sheets, I cup my Birth-blessing pendant to my chest. It's the only thing I have with me from home. Squeezing my eyes shut against the sting of the tears, I picture Baba and Tien in the house, how they might be coping, and it breaks something deep within me. The word itself—*home*—is a blade in my gut.

It's a call, a song. One I can't answer anymore.

On nights when I couldn't sleep back in Xienzo, I used to lie exactly the same way I'm lying now, hands over my heart, my pendant safely nestled in the curve of my palms. I would pass the time by imagining what word could be hidden inside, and there was something comforting in it. The idea of being looked after, almost. A promise of a future so beautiful I couldn't even dream it yet.

But on the occasional night, my mind would fill the darkness with words just as black. Because whatever I want to believe, it is possible that my pendant holds a future I will not be grateful to receive.

And tonight that's never felt more likely.

SEVEN

WHEN THE GONG SOUNDS THE NEXT morning, I've already been up for hours.

It was the nightmare again. The kind you can't banish with assurances that it's all make-believe. That you can't wake from and let the bright sureness of your life slowly melt the darkness away. This was the kind of nightmare whose monsters you can never outrun, that are still there when you open your eyes.

The worst kind of nightmare, because its monsters are real.

It hit me hard and fast, almost as soon as I'd closed my eyes, thrusting me straight into the fire and screaming. The roar of demon soldiers. Fragments of memory, barely smudged by age: the way Mama cried my name; splashes of blood on the floor, as vivid as paint; the bodies I tripped over trying to get back to my parents.

Afterward—only returning home with one.

I knew I wouldn't get back to sleep after the nightmare, so I spent the rest of the night pacing the small rectangular patch of my room, feet almost silent on the soft bamboo mat floor, until my pulse returned to normal and my breathing slowed. And as I paced, a new idea started to emerge: that maybe it's a sign that on my first night in the palace I dreamed of Mama. Here I am, so far from home, in a place where she could have also been.

Instead of sleeping, I take one slow lap of my room after another. Did the soles of her feet kiss the ground here, too, once? There's got to be some way I can find out more about her while I'm in the palace. Someone who might know what happened to her. If nothing else good can come from being here, at least I might be able to get some closure about that.

How incredible would it be to be taken from one half of my family only to find the other half here on the opposite side of the kingdom?

As the morning starts to fill with the sounds of daily life, I move to the window. Outside, the sun is rising, burning away the last scatters of raindrops from the night's storm. My room looks out over the northeast side of Women's Court. I'd been imagining small gardens from what Mistress Eira told us last night, but the daylight reveals them to be vast, an undulating landscape filled with trees and ponds and lush wildflower meadows. Winged roofs of pagodas poke through the treetops. The grounds stretch so far into the distance that the palace walls are barely visible, but my gaze is still drawn to them: a severe line of black, like an angry brushstroke blotting the horizon.

A flock of birds scatter into the air. I follow their wheeling formation over the trees before they fly beyond the wall.

I turn from the window, a sour taste in my mouth. It doesn't matter how beautiful the cage is. It's still a prison.

There's a tap on the doorframe. Lill bounds in a second later, far more excitable than is decent for this time of day. "Good morning, Mistress! Did you sleep well?"

"Pretty well," I lie.

She beams. "Great! Because you've got a busy day ahead. We need to start getting ready." She clasps my hand and pulls me out of the room, leading me down the corridor. "First stop—the bathing courtyard."

"Um…I usually bathe at the end of the day. You know, *after* I've had time to get dirty?"

She sighs and says as if it were obvious, "Paper Girls wash in the mornings. It's one of the rules. Mistress Eira says it's symbolic. Something about purifying yourself for the day ahead. Getting rid of negative qi from bad dreams."

Thinking of last night, I repress a grim laugh. I'd need a whole *lake* for that.

We turn the corner to the bathing courtyard, a rush of hot air instantly moistening my skin. I raise my hand against the sun as we step down into a sunken courtyard dotted with big wooden barrels. Fronds of swaying bamboo line the walls. I pick up the scents of sweet rosewater and ylang-ylang, the ocean tang of seaweed, and homesickness darts through me as the fragrances take me back to my herb shop.

Through the steam, I notice that some of the tubs are already occupied. Most of the girls are submerged up to the neck, but when they move, they reveal flashes of skin that draw my eyes—the naked curve of a breast, the slope of a thigh.

I drop my eyes quickly to the floor and keep them trained on my feet as we cross the courtyard. Nakedness must be something everyone from affluent families is used to. Most of these girls probably had maids since they were young. Maybe they had places like this in their own houses, instead of a tiny room downstairs at the back of a shop-house where you had to use a sponge and water heated from a kettle to clean yourself, crouched in a corner so water wouldn't spill under the door.

Thankfully, Lill brings me to a barrel tucked into a corner that's well hidden by the clouds of steam. I shrug off my night robe before she can help, then practically dive into the tub.

"Don't worry, Mistress," she giggles when I emerge, peeking my head up above the water. "You'll get used to it."

Once we're back in my room, she dries my hair with a towel before dressing me in simple midnight-blue robes. Lill is just crouching at my feet, helping me into the socklike indoor slippers the women here wear to keep their soles smooth, when the clicks of talons sound in the hallway.

"Hurry up!" Madam Himura calls. "The others are waiting."

With one last encouraging look from Lill, I lift my chin and step out into the hall—and immediately trip.

I flail sideways, throwing a hand to the wall to catch myself. A few of the girls titter.

"It's…the shoes," I mumble, righting myself. "I'm not used to them."

"Of course you aren't," Madam Himura says. With a sigh, she turns, motioning for us to follow her. Even the snap of her cane manages to sound disapproving.

Aoki comes over as soon as she's gone, lacing an arm through mine. "I'm struggling with them, too," she whispers. "It's weird to have your feet all squashed like this. My sisters would laugh so much if they could see."

Most of the other girls have left, but Blue hangs back. "Perhaps it's good you're here after all, Nine," she says silkily. "You make even little Aoki here look graceful."

I make a rude gesture with my hands when her back is turned, and Aoki suppresses a laugh.

After some more stumbling, Aoki and I catch up with the girls. We're taken to the same parlor we were in last night. A set of sliding doors has been opened, letting in sunlight and the sound of leaves rustling in the garden beyond. Madam Himura leaves us without explanation. We wait until the rap of her talons has faded away before erupting into anxious whispers.

"I wish I knew what the assessments are," Aoki says, chewing her bottom lip. Around us, the other girls are speculating on the same topic. "Nothing too physical, I hope. I…I have some scars." Her emerald eyes shimmer. "Lei, do you think they'll send me home because of them? I can't be thrown out before I've even met the King!"

I take her hand and give it a squeeze. "I'm sure you'll be fine, Aoki. They chose you. They want you here."

"But what if they've changed their minds? Maybe now that they've seen me with the other girls they've realized they made a mistake picking me. Maybe—"

"Tell me about the selection process," I interrupt, realizing she's on the verge of a meltdown. "How does it work?"

She blinks. "Haven't you followed any of the selections?"

I shrug. "My village doesn't pay much attention to the court. It's just…so far away." I don't add the other reason—that we don't want anything to do with it. That what the King gets up to isn't important to us, as long as he leaves us alone.

"I thought everyone in Ikhara follows them!" Aoki exclaims, and seeming to forget her nerves, she launches into a thorough explanation.

I learn that the selection for Paper Girls begins on the first day of the third month each year. The process is split into two halves. The first, which runs for six weeks, invites families to bring their eligible daughters—Paper caste, of course, and at least sixteen years old by the time they would be inducted in the palace—to the court representatives in their province. The representatives evaluate candidates based on their ancestry, social standing, and nu skills, as well as their appearance. Scouts also travel throughout Ikhara to find suitable girls whose families didn't put them forward. The number discovered this way is surprisingly high.

Or perhaps not so surprising. Most Paper castes aren't exactly the King's biggest fans.

Once the six weeks are up, the representatives put forward their recommendations, shortlisting one hundred girls. The King is shown the selection to allow him to rule out any he deems unsuitable, and occasionally, to highlight ones he particularly likes the look of. A final thirty girls are invited to Han's capital for a presence with delegates from the royal court.

Aoki tells me her family are rice-paddy farmers in a remote part of eastern Shomu. The banquet was her first time out of the fields. "I wasn't myself at all, which is probably why they liked me. My quietness must have come across as dignified. But really I was just keeping my mouth shut so I didn't throw up! None of us could believe it when a royal messenger delivered my letter of acceptance—sealed by the King himself. *I* still can't believe it," she adds, her thick lashes tilted down. "I keep waiting for someone to tell me it's all been a joke."

"Don't say that. You earned your place here. Just like the others."

She grins. "You did, too, Lei! You're extra special for them to make such a big exception for you."

I bristle at the idea that I should be honored to be here. But the look she gives me is so earnest I swallow my retort.

Just then, the door opens, a maid announcing Madam Himura's return. In an instant, the room falls quiet.

The eagle-woman waves a hand irritably. "Blue," she croaks from the doorway. "You're first."

Blue rises to her feet with a look that says, *Of course I am.*

I didn't think Madam Himura would take long to come back, but two hours pass before the next girl is called, and another two until the next. Maids come in to serve us lunch, which I practically wolf down without chewing. It's been a long time since my last proper meal and the palace food is delicious. Some of the dishes are recognizable to me, if far more delicate than how I've tasted them before: steaming bowls of coconut rice jeweled with pomegranate seeds; marinated eel slices; a whole roasted duck glistening with dark sauce. But far more are unfamiliar, and even though my stomach rounds, I make sure I try at least one mouthful of everything.

By the evening, the superior-looking girl with the catlike eyes and I are the only ones left.

"Best till last, right?" I say when we've been sitting in silence for over an hour.

Cat-girl doesn't reply, watching me with her haughty look before turning pointedly away.

Uncomfortable silence it is, then. Glaring down at my plate, I stab at a sugared glutinous rice-ball a bit too aggressively. The little cake skids off the plate and plops onto the floor.

A snort of laughter.

I look up to find Cat-girl watching, eyebrows arched, her lips tucked up. Then, seeming to remember herself, her expression returns smoothly to neutral. "The chopsticks here must be different from the ones in Xienzo," she says coolly.

It's the first time I've heard her speak. Her voice is lower than I expected, and husky. It carries the elegant intonation of an aristocratic family. Lilting vowels, slow pacing.

"Yes," I mutter under my breath. "The ones here seem to be used as sticks up everyone's—"

Her eyes glide back to me. "What was that?"

"Nothing!" I sing, and luckily Madam Himura chooses that moment to return, calling finally for me.

I leave without saying good-bye to Cat-girl. Madam Himura leads me to a small room, a high, bare table in its center. A tall figure stands beside it with his back to us, and I catch an animal scent, something musty and sharp.

Nerves ripple through me.

"Doctor Uo," Madam Himura says, pushing me forward. "The next girl is here."

I force myself to stand steadily as the doctor turns, fixing me with a beady-eyed stare. He's a boar demon, Moon caste. Two short tusks grow from either side of a snoutlike nose. His skin is coated in tawny-colored hair, wizened with age, and a pair of jade spectacles perch at the end of his nose.

"Lei-zhi is the one I told you about, Doctor," Madam Himura continues. "This year's additional girl. Since she didn't go through the official selection process, please be sure to inspect her even more thoroughly."

The doctor's nostrils twitch. "Of course, Madam." His voice is as scratchy-sounding as his hair looks. As Madam Himura moves aside, he steps closer, hunching to bring his face in line with mine. Then, before I can process what he's doing, he reaches out and tugs my sash free.

My robes loosen. The doctor pulls to open them and I grapple against him to keep them shut, the blood rushing in my ears.

"W-what's going on?" I gasp, looking past the doctor to where Madam Himura is settling herself in the corner of the room, a scroll unfurled on the floor in front of her.

"Stop struggling, girl," she commands, not even glancing from her reading. A maid crouches in front of her, lifting a teapot. "Let the doctor inspect you."

"But—"

"Navya! Go help."

Jumping up, the maid rushes over. "Please, Mistress," she pleads, clasping my arms. "The doctor won't hurt you."

But I continue to struggle as the robes are ripped from my body, first the outer layer, then the inner. The maid is Steel caste, like Lill—most of the servants here are—and even though her jackal eyes are kind and she doesn't seem to enjoy herself as she helps the doctor undress me, my face burns with humiliation at my disrobing by two demons. It's as though I'm somehow doubly unclothed in their presence, lacking in robes *and* demon adornments, and I feel very clearly in this moment what it means to be a Paper caste. To have a body sheathed in something so delicate and easily damaged.

"On the table," the doctor orders.

Head low, tears stinging my eyes, I do as he says.

"Hold her."

The maid pins my arms down, though she needn't bother. I lie still from then on no matter how private the places the doctor touches are, Mistress Eira's words from last night playing in my mind.

Your lives belong to the court now, girls. The sooner you understand that, the better.

Lying there on the doctor's table, the dark truth of what she said hits me. It makes me imagine another time I might be lying naked for a demon, and the horror is so real then that I have to clamp my eyes shut, wish myself away.

When the inspection is finally over, I sit up and wrap my arms around my body. Tears leak from the corners of my eyes. The doctor moves away, but the young maid hovers nearby, watching me with her chin tipped down, hands clasped in front of her.

"Get dressed," Madam Himura snaps. Her feathers rustle as she gets to her feet. "We don't have all night."

The rest of the assessments pass in a blur. There are a fortune-teller's analysis and a meeting with the court's most reputable astrologer, and a royal shaman checks for any magic I might have used to change my appearance. There's also another doctor's examination, though this time by a qi doctor, who, thankfully, doesn't require me to take my clothes off.

It's past midnight by the time I get back to my room, so I'm surprised to find Lill waiting for me. She leaps up to hug me the second I walk through the door. "I was so worried!" she cries.

"Has something happened?" I ask, untangling from her. The tone of my voice is hollow. Just as I feel.

Her doe ears drop. "I—I thought you'd have heard, Mistress. One of the girls…she didn't come back from her inspection. She must have used an enchantment on herself during the selection process and the royal shaman found out. Apparently it's happened before, but not for many years." She adds shakily, "You were taking so long I got worried that something had happened to *you*, too."

"They were just extra thorough with my assessments," I explain. I think of Aoki. Cat-girl. "Which girl was it?"

"Mistress Rue. The girl from Rain. She seemed nice."

A hazy memory returns to me from last night of a pale petite girl in an ice-blue dress. She had seemed shy, not meeting anyone's eyes, but I noticed the quiet dignity in the way she held herself, her humble demeanor.

My belly knots. I didn't even get a chance to speak to her.

Though I'm not sure I want to know the answer, I wet my lips and ask, "What's going to happen to her?"

"Nothing good," Lill says, long lashes hiding her eyes as her gaze drops, and I somehow know that we will never hear of Rue again.

EIGHT

I THOUGHT BLUE MIGHT STOP CALLING me Nine now that our numbers have dropped back down to the usual eight, but it's the first thing she does when I arrive in the bathing courtyard the following morning.

"You let me down, Nine," she says, thin lips curving. "I bet the others you'd be the one to be thrown out."

I stiffen. Lill tugs on my elbow. "Ignore her, Mistress," she mumbles. She tries to pull me onward, but I don't move.

Blue is lying back in her tub, arms slung over its sides. Her collarbones are as sharp as a pair of featherless wings, stretched across her narrow chest like a necklace, and her breasts below—which she exposes without any hint of self-consciousness—are just as pointed.

Blue is all angles. Mind *and* body.

I meet her eyes with my own narrowed. "I hope you didn't bet a lot. From what Madam Himura said, it doesn't sound like your father will help you with your debts."

The easy chatter of the courtyard drops in an instant. The only sounds are the coos of birds nesting in the eaves, the splash of water as the other girls shift uncomfortably.

Blue's lip curls. "Don't pretend to know anything about my life. What could an herb-shop owner's daughter from Xienzo know? Especially one whose own mother left her family to become a whore."

Her words hit me like a slap.

"*What* did you say?"

"News travels fast in the palace, Nine. Better get used to it." She rises out of the barrel, wearing her nakedness proudly, like armor, eyeing me with a stare that dares me to look away. "It's a shame your mother didn't stick around," she adds, picking a bathrobe from the nearest maid and wrapping it around her slim frame. "I bet she'd be so *proud* to see her daughter following in her footsteps."

And then I'm running at her, snarling, my fingers flexing as though they could grow claws. I'm inches away from scraping her face off—that horrible, smug face, how *dare* she—when there's a blur of movement at my side. Before I can react, a pair of arms encircle me, pulling me off my feet.

"Let go!" I yell, kicking out, but the girl's grip is strong. She pins me against her, one elbow hooked at my waist, the other across the front of my body. A scent unfurls from her skin: something fresh, oceanlike.

Somehow I know it's Cat-girl.

Blue's face, shaken for a moment, settles quickly back into a sneer. "Well," she says, fixing the tie of her bathrobe. "That's no way for a Paper Girl to behave."

"Enough, Blue," Cat-girl snaps. "Before Madam Himura or Mistress Eira hear."

I expect Blue to shoot back a scathing comment, or at least take offense at the way Cat-girl spoke to her. But after glaring at me a while more, she shrugs. "I suppose you're right. No point wasting their time over something so petty."

My hands wrap into fists. "Calling my mother a whore isn't petty!" I shout.

Blue rounds on me again, then stops at the look Cat-girl gives her. With a toss of her hair, she stalks back into the house, leaving a trail of wet footprints across the courtyard's boarded floor.

As soon as Cat-girl releases me, I whirl around to face her. "You should've let me claw her face off!" I growl.

She regards me coolly. "Perhaps." Then she turns to leave, pausing first to add, "I *am* getting tired of that sneer."

The comment—almost humorous—disarms me, and I watch her go in silence. Damp hair cascades in a tousle to the low dip of her back. Her bathrobe has come off one shoulder to reveal a curve of smooth tanned skin, rosy-brown. I gave her the nickname Cat-girl because of the shape of her eyes, the keen, feline intelligence in them. But the way she moves is catlike, too. My eyes track her shifting hips, an unfamiliar warmth turning my belly.

"Mistress!" Lill grabs my arm, making me start. "Are you all right?"

"What's that girl's name?" I ask distractedly.

She follows my gaze. "Oh, Mistress Wren? I thought you might have heard of her already."

This makes me look round. "Why?"

"Mistress Wren is the daughter of Lord and Lady Hanno."

I recall the two blue-caped men on horseback I saw on the road to the palace. No wonder Blue listens to Cat-girl. If she really is a Hanno, the most powerful Paper caste clan in the kingdom—and daughter of their leader, no less—it explains why she's been acting so superior.

Not that it condones it.

"Wren," I murmur to myself, testing the name. It's wrong, too gentle on the tongue. Wrens are the noisy little birds that fly in pairs around our house in Xienzo, all chirping and dull brown feathers.

The word doesn't seem to fit this silent, solitary girl, who is more like the cat that would stalk the birds before pouncing.

After breakfast, Mistress Eira calls us for our first lesson. Lill prepares me carefully. She fixes my hair into a sleek double-knot at the nape of my neck before dressing me in a fuchsia ruqun—a wrap-front shirt with draped sleeves and a floor-length skirt, secured by a sash that falls down its front in a long-tailed bow. Apparently it's another clothing style popular with central Ikhara's high-class clans, but I am stiff and self-conscious in it, even though the fabric is soft.

"I'm not even leaving the house!" I say as Lill fusses over the bow for a good few minutes. "Does it have to be perfect?"

She shoots me a surprisingly stern look. "You're a Paper Girl now, Mistress. You never know who you might run into. Who is judging you at any time." Then she lightens. "You know, it's important you win the favor of the court if you want to win the Demon King's heart."

"Like he even *has* one," I mutter when she's out of earshot.

The other girls are already there when I arrive at Mistress Eira's suite. They're kneeling around a table with a stove set into the middle, steam rising from a copper kettle. On the walls are richly colored rolls of velvet and embroidered satin, all fluttering in the breeze coming in through the open doors at the back of the room. Through them, I glimpse the green of a courtyard garden, speckled with morning light.

"Lei-zhi, what a beautiful outfit," Mistress Eira says with a smile. She motions to a space next to Aoki. "Would you like some barley tea? I know how you girls must be feeling after yesterday's assessments. There's nothing better for nerves."

I kneel, careful to fold my skirt under the back of my legs so it won't fan out. Then, realizing what I'm doing, I let out a disbelieving laugh. Just a week ago I was squatting in a mixing tub, covered in dirt. Manners and etiquette were the last things on my mind.

Mistress Eira lifts a brow. "Something amusing, Lei-zhi?"

"Oh." I pick at the tails of my bow under the table. "I was just... remembering something that happened earlier."

A few of the girls stiffen—they must be worried I'm going to bring up what happened in the bathing courtyard. But that's the last thing I want Mistress Eira to know about. I highly doubt fighting is on the list of skills a Paper Girl should cultivate. *Oh, hey, King! Check out my amazing whip kick!*

"I keep tripping in my shoes," I make up lamely.

Mistress Eira nods. "Ah, yes. I remember. It took me a long time to get used to them, too." She looks around the table, and even this, the simple sweep of her head, has an elegance to it, a precision. "I don't know how much you all know about my heritage. Most of you are from prominent families. You've grown up with the customs of the court. But I spent my childhood working for my family's sari-making business in southern Kitori. When I first arrived at the palace, I was as graceful as a duck drunk on plum wine, heavens help me."

A few of the girls titter.

"No one would know, Mistress," Blue says, her tone honeyed. "My father told me you were the King's favorite."

Aoki lets out a cough that sounds suspiciously like a snort.

Ignoring her, Blue continues, "Didn't he personally choose you to become the Paper Girl mentor so we could all learn to be like you?"

"Well, I'm not sure about that," Mistress Eira replies with a half smile. "But it's true my transformation was pronounced. It took a lot of hard work and dedication to prove myself. That's why I take my job as your mentor so seriously. Whatever your backgrounds, you start at the same level here. Madam Himura and I have organized a rigorous timetable of lessons. You'll be replaced by new girls next year, but you're still expected to work in the court—as performers, or escorts for the King's guests, and so on—so it's important to keep cultivating your nu skills."

Just then, one of the girls speaks up. "Will we have any time off, Mistress Eira? I have a cousin who works in City Court. I promised my parents I'd visit her."

It takes me a moment to recall her name: Chenna, the dark-skinned girl who was wearing an orange dress—a sari, as Lill later explained, a style popular in the Southern provinces—the night we arrived. Today, her sari is citrus-yellow. It sets off the smooth gloss of her skin, the coal shade of her wide, heavy-lashed eyes.

"You'll have some time between your lessons and engagements with the court," Mistress Eira answers, "but it's important for you"—she turns to us—"for *all* of you, to understand that you don't have free time to yourselves here in the palace. You can't just leave Women's Court as and when you like." Her voice softens. "Don't get me wrong. You can live very happy lives as Paper Girls, I assure you. I myself have. But we are all part of the rhythms and workings of the palace, and so we must play the parts expected of us."

She begins a lecture on some of the palace's many rules and regu-lations. There are rules for things I wouldn't even have thought of, such as the depth of a bow or the speed at which we should walk in different areas of the palace.

"Soon she'll say we have to regulate our bowel movements, too," I whisper to Aoki, who stifles a giggle.

"This is just an introduction, of course," Mistress Eira says once she's finished with the lesson, a full hour later. "You'll learn every-thing else you need to know from your teachers in due course. But does anyone have any questions for now?"

Only about everything. But I don't admit it.

"I have one," one of the twins announces. After Mistress Eira nods, she leans forward and drops her voice a fraction. "Is it true that there is a Demon Queen?"

Murmurs ripple through the room. Nonplussed, I glance at Aoki. She shrugs. It seems the two of us are the only ones who haven't heard of her before.

Mistress Eira waits for quiet. Then she answers, "Yes." A pulse of expectant stillness falls over the table. "Most people outside the palace aren't aware of her existence because she's hidden. Kept in private quarters in Royal Court for the sole purpose of breeding."

"My father told me there is more than one queen," Blue says.

"Then he was misinformed," Mistress Eira answers, and Blue's face does a little spasm as she tries to look like she didn't mind being wrong. "There is only one. The royal fortune-tellers and advisers couple her carefully with each new King when he takes the throne to ensure a union the heavens will smile upon."

I swallow, glancing round the table. "None—none of *us* could become the queen, could we?"

"Certainly not. You are Paper castes. It is impossible for you to produce the Moon caste heir that would be required. In fact, each time you spend a night with the King, you will be given medicine to keep you from becoming pregnant."

While I don't know much about inter-caste procreation, I do know that although it is difficult for a man and woman from different castes to conceive, especially a Paper caste female and a Moon caste male, it's still possible. I suppose the King wouldn't want to lose his concubines to miscarriages. Or worse, give him a low-caste baby. In a coupling, the higher caste's gene is usually dominant, but we've all heard the stories of couples being taken by surprise.

"Has the current queen given the King any children yet?" Chenna asks from across the table.

Blue's eyes go wide. She shares a look with the short-haired girl sitting next to her.

Mistress Eira lifts a hand. "That is a private matter between them, not to mention a...sensitive issue. I strongly suggest none of you inquire into it any further." She tilts her head, her face relaxing. "Let's eat. You must all be hungry."

As lunch is served, we chatter easily at the table. Maids duck between us to keep our plates and cups full. Perhaps Mistress Eira's barley tea really does work, because halfway through the meal my nerves have calmed. I'm starting to enjoy the afternoon—the serene comfort of Mistress Eira's suite, the food, the company of the other girls.

It's the first chance I've really had to get to know them. Besides Aoki, Blue, and Wren, there is Chenna, who I learn is from Jana's capital, Uazu, in the South and is the only daughter of a rich mine owner. I like her immediately. She comes across as reserved, though not shy. When one of the other girls asks her whether she misses her family, she says yes without hesitation.

The twins are Zhen and Zhin. Their delicate features and alabaster skin are so similar I can barely tell them apart. I overhear them telling Chenna about their aristocratic family in Han, which, judging by her reaction, is apparently well known in Ikhara. Of course it would be—aristocratic Paper caste families are rare. Enterprise and government are areas for Moon castes. Even Steels are mostly limited to industry and trade. Paper castes usually occupy the lowest roles: servants, farmers, manual laborers. Sometimes the caste lines are crossed. Zhen and Zhin's family, as well as Blue's and Wren's, are testaments to that. But it's uncommon.

And still, there's always the knowledge that no matter how high a human might rise, demons will always be superior.

The last in our group is Mariko, a curvaceous girl with full lips and a perfectly oval face, enhanced by cropped hair that cups her chin in two winglike sweeps. Mariko and Blue seem to have become friends. They drop their heads together to whisper often, shooting me smug looks over the table. I get so fed up of this that the next time they cut their eyes to me I beam back, waving.

There's a snort. I glance round to find Wren watching me, her eyes lit with amusement. But as soon as she sees me notice, the smile drops from her face. She crooks her neck round, shoulders stiff.

"What's her problem?" I ask Aoki under my breath, scowling in Wren's direction. "She's barely said a word to anyone. It's like she *wants* us to dislike her."

Aoki leans her head close. "Well, you know what they say about the Hannos." At my blank look, she goes on, "You know how most Paper castes hate them for being so close to the King? She must be aware of that. I can't imagine it's easy."

It takes me a moment to understand what she's telling me. That Wren may act like she hates all of us, but maybe it's because she's worried that *we* hate *her*.

After lunch, Mistress Eira takes us out to her small courtyard garden. It's beautiful. The trees and bushes are strung with colorful beads, yellow flowers dotting the green like precious jewels. Gilded cages hang from the eaves. The twitters of the birds inside rise above the babbling pool that loops round a central island mounted by a small pagoda. Something about the place reminds me of my garden back in Xienzo, the slightly overgrown edges, or maybe just the sound of birdsong and the warm sunshine on my face.

Eyes stinging, I hurry away from the other girls, heading down a narrow stone path, suddenly wanting to be alone. I settle on a bench half hidden by a magnolia tree. Curling cups of pink-white leaves form a ceiling overhead. The afternoon air is rich and sweet, full of the scents of blossom and sun-warmed wood and the conversations of the other girls. I recognize the voices of Chenna and Aoki, just around the corner.

"So you've heard about them, too?" Chenna says.

"I thought they were only happening in the North. There was one not far from where we live in the East of Shomu, and I heard reports of others in the rest of our province. Xienzo and Noei, too."

"I think it's all the periphery provinces. We've had some in Jana, too." "My Ahma told me the King's patrols have always performed raids," Aoki replies. "Especially on villages where Paper caste clans live. But there's more now. And from what we hear, they're...different. Even worse."

"Has anyone you know..." Chenna's voice trails off.

I imagine Aoki shaking her head. "You?"

"No. The court would never attack the capitals." There's a pause, and then Chenna goes on, "But on my way to the palace we passed a town near the northern border—or what *was* a town. There was barely anything of it left. My mother told me she had a friend who had family there. Kunih help their souls," she blesses quietly.

"I saw places like that on my way here, too," Aoki murmurs.

"Do you think it has anything to do with the Sickness?"

"I don't know. But I *do* know that the Sickness has been getting worse. My parents told me our taxes have gone up, and more and more of our crops are getting seized by royal soldiers every year. It must be getting pretty bad in some places."

They move away, and my thoughts drift with them. I don't know what the Sickness is, but they were talking about the raids, like the one that happened to my village, and the ruined town I saw on my way to the palace. It must be happening all over Ikhara. General Yu said the one we saw in Xienzo had to do with a rebel group. Is that why other places are being attacked, too? And was that what he meant when he said to Mistress Eira that the kingdom is facing hard times? Increased rebel activity, and whatever this Sickness is?

"What do you think?"

Mistress Eira's voice surprises me from my thoughts. I hurriedly stand and give her a bow, which she waves me out of, smiling.

"A-about the raids?" I ask, before realizing she doesn't know what I overheard Aoki and Chenna discussing.

"About my garden," she corrects with a frown. "Do you like it?"

I nod. "It's lovely."

She sits down on the bench, motioning for me to join her. "I'm so glad you like it. Sometimes in summer I sleep out here in the pagoda. It reminds me of my childhood. We used to do that, too, when the weather was good."

"You said your family were sari-makers from Kitori?"

Mistress Eira nods. "We were well known in the region. There was always lots of work. My cousins and I would tell jokes, exchange gossip as we washed in the river after work to get the dyes out of our skin." She raises her palms and adds, muted, "Sometimes I dream about being unable to get the colors out. When I wake up and find my hands bare, it almost makes me want to cry." She lets out a little laugh and shakes her head. "I'm being nostalgic."

"Do you miss it?" I ask gently. "Your home?"

There's a beat of hesitation before she replies. "This is my home now, Lei-zhi." She lays a hand on my shoulder. "You should try to start thinking of it that way, too."

I look away. "My home is Xienzo. My parents' house. It always will be."

Even after Mama was taken, Baba, Tien, and I kept it going. We made a new family. We kept our home alive. How can I just let go of that?

I remember the promise I made to myself on the way to the palace. I *won't* let go of it. Whatever it takes, I'm going to get back.

"Mistress," I say quickly, an idea coming to me. "Do you think I could write to them? My father and Tien? Just let them know I'm well. Nothing more, I promise."

At first it seems like she's going to say no. But with a half smile, she replies, "Of course, Lei. What a nice idea. I'll make sure you're given paper and ink."

I grin, forcing myself to remain dignified and not throw my arms around her in a giant bear hug. I picture my father and Tien reading my letters together. Even from the other side of the kingdom they'll be able to touch something I've touched, feel my presence in each indent on the paper. They'll know I'm safe. And, always, that I am thinking of them.

"Make sure to bring your letters to me when they're done," Mistress Eira instructs. "I'll give them to my most trusted messenger to deliver."

"Of course. Thank you, Mistress. You don't know how much this means to me."

She returns my smile. But just before she turns away something flutters across her eyes: the barest shadow of sadness. Perhaps it's all this talk about the past, about life before the palace. I recall what Mistress Eira said about waking up from dreams of her childhood, her once dye-stained hands delicate and bare, and comprehend that although she might have avoided answering my question about whether she misses her home, I am sure of what the answer would be anyway.

I know what it means to dream about the past.

To dream about things you have loved, and lost.

NINE

Paper House is already busy when I wake the next day, the sunlit air bright with the sound of maids hurrying in the hallways, orders being called from room to room. Excitement carries through the air, an electric hum. It takes me back to festivals in our village, when every street would be draped with crimson banners during the fifteen days of the New Year, or lit with sparklers and firecrackers for spirit-warding ceremonies in the winter. Tonight, cities across the kingdom will be celebrating in our honor as we participate in the Unveiling Ceremony, where the Paper Girls are officially presented to the court.

I can still hardly believe that this year that includes *me*.

Lill is so excited about the ceremony she barely pauses for breath from the minute she comes to take me for my morning bath. "I haven't been able to visit my parents and tell them about becoming your maid yet," she chatters as I soak, her fluted deer ears quivering. "They're not going to believe it! Mistress, you might even see them during the procession! I wish I could be with you. The look on their faces if they knew…"

I float my hands out, scooping the bubbles on the surface of the water. "When was the last time you saw them?"

"Oh. It's been quite long. Almost half a year."

I splash round. "Half a *year?* But they live here, right? In the palace?"

Lill nods. "I lived with them in Mortal Court before I moved here. And they work in City Court, which is just south of here. I just don't get many days off. Not that I'm complaining," she says hurriedly. "The ones I do, I spend with them. I have a little brother and sister, too. I try to bring them treats from the kitchens whenever I visit—" She cuts off, blanching.

"Don't worry. If anyone notices, tell them it was me. The portions here are way too small." Lill's smile comes back, grateful, even though this sweet girl shouldn't have to worry about stealing a few bits of food to bring to her siblings. "I hope you can see them soon," I add.

She bows her head. "Thank you, Mistress."

I place my wet hand over hers where she's holding the edge of the tub. "You know, I had a Steel caste friend back in Xienzo, too. She worked in my family's herb shop."

"Really?" Lill's eyes widen. "We were told castes don't ever work for ones below them outside the palace." She blushes and goes on quickly, her head lowered, "Oh, I didn't mean that it's wrong for me to be working for you. It's a huge privilege, Mistress. It's just, Mistress Eira told us it's an exception that the Paper Girls have demons as servants. She said the King himself requested it. Only Steels, though." She glances up at me from under thick lashes. "I—I'm sorry I'm not Moon."

I almost laugh, the notion that I would prefer a Moon caste for a maid—or just anyone other than her.

"You're perfect, Lill," I tell her, and the beam of her grin is so luminous it seems to wash the whole courtyard with gold.

*   *   *

Following tradition, each of us is dressed in silver for tonight's ceremony. Silver is a powerful color: a symbol of strength, success, wealth. Yet because of its closeness to white, the mourning color shared by all Ikharan cultures, it is sometimes thought to bring bad luck. When Lill tells me about this tradition, I understand the message it is sending to the kingdom.

Support the King, and you will be rewarded.

Cross him, and you will suffer.

As it's Lill's first time being a Paper Girl's maid, her preparations are overseen by one of the other maids—Chiho, a serious-looking Steel caste lizard-girl, human in appearance apart from the coating of sleek pine-green scales along her bony arms and neck. Chiho dashes between rooms, trying to teach Lill while getting her own girl ready, until Lill suggests we get ready together. I can't remember which girl Chiho is a maid to, so when she appears in the doorway with Wren behind her, I stiffen.

Though still in her bathrobe and only half made up, Wren looks striking. Her cheeks have been colored a deep plum shade that brings out the dark sheen of her eyes and lips, and her hair cascades over one shoulder in flowing waves. She picks up the hem of her bathrobe as she steps inside. My eyes are drawn to the movement, and I do a double take.

Wren's feet are worn, their soles hard and calloused. They're more like my own feet. Workers' feet. Not the delicate kind you'd expect from the pampered daughter of the Hannos.

Catching me looking, she releases her robe and the hem drops to the floor.

"Right," Chiho says to Lill. "Let's continue."

Wren avoids my gaze as she kneels in front of me. I fight the childish urge to shout at her, to make her look at me. I remember what Aoki told me about Wren being aware of people hating her. Well, she isn't exactly helping the matter, is she?

It takes an hour for Chiho and Lill to finish with our faces. Coated with polish, my eyelids and lips are sticky. The first thing I do when they step back is lift a hand to rub my eyes, causing Lill to have a mini panic attack and assess closely for damage, even though I hadn't touched them yet.

Chiho circles me, making one final inspection. "Good," she says eventually, and Lill beams.

My eyes cut to Wren, who still hasn't said anything all this time. As she gets up to leave, I lift my chin and blurt out brusquely, "Well? How do I look?"

I want to take it back immediately—I sound petulant and stupid, and I'm not even sure why I care about her opinion. But Wren has already stopped. She glances over her shoulder, dark eyes under heavily glossed lids finally meeting mine. "Like you're not ready," she says bluntly, her face expressionless, before following Chiho out of the room.

Her words sting. I look away, my cheeks glowing.

Lill leaves the room, returning a few minutes later with a silk-wrapped package. "Your dress," she announces, almost reverently, as she hands it to me. "The royal tailors were given the results of your assessments and told to create unique pieces for each of you. It's meant to be a statement to the court about who you are. Something to give the King an idea about what you're like." She beams. "Go on, Mistress! Open it!"

Rolling my eyes at her excitement, I pull aside the folds of silk. There's the wink of metallic silver. Carefully, I lift the dress out and lay it on the floor.

It's the most exquisite dress I have ever seen. Not that that's hard—I haven't seen many. But even including the outfits the other girls wore on the first night at the palace, this one outshines them all. Cut long and slender, sleeveless, with a high collar, silver threads woven through flicker like running water when they catch the light. The delicate silk fabric is almost sheer. A scattering of moonstones, and diamonds wind along the hips and chest.

I stare down at myself, my belly doing a low flop. Just a handful of these jewels would be enough to support my family for life.

Lill lets out a squeal so high-pitched it almost shatters my ear-drums. "Oh, it's so beautiful! Try it on, Mistress!"

Many awkward wiggling movements later, the cheongsam—as I know now this modern style of dress is called—is on. It fits per-fectly, clinging to my frame like a second skin. Despite the jewels, the material is light, mere brushings of gossamer across my skin. Magic thrums in the fabric. Whatever enchantment has been placed on the dress also makes it glow. Every movement I make sends out scatters of silvery light, as pale as moonbeams.

I raise a brow at Lill's expression. "This is the first time you've not had anything to say."

She giggles. "Better enjoy it, Mistress! I don't know how long it'll last."

After a final once-over, we head through Paper House to its main entrance, where the procession will start. Though the dress fits per-fectly, less perfect is my ability to move in it, and it takes me a while to get used to wearing something this formfitting. Not to mention, it feels so expensive I'm worried about damaging it; every table corner glints threateningly. As the muffled buzz of voices and music outside grows louder, my heart thuds harder. Maids bow as I pass, some holding up good-luck offerings of red flowers, others sprinkling salt in my path, a custom I've never seen before. We would never waste salt in my house like this.

When we're almost at the entrance, I spot the familiar blaze of auburn hair. "Aoki!" I call, and she turns, breaking into a grin.

"Lei! Oh, you—you look…" Something shifts in her tone, a twist of envy. One hand fingers the collar of her own dress as her gaze travels slowly down mine.

"You look amazing!" I say quickly. "What a beautiful ruqun." I look it over appreciatively. The layered sheets of material are shimmery and light, decorated with patterns of leaves in thick brushstrokes. When I run my fingers over them, the leaves seem to ripple, swirling as if in a wind. More magic.

She tucks her chin, lashes low. "They say they're designed to reflect our personalities. It sounds silly, but as soon as I put it on, I felt like I was home. Like I have a part of the countryside with me. But you…" She reaches for my dress, then stops short. "You look like a *queen*."

Her words send a shudder through me. That's the last thing I want to look like. I think of Baba and Tien. What would they say if they saw me in this dress, my face and hair decorated even more elaborately than our entire village during New Year celebrations?

If I were a queen, then that would mean I would belong in the palace. And I don't.

As Aoki and I walk down the last few corridors together, the sound of cheering grows so loud now it vibrates in my rib cage. We step out onto the porch into sunlight and a clapping crowd. The streets around Paper House are packed. My breath hitches. I've never been in the midst of so many people—let alone Steel and Moon castes, all crammed together—and even though their applause and shouts are friendly, the sheer number of them makes me uneasy.

Along one of the streets, the crowd is parting to let through a train of ornate carriages carried by muscled oryx-form demons in red and black robes. The King's colors. Aoki nudges me excitedly as they advance. Wind flutters the ribbons draped over their open sides. Every step they take makes the bells hanging from their horns sing.

They come to a stop in front of Paper House. Madam Himura moves forward, shouting to be heard over the noise. "Presenting Mistress Aoki-zhi of Shomu!"

A servant comes to take Aoki to her carriage. She gives me a quick look—her jade-stone eyes gleaming, whether from excitement or fear I can't tell—and our fingers brush before she's led away.

Next, Madam Himura calls Blue, then Chenna. All too soon it's my turn.

I stumble forward, head low against the stare of the crowd. With a bow, the oryx drop to their knees. A servant helps me up into the lowered palanquin. The interior reminds me of the carriage I traveled in with General Yu, with its plush, perfumed cushions and elegant wood paneling. As I settle on the bench, my breath grows tighter. That carriage stole me away from my home—what kind of life am I about to be led into with *this* journey? In this beautiful cheongsam, being carried on the backs of demons, I feel like a dish being served for the King's dinner, and a shiver runs down my spine.

Just when will he choose to devour me?

TEN

M Y VIEW IS OBSTRUCTED BY THE long sashes hanging over the palanquin's open sides, so this is how I see the palace properly for the first time: in snatched glimpses, the blur of movement and color. The lowering sun tints everything in a golden haze. It looks dreamlike, and feels it, too, as though I were looking out through someone else's eyes. I'm about to become a Paper Girl. The concept is still ridiculous and ungraspable, even though here I am, sheathed in silver, hundreds of humans and demons watching my carriage pass, craning for one look at my face.

Yesterday Mistress Eira showed us a map of the palace. I picture it now, trying to keep track of where we're going. I haven't forgotten about finding my mother. Maybe I'll see something that will give me a clue as to where she might be.

The palace grounds are arranged in a gridlike system, divided into courts, which are further separated into two areas: the Outer Courts, where all the daily services, work, and residential areas are, and the private Inner Courts, where only those of certain positions are allowed. Women's Court is in the northeast block of the palace, in the Outer Courts. We first travel south, passing through City

Court, a vast, bustling area of trade, markets, and restaurants. Then we head west through Ceremony Court, the square behind the main gates where I arrived with the General, and on to Industry Court, with its smoking forges and leather-tanning houses. Next, we move up the west side of the palace. We pass through Mortal Court— Lill's family's home, another citylike area where the maids, servants, and low-level government officials live—and then Military Court, home to the training grounds and army barracks.

There are two areas in the Outer Courts we don't visit. At the northwest tip of the palace, Ghost Court is the official burial grounds. It would be bad luck to pass through such a place on a night of celebration. We also avoid Temple Court, which is within the exterior walls of the palace itself. The royal shamans must never be disturbed; only with the King's permission can one enter their holy grounds. At one point, though, when we take a perimeter road through one of the courts that takes us right up to the wall, a warm, prickly sensation ripples across my body, the thrum of magic imbued in my dress seeming to shiver and rustle in response.

Night has fallen by the time we arrive at the Inner Courts. At once, the crowds thin out. It's still busy, with every court official and their servants out to greet us, but the grounds here are more spacious, so the effect is of a sudden dampening, like a thick fog pillowing the world. The quiet comes as a shock after the jubilant atmosphere of the Outer Courts, and suddenly I miss the noise and chaos. I watch the darkening grounds through the window with a growing sense of unease, my tongue padded and dry in my mouth.

We're almost there.

The landscape of the Inner Courts is a mix of lantern-lit streets, elegant pearl-white squares, and manicured gardens, the perfume of flowers cloying in the air. Moonlight reflects off a sweeping crescent of water that loops in and out of sight as we travel—the River of Infinity. It flows in a figure eight through Royal Court, the area at the heart of the palace, designed to bring the heavens' fortune on the King.

The last part of our journey is marked when we pass over the central-most point of the river where the four curves meet. A gilded bridge arches over the water, lined with onlookers. They toss red blossoms at us, the petals catching in the wind and swirling around our carriages like a blood-drenched snowstorm.

"Heavens' blessings!"

"May the gods smile down upon you!"

Their words are well meaning, but much less exuberant than those of the Outer Courts. The closeness of all these demons makes me press back from the window. We're almost over the bridge when there's the thud of something ramming the carriage.

I fling out my arms as it jerks to the left.

Another thud.

This time the carriage lurches sideways, almost tipping over. I smash into the side, fingers scrabbling for hold just in time. A few seconds later and I would have fallen through the open side. As the oryx right the carriage, I steady myself, rubbing my right shoulder where it hit the wood. Yells and shouts are coming from outside. Still cradling my shoulder, I cross the floor and peer out through the fluttering ribbons.

And gasp.

A human—Paper caste, her furless, scaleless, clawless body standing out against the otherness of the demons all around—is being pinned to the ground by two guards. Her robes are thin and worn. Servants' clothes. Paper caste servants aren't allowed in the Inner Courts; she must have snuck in somehow.

Just then, she lifts her head and our eyes meet. I don't know what I was expecting. That they'd be filled with compassion, maybe, a kindred connection from one human to another. But instead, her look is fire.

"*Dzarja!*" she shrieks. Flickering lantern-light distorts her face, making her mouth seem too wide, her cheeks sunken hollows. "Dirty sluts! You shame us all!"

Above her, a guard lifts a club.

I look away, but not quickly enough. The heavy crunch rings in my ears. The accusatory glare in her eyes just before the club was brought down on her skull shimmers on the back of my eyelids, a ghostly afterimage. Lowering my lashes, I hover my fingers at my chest, then turn them outward with my thumbs crossed: the sky gods salute for a newly departed soul.

"Mistress, are you all right?"

I jolt as a horned face, part rhino, skin thick like hide, appears through the ribbons.

I open my mouth a few times before finding my voice. "Y-yes."

"Apologies for the disruption. You will be continuing on your way now." The guard bows.

"Wait!" I say as he turns to leave. "The woman. Why did—why was she—"

His expression doesn't change. "Why was she killed?"

I swallow. "Yes."

"She was a slave. She wasn't permitted to be in the Inner Courts. And she posed a threat to the King's property."

It takes me a moment to realize he means me.

"But—you could have arrested her. You didn't have to...to *kill* her."

"Guards are permitted to execute Paper castes on the spot." The leathery skin of his forehead wrinkles. "Is that all, Mistress?"

The tone of his voice makes me stiffen. He says it so easily, so bluntly, as though it weren't anything at all.

"Mistress?" he repeats at my silence. "Is that all?"

I go to nod, then change it to a shake at the memory of the searing look in her eyes. "The woman, she—she called me something. Dzarja. What does it mean?"

He scowls. "It is an ugly expression."

"For what?"

"'Traitor,'" he says, and lowers his hand, ducking his head out of the carriage, the ribbons fluttering back into place.

Dzarja. The word haunts me as our procession starts back up. How easily the guard took the woman's life, just the arc of a muscled arm. She wasn't that much older than my mother when she was stolen, and I get a flash of a Paper caste face—Mama's this time—mouth wide with terror as she is pinned down by a demon guard. I've been so focused on the thought that all she needed was to survive the journey here that I didn't consider how difficult it might be for her to survive once she *arrived*.

Ten minutes later, my stomach is still churning when we pass through a set of tall gates into a barren plaza. A single road cuts down the center. Ahead looms a grand fortress, carved from flecked rock dark as a raven's coat. Banners marked with the King's bull-skull symbol snap in the wind. On every balcony and along the base of the building, guards stand watch, weapons at the ready. The quiet is uneasy, and the hoof-fall of the oryx demons echoes through the desolate square, my own pulse matching the rhythm and even their weight, each beat so heavy and terse it's like my heart is clamping around a stone.

As we make our approach, I flex my fingers, trying to bring blood back to them. My muscles are as frozen as the rock of the royal palace looks.

Our procession comes to a stop at the bottom of a grand set of marble stairs leading up to a high, vaulted entranceway. At first everything is still. Then a band of gold unfurls itself from the entranceway. In one luxurious sweep, it rolls down the staircase, viscous and fluid, like some kind of charmed waterfall, and sure enough, I pick up the telltale vibration of magic in the air.

The door of my carriage swings open. "Mistress Lei-zhi," greets a servant, holding out a hand to help me down.

The golden spill has painted the ground around the carriages in a shimmering metallic carpet. As my feet meet the floor, I look down to see ripples flowing out around me. But despite the beauty of it, I'm still reeling from what just happened on the bridge, and I follow the rest of the girls up the stairs, eyes trained on my feet to avoid the stares of the guards.

The world seems to grow even quieter when we enter the palace, though maybe I'm imagining it, the hush that sinks over us, reverent almost. As we march, I take in our surroundings in silent awe. There are echoing halls and narrow corridors. Indoor gardens with magical ceilings that mimic the night sky. Long staircases that wind steeply from floor to floor. Everything is carved out of the same black stone as the exterior, and though undeniably beautiful, it gives the place a clammy, imposing feel, like a mausoleum.

I think of the Paper Girls who came before me. The dreams of theirs that might have died within these very walls.

We have been walking for over twenty minutes when we are finally told to stop. A vaulted archway looms before us, the room beyond hidden by a heavy black curtain.

We're still in a line ordered by our names. In front of me, Chenna's thick hair falls down in its usual braid, though tonight it has been threaded with tiny silver flowers that make it look as if she'd been dancing between the galaxies, catching stars. Her shoulders rise and drop with shallow breaths. I'm about to step forward, offer some words of comfort, when there's a groan behind me.

"Oh, gods," Mariko moans. "I think I'm going to be sick."

I pivot round to find her doubled over, her face white.

"Take a deep inhale," I say, laying a hand on her arm, but she shoves me away.

"I don't need the help of a peasant!" she snaps.

I draw back. "Fine, then." I'm about to turn away when, over Mariko's bowed head, Wren catches my gaze.

I freeze. She looks so astonishing it's almost unreal, as though she'd slipped out of a painting perfectly formed, a thing of beauty, of art—of bright, vivid life in this cold, still place. The design of her cheongsam is the exact opposite of mine. Where the collar of mine is high, hers runs low, exposing the deep shadow of her cleavage. My dress has a slit up the side; hers is tight all the way down her legs, emphasizing their length and muscled shape. Unlike my sheer fabric, hers is a dark gunmetal silver, dangerous and enticing, evocative of armor.

Faintly, I remember what Lill said about our dresses representing our personalities. Underneath my wonder at her beauty, curiosity stirs.

As usual, Wren is the one to break eye contact. But to my surprise, she does so to lean forward to speak into Mariko's ear. "I don't know about you," she murmurs, "but I have never seen a peasant who looked like that." She looks up at me, a half smile touching her lips. "*Now* you look ready," she says, just as a gong sounds from beyond the archway.

I whip back round to see the curtain floating aside. "Heavenly Master and honorable members of the court," a magnified voice announces from the room beyond. "Presenting this year's Paper Girls!"

In front of me, Chenna straightens, rolling her shoulders back. I follow her resolve, releasing a long exhale to steady myself as best as I can despite the spike of my pulse as, one by one, we step through the archway.

We emerge into a columned hall, deep and cavernlike, draped with garlands of vermilion silk. The walls look hollowed out of a marble cave. Rows of sheer steps on all sides lead down to a sunken pool. Ink-black water glitters with the reflection of lanterns overhead. From balconies ringing the room, hundreds of demon faces leer down at us. Our steps echo as we fan out in a row at the top of the steps, and I find it difficult to move, as if the expectant hush of the watching crowd had a weight, a solidity that thickens the atmosphere, lends an extra tug to gravity just here in this hall.

At first I keep my eyes low, trained on the floor. But something soon pulls their attention. Something draws them down the steps, across the pool, and to the podium on the far side. And I know before I see him what—or rather *who*—it will be.

The Demon King.

Lounging, almost, on his marbled gold throne. Or at least, there is something casual in the way he occupies it, some smug, almost irreverent quality to the way he sits, hips sloped a little too low, arms slung over the sides, head tilted back just enough to make it seem as if he were looking down at us even though we are much higher up the steps.

This is the first thing about him that surprises me. The King's pose is particularly at odds with the formal, straight-backed stances of the three soldiers flanking him—a gray wolf-man, a huge moss-colored crocodile-man, and a white fox female, all Moon caste.

Also unexpected is how slender he is. Particularly in comparison with the crocodile demon who towers behind the throne, the King's muscles are lean, roped, a bull's strength bound through manlike limbs, and hidden under layered black robes with gold trim. In a fight between him and his crocodile guard, I wouldn't rate the King's chances very high…*except*. There is an energy about him. Coiled and alert, a magnetic pull that commands attention and power. Ice-blue eyes watch from under long lashes. Above his ears, thick horns unwind, etched with grooves inlaid with gold. And as I take in his face from a distance, there is a third thing that surprises me.

The King is handsome.

I was expecting an old King. Some weary, war-torn bull. But he looks young, not far past his teens. There's an elegance to his face. Whereas General Yu's was an ugly clash of imposing bull features, the King's face is long, almost delicate in shape, with a defined jaw and wide, graceful mouth, a cupid's bow peaking perfectly in its middle.

A lazy smile sharpens into a grin. The King leans forward, lantern light lending his walnut coat a glossy sheen. "My new Paper Girls," he drawls. "Welcome."

His voice is deep, heavy as night.

Quickly, we drop to the floor in low bows. The marble is cool against my palms. I feel the King's gaze upon us like a touch and keep my head down, breathing hard.

"Presenting Mistress Aoki-zhi of Shomu!" comes the announcer's voice.

There's the sound of Aoki getting to her feet. Her tentative footsteps, then the unmistakable swish of water as she enters the pool. Mistress Eira told us that the water is part of the ritual, symbolic of purifying our bodies before we meet the King. It's been enchanted so it won't affect our appearance. A short while later Aoki's wavering voice rings out with the greeting Mistress Eira taught us.

"How sweet," comes the sound of the King's voice, quieter now but still heavy and deep. "What a cute nose."

I grind my teeth. He makes it sound as if she were a toy, a plaything for him to toss aside once he grows bored.

Which is exactly what she is, I remind myself, pressing my fingertips firmer against the cold stone.

What we all are.

The King takes more time with Blue, who is called next, and with Chenna, until all too soon, the announcer sings, "Presenting Mistress Lei-zhi of Xienzo!"

I get to my feet, awkward in this ridiculous dress, my right shoulder still stiff from where it bashed into the carriage wall earlier. The chamber is deafeningly quiet. The silence seems to spool around me, catlike, coaxing my nerves. I walk forward, trying to mimic Mistress Eira's light way of moving. But my steps are heavy. Like in the carriage, the whole situation has a dreamlike tint to it, and my heart surges with the hopeless desire for that to be all this is.

I've learned how to live with nightmares. I could cope with one more.

Though I keep my eyes firmly tracked on the stairs I'm making my way down—it's all I can do not to trip over in this ridiculous dress—I sense the eyes of the crowd following me. *Dzarja.* The word bounds into my head. Is that what I am? Is that what the demons see, a girl who is a traitor to her own people?

When I reach the bottom of the steps, I let out a relieved puff of air—just as I take my first step into the pool and stand on the hem of my dress.

The crowd gasps as I lurch forward. My arms fling out inelegantly, and I grimace as I hit the surface of the water with a smack. It's cold, a fist of ice. I expect to choke, but the water is like viscous air, and I wrestle my panic down, regaining my composure. Or at least, whatever passes for composure when you've lost all traces of dignity. I scramble up and stride on, the dark liquid of the enchanted pool flowing around me like smoke. I do my best at getting out the other side somewhat gracefully. When I climb onto the podium, I drop to my knees at the King's feet without daring to look at him.

"I—I am honored to serve you, Heavenly Master," I recite into the shocked silence.

More silence.

And then the room erupts with the King's laughter.

"Look at the poor thing!" he cries, his sonorous voice echoing off the cavernous walls. "Dressed like a queen when she cannot even walk a straight line. How much liquor did you ply her with to calm her nerves, Madam Himura?" he jokes, and the crowd joins in, the hall reverberating with demon laughter as a servant darts forward to hurry me on, and I stumble away, face burning.

ELEVEN

"MARIKO ALMOST THREW UP ON HIS FEET."

"But she didn't."

"I think Zhen bowed wrong. It looked funny from where I was, anyway."

"Aoki, I fell flat on my face. In front of the entire court."

She sighs. "You're right," she admits. "It was a complete disaster."

I break a smile, and she nudges me with her shoulder, green eyes glittering.

It's early the next morning. The two of us are sitting on the steps to the bathing courtyard, wrapped in gray light and predawn hush. The calm is at odds with the busyness of the house yesterday, and I'm glad for this moment with Aoki before the day, our first as official Paper Girls, begins.

Last night, all I wanted to do was curl up in a ball of embarrassment after my display at the ceremony. Not just because of how humiliating it was, falling over in front of the whole court, but because of how it made me look to the King. Before last night, I thought I didn't care what he'd think of me.

And then he laughed at me. *Laughed*, like I was a joke. And I want him—*need* him—to know that I am not.

To know that I am strong.

To know that whatever happens, whatever the official position says, I do *not* belong to him.

But as soon as we got back to Paper House, Madam Himura rounded on me, so incensed she could barely get a word out. "You didn't just shame yourself, you shamed *us!* You shamed *me!*" she cried, before sending me to my room, Lill hurrying behind me, her cheeks as red as mine.

"Maybe it was a blessing in disguise," I say now to Aoki. I sit straighter, scraping back the hair from my brow. "Now he definitely won't call me first. Maybe he'll never call me at all."

She tilts to the side so she can look at me. "You don't want him to?"

"No!" I say it a little too forcefully, and I steal a glance over my shoulder, as though Madam Himura could have snuck up behind us. Voice lowered, I ask, "Do you?"

"Of course!" she answers, also a little too hard. She takes a breath. "I mean...I'm not sure. I—I think so. He's the King, Lei. It's a privilege." This part at least sounds like she believes it.

"But even so," I press, "is this really what you want? What you hoped for of your life?"

Aoki twines her fingers in her lap, her teeth softly working her bottom lip. "I miss my family so much. I really do. But if I hadn't been chosen, I would have been stuck in our tiny village for the rest of my life. Maybe I would have been happy there. But *look* at this, Lei," she says, sweeping her arm at the empty courtyard, and I know she means not just here but the house, the palace, the beauty and extravagance of it all.

Unmoved, I mutter, "I'd rather be back in Xienzo."

"Even though your family is taken care of now?"

I open my mouth to retort, stopping myself at the last moment. Aoki's from a poor village, too. She has also known hunger and struggle, experienced the fierce bite of the cold and the heavy ache of exhaustion after a long day's work, so deep you feel it in your bones.

Even so. *I* was meant to take care of them, my father and Tien. Me. Not the King.

Dzarja.

His money is dirty. Blood money.

"I wonder who he'll pick first," Aoki murmurs a few moments later.

Her question hangs coiled between us.

I flash her a sideways smirk. "I bet it's Blue."

She groans. "Oh, gods, no! We'd never hear the end of it."

As we both snort, a maid hurries into the courtyard from the opposite side, hair still mussed from sleep and her night robe tied messily. She drops to the floor as soon as she spots us. "So sorry, Mistresses!" she stammers. "I—I didn't know you would be up."

"Oh, don't worry—" I start, getting to my feet, but she darts off before I can finish. I turn to Aoki. "I'm not sure I'll ever get used to that. 'Mistresses.' It sounds so…"

"Old? Formal?" She giggles. "I guess that's something else the other girls are used to. They were probably called Mistress since they were babies." She puts on a posh accent, fluting her wrist fancily. "Mistress Blue, would you care for some honey in your mother's breast milk?"

We burst into laughter, stopping at the sound of voices from inside the house.

"We'd better go," I say. "It's almost time to get ready."

We walk back to our rooms in silence, and slowly the significance of Aoki's earlier question settles onto our shoulders, gaining a little more weight with each step. After my performance last night, I'm sure the King won't choose me first. But still, I pray silently with every fiber of my being that I'm right.

Paper Girl life, it transpires, consists of a *lot* of studying—something my old life in Xienzo had barely any of. Mistress Eira warned us we would have a busy schedule of lessons to develop our nu skills, ranging from etiquette classes to calligraphy to music practice to Ikharan history, but I didn't realize how tiring it would be. Maybe it's because I never went to school. I was helping my parents with the shop from pretty much the moment I could walk, and as one of my only teachers, Tien would be the first to complain about my attention span. *The problem, little nuisance,* she'd say, *is that you have none.*

By the time we head back to Paper House for lunch, my head is stuffed with four hours' worth of information from our morning classes. Most of the other girls are busy chatting, but I'm dazed, going over everything our teachers said, hoping to somehow imprint it all into my brain through sheer will. I'm still so focused that when we take our seats around Madam Himura's table and she says something that causes the other girls to become quiet, it takes me a few moments to register what is happening.

The King has made his first choice.

"Who is it?" Blue speaks up immediately, adding a quick, "Madam Himura," at the eagle-woman's piercing look.

I glance at Aoki, but she's focused hard on Madam Himura, her mouth pressed small. Then my eyes flick to Wren. Unlike the others, she doesn't seem to be paying much attention to what's going on. She looks younger than she did last night, when she'd been glossed with makeup and wrapped in *that* dress, but there's still a stoic quality to the way she is poised, chin lifted, eyes cast away. Suddenly, I'm certain that it will be her name Madam Himura will announce.

The way she looked last night, how could it *not* be?

"The name of the King's chosen girl will be delivered by royal messenger on the days he requests company that evening," Madam Himura explains into the expectant hush. "It goes without saying that if it is you who is summoned, you must obey his call." With a rustle of feathers, she unwraps a silk-bound package and slides its contents—a small bamboo chip—into the center of the table with one curving talon. Then, the room in absolute silence now, she moves her hand away to reveal the name printed across it.

Chenna-zhi

The calligraphy ink is red, like a splatter of blood.

Relief clangs through me, so strongly I instinctively brace as if it were audible. But all the girls are looking at Chenna. Even Wren. Her eyes are lit with something unexpected and sharp, though not at all like the jealousy or relief playing in the other girls' gazes. It's more...steely. Challenging, almost.

Chenna herself doesn't react. Or at least, not visibly. Her expression is calm, her posture straight-backed, the image of perfect Paper Girl. She keeps her eyes trained on the chip.

"Congratulations, Chenna," Madam Himura croaks into the quiet. She glares pointedly around at us.

"Congratulations, Chenna," Wren echoes smoothly.

"Y-yes, congratulations," Aoki stammers with a faltering smile.

The rest of us follow suit until it's only Blue left. Her mouth is set, but she manages a quick curve of her lips. "Yes, well done, Chenna." Then she taps her empty bowl and snaps, "Well? Is lunch going to come anytime soon?" earning a scolding from Madam Himura that she seems almost grateful to receive.

The rest of the meal passes in near silence. There's a stiffness to the girls' interactions, everyone's eyes frequently sliding back to Chenna, and even I find myself watching her, trying to see through her serene exterior. But she keeps her face calm, a glaze over her eyes as she focuses on her food, eating slowly but steadily.

"Chenna," Madam Himura orders when it's time for us to leave for our afternoon lessons. "You stay with me."

And that's when I see it. For the first time since her name was revealed on the bamboo chip: a tremor runs through her hands.

She turns her cheek as we file out of the room, making a strange, fleeting gesture with her fingertips across her brow that perhaps could be something religious—or could also just be her brushing aside a stray hair—before one of the maids closes the door behind us.

Even though I can sense they want to discuss what just happened, the girls manage to keep from talking as we trail down the corridor. But as soon as we turn the corner, Blue speaks up. "That was a surprise."

A few of the girls make noncommittal murmurs. Though I hate to admit it, I can tell most of the girls agree with her. Still, I bristle at the way she puts it.

"I wonder what his reasoning was," Mariko says with a purse of her lips. She shifts, hips jutting to one side. "Chenna is beautiful enough, I suppose. And her family is somewhat prestigious. At least for Jana."

"Maybe that's it," Zhen, one of the twins, offers. "He wanted to connect with a part of his heritage."

Blue scowls at her. "What part? Desert slum?"

"I just mean," Zhen continues, though her cheeks are pink now, "that Jana is where the original Bull King was from—"

"And is now where half the rebel nomads are hiding," Blue interrupts. "Or at least according to the rumors. I doubt that's something the King wants to align himself with."

Zhen lifts a shoulder. "Maybe he's trying to send a message to them, then."

"Or maybe," her sister, Zhin, speaks up, with a cool glance at Blue, "politics has nothing to do with it. He could just be picking the girl he was most attracted to."

"I agree," I reply. "Chenna *is* beautiful, and she seems smart, and interesting. No wonder the King liked her."

The twins nod, smiling at me, and I see Wren look my way, something curious in her warm brown irises. Beside me, Aoki is silent.

Blue and Mariko swap smug looks. But if they want to throw an insult my way, they manage to refrain. "Anyway," Blue says, in a crisp tone that makes it clear we are done with this discussion, "the first few choices are just based on his initial impressions of us. I'm more interested to see who he continues to pick." Her eyes slide to me. "And who he doesn't choose at all."

TWELVE

I'M STILL BLURRY FROM SLEEP WHEN I'm woken the next morning by the slide of doors. There's the patter of bare feet in the hall outside, then muffled voices, excitement barely constrained by whispers. With a yawn, I untangle from my sheets and pad out blearily into the corridor, arms folded across my waist.

"What was he like?"

"Did he tell you any secrets about the court?"

"One of the maids told me his bedchamber is covered completely in moonstones and opals—is it true?"

Chenna's room is at the opposite end of the hall, and though I can't see her past the backs of Zhen, Zhin, Mariko, and Aoki crowding in her doorway, I assume she's somewhere inside. Sure enough, her voice floats out a second later.

"I don't want to talk about it."

I roll my neck as I amble over, easing out the crick from sleeping. Wren's door is shut, and so is Blue's, but as I step in front of her room, there's a movement behind the rice-paper screen and I notice the very Blue-shaped shadow bunched at the edge of the door. I push down the urge to call her out, instead turning to where the other girls are clustered in the doorway across the hall. Zhen and Zhin greet me as I join them, but Aoki and Mariko don't look away from Chenna.

"Just a few details," Mariko presses, leaning in, the shoulder of her robe slinking down her arm. She flips it back up distractedly. "We'll find out for ourselves soon enough."

"Exactly." Chenna's face is tight, a slight flush of color darkening the apples of her cheeks. But apart from that, she looks just as she did the day before—unruffled. The picture of composure. "So you don't have long to wait."

Mariko pouts at this, but the twins nod.

"We're sorry," Zhin says. "You don't have to tell us anything if you don't want to."

"But if you do need to talk," Zhen adds, "we're here."

With a kind smile, the twins return to their rooms with their arms linked, heads close. As Mariko huffs and moves away, I slip in beside Aoki. She blinks, barely registering me.

"Oh! Hi, Lei." Her eyes click back to Chenna. "Well, thanks anyway…" she mumbles before heading off.

"Lei," Chenna greets me unsmilingly. "I suppose you have a hundred questions, too?"

"Actually, just one." I drop my voice. "How do you feel? I hope… I hope you're all right."

Chenna blinks at me. She smiles, though it's stiff. "I'm just fine. Thank you for asking."

Her eyes glide past my shoulder as the door behind me opens. I brace myself for the cutting remark that's surely about to come, but instead Blue's voice floats out calmly and politely.

"Good morning, Chenna. Nine."

I lift a brow, glancing round to see Blue slink down the corridor, her long azure hair swishing.

"Wow," Chenna says once she's gone. "She's *really* annoyed."

I give her a wry smile. "She was so sure she was going to be picked first."

A frown puckers Chenna's forehead. "You know, I thought so, too, what with her father's position in the court. But when I asked the King why he chose me, he said it was because of some dream he had the night before. He'd been in Jana, flying over the southern deserts. He thought it was a sign from the heavenly rulers that they wanted him to select me."

"Maybe I can bribe a shaman to keep his dreams out of Xienzo," I murmur.

As she goes to shut the door, Chenna adds, eyes not quite meeting mine, "Or all of Ikhara, for that matter."

As the days sift past, my life dissolves into a blur of routine and ritual. It surprises me how quickly I fall into the palace's rhythms, the shape of my world before coming here erased as though by water on ink and replaced with a new life of lessons and gossip, banquets and ceremonies, rules and rituals. I don't forget about wanting to find out what happened to my mother, but I'm so busy I don't get the chance. I also know that kind of thing won't go unnoticed, and General Yu's threat is still fresh in my mind.

You are going to try, and you are going to succeed! Or else your family—what pitiful part that's left of it—will be punished. Make no mistake, keeda. Their blood will be here. Do you understand me?

On your hands.

Any time I have the urge to give up or defy Madam Himura's orders, the General's cool voice slinks back into my ears, and I know the only option is to keep going.

At least, for now.

Each day as a Paper Girl begins with the morning gong. The maids will have woken earlier to ready the braziers and bathing barrels and light incense, their smoky-sweet scent always in the air. Lill takes me to the bathing courtyard to wash before dressing me in simple cotton robes, my hair swept into a tight bun on the top of my head. Once we're ready, we have breakfast—usually rice balls, pickled vegetables and salted fish, and delicate cuts of fresh fruit: peaches, papaya, honey apple, winter melon—before heading to our first lesson of the day.

After my embarrassing performance at the Unveiling Ceremony, most of the teachers don't seem to expect much of me. One of them especially takes an instant dislike to me. Mistress Tunga is a broad-hipped woman with wide-set eyes who leads our lessons in movement, covering everything from how to walk elegantly to the proper way to kneel in robes. She often singles me out as an example of how *not* to do things. She'll have me pace the length of the room in front of the other girls, a practice block held between my knees, while she points out every mistake. "No, no, walk taller, Lei-zhi! Remember what I said last week? Imagine a thread running from the base of your feet to the top of your head. Now, lean back just so and let your hips jut out the tiniest amount....Not like that! You look as though you're about to keel over from too much sake. After what happened at the Unveiling Ceremony, that's the last thing you want others to think of you. All right, settle down, girls! Sniggering isn't becoming."

Just as bad are our dance classes. They're taught by Madam Chu, a dignified old swan-form demon, the pearly feathers flowing over her slender body tinged with gray. She flits around us, feathers rustling as she sets us into place. This isn't dancing the way I saw it done back home, all abandon and laughter and loose limbs. This is a kind of clockwork, technical thing. Every flute of a wrist, every curve and bend of a limb is measured—or not, as it often applies to me.

After our morning classes we return to Paper House for lunch, either with Mistress Eira or Madam Himura, to update them on our progress. If the King desires the company of one of the girls, this is usually when we're notified, and that girl is taken away for preparations. For the rest of us, it's back for more lessons until sunset. By then I'm desperate for sleep, but our nights are just as busy. There are banquets with court officials, trips to plays and dance recitals, ceremonies to attend.

By the time we finally return to our rooms, it's often past midnight. Despite our tiredness, Aoki and I usually stay up for a while, sipping tea and snacking on pineapple tarts Lill sneaks us from the kitchens. In these stolen moments, all the stress of our lessons, of being away from our families and having to adjust to this new way of life, melts away, and I go to sleep afterward with a smile on my lips and warmth in my chest that feels a lot like happiness.

And yet.

As the days go by without my name appearing on the bamboo chip, an uncomfortable notion starts to grow inside me: that it never will. And while part of me, most of me, is relieved, there is also shame, and the bright, cruel sear of failure.

Even though Aoki still hasn't been chosen, either, it's me Madam Himura scolds. Every day she reminds me what a disappointment I am. "You'd better find a way to show him those heavens-blessed eyes of yours soon, before I throw you out like the waste of space you've so far proven to be."

Once, I dream of the Unveiling Ceremony. But when I stagger out of the enchanted pool, it's General Yu who gazes down at me from the King's throne, a half smile twisting his face.

"Look what you've done." He holds up his arms. From his hands, my father's and Tien's severed heads hang, blood dripping to the floor. "Catch," he calls, and throws them to me.

I wake up, a scream dying on my lips.

There's nothing more I'd like to do than try to escape. To go back home. But every time I consider it, the General's threat comes back to me, along with the sound of the guard's club coming down onto the servant woman's head on the bridge outside Royal Court. And I remember that if I fail, I might not even *have* a home to return to.

After a month at the palace, I've barely improved in any of our lessons. When my attempt at the fan dance Madam Chu is teaching us ends with my fan flinging from my grip after I shake it too vigorously and hitting her between the eyes—which unfortunately she couldn't see the funny side of—she keeps me behind after class.

"But lunch—" I start hopelessly.

She flutters a winged arm. "Don't you have a banquet tonight? You can miss one little meal." Then, raising her voice, she calls, "You too, Wren-zhi."

Wren pauses in the doorway, the other girls filing out past her. "Madam Chu?" she asks, turning.

"Practice with Lei-zhi. Maybe she'll pick something up from you." Then the swan-woman strides out the door, her feathers ruffling.

"Well," I say into the silence. "At least we've got a Blue-free hour."

Wren doesn't laugh, but when she approaches me, her expression is a little softer than usual. "So, what are you having trouble with?"

"Um…all of it?"

She arches a brow. "Helpful."

I sigh. "I don't know. It's just so…precise. I can't control my body the way you can."

"That's what it looks like when I dance?" she says, a wrinkle creasing the tip of her nose. "Controlled?" I'm surprised—there's hurt in her voice.

"No!" I say quickly. "That's the point. You're in control, but it's like you're not. Natural, that's what I mean. It seems so natural to you."

It's true. I've watched Wren in our classes, and though she excels in all our lessons, dancing is where she comes alive. There's an effort-lessness about the way she moves that reminds me of the bird-form demons I used to watch flying over the mountains beyond our village. She is graceful. Free. When she dances, she loses her usual haughty, absent look, something gentle taking over her features—and send-ing a warm new sensation through me that I can't quite place.

Wren collects a fan from the cabinet at the side of the room and flicks it open. "All right. Let's start with something simple." Her posture loosens, a slight bend in the knees, a tilt to her hips. Clos-ing her eyes, she holds both arms to one side. She pauses here, and her stillness is as purposeful as movement. A shaft of muffled light filters in through the rice-paper walls of the rehearsal room, casting her outline in an amber glow, and my eyes trace the high arches of her cheekbones, limned in gold. As graceful as all the times I've watched her before, she draws the fan across her chest, rippling it like a wave.

Then she opens her eyes. "Your turn."

"*That's* simple?" I grumble as she hands the fan to me, our fingers brushing.

"Just try it." But I've barely gotten into position when Wren stops me. "Not like that. You're too forceful with your movements. You have to move more lightly. See?" Her eyes travel over my body. "Even the way you're standing is wrong."

A ripple of irritation runs through me. "I didn't realize *standing* was on the list of Paper Girl requirements," I retort. "I thought the King was more interested in the lying-down kind of activities."

Her lips purse. "You don't need to say it like that."

"It's true, though, isn't it? What's the point of all this, all these stupid lessons? There's only one thing we're really here to do."

And I haven't even been wanted for that.

The thought squirms into my head before I can stop it.

"You have to think about the future," Wren says, frowning at me. "After this year, you'll still have some role to play in the court. What do you want to do? Who do you want to *be?*"

"Not a dancer, that's for sure."

That earns a half smile from her. "Come on. At least *try*. You might be better at it than you know if you just focus. And you'll never get better if you don't give yourself a chance."

I open my mouth to argue but catch myself. Because she's right. I *haven't* been giving it my all. Even though I've fallen into the routine of palace life, my heart isn't in it.

How can it be? It's still back in Xienzo, with my father and Tien, and a life I wish every day was still mine.

"Oh, *fine*," I mutter, glowering. Tears are pricking my eyes now, and the last thing I want is to cry in front of Wren. Gritting my teeth, I give the movement she demonstrated a few more tries while she hovers nearby, providing pointers. I try to concentrate on the wave of my wrist, the tilt of my hips, but I can't seem to get it right, I grow more frustrated with every minute. Without warning, Wren moves in close. Her fingers curl round my arm to pull it into position, and the intimacy of her touch, her nearness, flusters me, and I drop the fan.

"Focus!" she snaps.

I clench my jaw. "I *am*."

"No, you're not."

I shrug her away from me. "Well, maybe I don't want to perform well. Maybe I don't want any of this."

"And you think I *do?*" Underneath her usual stern tone there's something delicate, almost broken. Her chin lifts, rich brown eyes regarding me. "None of us had a choice in this. But we do it for our families, because otherwise the King will—"

She stops abruptly. The end of her sentence hangs in the air between us.

I recall General Yu's threat. Maybe it wasn't just me that received one. Maybe the coins and riches showered on Paper Girls' families are less a reward and more a reminder that the King has bought their daughters' obedience. And if they break it…

"All right," I sigh, picking up the fan. "Let's try again."

Half an hour—and many dropped fan incidents—later, Wren and I head back to Paper House. From outside Mistress Eira's suite comes the chatter of the girls, the muffled footsteps of maids. Delicious food smells waft out, making my stomach growl. But when Wren moves to head straight in, I hold out a hand to stop her.

"Thank you," I say. "For helping me. You were right. I haven't really been trying." I puff out air, rubbing the back of my neck. "I guess it felt like I'd be letting my family down or something. Like I was happy to be here."

Her eyes move away. "I don't think any of us are truly happy to be here."

"Excuse me? Have you *met* Blue?"

"Right," she replies with a lift of her brows. "Because she's so happy all the time."

I blink, and Wren opens the door, something closing back over her expression. Following her inside, I send a quick bow in Mistress Eira's direction before kneeling down beside Aoki. "Thank the gods there's food left," I murmur, picking up my chopsticks. "I'm starving."

She doesn't look up. Her face is frozen, eyes locked on something small in her hands, and when I peer round to see what it is, my own expression freezes.

Red calligraphy; a scarlet summons.

Aoki-zhi

Slowly, I set my chopsticks down. "Are you all right?" I ask in a whisper.

She gives a jerk of her head that I take to be a nod.

Zhin's voice pipes up from across the table. "You must be excited, Aoki!" A sincere smile lifts her cheeks.

Still staring down at her hands, Aoki gives another stiff nod. I notice that her fingers are trembling. Underneath the table I press my thigh to hers.

There's a harsh laugh. "Looks like our little Aoki is finally about to become a woman," Blue purrs. "And at only sixteen." She looks round the table, purposefully avoiding my eyes. "That's all of us now, isn't it?"

"You're forgetting Lei," Mariko sniggers.

Blue's dark irises flick my way. "Oh, yes. I forgot all about her."

My fingers knot, but before I can say anything, Mistress Eira stands up. "I wasn't called by the King for two whole months after our ceremony," she announces smoothly, giving me a smile across the table.

That makes Blue's and Mariko's smirks drop.

"With some girls," Mistress Eira continues, "he enjoys the wait." She steps over, holding out a hand. "Come, Aoki. I'll help you get ready."

Aoki winces. With a jagged breath, she looks at me, a white tinge to her lips where she sucks them in. "It's what I wanted," she breathes as she gets to her feet, a whisper that only the two of us hear, and I'm not entirely sure which one of us she's trying to convince.

That night as I stay up waiting for Aoki to get back, I write home.

> Dear Baba,
>
> It's been over a month since my first letter and I still haven't heard from you. I'm hoping this is because the shop is so busy now and you've become such a celebrity in Xienzo that you don't have time for your daughter anymore (remember her?). Or maybe Tien's just been working you too hard (more likely). Whatever it is, please write soon. I miss you.
>
> Palace life is highly overrated. There are hours of preparation before you can even leave your room, and there are rules for everything. Tien would love it. Also, the food is awful.
>
> All right, not really. But I'd still trade it all for one of your pork dumplings any day.
>
> > All my love,
> > Lei

My brush hovers over the paper, wanting to add more. But Mistress Eira made it clear that I wasn't to give out any details about

the palace or my life here. Anyway, I wouldn't want my father and
Tien to know how difficult I'm finding things. I set the brush down,
waiting until the ink dries before touching my fingers to it. As I
trace each character, I imagine Baba's and Tien's hands doing the
same in a few days. I bring the paper to my lips for a kiss. Then I
roll the letter up, fastening it with a ribbon.

At this hour, the only light comes from the lantern in the corner
of my room. Pattering rainfall fills the midnight hush. I sit back
on my sleeping mat, pulling my legs to my chest. This is the third
letter I've written to home, and I still haven't heard anything back. I
probably shouldn't read too much into it—there are so many expla-
nations as to why they haven't responded yet. But I can't help it.
Maybe Madam Himura found out about the letters and stopped
them from being sent as a punishment for my embarrassing her
at the Unveiling Ceremony. Guilt wrings my belly as I remember
Wren's warning earlier today. Maybe, if I was performing better in
my classes…

The sound of movement in the hallway snaps off the thought.

I get up, tucking my hair behind my ears, and move to the door. A
figure passes, footsteps light.

Aoki's back.

Clutching the silk of my night robe tighter around me, I glide
the door open. The air is fresh from the rain, the floorboards cool
beneath my bare soles. "Aoki?" I call softly after the retreating figure.

She doesn't stop.

I hurry after her. She turns the corner, disappearing through a
door that leads to the gardens at the back of the house. I hesitate.
We're not supposed to leave our rooms at night, let alone go outside.
And if Aoki wanted me to go with her, wouldn't she have left the
door open?

Unsure now, I slide the door ajar. Rain-cooled air greets me. Beyond the house are gardens, graduating from manicured lawns and flowerbeds to a dense pine forest in the distance, moonlight silvering the treetops. I spot Aoki's retreating figure just before she's swallowed up by the dark line of the forest.

Only it isn't Aoki.

It's Wren.

Under the moonlight, her outline is unmistakable: long-limbed and broad-shouldered, with that slinking, feline prowl.

I stare at the spot where she disappeared between the trees, battling the urge to charge after her. Because while being caught wandering the house at night might earn us a slap and a lecture from Madam Himura, actually leaving the house to go gods-know-where and with gods-know-who will certainly have more serious consequences.

My lips press tight. And after her telling *me* to be careful.

I tiptoe back to my room. Sleep doesn't come for a long time. I keep picturing Wren moving through the forest, winding her way easily through the pines, smiling as she spots the person she's snuck out even in the rain to meet. In my head it's a tall, shadowy man. He opens his arms and she wraps herself around him, dissolving into his touch, and in the pit of my belly, something dark stirs.

THIRTEEN

I DON'T GET A CHANCE TO speak to Aoki until the following morning. She comes to my side as we head down the raised walkways
to the lake in the south of Women's Court where our qi arts
teacher, Master Tekoa, holds his classes. It's a beautiful midsummer
morning, bright and crisp, drops of rain from last night's shower
nestling in the cupped palms of leaves and the wooden buildings
still stained dark. Yet the daylight shows how tired Aoki looks. Her
eyes are puffy, her lips chapped.

Before I can say anything, Blue looks round. "Little Aoki!" she says,
striding over. "How are you feeling after your special night?" Her grin
is all teeth. "I'm surprised you're even able to walk," she goes on with a
glance at Mariko. "I thought the King would have broken you."

Mariko titters, but the other girls are quiet.

"Go away, Blue," I snap, threading my fingers through Aoki's.

Blue arches a brow. "Don't you want to hear the saucy details,
Nine? I'm surprised. I thought, since you still haven't had any *sauci-
ness* yourself..."

"Well, you thought wrong. Nothing new there," I add, and I
notice Wren at the back of the group, her lips quirking.

Blue ignores me. "Come on, Aoki. Give us the details."

"Yes, tell us!" Mariko chimes in. "Was he gentle with you? Or did he want it rough?"

Aoki's cheeks grow splotchy, her freckles disappearing under the pink. "It's—it's private," she stammers. She tucks her chin, a lock of auburn hair falling across her face.

"Private?" Blue regards her through squinted eyes. "Don't you remember what Mistress Eira told us? There's no such thing as private when it comes to being a Paper Girl." And though I could be imagining it, I detect a note of bitterness in her voice.

"Ignore them," I say, and tug on Aoki's hand. "Let's get out of here." My eyes meet Wren's. Before I can question what I'm doing, I march past the other girls toward her, pulling Aoki with me. "Could you send Master Tekoa our apologies for missing his lesson?" I ask her in a low voice. "Say there's been a…female emergency."

Though Wren's eyebrows knit just a fraction, she gives a curt nod. "Sure."

"Thank you," I say.

She shrugs. "It's nothing," she says, even though it's not. If Master Tekoa decides to inquire into our absence, he'll know Wren lied to him. She'd be punished along with Aoki and me. But I'm counting on the fact that the notion of a female emergency will be too embarrassing for him to press further. Master Tekoa is our only male teacher. The King gives him special permission to come into Women's Court because Madam Himura insists, claiming he's the best qi arts practitioner in the whole palace.

The rest of the girls are still watching us, most looking apprehensive. Chenna and the twins get on well with Aoki, and unlike me, they must know what she's going through. All the girls were sullen the day after their first night with the King—even Mariko and Blue, though I'm sure they wouldn't admit it now.

With a pointed look in Blue's direction, as though defying her to intervene, Chenna comes over to us. "I cried all night after the first time," she says, bending to clasp Aoki's shoulders.

Aoki blinks, looking up with a sniff. "Really?"

Chenna nods. "It wasn't easy for me, either."

Over her head, Wren turns to me. "It's all right, Lei," she says. "Go."

As her eyes meet mine, a spark of heat stirs in my chest. It takes me a moment to realize it's the first time she's spoken my name. My single syllable is surprisingly soft on her tongue, light, like a drop of rain. I think of her in the gardens last night, lit by moonlight. What she might have left Paper House for. Not just what—*who?*

And more: why do I care so much?

I break her gaze and mutter a thanks, quickly leading Aoki away.

The two of us find a secluded veranda at the back of a nearby teahouse to wait out the lesson. It overlooks a rock garden, an old gardener in a wide-brimmed straw hat sweeping the stones with a rake. She doesn't look up as we kneel side by side on the edge of the porch, and the rhythm of her rake is comforting, a steady scrape that plays under the soundtrack of the teahouse, the chirp of birds in nearby trees.

"You don't need to tell me about it," I say into Aoki's silence. She's still avoiding my gaze, staring down where she's playing with the sash at her waist. "I just thought you could use some time away from the others."

She nods. Tears spring to her eyes. She swipes them away with her sleeve and mumbles thickly, "It's stupid. It had to happen at some point, and it's not like I didn't want it to. I did. I mean, he's the King. But…" Her voice wavers. "I never guessed it would feel like this."

I lace my arm round her shoulder. "It was your first time, Aoki. It was bound to affect you. I guess that's why we're meant to wait until marriage," I say, trying to sound like I know what I'm talking about. "So we are sure of the other person. So we're sure of *ourselves*."

Aoki sniffs. "I overheard one of my older sisters talking about it with her friend once. My parents were arranging for her to marry this boy from the neighboring village, and she met with him in secret one night before the deal was final." She tucks her hair behind one ear and shoots me a wobbly smile. "They did…things. Not everything. But enough that I knew she'd be in serious trouble if my parents found out. But she told my parents the next day that she was happy to marry him." Her smile disappears. "It must have been a good night," she adds, muted. Then, even quieter, "I was so scared."

I gather her to me, something hot flaring to life in my chest. How *dare* he scare her. Even though I haven't seen him since the Unveiling Ceremony, I can still picture the King's handsome face clearly.

I imagine punching it.

Rubbing her nose with one hand, Aoki looks up at me from under tear-wet lashes. "Are *you* scared? For when it's your turn?"

Something in the tone of her voice sends a prickle down my spine. "Should I be?"

Aoki turns to the garden with unfocused eyes. "There was this boy in my village," she starts. "Jun. He worked on the paddy fields, too. We didn't talk much, but every time I saw him—any time I was *near* him—my whole body got all hot and I'd be so nervous I could never think what to say. He'd be smiling and I'd just be blushing like an idiot. Each look he gave me was like…like sunlight sweeping over me." Her voice falters, and tears trace wet paths down her cheeks. Still twisting the sash in her fingers, she murmurs, "I—I thought it would be like that with the King."

"Maybe you'll feel that way next time," I try, swiping her tears away with my fingertips. "Maybe with some people it just takes time."

"Maybe," she agrees.

But I can tell she doesn't believe it.

For the rest of the day, Aoki is sullen. I didn't realize how much I depended on her happy chatter, for her bubbly mood to lift my own. I try to cheer her up, whispering jokes when our teachers' backs are turned and stealing for her sugared hopia pastries filled with peanut paste, one of her favorite sweets. But she says she isn't hungry.

This, coming from a girl who can usually eat ten of these in one sitting and still have room for more.

As if mirroring Aoki's mood, the weather turns over the course of the day. Heavy clouds roll in, so low I could jump up and touch them. We rush back from our last lesson, making it to Paper House just as it starts to pour.

I bump into Chenna on my way to the toilet. She gives me a nod as she passes, but I touch her shoulder to stop her. "Thank you," I say. "For earlier."

She gives me her usual half smile. "It's all right. I have a little cousin back home. Aoki really reminds me of her. I know she's sixteen, but she seems so much younger sometimes."

I nod. "If only Blue and Mariko could leave her alone."

"Like they do the rest of us?"

Chenna's face is straight, so it takes me a moment to catch her joke. I let out a laugh. "You're right. I shouldn't hold my breath."

"Anyway," she says, "Mariko's actually pretty nice when she's not around Blue. And I wouldn't care too much what Blue says." She looks like she's about to say something more, so I lean forward, brow furrowing.

"What is it?" I press.

"Well, I don't really like to talk about other people's business. But seeing as it's Blue..." She wets her lips. "Do you know who her father is?"

"Someone important at court, right?"

"Not just someone important—he's the King's *only* Paper caste adviser. Even the Hannos aren't involved with the King's council. Everyone knows the King is paranoid when it comes to dealing with the clans. Probably worried he'll upset them one day and they'll turn on him. But Blue's father was exiled from his clan years ago."

"Why?" I ask.

Chenna shrugs. "There are lots of different rumors. But whatever it was, he ended up here, and because he's a free agent, the King seems to trust him more than most."

"What's this got to do with Blue?"

"Everyone knows her father is after a promotion. The King's first adviser died earlier this year and he still hasn't appointed a successor." Chenna's coal-black irises don't leave mine. "Blue is eighteen. She could have been entered into the Paper Girl selection before now. So her father putting her forward for the first time this year seems rather convenient, don't you think?"

I frown. "But the selection process—"

"Is not mandatory for daughters of court officials." She nods. "Not that there are many Paper caste court officials anyway, of course. But for the few who are, they're granted an exception. Unless—"

"The family *wants* them to be considered, and enters them voluntarily," I finish.

"What's more," Chenna goes on, "I heard some of the maids talking about how it was common knowledge Blue didn't *want* to be put forward as a Paper Girl."

Silence unfolds at this. Out of all the girls, Blue is the one I would have bet on for fighting tooth and nail to be selected. I imagined her following the selection of the Paper Girls since she was young, playing dress-up with her maids, pretending she was one of the chosen.

"Her father used her," I state, hollow.

"It's exactly what Blue would have done herself," Chenna replies with a lift of a shoulder.

The coolness in her voice makes me wince. Tien had told me how Paper caste families offer up their daughters in the hopes of gaining favor with the court. But hearing Chenna talk so frankly about it...

Being traded against your will by your own father can't feel nice. Even for someone like Blue.

"Chenna," I say as she moves away, "how do you know all this?"

Something flickers in her dark eyes. "The King talks a lot," she answers, an edge to her voice. "Especially after a few glasses of sake."

It's not until I'm coming back from the toilet that I comprehend the significance of Chenna's words.

Maybe the one person who can tell me what happened to my mother is the last person I'd ever want to ask.

At dinner, Madam Himura tells us we'll be attending a dance performance later that evening. "The King will be in attendance," she says. Her yellow eyes cut to me. "So no mistakes."

An excited thrum runs through the room. Zhen and Zhin lean their heads in, whispering, and Blue and Mariko swap knowing looks. It's the first time we'll be crossing paths with the King in public, and while some of the girls seem happy by this news, a coldness slithers over me at the mention of him.

I glance across the table in Aoki's direction. She doesn't make any sign that she's heard, still poking her food with her chopsticks, head propped on one hand.

When we get up to leave, I notice Blue hanging back. I hover in the doorway, pretending to be adjusting my shoes. As Madam Himura rises from the table, Blue approaches her in a purposeful stride.

"What is it?" the eagle-woman snaps.

Blue rolls her shoulders. "I—I want to know whether my father will be attending the performance tonight," she declares.

"It's not my duty to memorize guest lists, girl."

"But—"

"Send a messenger to ask."

Blue mumbles something.

"Well," replies Madam Himura, waving a feathered arm, "that's not my problem. Your father is an important man. He'll respond when he sees fit."

I hurry away before they catch me listening. Something sour turns my stomach, remembering my conversation with Chenna, but it takes me a while to place the feeling because it's not something I ever thought I'd associate with Blue.

Pity.

Back in my room, Lill hums as she dresses me in velvety amethyst-colored hanfu robes stitched with a floral print. "Tonight, Mistress," she announces with a grin, "you're going to look so beautiful the King won't be able to take his eyes off you."

I arch a brow. "That's what you said last time. Remember what happened?"

"Don't remind me!" As she fusses with the positioning of the layered fabrics, she adds, "I overheard one of the court messengers speaking to Madam Himura." Her grin creeps wider.

"Oh, no." I grimace. "What now?"

With a clap of her hands, Lill does a little dance on her tiptoes before bursting out, "You've been chosen to sit next to the King tonight!"

I look away jerkily, and Lill falters.

"Aren't...aren't you happy?"

I answer her through gritted teeth. "Can't wait."

"Don't worry, Mistress," she says. Her small hand lands on my own. "He's bound to pick you tomorrow after seeing you like this. I'm sure of it."

What I don't tell her is that's exactly what I'm afraid of.

I can't deny that every time the royal messenger delivers the bamboo chip and my name isn't the one on it, it's started to bring a twist of shame. Along with Blue's snide comments and Madam Himura's constant admonishments, it hasn't been easy being the unchosen girl. Every day I think of General Yu's threat. How long will they keep me in the palace without being chosen by the King? What happens if he *never* picks me? Will they throw me out? Somehow I can't imagine Madam Himura sending me merrily on my way, a packed lunch and some money in my pocket, wishing me and my family all the best for the future.

But even the fear of what could happen has been outshadowed by relief. Of not having to face the King for one more day, at least. Of being able to ignore the real reason I'm in the palace in the first place. And while I've discovered that a month is not long enough to forget a face such as his, it *is* enough time to create distance from that face, and the demon it belongs to.

Later that evening, as we travel through the palace to where the dance recital is being held, his presence starts to reveal itself, like smoke on the wind, a bitter taste that knots my stomach.

Rain pounds on the carriages as we pull up to one of the Inner Court theaters. The dark wood walls of the theater are slick from the deluge. Over the sound of the storm, music thrums from within: the melancholy song of an erhu, piping reeds, low drumbeats. A troop of umbrella-wielding servants usher us inside. We file into the theater's main hall, a grand, circular room. At the center is a round stage ringed by cushions.

Mistress Eira takes my arm. "You're with me, Lei." She smiles, leading me to the front row.

Around us, court members in an array of demon forms are taking their places, shadows distorted by the lantern glow. My breaths come more shallowly as we kneel on our cushions, and I hold myself stiffly, trying not to flinch each time I hear the heavy drop of hooves. To distract myself, I focus on the stage. There's a dusting of snowlike powder sprinkled across it.

Mistress Eira follows my gaze. "Sugar dust," she says.

I look round. "What is it for?"

"The dancers kick it up with their movements so it settles onto our clothes and skin. It's more for display, really. But it's also said to encourage sensual thoughts." Her voice drops. "Men and women will know their lovers' skin will taste sweet later tonight."

An image flares into my mind: the King, leaning in close, a thick tongue sliding out to run along my bare collarbones.

"I—I can't do it," I say suddenly. Pushing my palms into the floor, I start to my feet. "I can't, I *won't*—"

Mistress Eira seizes my arm. "Hush, Lei!" she hisses, yanking me back down with pinching fingers. "You can never speak this way in public. *Never*. Do you understand? Imagine if word got back to Madam Himura. To the King." She waits as an elegant-looking lion-form demon strides past, his arm looped over the shoulder of a smaller lion-form male. They share a chaste press of their snouted noses as they pass. Relaxing her grip a little, Mistress Eira continues, "I understand your fear, but you have to see it as just another aspect of your job. Not even one that takes too long—a few hours and you'll be back in Paper House. And while I can't promise that you'll enjoy it, it might not be as bad as you feared. Remember, even that which seems impossible at first can be overcome by strength of mind and heart."

It's an old saying, one everybody in Ikhara is familiar with. I turn it over on my tongue, hunting for comfort in its words. For some reason, it makes me think of Wren. The way her eyes often gaze into the distance during dinners and lessons, as though she's retreating somewhere deep within herself. Is this how she copes with sleeping with the King? Protecting her true self by folding it away where he can't reach?

I look across the stage to where she's sat opposite me, expecting to find her staring off into the distance. But my breath catches—because she's looking straight at me. And this time, instead of emptiness, Wren's eyes shimmer brightly with fire.

Then a voice rings out through the theater, and our connection breaks. "Honorable members of the court, presenting our Heavenly Master, our gods' blessed ruler and commander of all beings who walk the mortal realm, the King!"

Every member of the audience drops into a bow. My cheeks are still flushed from Wren's look as I lower my forehead to the floor, but the rest of my body is clammy. Silence claims the hall. The only sounds are the rustling of fabric and the thrum of rain on the roof. And, beneath my ribs, the frantic slam of my heart. It seems impossible that no one else can hear it. Even now, Baba and Tien must be raising their heads in Xienzo from their late dinner after another busy day to wonder what that distant drumming sound is.

The hall is quiet for a few moments more. Then—hoof-fall.

I fight the urge to jump up as they approach in a slow gait, coming to a stop right beside me. Heat ripples from the King's body as he kneels down, close, not touching but so near his presence is as heavy as a sky full of storm clouds, and the smell of him fills my nose; that sharp scent of bull, raw and masculine.

"Heavenly Master," I murmur along with the rest of the room. There are rustling sounds as everyone in the audience sits back up. I straighten, my eyes locked on the floor, aware of his stare.

"Lei-zhi," he says, drawing the letters out. There's a smirk in his voice. "Am I to always find you face-first on the floor?"

"If that is where you want me." I inject the words with as much derision as I dare, adding a quick "Heavenly Master" for good measure.

His boom of laughter shudders deep, right down to my bones. "So, how have you found your first month at the palace? I hope it has been enjoyable."

"In ... some ways," I answer carefully.

"In some ways! Tell me those that disagree with you, and I'll see what I can do."

Oh, just the small fact that I'm a *prisoner* here. But I keep my eyes down and mumble instead, "The days start very early. And we have a lot of lessons. And the food could be better, I suppose."

Again, his laughter rattles me. "Now, I know at least that last one's a lie. We have the most superior chefs in all of Ikhara. I challenge you to find better. But perhaps," he goes on, his tone cooling somewhat, "your tongue hasn't become accustomed to fine food yet. I can only imagine what your meals were like in Xienzo. Do not worry, Lei-zhi. I am sure your tongue will become accustomed to palace delicacies soon enough."

The double meaning in his words jolts me, but I only have a few seconds to falter before he speaks again, his voice flat and serious now.

"The court tells me you're blessed with eyes leant by the Moon Goddess herself. Show them to me."

With a deep inhalation, arranging my face into as calm an

expression as I can muster, I lift my chin. And finally, after all these weeks, the King's cool gaze meets mine.

His spine stiffens. Not in fear, or even surprise. But the way a cat goes still when it's spotted a mouse. How the world grows silent before the roar of a storm. His stillness seems to ripple through the room until everything is frozen, everyone focused on the two of us, the fix of golden eyes on blue.

A smile sneaks across his lips, accenting his pointed cupid's bow. "So. They weren't exaggerating."

I bow my head. "I am humbled by your compliment, Heavenly Master," I force out.

There's a pause. "You haven't thanked me for my other one."

I jerk my chin up. "The—the other one?"

"You must have been wondering why I haven't called you to me yet, no?" The King leans down until his face is just a hairsbreadth from mine and curls a hand round my cheek, holding me with just a fraction too much pressure. "Didn't you know, Lei-zhi," he murmurs, grin sharpening, "I always save the best for last."

The announcer's voice sounds again, signaling the start of the show. But the King doesn't look away—and I don't dare to.

Out of the corner of my eye, I spot a sleek dog-form dancer entering the stage. A lone string melody starts up. The dog-girl launches into movement. Scarlet ribbons tied round her wrists fly out in long, rippling waves. She dances across the stage, lifts high with fast kicks of her slender haunches, turning the air around her into a whirl of red.

A shower of sugar dust falls over us. Slowly, not taking his eyes off mine, the King runs a thumb over my lips and raises it to his own, tasting it with his tongue.

"Delicious," he growls.

The next day, the name painted on the bamboo chip is mine.

FOURTEEN

THE TABLE ERUPTS, ALL THE GIRLS talking at once. Madam Himura has to slam her hands down to shock them into silence. "This is not some housewives' mahjong party!" she cries, yellow eyes blazing. "Are you forgetting who you are?" She points a taloned finger at the door. "Go! Mistress Tunga is expecting you." When I start to stand, she gives an exasperated sigh. "Not *you*, Lei."

Whispering, the girls file from the room. Aoki looks over her shoulder as she goes, offering me a smile I can't return. Wren also pauses in the doorway. She looks round. Just like last night when our gazes caught across the stage, there is a radiance in her eyes that pulls something in the pit of my stomach into life.

"Good luck, Lei," she says. "I'll be thinking of you."

I blink after her as she slides the door shut.

"So. The King has finally summoned you."

Madam Himura's voice cuts through the quiet. I look down at my lap, where my fingers twine together.

"Mistress Eira predicted it," she goes on. "Apparently he was quite taken with you at the dance recital last night." With a rustle of feathers, she comes round the table to kneel beside me. "It's nothing to be ashamed of, Lei-zhi. Being scared of your first time is normal. All girls are."

I bite my lip. "Is there…is there any way—"

She clicks her beak. "Do not ask the impossible of me. The King's decision is final." A clawed hand lands on my shoulder with surprising gentleness. "You'll feel better once it's over. You might even grow to enjoy it in time."

I remember Aoki's tear-streaked face.

"I doubt it," I mutter.

Madam Himura snatches back her hand, the callous tone returning to her voice just as quickly as it went. "Whether you enjoy it or not is beside the point. This is your job. And as with all your duties, you will perform to the best of your abilities. Even if *your* abilities don't seem much." She jabs her cane against the floor. "Rika!" she barks at one of the maids. "Take Lei for her ye lesson."

I frown. "Ye lesson?"

"Night skills," Madam Himura responds curtly. "To prepare you for tonight."

She doesn't say it, but the word is in the air with us, sharp and cutting and cold.

Sex.

I'm finally about to be trained for the most important role of a Paper Girl—and the one I've been dreading the most.

Hidden in the southeastern corner of Women's Court, beyond high walls and set deep within gardens scented with the rich, heady fragrance of jasmine and frangipani, are the buildings where the palace courtesans live. The Night Houses. During her description of the different areas of the palace when we first arrived, Mistress Eira didn't go into any further detail, telling us only that they are strictly out of bounds unless we're given explicit permission from her or Madam Himura. Now, pulling up outside the concubines' home, I wonder why. It's not as if we'd just be able to saunter in. Along with the steep walls, dozens of soldiers line the deep gate leading into the grounds. Sunlight glances off their leather armor, the elaborate sheaths of the jian crossed at their chests.

Rika, Madam Himura's maid, helps me down from the carriage. The guards don't move, but their gazes flick over me. I catch the eye of a tall cheetah-form soldier as we pass. She has a surprisingly sweet face, sandy fur almost as pale as skin, looped black markings around each eye. She gives me a smile, friendly somehow despite the glint of canines.

My eyes shift from her to the demon next to her, then the next. I turn to Rika. "They're all female!" I say.

She nods. "Male guards aren't allowed permanent fixtures in Women's Court."

"But what about the visitors? Aren't they men?"

"There's an entrance on the side that leads directly from City Court for them to use." Then she adds, almost as an afterthought, "That's where the house with the male courtesans is, too."

"Male courtesans? For the female court members, you mean?"

"No, Mistress. They are also for male court members."

We fall silent. I can't say I'm that surprised by this news. At our nightly events there have sometimes been male demons who have had other men as their escorts, like the two lion-men last night. But I've never seen it the other way round—two female lovers.

We don't say any more as we head along a winding path through the gardens. It's peaceful here among the trees, the floor dappled with sunlight. The grounds are lush and wild, with willowy trees and tangled knots of flowering shrubs, vibrant after last night's storm. Red saga seeds pepper the grass. There's the trill of bird-song, the rustle and rush of breeze-blown leaves. The violet beams of half hidden pavilions wink from deep in the foliage. As we pass one, movement from inside draws my attention. The view is partially blocked by the swaying leaves of a ginkgo tree, but I make out the form of a naked woman beyond the latticed balcony.

Her long raven hair tumbles to the floor. Two elklike antlers twine elegantly from the crown of her head. Tossing her head back, she shifts, and the brown-haired body of some kind of bear-form demon sits up from under her. His hands grip her shoulders as she moves on top of him. I can't hear their noises from here, but it's clear what they're doing.

My cheeks burn. I look quickly away, hurrying down the path with my eyes fixed on the ground.

After a few more minutes the gardens open onto a square populated with a cluster of low, two-tiered buildings. Moss crawls up their green-and-red walls. Over their open entrances hang banners marked in sweeping calligraphy, each displaying the same character: *ye.*

A figure emerges from the middle house. "You're late."

The woman cocks her head to one side, arms folded across her chest. She's a dog-form demon, Moon caste, the spotted umber hair flowing over her lithe frame just showing the beginnings of gray. Long legs—a meld of human limbs and dog haunches—show through the split in her maroon robes. Though her ears are floppy, any softness this adds to her appearance is countered by the keen contours of her face and the flint-colored stare she gives us as we approach.

Rika bows. "Our sincerest apologies, Mistress Azami."

Just as I start to mumble a greeting, the dog-woman strides forward and grabs my arm. "Your job during these lessons is not to talk," she snaps, yanking me up the steps into the house. "It's to listen. *Only* listen. Can you do that? Can you keep that pretty mouth of yours shut for the next few hours?"

I almost trip on the lip of a step. "Y-yes, Mistress."

"What did I *just* say? Aiyah, you're a slow learner, aren't you? Let's hope you have some talent between the sheets to make up for it."

With an irritable click of her tongue, she drags me up a flight of stairs to the upper floor and down a narrow hallway. I get only a quick impression of the building's interior; low, shadowed corridors, glimpses of moving figures from behind thin rice-paper screens, and sounds, unfamiliar but somehow... not. Heavy groans. A stifled moan.

Mistress Azami raps on one of the doors. "Zelle!" she barks. "Open up! Your Paper Girl is here for her lesson."

A silky voice answers from inside. "Why don't you ever ask nicely, Mistress?"

"And why don't *you* ever just do as you're told?" Grumbling, the dog-woman opens the door and shoves me through. "Three hours. The basics. Go."

She shuts the door with a slam.

I stumble to a stop, hastily smoothing down my clothes. My eyes meet with those of a Paper caste girl just a few years older than me. She's leaning by the window, dusky light from the half closed shutters painting her slim outline in gold. A slit travels up one side of her indigo skirt, exposing the lean length of her legs.

The girl gives me a lopsided smile. "The famous Nine. I've been looking forward to meeting you."

I flinch at her use of Blue's nickname for me but force a bow. "I'm honored to learn from you today, Mistress Zelle."

"Please," she sighs, rolling her eyes. "Just Zelle. *Mistress* makes me feel so *old*." With a swish of her robes, she comes forward to kneel on the bamboo-mat floor, gesturing for me to join her. "Don't you ever got bored of it? All the *Mistress* this, *Madam* that. At least in my job I'm not expected to make small talk. Unless, of course, it's a customer's preference." She winks.

I don't know how to respond to that. Instead I look round her room. It's so different from my own in Paper House. Paintings and calligraphy scrolls hang on the walls, and the cabinets and side tables are richly detailed, carved from polished teak and mahogany and inlaid with mother-of-pearl. To one side of the room hangs a swath of gauzy fabric, rippling in the breeze coming through the window. The fabric is sheer enough to make out a bed behind it, low and wide, mounds of pillows thrown across its top.

"You're from Xienzo, yes?" Zelle says, following my gaze. "I guess you haven't seen one before."

"A bed?" I shake my head. "We used sleeping mats back home. And in our rooms here."

She snorts. "Of course you do. They wouldn't want to encourage you bringing lovers back. Though that doesn't stop *all* the girls."

A crooked grin darts across her lips, and I find myself returning it. There's something friendly about this girl, with her sparkling eyes and teasing voice.

"So," she murmurs, gazing at me. "What to teach you…"

"Mistress Azami said the basics?"

Zelle flaps a hand. "Basics are boring. I could tell you how it works, where certain parts need to go, the anatomy and mechanics of it all. But what's the point? You'll know all that anyway once it happens. The best sex is natural. Instinctive. It's about letting go, not running through a list of actions in your mind. That's why I hate all these formalities and etiquette. They spoil it—the rawness. The passion." She pauses. "Think of it as a simple case of action and reaction. Touch and response."

With an impish smile, she leans forward to grasp my hand. As she does so, her collar shifts, exposing the shadow of her cleavage. Zelle doesn't seem to notice. Pushing back my sleeve, she holds a fingertip to my inner elbow and, her thick-lashed eyes never leaving mine, she traces her finger down my arm.

Slowly. Lightly. Teasingly.

Heat stirs between my legs.

"How does this make you feel?" she asks in a glossy voice, watching me.

I swallow. "I—I guess it's nice."

Zelle laughs, though not unkindly. "There's no lying when it comes to sex, Nine. Your body will always betray you." Touching my cheek, she murmurs, "Look how deeply you're blushing." Her fingers brush my lips. "Your mouth is parted, expectant. Ready to be kissed." Her palm rests against my breastbone, her skin hot on mine. "Your heartbeat is fast. Excited. What would I find if I slipped my hand between your legs? Would your body betray you there, too?"

I drop my gaze, and Zelle shifts back.

"There's nothing to be ashamed of," she says, gentler now. "You can be honest with me. Many of us yearn to be touched. To be loved."

"Well," I say, glowering, "I *don't* yearn for the Demon King."

It comes out louder and harsher than I meant it to.

"I—I mean," I go on, "he's a demon. And I'm not."

Zelle rubs a lock of her hair between her thumb and finger. "A lot of the girls have trouble understanding that," she says with a nod. "The attraction between castes. But it isn't actually as rare as you might expect."

"It isn't?"

"Think of it this way. Moon castes came from Paper, according to the old myths of the *Mae Scripts*, am I right? And Steels are what resulted from the mix of Paper and Moon. So really, Paper, Steel, and Moon aren't that separate fundamentally. We're just at various levels on the scales. So we look a little different." She shrugs. "Fur, feathers—it's just decoration, really. Our basic makeup and structure are the same."

Her words remind me of what Mama told me about humans and demons sharing the same blood. And being reminded of my mother leads me to think of that day seven years ago, the day I stopped believing in her words because how *could* we be the same when demons could do *that?*

"But if they think they are so superior to us," I scowl, "why would they even *want* us in that way?"

Zelle cocks a shoulder. "Part of it is the temptation of the forbidden, I suppose. The excitement of breaking the rules. Especially somewhere like here, the palace, a place full of Moon and Steel castes—maybe the delicate features of human girls have an exotic lure." Something hardens in her expression. "But mostly, I think, it's about power. Demon men can take what they want. Our homes. Our lives. Our bodies." Then, as abruptly as it went, her lighthearted demeanor returns. "And of course, there's our sheer beauty. I mean, who can resist this?" She flips her hair, shoots me a wink. "Anyway, the real issue is how do we help *you* feel at ease with the King."

I shift uncomfortably, remembering last night—the closeness of the King, his thumb tracing my lips, the way he touched me with the intimacy, the sureness of someone who has already known others' bodies.

Or, perhaps, of someone who is comfortable with taking things as his own.

Revulsion swirls through me, edged with something fire-hot. I want to jump up, scream at Zelle. Isn't it obvious? Isn't it understandable how maybe I *wouldn't* want a stranger's body pressed against mine, especially not a demon whose power has brought so much pain to Ikhara, to families like mine?

Dzarja. It *is* a betrayal.

Every day I'm here in the palace is a betrayal.

But I swallow my words, unsure of how Zelle would respond. Instead, I make up, "I know nothing about him. We've had one conversation. Barely. How am I supposed to be attracted to someone I don't know?"

"You're really telling me you've never been drawn to someone because of the way they look?" Zelle asks with an arch of her brow. "It's not shallow, Nine. Attraction is an honest, instinctive part of life. And a person's appearance is much more than just their features. It's how they hold themselves. The way they move. The things you can tell about them without words. You're how old?"

"Seventeen."

"Seventeen," she repeats, something a little wistful in her voice, even though it couldn't have been more than a few years ago for her. "Such a good age. Still fresh enough that attraction and desire feel new to you, but old enough to understand what to do with them. You must have watched someone by now and wished you could know them. Wondered whether their thoughts might stray to you."

And all at once my face gets hot—because it's a perfect description of the way I've been feeling about someone.

Wren.

Understanding arrives then the way twilight falls: instantaneously. Just a blink, a skip in time, leaving only the before and the after, and the inescapable ripples of change.

Every lingering glance, every stolen moment watching her out of the corner of my eye clicks into place. How flustered I always feel around her. How jealous I was at the thought of her with a lover. The way watching her dance makes something inside me physically *ache*. And even though we've not spoken that much—Wren still carries herself with that infuriating aloofness that separates her from the group—Zelle is right. I *can* tell things about her just from the way she behaves. She's not as unknowable as she might like to think. I've noticed the way she relaxes anytime we have a physical-based lesson, as though grateful for the time to move in her own body. The way she hides her nakedness in the bathing courtyard, less out of modesty but more, it seems, as a sense of maintaining the distance she has crafted between herself and the rest of us.

And I've noticed the way she's begun to watch me sometimes, and how—with burning eyes.

Something I haven't felt for a long time flutters into life in the pit of my belly. Hope. Because, maybe, Wren has already come to her understanding.

Maybe her eyes were showing me what I'm only just realizing now.

Zelle watches me patiently, her lips quirked. "See? Your body doesn't lie. There *is* someone."

Breath quiet, I palm my hands down the fabric of my skirt and answer, tentative, "But…it's not the King." I want to add, *And it's not a man, either,* but that seems too telling.

"So?" she says. "You're not expected to be attracted to the person you're being forced to sleep with. Look at my clients. Most of them are government dogs." Zelle snorts. "Sometimes literally. But every now and then, someone comes along...." Her face glimmers with a secret memory, perhaps of kinder, less selfish hands and mouths. "You need to find ways to arouse those feelings even when you're with someone who repulses you. It might sound impossible, but it's actually quite simple once you know how. I'll show you. Take off your clothes," she commands brusquely.

Instinctively, I clasp the collar of my robes. "W-what?"

"There's no use being coy, Nine. I work *here*, remember? I've seen it all. Besides, if you can't undress in front of me, what hope do you have when it comes to the King?"

Her words send a shudder down my spine. Not just because of how she means it, but for the second meaning hidden within, too. Because the answer to her question is easy: none. I have no hope. No hope of being free, no hope of escaping what's to come tonight.

But if there's one thing palace life has taught me, it's how to follow orders. Even if on the inside, you're raging against them.

Chin low, I pull my sash free. Then, slowly, I draw my cotton robes off my shoulders. I stare down at the floor, feeling as exposed as I look.

"Gods," Zelle murmurs. "That was about as sensual as a tooth extraction. You'd better watch closely."

She casts her face to the side, her gaze blurring, unfocused. She undresses from her hanfu leisurely, and I can't help but be amazed at the transformation in her demeanor. She becomes a woman in love. Every movement is filled with yearning. Desire in the quickening of her breaths as the robes tumble from her body; coyness in the way she catches my eyes before dropping her gaze to the floor. In her parted lips: longing.

Then she grins, and the mirage is broken.

"That was amazing," I admit.

With a shrug, Zelle glides her robes back on, though there is real pride in her voice. "Of course it was. You wouldn't expect anything less from the highest-paid courtesan in the palace, would you? Now, get dressed and try it again. Imagine that you're with the person you desire. You're undressing in front of them for the first time. How would you feel? How would *they* feel? Use the thought of their lust to fuel your own."

I close my eyes and do as she says, dreaming of Wren.

Over the next few hours, Zelle teaches me more techniques for the King's bedchamber, from ways to be touched she's heard he likes from previous Paper Girls to exercises for me to practice to become more aware of my own sensuality. Sometimes she looks at me in a way that makes it seem like she can tell what I'm thinking about. Or, more specifically—*who.*

"Will we have more lessons?" I ask once the lesson is over, gathering up the hem of my robes and starting to my feet.

"Anytime the King calls for you," Zelle replies. "Though there won't be that much more to teach you. Like I said, it's natural, really. You just need practice. But Madam Himura thinks there's benefit in you all having lessons with me, and I get to take a few hours out from seeing clients." She smiles up at me. "I'm looking forward to hearing how tonight goes, Nine. I think you'll do well."

Heat—and not the good kind—crawls across my skin at the thought of the King's hands on my body. Everyone talks about our job as though it were totally normal. As though physical intimacy were something to be demanded, not offered or shared. Not with love, the way I'd dreamed of it since I was young, thinking marriage was the sweet kisses my parents shared when they thought I wasn't looking, the way they sat side by side many nights on the back porch, in silence but somehow making the air feel full of words.

Something narrows in my throat. "I still don't feel ready."

"I know I've thrown a lot of information at you today," Zelle says gently. "Just remember that it's your first time. The King isn't expecting you to be highly skilled. In fact, he's probably looking forward to your inexperience. Many men enjoy that, taking a girl's virginity."

"Why?" The word comes out bitter. All the bad things in my life have happened because of men's greed—first when they took Mama, and then when they came back seven years later for me. My voice is rough as I add, "They have all the power, anyway."

The look Zelle gives me is sharp. "Do they? Yes, they like to think they're in charge, ordering us around and taking women for their own whenever they fancy. But is that true power? They can take and steal and break all they want, but there is one thing they have no control over. Our *emotions*," she says at my nonplussed look. "Our feelings. Our thoughts. None of them will ever be able to control the way we feel. Our minds and hearts are our own. That is our power, Nine. Never forget it."

There's an odd calmness to her expression, though something dark surges behind her eyes. Just as I'm about to leave, I pause, glancing back from the doorway. "About my nickname..."

Zelle nods, guessing what I'm about to ask. "I did get it from Blue. But I don't use it in the same way."

"How *do* you use it?"

She flashes her crooked smile. "As a compliment, of course."

FIFTEEN

Back at Paper House, I spend two uncomfortable hours being polished and plucked by a group of chattering maids before being left to soak in a bath of honeyed milk and spices. It's supposed to soften my skin, perfume it, but it only heightens the sense that I'm some animal being prepared for a feast, and as I float in the bath, this unsettling vision hits me of the scented liquid seeping into my body through my pores, right down into my bones, until I'm nothing but fragrance and softness. As if I might disappear at the lightest touch.

Afterward, Lill dresses me in a long embroidered skirt of cream and charcoal black, tied at my waist with a ribbon of velvet over a gauzy pearl-colored shirt with draped sleeves. It's a teasing mix of conservative and sensual. The full skirt hides my legs, but the sheerness of the top exposes the shape of my breasts and the slender slope of my shoulders. It makes me intensely aware of what I'm wearing it for.

Or rather, what I'm wearing it *before*.

Lill is quiet as she works, sensing my mood. Before we leave, she places a leaf-wrapped bundle at the head of my sleeping mat. "I'm supposed to remind you to mix these with water as soon as you get back," she says, avoiding my eyes. "And you have to drink the whole thing, Mistress. Even if it tastes bad."

The herbs to stop pregnancy. I'd forgotten about them.

I nod to show Lill I understand. But my stomach is already churning, and I have no idea if I'll even be able to keep down a few sips after what's about to happen. As Lill leads me through Paper House to where a palanquin is waiting, it takes all my effort not to be sick right here and now.

The small burst of courage Zelle's lesson gave me slips away even more with each moment drawing me closer to the King: Lill wishing me luck as I climb into the palanquin; the swaying stride of the oryx on the journey through the darkening palace. Arriving at Royal Court, the line of soldiers standing guard outside the King's fortress is just as intimidating as my first visit, a row of armor and horns. Inside, I'm taken to a windowless room for a purification ceremony. A group of royal shamans move in a ring around me, swinging gold thuribles as they chant, incense twining into ropelike tendrils around my body, a physical manifestation of how trapped I feel.

By the time I'm brought to the King's private rooms, my panic is deep, a physical thing. Everything in me wants to turn. Run away. But I force myself to recall General Yu's threat, and Wren's reminder that our actions impact not only us but our families, too.

I have to keep Baba and Tien safe. And, just maybe, the King will have some answers about my mother.

The soldiers escorting me are led by a Moon caste fox female who I recognize as one of the demons at the King's side during the Unveiling Ceremony. She must be one of his personal guards. She is undoubtedly beautiful, with sharp, vulpine eyes, and a slender body, human and fox blended seamlessly under a coating of sleek fur the color of freshly laid snow. Something about her stirs a deep current of unease in me. Through life in the palace, I've been slowly getting used to the presence of demons, but being so close to them still unnerves me. Especially Moon castes, with the promise of power in their animal-like limbs. The sense that they could tear me apart any second they chose.

We stop at a set of heavy opal doors set into an arched recess in the stone. The fox raps her knuckles against them and they glide slowly open, revealing a high-ceilinged black tunnel. I gag on the warm, perfumed air that rushes out.

The fox female glares down her powder-white nose at me. "The King is ready for you." Her voice rings high and cold, every syllable injected with disgust. Clearly she hates the fact that her precious King takes Paper caste girls to his bed.

Well, fox, I want to tell her, I'm not so keen on it, either. But I don't say, can't say, anything. The darkness of the tunnel fixes my gaze. It seems to pull at me, coaxing me forward. But my feet stay rooted.

The King is in there.

Waiting for *me*.

The fox makes a hissing sound with her teeth. "What," she snarls with a flick of her tail, "have you never seen a door before? Oh. Of course. I forgot you're from Xienzo. I suppose you keeda peasants can't afford them." Then she grabs me, whispering into my ear so only I can hear—"Whore!"—before shoving me inside.

I pitch forward, just managing to stop myself from falling as the doors shut with a weighty thud behind me. The tunnel is dark. The heaviness of the air seems to press on me from all sides, and I hug my arms around myself, my breathing loud. The idea that I could just stand here and not move is tempting, but it would just be delaying the inevitable. With a shaky inhale, I straighten my spine and start forward.

Soon I make out a faint red light up ahead. I move a little faster. A few moments later I emerge into a high, vaulted room. The ruby glow is coming from the hundreds of candles peppering the room—along the floor, in clusters on top of cabinets and side tables, even floating in the air—giving off heat and a cloyingly sweet aroma that makes my gut cramp. And there, in the center of the room on an enormous golden throne—

The King.

He's dressed in his usual black-and-gold robes, but tonight they're tied loosely, cutting a deep V down his torso, revealing chestnut-brown hair and the ripple of muscles. It strikes me again how humanlike his body is, and I recall Zelle's words earlier about how similar the castes actually are. If you ignored his bull's coat and the elongated pull of his jaw, the King could almost pass for human. Then my eyes travel down, to the muscled calves tapering into gold-plated gray hooves, as big as a pair of stone weights, and I remember seven years ago, the sound of demon footfall so alien to our village.

I lower into a bow, knees and forehead to the floor. The polished rock is frozen against my skin. "H-heavenly Master," I greet, and I'm furious with myself for the shake in my voice, the way it echoes weakly in the vast room.

"Come, now, Lei-zhi," the King says smoothly. "There's no need to be so formal. Not when it's just the two of us." His tone is light, but the command in his words is clear. When I unravel from my bow, he beckons me forward, gesturing to the table in front of the throne. "The royal chefs have prepared us dinner. I took the time to find out what your favorite dishes are." Candlelight picks out the copper hairs in his coat. He cocks a smile. It's wonky, almost boyish, at odds with the deepness of his voice. "Sugared almonds are a particular weakness of mine, too."

My eyes take a quick sweep of the bowls and plates spread across the table. There are prawn dumplings and scallion pancakes, steamed turnip cakes and cuts of roasted chicken breasts glistening with sauce, wine-steeped dates and fried red bean dough balls covered in syrup and coconut flakes. A glass carafe of sake sits to one side, along with two bowls for serving. But even though the food looks delicious, I can't smell anything over the horrible sweet perfume of the candles. My veins are clotted with it.

Keeping my head low, I kneel at the table across from the King, still battling the urge to be sick. "I'm humbled by your thoughtfulness, Heavenly Master," I murmur.

He slaps his hand down onto the arm of his throne. "What did I *just* say?" His raised voice booms through the chamberlike room. "All you girls are the same. *Heavenly Master* this, *Heavenly Master* that. It's tiring. Sometimes I think these rules were made just to bore me." He leans forward, fixing me with his iced stare, the gold tips of his horns catching the light. "Do you know why my ancestor, the first Demon King of Ikhara, had the title Heavenly Master instated?"

"N-no."

He eases back in his throne. "Other warlords and clan leaders are known individually by their names, the families they descended from. It allows for easy infamy. For reverence. But it also means anyone can make a name for themselves. After emerging victorious from the Night War, the Bull King chose to shed his name completely. He saw it as symbolic. A way to elevate his status. Instead of mere mortals, he and his successors would be revered as an all-powerful entity. We would be gods." Something ugly wrings the King's face. "Yet tell me, Lei-zhi, what is the point of a god whose people know nothing about him? Whose followers cannot call upon him by his own name?" He snorts. "It's like worshipping a ghost."

I wrestle down a scowl. *If only you were one.*

"And do you know," he goes on, "when sons of the King are born they're known only by the sequence in which they were birthed? Before I took over my father's reign, I was Third Son. *Third Son!*" Again, he slaps his hand down, making me flinch. The sound rings through the room like a thunderclap. "As if anything about me is third-best!" But a muscle twitches in his temple, and there's a broken edge to his voice. Behind the anger is something more. Regret? Fear?

"What happened to your older brothers?" I ask tentatively.

The King licks his lips. "I killed them so I could take the throne." His words chill the air, power emanating from him like heat-shimmer. Then, abruptly, his face switches back to its wide, tooth-filled smile. "How about we start? You must be hungry, and I wouldn't want the food to go cold."

As we were taught, I reach for the vial of sake to pour it for him. But he waves my hand away.

"You're my guest, Lei-zhi. Let me take care of you."

He pours two big helpings. Handing a bowl to me, his furred fingers brush mine for a brief moment, sending a wave of goose bumps across my arms. We hold them up, bowing our foreheads to the rim of the bowls, before bringing them to our lips. The King drains his drink in one. I try to match him; we've been taught it's the polite thing to do. But I get only halfway through before my throat burns and I set my bowl down, eyes watering.

"You don't drink?" he asks.

"Only on certain occasions." My voice is still hoarse from the alcohol. I cough to clear it. "Otherwise we're not allowed."

"Sometimes it's necessary to break the rules," the King replies. The corner of his mouth tugs up into a feral smile. "They tell me I'm not allowed to leave the Inner Courts without my guards. But I have my ways."

It sounds like a threat. Suddenly I'm all too aware of my skin, of how much is on show through my shirt. I start to pull my hair forward over my collarbones, but the King's voice rings out.

"Stop."

I freeze at the command.

"You look better with your hair back. It shows off your beauty. Your eyes."

My pulse skitters as I drop my arms to let him look at me. The closeness of the room and the nearness of the King clamps tight, the air as heavy and unnourishing as concrete. My lashes are low, but I still feel the roam of his leer grazing my skin, like the projection of his touch, and I fixate on a spot on my skirt, trying to steady my breaths.

"Let us eat," he says eventually.

For the next half an hour I force down helpings of dish after dish. The King talks the whole time. Like the food, I don't register most of it. I'm so busy trying not to think of what'll happen after dinner that it's become the *only* thing I can think of. But at the mention of General Yu's name, my ears prick up.

"…his gift. I have to say, I was surprised. I didn't expect much of him, especially after his abysmal performance in Jana."

I swallow the piece of salted fish I've been chewing on. "Heavenly Master," I start, but at the look he cuts me, I amend quickly, "I mean, my King…"

It seems to be the right thing to say. He leans in a little, something satisfied uncoiling in his expression. "Yes?"

"About General Yu. If you don't mind me asking, on the journey here he mentioned something about a...a raid. On my village, seven years ago. I was wondering if you—"

In an instant, the King's face hardens. "Why would you want to know about that?" he growls before I can finish.

"Oh. I was...I was just hoping—"

"Order has to be maintained. Are you suggesting I allow everyone in the kingdom to do exactly as they please?"

"No, of course not—"

"Or that I will tell you anything, just because we are to share a bed?"

I flush. "*No.* I just meant—"

The King edges forward in his throne, the muscles on his neck taut. "Do not underestimate me, Lei-zhi. I may be young, but I know how to be a King. I was *born* one. I don't need a Paper Girl asking stupid questions about something she knows nothing about."

Under the fear, a spark of anger bursts to life. Something I know *nothing* about?

I push out a long exhale. Then, as carefully as possible, I go on, "I'm sorry, my King. But my mother was taken during that raid."

There's a pocket of silence. "That is a shame," he replies stiffly.

"Do you know what might have happened to her?" I clasp my hands in my lap and force the most deferential look I can muster across my face. "I'd like to know. For my own peace of mind."

He watches me in silence a few seconds more. Then he gives a small tilt of his head, scarlet light catching on the curve of his gilded horns. "Check the Night Houses' list of courtesans." He reaches with his chopsticks for a slice of barbecued pork belly and pops it into his mouth, the sauce glossy on his dark, bowed lips. "If she was brought back to the palace," he mutters between chews, "that's where she'd be."

I drop into a bow, half to hide the sudden rush of hope that's spiraling through me, and stammer a thank-you to the floor.

"See?" the King says, silky. There's the rustle of clothes as he gets to his feet, the thud of hooves as he steps around the table. "I'm good to my Paper Girls, if they are good to me. Now, Lei-zhi. To bed."

The words crawl along my skin. He offers a hand, and there's nothing I can do but take it. As his fingers close around mine—my palm tiny in his—the ground seems to shift under me, throwing everything off-balance, and even though it's the last thing I want to do, I let him lift me to my feet.

The King's bedroom is another deep chamber. An immense bed dominates the room, the posts at each corner strung with charms and copper bells that I can guess at the purpose of. Then I realize that the room isn't actually so large—it's a trick of the mirrors, which cover the walls and ceiling. There are broken mirrors, speckled and old, with deep, jagged cracks, and ones as polished as the surface of a lake. They refract and reflect everything in a dizzying kaleidoscope of images: the flicker of candles, the sliding muscles of the King's bare chest as he comes closer, the tensed line of my jaw as I turn away.

"*Look* at me," he growls.

I do as he says, heart wild.

Calloused fingers caress my cheek. "I've bedded so many women during my reign," he muses, one hand trailing down my neck to the front of my shirt, where my skirt is tied. "And yet there is always something new to discover in each one. I've come to learn that beauty isn't exhaustive. Desire cannot be tamed."

You're right. I want to shove him away, scream at him, *Tame this!* But fear grips me in place.

Then his fingers find the bow fastening my skirt.

"Please," I breathe. "Don't—"

He roars. "You do not command the King!"

With a sudden movement, he rips the bow away. My skirt falls open. A half sob, half growl escapes me. I grab his hands, trying to peel them off me, but he bats me aside, hooks a finger on the front of my blouse, and tears it straight down the middle.

Tears streak my cheeks. I cover myself with my hands, but he pries them away and shoves me back onto the bed. The bells cry out as he climbs on top of me and starts drawing off his robes. I squeeze my eyes shut. His body is hard all over, wired with muscle, but the hardest part of him pushes against my leg.

I jerk back, recoiling.

"Let's see if you taste as delicious as last night," he purrs huskily, and lowers his mouth to my neck. His tongue flicks out—rough. Hot.

Revulsion sings in my bloodstream. I beat my fists against him, but it makes no difference; he's too big, too heavy.

His mouth roams downward. One of his horns presses into the soft underside of my chin: a knife edge, a silent threat.

My heart is drumming hard enough to burst through my ribs. This is wrong. All wrong. Everything Zelle taught me earlier seems ungraspable, childish in the face of this ugly reality, far worse than anything I imagined. I think desperately of Wren, but I can't even picture her face, and the tears come harder, my breaths faster, and I know then that I can't do this. I'll die if I have to endure even one more second.

The King moves down past my navel. As he shifts his position, the balance of weight tips just enough for me to move.

I slam into him.

Shove him back.

I roll off the bed with a grunt. Pain fissures up my back as I hit the floor. I scramble to my feet. There's a rage-filled roar—the King—so deep it shudders my bones, but I'm already running, faster than he can come after me, desperation fueling my steps, and I sprint out the bedroom and into the main chamber, the floating tide of candles rippling away from me in waves.

I race down the hallway. The door at the end swings open as I get to it. I barrel past the waiting soldiers and servants, who cry out in surprise, not caring that I'm half dressed or that I have no clue where to go, only focused on getting out, out, *out*—

Something cracks against the back of my head.

I crash to the floor, collapsing headfirst into darkness.

SIXTEEN

WHEN I WAS YOUNG, MAMA TAUGHT me a method for dealing with situations that upset me. "It's all about yin and yang," she said, stroking my hair in her slow, calming way, her voice as sweet and delicate as summer rain. "Balancing your energy. When you're angry or upset, stop for a moment and close your eyes. Breathe in slowly. Imagine as you do that the air you take in is bright and golden, as lovely and light as your eyes. Let that brightness fill your belly. Then, when you exhale, picture the darkness that had been within you—whatever it was that upset you—and visualize it leaving your body as you release your breath. Joyful, golden light comes in…darkness goes out. Try it with me now."

I've always pictured happiness this way—as a light, something to summon at will to flush out the darkness poisoning my insides. But as I wake, the memory of the King's touch is so oppressive I can't imagine how it will ever leave me. It's more than just a bit of blackness.

It is a whole night sky, starless and cold.

I come to slowly, disoriented. I'm lying on a sleeping mat. Someone has dressed me in a night robe, clean and cool against my skin.

I must be back in Paper House, though I haven't seen this room before. It's small, plainly furnished like mine. Lantern light comes in through the gridlike pattern of a sliding shoji door. The building is muted, the room shadowed. It's still night.

For a while I lie unmoving, limbs so heavy they feel like lead, while at the same time I'm hollow, emptied of whatever vital force usually keeps our blood flowing and muscles moving. There's a dull ache where I slammed into the stone floor of the King's bedchamber, and the back of my head hurts. I recall the sudden crack. Crumpling to my feet. One of the soldiers must have hit me.

Grimacing, I try to sit up, but something is weighing me down. At first I think it's my own weight, that I'm just laden with exhaustion. Then I notice the gold bands circling my wrists. With awkward, jerky movements, I manage to prop myself up on my elbows, and I spot the same bands laced around my ankles; two pairs of gold circles, slender as twine, warm with magic. But though they look delicate, they are so heavy I can barely lift them.

Shamans' work.

I sit up again, this time carefully, my arms deadweight at my sides, just as hurried footsteps sound in the hallway.

"Please, let her recover—"

"You've been too soft on that girl since she arrived! I don't care what the King's orders are. She needs to be taught a lesson! Can you imagine? Denying the King? Who does she think she is?"

"She was scared—"

"They all are! That didn't stop the rest of them from doing their job!"

The door slams open. Madam Himura strides inside, Mistress Eira close behind. I shrink back against the wall, but the eagle-woman is on me in seconds, one wing-hand grasping the collar of my robe and lifting me off the floor. The other slaps me so hard my neck snaps round.

"You're lucky he didn't kill you!" she shrieks, spit flecking my face. "Stupid girl! Did you think that you're somehow above your duties because of the special treatment we granted you to be here? How dare you! You've shamed us in front of the King himself. And after everything we've done for you!"

She hits me again, so hard it fractures my vision. The silver of her rings cut my cheek. There's the warm trickle of blood, a kiss on my skin.

"Himura, you'll kill her!" Mistress Eira cries.

"It's the least she deserves!"

"Well, think of the damage you'll do to her face!"

"The shamans can heal her. Don't worry, Eira, she'll be as pretty as before—though hopefully not as stupid!"

Madam Himura's arm flies back and she hits me again. She hits me until lights are sparking in my eyes and my ears ring and my mouth is filled with blood. Just when I'm close to passing out, she throws me to the floor.

I curl into a ball, expecting more. When it doesn't come, I look up through swollen eyes, spit flecking my chin.

"I—I'm sorry," I stammer thickly.

"Don't you dare speak to me!" Chest heaving, Madam Himura draws down on me, a talon prodding my ribs. Her yellow eyes bore into me with their cold, unblinking stare. "Let me explain what's going to happen. The only reason the King didn't have you killed was because he still desires you, heavens know why. He has ordered you to be kept in isolation for one week with no food or comforts. Do not even *think* about escaping. Those enchanted bands will make running impossible, and a guard will be stationed outside this room at all times. You will return to your schedule once the week is over. The King will call you to his bedchamber from then on once he's ready, and that time, you won't deny him." Her voice is harsh. "I comforted you yesterday. Do not ever expect kindness from me again." With one last scathing look, she sweeps from the room.

Mistress Eira hangs back. In silence, she comes over and helps me lie down, pulling a blanket gently over me. She rests a hand on my brow, careful not to touch anywhere I was hit.

"Oh, Lei," she sighs. "What have you done?"

"I—I couldn't bear it." My voice is a rasp.

Mistress Eira brushes a thumb over my hairline. "You have to, dear girl. You don't have a choice."

"Please, Mistress." I rake in an inhale, fixing her with my watery gaze. "Tell me honestly. Does it get better?"

She gives me a half smile. "It does. That I promise you."

But I look away, unable to believe her.

"Eira! Come!"

At Madam Himura's call, Mistress Eira starts to her feet. "I'm so sorry, Lei," she whispers. "There's nothing I can do. You'll have to find a way to bear it—and I know you will. You are stronger than most of the girls who come here."

As she turns to go, I strain against the bands to lift my head. "My father," I say. "Tien. This won't affect them, will it? They won't be harmed?"

She hesitates. "I don't think so. At least, the King hasn't shared any such plans with us."

Relief wings through me. Then I add, "Do you know if your messenger managed to deliver my messages home? I still haven't had any replies, and it's been over a month now…"

"I'll be sure to check," Mistress Eira replies, already turning. "Now, I really must go."

After the door closes behind her, there's the thud of boots outside—a guard taking watch.

I slump back. Squeezing my eyes shut, I try to slow my breathing. Light in, darkness out, I remind myself. My father and Tien are safe. The King gave me a lead about Mama. Things aren't so bad. Light in, darkness out.

But no matter how hard I try, it doesn't work. As the minutes tick by, I draw in breath after breath, and all my lungs find is darkness.

I dream of home that night.

Not the nightmare—this dream is quiet and calm, a stitched patchwork of glimpses from my past life, the small world in which I lived before coming to the palace. Wind stirring leaves in the garden. The smell of herbs. Tien's pattering footsteps in the shop. A cough from a room above. Baba? Mama, even, before she was taken? Throughout, I stand like an echo in the middle of it all, unable to move and feeling only the edges of tears in my eyes.

Odd, how time works. On long days in the shop, I've known it to stretch out forever, as thick and heavy as molasses. Other days—days filled with fun errands or festivals—time would take on a brittle, icelike quality. I'd race through it and it'd snap into pieces around me, crystalline moments of happiness and laughter, and before I knew it, the day would be gone.

The time I spend locked in the room passes so slowly I begin to forget what life was like before my imprisonment. Hunger gnaws my belly. I'm given a bowl of water each day, and sipping it gives me some relief, but I still feel hollowed out, as though someone had scooped my insides with a giant ladle, fed my core to the earth.

And I miss the girls. Not Blue, of course, or Mariko. But the others. Since coming to the palace, I've been surrounded by so many women that I'm only alone at night, and even then I can hear the soft sleeping sounds of the girls in their rooms nearby, sense their closeness, the dreams flitting behind their eyelids. I didn't realize how much I'd miss that before it was taken away.

Over time that realization leads to another: that I have made a home here. Somehow, these walls, these rooms, have become as familiar and comfortable to me as my little shop-house back in Xienzo. And the girls within them, too. Because though I haven't managed to find my mother yet, I've found something else during my time here.

Friends. A new kind of family, even, albeit a weird, dysfunctional, at times infuriating one.

Still. Family. A home.

The guilt is so strong I double over, gritting my teeth to stop the tears.

On my fourth night of confinement I'm struggling to sleep. It's been hot all day, and without windows, the air in the room is trapped and close. To cool down, I've loosened my robe and am lying spread out on the floor, skin begging for just the slightest brush of a cool breeze. I watch the ceiling through half closed eyes. There's cricket song from the grasses beyond the house, but other than that the night is quiet. So I notice it immediately when the tread of the guard's boots outside my room disappears down the corridor.

I sit up with a struggle, weighed down by the bands at my ankles and wrists. For a few moments, nothing happens. Then I sense movement in the hallway.

The hair stands up on my arms. It could be the Demon King. He told me he has ways to get into Women's Court. Perhaps he's decided he doesn't want to wait anymore and has come to take what I refused him.

I stagger to my feet. It's not graceful, and I'm hunched over from the weight of the bangles, puffing heavily, my vision swimming. Yet I blow out an exhale and force myself to stand steady. I'll face him on my feet even if it kills me. But when the door glides open a few moments later, the figure that steals inside is smaller than the King, and infinitely more lovely.

"Lei?" a low, husky voice whispers.

"Wren?"

I move forward, realizing just as I do so that four days of no food is really not conducive to a person's ability to keep herself upright.

Wren catches me just as my knees buckle. Looping an arm round my shoulders, she helps me to the floor. She doesn't let go straightaway, and a tremor runs through me at how close she is, her warm hands on me. The fresh, oceanlike scent of her unwinds in the air, stirring something deep in my chest.

"What are you doing here?" I ask, keeping my voice down. "The guard could be back any minute."

She shakes her head. "Not for a while."

"How do you know?"

"I've watched him," she says simply, as though it were nothing. As though spying on royal guards were completely normal. "He always leaves around now for half an hour or so. There's a girl here he goes to."

"One of us?"

She doesn't answer. Instead, she digs into the folds of her robes, pulling out a small package wrapped in a banana leaf. "Here. I thought you might be hungry."

Her fingers graze mine as she hands the package to me. I peel the leaf back to see a bundle of rice peppered with roasted peanuts and tiny fried fish. The fragrance of the coconut-steamed rice rises out, hot and sweet, already liquid on my tongue. I've never smelled anything more delicious.

I battle the urge to immediately inhale the whole thing. "I don't know what to say," I murmur, and Wren smiles, eyes shimmering in the darkness.

"Good," she replies. "You're not supposed to say anything. You're supposed to *eat.*"

The room is windowless, the only light coming through the rice-paper panels in the door, and even that is weak, an amber tint from the sole lantern in the hall. In the shadows, it's hard to make out the details of Wren's face. Still, something about her seems different. It takes me a few moments to realize that it's the first time I've seen her smile. Properly, I mean. Openly, widely.

Unguarded.

It completely transforms her. Gone is the hard, closed mask she usually wears, replaced instead with a lightness so beautiful it's dazzling. Her eyes are upturned, crinkled. She even has *dimples.*

"What?" Wren asks with a lift of a brow.

"It's just…I've never seen you look happy before." In an instant her smile vanishes. "Oh. I'm sorry."

"I guess I haven't had many reasons to feel happy since coming to the palace," she replies after a pause. Then she nods at the food. "You should eat, or there won't be time for sweets."

It's my turn to raise my eyebrows. "You brought sweets?"

She digs out another leaf-wrapped package from her robes. "I thought you'd like them. I know your province is renowned for having the best in the kingdom."

I unpeel the leaf to find four small diamonds of green-and-white coconut kuih. The last time I'd eaten these was at breakfast with Baba and Tien the morning I was taken.

For a while, I'm too choked to speak.

"Thank you," I say eventually.

"It's nothing."

"Wren. You've snuck here in the middle of the night against Madam Himura's orders—let alone the King's—to bring me food you've stolen, and you think it's *nothing?*"

She smiles again, that brilliant sunburst of a smile that illuminates her whole face and seems to warm the darkness, even just for a moment. "Well, when you put it like that…"

She laughs, but I don't join her. "Why do you do it?" I ask.

Her forehead pinches. "Do what?"

"Put on a mask in front of the other girls." As Wren goes to interject, I carry on, "Don't you want to get to know us?"

"Of course I do."

"Then why do you distance yourself so much?"

She falters. Glancing away, her long lashes hide her dark eyes. "Before I came here, I promised myself that I wouldn't make friends. I thought it'd be easier to shut myself off from everyone. To go through this alone."

"So why are you helping me?"

"Because you *tried.* Because you were brave." Wren leans in, voice fierce even in a whisper. "Our lives here are defined by others, every decision made for us, every turn of fate pushed by the hands of others. But you stood up and said *no.* Even though you knew what it could cost you. You have integrity, Lei. You have fight. I respect that."

I drop my gaze to my lap. "It's not like anything came of it. The King…he'll call for me again one day. And this time I won't be able to refuse."

She shakes her head. "Don't devalue what you did." Then, stiffly, she reaches for my hand.

There's a moment of awkwardness. I almost pull away—more from surprise than anything. But then we relax and our fingers twine together. The race of Wren's pulse against mine sends a jolt of something electric down my bloodstream.

"You fought against the Demon King, Lei. There aren't many people in the kingdom who can say that, let alone a Paper Girl."

When she lets go, my skin sears where she touched me.

We talk in whispers while I eat. For the first time, there are no walls up between us. No masks. Honesty comes easily after her hand in mine, our closeness in the dark, hushed room. I tell Wren about my past, and in turn she tells me about hers. Life as an only child in the Hannos' palace in Ang-Khen. Years of structure, routine, expectations. When she reveals how she was promised to the King by her father before she was even born, it makes me think of Blue.

"Did you want it?" I ask. "To become a Paper Girl?"

She hesitates, lips clamped. "Want doesn't come into it. My life has always been about duty. Always, and only."

"And your future?"

She answers matter-of-factly. "The King."

I can't imagine what it was like to grow up knowing that. To have never tasted freedom, never felt its golden, sun-bright wind beneath her wings.

"What would you have done?" I press. "If you hadn't been chosen as a Paper Girl."

At once, her expression turns rigid.

"I—I haven't really thought about it."

"You must have some ideas. Things you like to do, hobbies—"

"I don't have any hobbies."

She says it so seriously that I almost laugh, catching myself just in time. "What do you mean? Everyone has hobbies, Wren. All right, so I spent most of my time in the shop. But there were still things I liked to do when I got a chance. Playing with Bao, cooking with Tien…"

"Well," she says after a beat, "I didn't have any chances."

Her face is shadowed in the darkness, and I scan for answers among its strong lines and feline angles, the charcoal pools in the hollows of her cheeks. Not for the first time, I wonder what word was hidden in Wren's Birth-blessing pendant. At nineteen, she's already opened it. I try to picture her reaction when the gold shell parted. Whether she discovered something new inside, or whether the character just confirmed what she'd already known all along, some fate or truth she'd always felt, like an ache in her bones. The way she told me her life has always been about duty, and her future about the King, worries me that it wasn't what she'd hoped for. But asking about someone's Birth-blessing word is taboo, so I bite back my curiosity.

Before she leaves, Wren tucks the now-empty leaves back inside her robe so Madam Himura won't be suspicious.

"We can be honest with each other now, right?" I say as she helps me to my feet. At her nod, I wet my lips and go on, "I saw you leaving Paper House. A few nights ago. You went into the woods."

"You *followed* me?"

The hardness in her voice makes me flinch.

"No! I—I saw from the veranda. I don't know where you went—"

"Good!" she snaps.

My arms stiffen at my sides. "I'm only asking because it's dangerous, Wren. If you were caught—"

"I know what'll happen."

"Well, you should be more careful."

"I always am."

I blink, freezing in place. "So it's happened more than once?"

She looks away, a muscle pulsing in her neck.

"And you're going to do it again," I say dully.

Her silence is my answer.

My next question comes out quiet, barely more than a whisper. "Are you meeting with someone?"

"Of course not," she replies, eyes flicking back to meet mine.

"Then what, Wren? What could possibly be worth you risking Madam Himura finding out?"

Wren's face is touched gently on one side by the light from the corridor. Her features are set hard, but she closes her eyes for a brief second, taking a long breath, and the lantern glow across her right eyelid trembles, so soft looking I long to brush my thumb across it.

Finally she sighs, her shoulders curling forward. "I can't tell you, Lei. I'm sorry. Please just pretend you never saw me. Can you do that?" When I don't answer, she steps closer and adds, her voice gentler now, husky and low, "Have you never had a secret you needed to keep?"

Yes, I want to say. *These feelings for* you.

Instead, I look away.

Wren reaches out, her fingers grazing mine. "You're making this so hard for me," she says. "Do you know that?" And without waiting for an answer, she glides the door open and disappears into the corridor.

SEVENTEEN

THREE DAYS LATER, MISTRESS EIRA COMES to release me. She brings a shaman with her, and he removes the gold bands from my ankles and wrists, my skin warm and shivery from his magic. It only takes a few minutes. When he's gone, I lift my arms, rolling my hands, marveling at how light my limbs have suddenly become, as though they might float away from me. But when Mistress Eira helps me to my feet, I pitch forward. My body is just as heavy as if I were still wearing the bonds. I have to cling to her to stop from collapsing.

"You're weak," she says. "You need to eat. I got the kitchen to prepare you a special meal. It's waiting in your room."

"Just the one?"

She gives me a smile. "Today, Lei, you can have as many meals as you want."

With Mistress Eira's help, I shuffle to the door. She's only just started to slide it open when a teary-eyed Lill runs inside and barrels straight into me, knocking me half to my knees. "Mistress!" she cries, looping her arms around my waist. Her doe ears flutter against my cheek. "I'm so glad you're all right!"

I squeeze her back. There's the pinch of tears in my eyes and I blink quickly to stop them from coming. "Of course I am," I say, trying to keep my voice light. "I've handled Blue first thing in the mornings. Everything else is easy."

Lill doesn't laugh. From the doorway, Mistress Eira gives me a nod before leaving us alone.

I unravel myself from Lill. "It's so good to see you."

She doesn't return my smile. Though her young face is still lovely, there's something anxious in the pinch of her small mouth, and I notice dark patches beneath her eyes, like a pair of bruised figs. My heart gives a little kick.

"Has Madam Himura been cruel to you?" I ask, curving my hand round her shoulder.

"Not any more than usual." She bites her lip. "But I wouldn't have even noticed. Oh, I've been so worried, Mistress." Her gaze moves over me. "You look…"

"Radiant? Ravishing?" I mean it as a joke, but in an instant tears well over her lashes.

I swipe them from her cheeks with my fingers. "Oh, Lill," I say. "I'm sorry. And I'm so sorry for worrying you. I haven't had the best week, either." My stomach tangles with how much of an understatement that is. I force a smile. "But I'm fine now. I got through it, and so did you. That's what counts." She sniffs, and I pull her back against me, cupping my hand round the curve of her head. When I can tell she's stopped crying, I draw back. "Mistress Eira said there's food waiting in my room. Want to eat it with me?"

And finally—a smile.

Lill scrubs the back of her hand across her eyes. "If you don't inhale it all first," she murmurs with a sniff.

I laugh, such a strong rush of affection hitting me then that it temporarily pushes aside the exhaustion. And even though it takes us twice as long as it should to make the trip back through Paper House to my bedroom because my steps are shaky and I have to keep stopping to swallow down surges of nausea, I keep a smile on my face for her.

After we eat the food Mistress Eira ordered for me—and two more helpings after that—Lill takes me for an early bath. There's a while before the rest of the girls wake. Though the sun has just broken the horizon, night still clings to the air. Because of the late summer heat we've been experiencing, it's been easy to forget that autumn will arrive soon with the turn of the tenth month, but the days are noticeably shorter now. The morning air is crisp. Herb-fragranced steam rises from the bubbling tubs.

Taking care to be gentle, Lill helps me out of my grubby robes. The fresh air is as welcome as kisses on my skin.

Then I remember the last time I was naked.

Not kisses, but *teeth* on my skin.

I scramble into the water, slopping it over the sides of the barrel in my hurry. Lill comes forward to wash me, but I cup her hands and take the sponge from her. "I'd like to do it myself, if that's all right?" I ask, and she nods, seeming to understand.

Slowly, I draw the sponge over my body. I take my time, methodical, careful to reach every inch, every spot of pale skin. I'm not nearly as dirty as when I had the bath that first night I arrived at the palace. At least, not physically. But it's a similar feeling of cleansing as I wash, of my body becoming lighter the murkier the bathwater gets. And with the shrill song of the birds in the eaves and the familiar sounds of Paper House waking, I finally start to relax. It's so good to be able to move my limbs freely, especially now that my energy is coming back after that gigantic breakfast, and I tilt my chin up to the sky, swishing about in the tub as my hair fans around me in dark waves.

We get back to my room just as the morning gong sounds. Seconds later, my door slams open. Aoki bounds in, still in her nightdress and her short hair a mess.

"Lei!" she gasps. Just like Lill, she dives straight at me. Her heartbeat jangles against mine as she clutches me fiercely. "I was so scared when Madam Himura told us what you'd done! I thought... well, you don't want to know what I thought. When she said you were being confined for a week as punishment, I actually felt relieved."

"I guess I'm lucky the King didn't throw me out," I say as she lets me go.

Or kill me, I add silently.

Aoki's lips flatten. "He must really desire you." There's a strange constriction to her voice. Then she takes my hands and leans in, face gleaming. "Oh, it's been horrible without you here, Lei! Madam Himura's been even worse than usual, snapping at every little thing—"

"*What* have I been doing?"

Aoki's eyes almost pop out of her head.

She spins round. Framed in the doorway, Madam Himura glares down at us, her beaked chin jutting into the air.

"M-Madam Himura!" Aoki stutters. "I didn't mean—"

The eagle-woman jabs her cane on the floor. "Quiet, girl! It's too early for your blabbering." Glowering, her cool eyes fix mine. "I expect you to perform your best in every one of your lessons from now on, Lei-zhi. The teachers will be reporting to me on your progress after each class. And to make sure you've got the right kind of influence around you"—she cuts a scathing look in Aoki's direction—"I've ordered one of the other girls to accompany you for the next few weeks. You could do well to learn from her." She waves a taloned hand. "Now, get ready for your classes! And you—get to the bathing tubs. That filthy mouth of yours needs scrubbing."

As the eagle-woman drags her from the room, Aoki looks back over her shoulder, an expression of pure terror on her face.

I restrain a laugh. She might still be terrifying, but there are far worse things than getting shouted at by Madam Himura.

When I leave my room a while later, I find Wren waiting in the corridor. The memory of her closeness a few nights ago, how intimate we were with each other, makes me flush. She looks just as she did that night, face bare, hair relaxed and wavy, falling in soft drifts over her shoulders. My hand lifts toward her, an impulsive movement, and I quickly cover the gesture by smoothing down the collar of my robes.

"So you're the one who will be babysitting me."

"Who else would it be? Didn't you know, Lei, I'm at the top of the class?"

"Is that so?" Glancing round to make sure the other girls are out of earshot, I add, "Top of *what* class? Thievery?"

Her eyes glint, but she keeps her voice casual. "Yes, I heard about some food going missing from the kitchens. A real mystery. Do you have any idea where it went?"

I grin. "Into someone's belly, I expect."

"Well, I hope that person enjoyed them."

"I'm certain they did."

Wren smiles, a warm, honeyed curl of her lips that draws my eyes. Before we can say anything more, the door behind her opens.

"Lei!" Aoki calls, bustling out of her room and linking her arm through mine. "Come on, you can't be late on your first day back." And although she shoots a curious look at Wren, she doesn't say anything, just lifts her brows at me as if to say, *Well, all right, then.*

Lips cocked in amusement, Wren falls into step beside me, and together the three of us make our way down the corridor. Though we don't mention it again, I can sense the secret of what passed between Wren and me three nights ago like a cord, an invisible strand running from her body to mine. Whenever she makes a movement—even something as small as brushing a speck of dust from her hair or adjusting her sash—my eyes instinctively cut her way, and I wonder if she's noticing it, too, this tether, this pull between us.

During the first days of my confinement, I'd tried the breathing technique Mama taught me over and over again to no avail, unable to find comfort in it. Light in, darkness out. Trapped in that tiny room, there only seemed to be darkness, and though I wanted to be set free, I also knew that the moment I was, it would be straight back to my Paper Girl life.

And to the King.

But then Wren came along with her stolen food and warm hands, and a spark of something—the barest quiver of light—entered the room. And after that, my breaths came a little easier, a little brighter. Not quite golden, but...sun-touched.

Now I shoot Wren a look out of the corner of my eye, Aoki's chatter wrapping around us. She offers me a brief half smile in return.

"All right?" she mouths.

I nod.

And while it's not exactly the truth, it isn't a lie, either.

The pavilion where our qi lessons take place is an ornate, two-tiered building with red beams and a magenta-tiled roof, their colors vivid against the faded green of the surrounding gardens. It sits in the center of a shallow, circular lake. Sunlight glitters on its surface.

Birds dart low over the water, on the hunt for small fish and insects, their wingbeats casting ripples in the blue.

We step under the rustle of prayer sheets fluttering from the eaves of the pavilion. As usual, Master Tekoa is waiting for us on the floor. He's wearing loose wrap trousers, thighs crossed, his lean torso bare despite the chill. A monkey's tail protrudes from the top of his trousers—along with the wiry copper fur sheathing his legs, the only indication of his Steel status.

"Take your places," he says without rising.

Aoki, Wren, and I are the last to arrive. I haven't yet had to face the others this morning, and as I cross to the back of the pavilion, they're all staring at me. I keep my head low. The boost of energy from this morning's meal has been spent on the walk over here, and though I try to kneel down slowly when I get to my usual spot, it's more of an ungraceful drop. Although Madam Himura sent a shaman on my second day in confinement to clean my skin of any marks left by her or the King, she asked him to leave my pain as a reminder of my failings. Some of it has settled, a dull ache in the pits of my muscles. I roll my shoulders, trying to ease the rigidness in my back.

In front of me, Zhen and Zhin look over their shoulders.

"We were worried about you, Lei," Zhen murmurs, her short forehead furrowed.

Her sister nods. "How are you feeling?"

"Not too bad," I reply. "Thanks for asking. Did I miss anything important?"

The corner of Zhin's lip quirks. "Only if you count Mariko getting drunk at a dinner one night and almost setting herself on fire by falling into a row of lanterns."

I smother a laugh. "Definitely. Did she set anything else aflame, by chance?"

"Sadly not," Zhin sighs. "Though my maid told me she threw up in a bush outside Madam Himura's bedroom, and the whole of the next day Madam Himura was in such a mood because she didn't know where the bad smell was coming from."

This time I can't help a snort. The twins flash me matching smiles before turning back round.

We begin the lesson with breathing exercises to channel the flow of our internal energy. Qi arts is a meditative movement that blends internal and external manipulation of life energy. Master Tekoa's voice is light but commanding. I focus on his words to tune out the noises around us—chirruping birds, the rustle of wind as it combs the grasses. This is one of the only classes I enjoy, and I'm grateful to have its calming effect this morning. Unlike most of our other lessons, the skills Master Tekoa teaches us aren't about precision or performing to a certain standard, but about how to connect to ourselves, to find peace and strength within. It brings back distant memories of my parents practicing taoyin on the porch, limned in predawn light and set in perfect synchrony, their movements a smooth, underwater flow.

While we repeat the sequence of movements he's been teaching us, Master Tekoa walks around to observe. He usually prefers to hang back, demonstrating adjustments in silence, but when he gets to me, he stops. He stares for a moment before suddenly speaking.

"Fire. So much fire."

I falter midflow.

"Fire so hot it burns even ice to ashes. Fire like a wave to swallow the world whole."

The twins turn around, frowning. Master Tekoa's voice has taken on a rough, grating edge I've never heard before. As he stares unblinkingly in my direction, his eyes glaze over, and my stomach gives a kick as I notice that his pupils are expanding, creeping across his eyes to fill them with black, like dark blood spilling from a wound. A chill emanates from his body—and shivers through mine.

"S-something's wrong," I say as the other girls turn to look. "I think Master Tekoa's having some kind of fit...."

There's a trill of laughter. "What have you done to him, Nine?" Blue crows from the front of the pavilion. "You just can't allow men near you, can you? What's the problem? Don't tell me you prefer *girls*."

Wren is at my side at once. "Shut up, Blue," she snaps.

Blue blinks. "When did *you* two become friends?"

"Fire from within her," Master Tekoa rasps before Wren can retort. The air around him is frozen, and I want to move away from his horrible black stare, but my feet are rooted to the spot. His voice grows louder, gathering pace, his blank expression at odds with the intensity with which he is speaking. "Fire that sears her skin and all she touches. Fire bright enough to blind those who look at her."

With a dismissive flick of her wrist, Blue laughs. "Well, he can't be talking about you, then, Nine. You're not—"

"Red flames in the palace!" roars Master Tekoa, making all of us jolt. "Red flames, kindled from within! On the night of fire, more will come to scorch him!"

There's a moment of charged silence.

Then he blinks.

The darkness slips from his eyes like honey sliding off a spoon. Though the chill in the air around him disappears, my arms are still pricked with goose bumps. I hug them, staring openmouthed.

"You're—you're all out of form," Master Tekoa says, looking round with dull surprise at our stunned faces.

I clear my throat. "Master," I start, "are you feeling all right? You were talking about...fire."

He looks blankly at me before seeming to understand. "Ah. Yes. Qi fire, our internal energy. What you are practicing in these lessons to control." He steps to the front of the pavilion, the sunlight at his back outlining his edges in gold. "That will be enough for today."

Wren places a hand on my arm when I start to question him. "There's no point, Lei. I don't think he knows what just happened."

As soon as we leave the pavilion, Zhin addresses us all, looking worried. "We should tell Mistress Eira and Madam Himura. Something really seemed wrong with him."

Her sister nods.

"Maybe he's sick?" Mariko suggests.

"Or had some kind of magical fit?" Zhen offers.

Blue rolls her eyes. "Clearly."

"A spiritual trance is not something to joke about," Chenna says sharply, shooting Blue a stern look that makes her pout and look away.

"Well, I don't think we should tell them," Mariko says. "It's just another thing for Madam Himura to punish us for."

"You mean, punish *Nine*," Blue retorts. "It was *her* Master Tekoa was addressing, after all."

The other girls glance round to where I'm trailing at the back of the group. Though I can tell they don't like the way she said it, I can also see that they're not entirely unconvinced by what Blue said.

"Well," I say, in a voice much more casual than I feel, "at least we know Master Tekoa carries a…*flame*…for me."

The twins snort. Even Mariko stifles a laugh, and Blue shoots her a furious look. Only Wren and Chenna don't laugh.

At least my joke seems to have broken the tension somewhat. Before long, the eeriness of Master Tekoa's turn starts to drain away in the warmth of the day and the familiar surroundings of

Women's Court as we head back to Paper House. The events at the pavilion start to seem unreal, a strange, shared daydream. Aoki tells everyone about her brother's sleep-talking—"Once he was *convinced* I was a giraffe called Arif"—but I'm only half listening.

A memory has come back to me from a few summers ago, when a fortune-teller arrived in our village.

She was an old cat-form demon with ragged fur and blind eyes, filmed over like curdled milk. She set up a booth at the side of the main road, just a simple table with a hearth in its center. Even though I was meant to go straight back to the shop after my errand, I stayed to watch as a young woman from our village knelt down at her table and handed over a fistful of coins. There are many ways in which fortune-tellers divine insight: tea leaves, the lines in a person's hands or paws, burning paper offerings, the analysis of dreams. This one was an osteomancer. She made the young woman carve her question into a bone before tossing it into the hearth. I remember my shock at the black inklike spill that spread over the cat-woman's eyes as she drew the bone from the fire, running her clawed hands over it to read the cracks.

I was so spooked I ran all the way home. Some part of me always believed I had imagined it. That the change in her eyes was some trick of the light. But seeing it happen to Master Tekoa, I know now that it was real. It must be what happens when someone falls into a fortune-telling trance.

Despite the sunshine, a shiver runs down my neck. If Master Tekoa's prediction is right, fire is going to destroy the palace. But what's even scarier is that it seems he thinks the fire is already burning within—of all people—*me*.

EIGHTEEN

Slowly but surely, life blurs back into the routine of palace life.

With the King away on official business for over a month—something to do with rebel activity in the South, according to the rumors—and no strange happenings after Master Tekoa's prediction, I lose myself in our steady rhythm of classes and dinners and nightly entertainments. My teachers notice the improvement in my efforts, and Mistress Eira congratulates me about it one day, telling me she's proud that I used what happened with the King as a turning point. And she's right. It *was* a moment of awakening for me.

But not in the way she thinks.

Though it only takes me a couple of weeks to replace the weight I lost during my confinement, it takes me much longer to get back to my normal self—or at least something that passes for normal now. I'm cast in the shadow of that night with the King. The memory of it hovers close, a constant presence at the edge of my consciousness, like moon-shimmer on the surface of a lake.

Even though the King is out of the palace, I get the sensation sometimes that he's watching me. Yet when I turn around, it's only to find an empty corridor or the quizzical face of one of the girls.

"Are you sure you're all right?" Wren asks me one afternoon when I stop midconversation on our way to a lesson, looking round my shoulder with the certainty that the King will be there, just behind me, head cocked and a loose grin on his face.

Forcing down a shiver, I keep walking. "Yes. Sure. Never better."

"Lei." Her fingers brush my arm. "Be honest with me. You haven't been right since what happened with the King—"

"Of course not!" I hiss, jerking away. Aoki's chatting to Chenna a few steps in front of us, and she glances over her shoulder. Lowering my voice, I go on, "I mean, it was awful, Wren. And it's going to happen again someday. I hate this, this…*waiting*. I don't know if I can keep it up."

Wren nods. "It's the same for me. But it's all we can do."

"Is it?" I reply quietly.

She stiffens, looking away with pressed lips.

I want to ask her how she can stand it. Whether she dreams of freedom the same way I do, in the small of the night, when the darkness is broken only by moon-silver and thoughts of home, and of her and the other girls—the futures we could be having, if only we could escape from the palace. But I swallow my words. I know her answer already, because it is the same thing that holds me back every time I dream of escape.

Their blood will be here. Do you understand me? On your hands.

We walk the rest of the way in silence.

Our history and politics teacher, Madam Tharazi, is an old lizard-form demon with dull scales the color of fallen leaves. Her room is on the ground floor of a house on the southwest side of Women's Court, small and warm, kept shadowed by lowered shutters and the gnarled trunk of a maple tree growing outside the window, its knotted branches reaching over the house like a tree spirit's bony arms. It always feels like dusk in her room, and I often catch the other girls dozing in her lessons. It doesn't help that Madam Tharazi is the most lax of our teachers, her eyes half glazed as she lectures on one topic or another. Most of the other girls probably know all about Ikhara's history and politics already. But I always pay attention. These lessons are one of the only times I get to learn about the world beyond the palace walls, and I cherish them, needing to remember that there *is* a world outside.

Not just a world. A *future*.

It's cold today, overcast. Gloomy light glances off Madam Tharazi's scales. Beside me, Aoki's chin drops and she gives a little start, looking up with a sheepish grin.

Today's lesson is on the Amala, the Cat Clan. "After the failure of the Kitori uprising," Madam Tharazi recounts, gazing out the window as if we weren't there, "their numbers dropped to almost half. The clan retreated to the southern deserts of Jana to recover, which is where they have lived nomadically since. Lord Kura's daughter, Lady Lova, took over rule of the clan a year later, after her father's death. She was only sixteen. Incidentally, it is the fourth time they have had a female leader. Unlike many clans, the Amala has a progressive attitude toward the females in its rank...."

"General Lova."

I glance sideways at Wren's whisper. Madam Tharazi's voice drones on, the tip of her tail twitching lazily as she speaks. Sometimes I think Madam Himura chose her to teach us on purpose. I doubt they want us to be too knowledgeable about politics; just enough to hold conversation at dinners with court officials, but not enough to get any ideas.

"What?" I whisper at Wren.

She blinks. She doesn't seem to realize she spoke out loud. "Oh. It's just that Lova goes by the title of General, not Lady. She's very adamant about it."

"You've met her?"

Wren nods. "My father was holding a council a few years ago for some of the leading clans. The King didn't want to invite the Cat Clan. You've heard about their disagreements. But my father insisted. He told the King it would do him well to keep a closer eye on them."

"What was she like?" I ask. "General Lova."

Something flickers across Wren's face. It takes me a moment to place it, because it's so unexpected coming from her—the hesitation, the flush in her cheeks.

She's embarrassed.

"Beautiful," she admits, and there's the echo of something wistful in her voice. "And strong. She'd just turned eighteen, so she'd only been ruling for two years, and most of the other clan leaders were at least double her age. But Lova walked in this way....It was as though she owned the place. As though daring anyone to doubt her reason for being there."

I hesitate. "Sounds like you spent a lot of time with her."

"Not really," Wren replies, but it doesn't sound like her. Her voice is too high, and I catch something bitter there, too, some undertone halfway between anger and sadness.

Later that day at dinner, Madam Himura reminds us that we won't be having any lessons tomorrow because of the koyo celebrations. On the first day of the tenth month, festivals are held across Ikhara to celebrate the arrival of autumn.

I can't believe it's been almost four months since I came to the palace. In the lush landscape of Women's Court, the turn of the season is a physical thing, marked in every tree and plant. Leaves flush crimson and ginger. Flowers scatter their petals to the ground. Over the last week, the gardens beyond my window have changed from a sea of green to one of fire and smolder.

"You'll be attending a party tomorrow night in the Inner Courts," Madam Himura tells us between mouthfuls, her chopsticks darting out to claim the last of the salted cuttlefish. "The King will be there. He arrived back at the palace early this morning. I heard it was a very tiring trip for him, so be on your best behavior."

I can sense Wren watching me from across the table. I avoid her eyes, taking a long sip of tea to try to ease the sudden swell of my throat. Memories flash: the King's roar; his long jaw wrested into a snarl. The rough grip of his fingers on my arms.

Aoki touches her shoulder to mine. "Are you all right?" she whispers.

I wet my lips. "I…will be."

"What will we do before the party?" Chenna asks from my other side.

"You're to stay in Paper House," Madam Himura replies. "Your maids will start preparing you in the afternoon."

A thrum of excitement runs through the room. We haven't had a day off yet. But while I'd like to rest just as much as the other girls, an idea comes to me for a better way to use this opportunity.

I wait until everyone is getting up to leave before approaching Madam Himura.

"What now?" she croaks, sensing me hovering over her.

"Madam Himura," I start in my politest tone, hands clasped at the small of my back, "I was wondering whether I could have an extra lesson tomorrow."

Still not looking up, she raps a taloned finger on the table. "There's no denying you need it. But none of your teachers will be working tomorrow. Everyone is off for the celebrations."

"Even the Night Houses?"

Her chin snaps up.

"Because that's what I'd like my lesson in," I go on hurriedly.

"With Zelle. Last time, I was so nervous I didn't really take much in, and after what happened with the..." I force a shy expression across my face. "I want to make amends."

Her eyes narrow. "The King hasn't called for you since then. Who knows when he will?"

"But he'll be at the koyo party. At least I can try to make a good impression on him there. Please, Madam Himura. I'm trying."

She regards me for one long moment. Then she flaps an arm, turning her attention back to the bowl in front of her. "I suppose it couldn't hurt."

Before she changes her mind, I shoot her a thanks and rush out of the room—bumping straight into Wren. My face flushes as we untangle, her hand lingering on my arm.

"What was that about?" she asks quietly.

"I'm going to have an extra lesson with Zelle tomorrow," I say.

She appraises me. "Why?"

"I just thought, since I'll be seeing the King again—"

"That's not why," she interrupts. Her fingers wind around my shoulder, and she drops her voice, head dipped close. "I know you, Lei. You don't want to please him."

"Yes, I do."

Wren stiffens. I avoid her eyes, but I sense her stare boring into me. When the silence is almost unbearable, I flick my eyes up, suddenly wanting to explain what my plan is. But I freeze at the look on her face. Her eyes are flinty. Hard-edged and hurt.

"Please don't lie," Wren says. Her fingers brush mine before she moves away, adding quietly, and low, "Not about that. Not to me."

I go to mutter something, but fall silent, letting her go. Because knowing I'll be facing the King tomorrow, I'm not ready to talk truthfully about how I feel yet. And if I can't offer her lies, there's nothing to say.

NINETEEN

"Y ou've made history, Nine," Zelle tells me when Mistress Azami takes me to her room the next morning.

She looks just as beautiful as last time. A rust-colored dress falls to her knees, exposing the slender shape of her calves, and a necklace of gold leaves adorns her collarbones. She props herself up one elbow and watches me with her head cocked as I kneel opposite her, drawing off my shawl and coat. Her room is warm. The shutters are drawn to keep out the wind, and in the corner a brazier flickers. The silk sheets on her bed have been traded for furs, a mark of how long ago it was I first came to her.

Two months. It feels like a lifetime, but also just yesterday, just a moment and a heartbeat ago.

I force a smile. "I have?"

Zelle grins. "You're the only Paper Girl I've taught who's refused the King."

The smile drops from my face.

"Oh," she says, and own smile vanishing. "I'm sorry. I thought you'd be proud to know that."

"Actually, I'd feel better knowing *every* Paper Girl tried to refuse him."

Her gaze sharpens. There's a beat before she murmurs, "Wouldn't that be something."

We start the lesson by running over what we covered last time. I try to appear focused, but as the minutes tick on, I snatch more and more looks at the door. I must be fidgeting so much that Zelle finally asks, "Is something wrong? Mistress Azami told me you personally asked for this lesson. If you've changed your mind—"

"That isn't it," I say quickly. "It's just...could I go to the toilet? I'm desperate."

She rolls her eyes. "Go on, then. But don't let Mistress Azami catch you. I'm not meant to let you out until the lesson is finished."

I hop to my feet and sing a thank-you as I dash outside. The house is muted at this time of day. My footsteps sound too loud, and I try to pad lightly, head down. On the stairs, a statuesque Moon caste panther-form demon glides past me, jewels adorning her feline ears, an amethyst-colored dress fallen off one shoulder to reveal her smooth, furred arm. She catches my eye, giving me a little shrug and a half smile as if to say, *Long night.*

When I reach the ground floor, instead of heading to the toilet, I cross the landing to the main corridor leading off it. I've not seen much of the Night Houses apart from Zelle's room, but if its layout is similar to other buildings in Women's Court, then, as the head of the household, Mistress Azami is likely to have a suite on the ground floor at the back of the house. I pass a few more quiet rooms—and some not so quiet—coming to a stop outside the door at the end of the hall.

I press my ear to the wood. Silence.

Preparing some excuse in case she *is* inside, I rap my knuckles on the door. Nothing. Carefully, I inch the door open a crack, wait again, then slide it wider and dart inside.

As I was expecting from someone so crisp and ordered, the room is spotless, all neat lines and bare surfaces. From the low table dominating the room, I guess that this is Mistress Azami's entertaining space. I move lightly to a set of doors on the far right side and, after listening for sounds from within, head through into what must be her office. Cabinets line the walls. A finger of smoke furls from an incense pot in the corner of the room, nestled in a shrine crowded with miniature jade statues of the heavenly rulers. There are only sky gods; Mistress Azami must be from the North, like me. I'm just moving to the nearest cabinet when there's a thud from the room above.

I freeze.

Another thud; boards creaking; the muffled sound of laughter. One of the courtesans and her guest. Glancing round the room as though Mistress Azami might dance out at any moment, I open the top drawer of the closest cabinet, my breathing shallow.

Inside are ordered scrolls, scraps of paper. I flick through them, but they just seem to be accounts of some sort, so I move on to the next drawer, then the next. I'm just about resigned to the fact that I'll have to head back to Zelle's room before she gets suspicious— and that my plan for having this lesson in the first place has failed— when I open a drawer of the last cabinet to find a set of beautifully bound scrolls wrapped in leather. Brushstrokes mark them as the records of the Night Houses courtesans.

The hairs on the back of my arms lift, remembering what the King told me. If my mother was taken back to the palace, this is where she'd be.

Each scroll is dated. I riffle through them, a jolt running up my spine when I find the one from seven years ago. Carefully, sending another glance over my shoulder, I unravel the bindings. I hardly dare to breathe. If I find Mama's name here, it could mean that she might still be alive—might even be here *still*, right here in one of these buildings.

The thought of being so close to her makes something deep at the core of me still.

As my eyes glide down the list of names, the paper trembles in my fingers. It was spring when the soldiers came to our village; there were blossom petals in the air. Her name should be one of the first. But by the end of the scroll, I haven't found it. I look over the names again and again, wishing hers to appear, hoping for some magic, some kind god to give me something good to hold on to.

Tears prick my eyes. I can barely make out the characters as I stare down at the scroll, battling the urge to tear it to shreds with my teeth.

"What are you doing?"

I whirl round. Zelle is standing in the doorway.

"I—I was just looking for something," I blurt, swiping a sleeve across my face as she walks over. My cheeks are wet from tears I hadn't realized were falling, and I sniff, trying to blink them away.

"I can see that." Her voice is hard, but not unkind. She squints at the scroll in my hands. "What exactly were you looking for?"

"My mother," I mumble thickly.

"Your mother is a piece of paper?"

I don't laugh. "She was taken from our village by soldiers seven years ago," I turn the paper for her to see. "This is the list of courtesans from that year. I—I thought her name might be on it."

Zelle's dark eyes glint. "And is it?" she asks quietly.

I choke the word out.

"No."

Just then, Mistress Azami's barking voice carries into the house from outside. In one swift movement, Zelle sweeps forward and snatches the scroll from me. She rolls it up in its leather sleeve with deft fingers before replacing it in the drawer, then, seizing my arm, she pulls me through Mistress Azami's rooms and into the hallway just as the dog-woman strides into the house.

Her pointed ears prick at the sound of our footsteps. "You're fin-ished already?" she asks, slanting gray eyes fixing on us.

Zelle heaves a sigh. "Not happy if we're late, not happy if we're early. Are you *ever* happy, Mistress Azami?"

"Not while you're around," she grumbles, though a curl of amuse-ment touches her lips. She beckons me forward. "Come on, girl. Your maid is outside."

I look over my shoulder before I leave, wanting to catch Zelle's eyes. But she's already walking away.

Outside, Rika greets me. She accompanies me back through the gardens of the Night Houses in silence, easily sensing my mood, and though I'm aware of my feet moving and the cool blow of the wind, all I can hear is blood rushing in my ears.

My mother wasn't—*isn't*—here.

I should be relieved. Mama wasn't forced to become a courtesan. She didn't have to suffer that. But as the King said, that would have been the only outcome of the soldiers bringing her to the palace, which means they probably didn't even bring her here at all. Which means...

At once, I double over, retching noisily.

"Mistress, what's wrong?" Rika asks, rubbing a hand on my back. "Are you sick?"

Yes. I'm sick. Sick of all this.

But instead I shake my head, forcing the nausea down. After a while I'm able to continue on, but as we walk, I jam my knuckles into my belly. There's a pain there, deep in the pit of me. A hard core, like a stone. It feels as though I've lost something. That I left something of mine behind in the Night Houses.

Something that was keeping me alive.

Something like hope.

TWENTY

THE KING'S KOYO CELEBRATIONS ARE BEING held in the Inner Courts, on a section of the river that follows a long, lazy curve, its bank bounded on one side by the feathered tops of trees and a paved pathway on the other. When our carriages pull up, I look out onto a sea of color. The river is crisscrossed with walkways, linked with little open-topped boats with candles lining their decks, and the roofs of pagodas and pavilions along the riverfront dance with hanging lanterns. More lights shine up at the trees across the water, showing off their autumn colors against the dark backdrop of the night. Music spirals through the air, carrying with it the laughter and chatter of the guests.

Everything is radiant and glittering. It's beautiful—maybe the most beautiful setting I've seen in the palace yet. But even as my eyes sweep over the scene, my head remains full of the rows and rows of names that weren't Mama's, the black brushstrokes clotting my vision.

"What's wrong?" Aoki asks, interrupting my thoughts as she comes to my side.

I blink. We're standing by the palanquins, a couple of servants hovering nearby, waiting for us.

"Lei?" she presses. "Did something happen in Zelle's lesson?"

I clear my throat. "I guess it just brought back everything that happened with the King," I say. I give her a smile, though it feels insincere. "But I'm fine. Honestly."

We amble toward the river. The rest of the girls are already ahead, Madam Himura ushering them to one of the larger platforms on the water, which has been set up as a tearoom. Lantern light glimmers over scattered velvet cushions and low tables.

"I keep wondering if it had something to do with what I said to you," Aoki admits quietly as we walk. She clasps her hands in front of her, lashes low. "You remember, the day after my first night with him. I was worried I scared you. That it was *my* fault you tried to escape."

"It wasn't," I tell her quickly. "Of course not. But...I hated seeing you like that. Has it...has it been any better since?" I ask, shooting her a sideways glance.

To my surprise, she nods.

The words tumble out of her in a rush then, an odd gleam on her face as she looks up at me. "I think I was just so scared that first night, Lei. I didn't know what to expect. I'd hardly spent any time with the King before, and straight after it happened, he sent me away. Like I'd done something wrong. And then with Blue and Mariko, you know, their teasing...but it's not actually been so bad since then."

I stare at her. "Really?"

She nods. "A lot of the time we just talk. The King tells me about what's going on in the kingdom—politics, all his trips and the people and things he's seen. He asks for my opinions. He shares his hopes for the kingdom. Even his fears." She bites her lip and looks down. "He...he makes me feel special."

Something chilled trickles down my spine.

"You can't mean that."

Aoki winces at the roughness in my voice. Her sweet face darkens. Avoiding my eyes, she licks her lips and goes on, "He asks about you sometimes. I know he doesn't show it, but it's not easy for him, dealing with everything. Having to look after an entire kingdom. And despite what you think, he really does want us to be happy." I snort at this, and she throws me a strange look, a stiff slant to her mouth. "Lei," she says, "he told me he's going to call for you soon."

The night is already cold. But at Aoki's words the air grows even colder. Stormy autumn winds spin around us, icy against my skin, and I clutch the fur shawl tighter around my neck.

I look ahead to where the other girls are sitting. The King is there, in his usual gold-and-black robes, throwing back his head to laugh at something Blue is saying to him. The sound is like a thunderclap, electric, cutting right through the air and into my bones. But the sight of him...*laughing* like that.

I stop. Aoki turns to me, forehead furrowed.

"I can't do it," I tell her, staring ahead at the King. My words are edged. Knifepoints.

The servants to either side of us keep their distance as they wait for us to continue, and the noise from the party is enough to hide our conversation. But I still keep my voice down, half whispering, half spitting, "I *won't* let him touch me again."

I don't realize it until I speak it. And it's different from the times I've said it before, or the way I've hoped it, as if dreaming something enough could birth it into being. I know it now with a certainty that has fitted into the lost core at the heart of me, as hard and angular as my hope was soft and shimmering.

The King will not have me.

Aoki's eyes are as wide as moons. "You're going to deny him again? This is your job, Lei. It's not so bad—"

I whirl round. *"Not so bad?* Remember how you felt the first time?"

"But I told you, it's gotten better. I think—I think I'm starting to enjoy being with him. To have the King's whole attention…" A glaze enters her eyes, something feverish in her glow. "How many people in the kingdom get to experience that?"

"The hundreds of girls he's bedded," I reply coolly, and pink spots her cheeks.

"You could at least be grateful for what the King has given you."

I goggle at her. "What he's *given* me? Aoki, he took us from our homes!"

"At least we were given a new one! The Hidden Palace, Lei! So many girls are forced into prostitution, or married off to some horrible man—"

"That sounds familiar."

We fall silent, glaring at each other. The sounds of the party drift around us like colored rain.

Aoki's the first to break it. "I'm sorry," she says. "That wasn't fair."

I grab her hands, offering a smile. "I'm sorry, too. Look, if you really want to be with the King, and he's as good to you as you say he is, then I'm happy for you. At least you can enjoy being here. But I don't."

"Maybe if you get to know him…"

"It's not enough."

After a glance to check the servants haven't come any closer, Aoki asks in a whisper, "Is there someone else?"

Wren's face flashes into my mind: her beautiful, dimpled smile, those smart, feline eyes.

"No," I lie. "Of course not."

Aoki looks relieved. "I don't know why I needed to ask. Where would you have found a man in Women's Court?"

Because it isn't a man. For some reason, a trill of annoyance runs through me. Everyone's assumption is for women and men to be together, and yet here we are, human girls, the Demon King's concubines. Surely love between two women wouldn't be so strange?

We are all the same really, little one. Deep down.

A tiny smile lifts my mouth. Mama would have understood. And the loss pierces me so freshly again that I have to push out a laugh to keep the tears away.

"Maybe," I tell Aoki, "I fancy old Master Tekoa."

She giggles, a hand flying to her mouth. "I knew it!"

But my smile drops as I focus again on the floating platform where the King is waiting. With a flex of my fingers, I start again toward it before I lose courage, Aoki hurrying to follow. We cross the short walkway onto the platform, and a servant announces our arrival.

At once, the conversations stop. The slap of water against the sides of the platform rises loud in the hush. A bark of laughter lifts from farther off in the party, and there's something threatening about it, a dare for anyone else to interrupt the moment. Aoki moves forward first, but it's me everyone is watching as we approach the King. I keep my own stare lowered to the floor, on the swishing tail of Aoki's cheongsam in front of me.

She greets him sweetly, an ingratiating furl in her voice I've never heard before. Then she steps aside. I lower to my knees as gracefully as I can in my long-skirted dress. I palm my hands to the floor. The memory of the last time I was like this in front of the King jolts through me, pricking goose bumps across my skin.

Two months gave me space and something almost resembling peace. But time has a way of folding itself, like a map, distances and journeys and hours and minutes tucked neatly away to leave just the realness of the before and the now, as close as hands pressed on either side of a rice-paper door.

"My King," I say into the quiet.

"Get up."

His voice is the same deep rumble I remember. I do as he says, barely able to breathe for the dashing of my heart against my rib cage. Finally, I gather the courage to lift my eyes to his, but the expression on his face takes me by surprise, because it's the last thing I expect to see.

Happiness.

He looks happy. To see *me*.

"Lei-zhi," he greets—as though we were old friends, all smiles and lightness. As though the last time I saw him he hadn't been chasing me through his chambers, half naked and roaring. "I've missed you. Let's take a walk, just you and me. I want to talk."

I get to my feet quickly, just in case he offers to help. Wren's eyes find mine, and then the King lays a hand on my shoulder to lead me off the platform. Whispers unspool into the silence like a cat slinking through the feet of a crowd. It must be common knowledge by now what happened between the King and me, and it's clear everyone is as surprised by his warm welcome as I am.

Surprised—and uneasy. Because what might his smile be hiding?

Lifting my chin against the stares, I follow the King into the party. Interconnected pathways run between the boats and floating hookah dens and teahouses, and we take a haphazard route through them. He seems intent on meandering. Breezily, he points out various guests, stopping to greet some, telling me about the banquet they had earlier and that I really must try the new sake he had imported from Shomu, matured for three years in total darkness! It's like nothing I've ever tasted before.

I mumble noncommittal responses. My pulse is still spiked at the closeness of him, the weight of his hand on my shoulder, and alongside the fear sparks something else: anger. Flame-hot and fierce. Because how can he speak like this to me after what happened the last time we met? The week of starvation and isolation he put me through?

"I owe you an apology, Lei-zhi."

Abruptly, the King stops. We're in the middle of a walkway. A pair of elegant gazelle-form men strolling arm in arm behind us almost bump into us, and they back away hastily, muttering apologies amidst fervent bows. Other guests ahead turn quickly around to take a different route. The noise of the party seems to dim now, wrapping its arms around the King and me, an intimate embrace. The blue of his eyes fixes me to the spot. They're an ice-cold color, shockingly bright against his golden-umber fur, like the sharpness of a cloudless winter sky.

"I suppose," he starts, "I'm used to being in control. Or at least, having to appear in control." He looses a long exhale. "I don't admit it often, but it's difficult. Being a King. Ruling. All of this"—he sweeps out an arm at the bustle of the party—"and more, the whole of Ikhara mine to look after. To protect. I try my best to be fair, but it's impossible. There will always be those who lose out." He rolls his shoulders, neck cording. "Ruling is like shaman's magic. You can only give when you have taken."

"Perhaps," I reply in a level voice, "it's about balancing who you take from."

The King looks down his slender bovine nose at me, light from the party embellishing his outline and picking out the elaborate patterns of his gilded horns. "A fair point, I suppose, if rather naive. Not everyone can have everything. And not everyone has the same needs, or rights."

I grit back a glower at this.

"And not everyone," he continues, "has the same to give in the first place." The King's face tightens. "Take my brothers, for example. They were one, two years older than me. But at the age of seven I already understood more than they about what makes a strong ruler. I knew that if I took their lives, it would prove to the heavenly rulers and the court that I was infinitely more capable of taking over my dying father's rule than either of them. They were put on this earth to give, while I was destined to take." A dark current threads his words, and I hold down the instinct to squeeze my arms around my chest, to back away. "I demonstrated my worth. And still no one has acknowledged the sacrifices I made. Everything I have given for this kingdom. I am not even allowed a name. It is only *Heavenly Master* this, *Heavenly Master* that, all the godsdamn time, as though I'm just that, some heavenly ruler everyone expects to grant their prayers."

I lick my lips, then say carefully, "Of course I'm no expert, my King, but...isn't that sort of what a King's job *is?*"

He regards me in silence from under full lashes, his face frozen in a rigid mask. For a second, it seems almost like he's going to strike me. "People do not ask of the gods without offering them things in return," he says stiffly.

Then he loosens. He offers me a smile, though it's a shadow of his usual lazy grin, and I notice then the heaviness in his expression, fatigue in the dark circles under his eyes. And underneath it all, a touch of something a little delirious. "Have you heard of the Sickness, Lei-zhi?"

"The Sickness?" The phrase nudges a distant memory, though I can't recall where I've heard it before.

"Something is making our land ill: forest fires in the mountains, earthquakes, crippling droughts in the southern provinces....More than three times last year, River Zebe burst its banks. Two of my battalions are still in Marazi to aid reconstruction efforts. The reports have been coming in too fast for me to keep track. On the trip I just returned from, I saw countless villages and farmlands affected. There was even a Steel clan forced to seek refuge with a neighboring Paper clan." He snorts. "The indignity of it. And with the increasing rebel activity, I've not had the time or resources to address it properly."

"But aren't those things natural?" I ask. "Earthquakes, droughts..."

"Indeed. But something is causing them to get worse. And I think I finally understand what it is." With a tilt of his head, the King raises his eyes to the sky.

I follow his gaze. The wind has blown the clouds away to reveal a sky brilliant with starlight and the crescent of the moon hanging right overhead, sharp as a scythe. At first, I don't understand what he's suggesting. Then it hits me.

"You mean the gods?"

"They're angry," the King growls, the familiar bite returning to his voice. A muscle tics in his jaw. "They're punishing us for something. See? Even Ahla takes her warrior form to taunt me." His eyes are shiny. "I need to appease them."

I remember what General Yu said to Mistress Eira about the King's superstitious nature, what Chenna told me about the reasoning behind his picking her first. Our belief in the gods is so organic and deep-rooted there can often be something customary about it. But there is nothing perfunctory about the fever-glow now on the

King's face. Though it would be blasphemous to speak out loud, the question comes to me, undeniable.

Is this magic or madness I'm seeing? Faith or desperation?

"How—how will you do that?" I ask in a hushed voice.

The King's bowed lips stretch, a grin more teeth than smile. "Punish those who disobey me," he says huskily. "Rid the kingdom of those who are not faithful." His frosted eyes slide my way, and the silence stretches out. Then, abruptly, the tension drains from his face. Slinging an arm around my shoulder, he spins us back round, the corners of his mouth lifted. "Come, Lei-zhi. We'd better get back to the others. I don't want them getting jealous."

And his chatter is once again so light and easy that I almost believe I imagined the threat in his words.

The party spirals on into the night in a whirl of laughter and starlight and the jewel-bright reflections of lantern light on water, everything colorful: the sounds, the conversations, the smiles, the dresses. It's the first time there's been such a big gathering, and from our corner of the floating tearoom, the girls swap gossip about the guests.

"Look!" Mariko cries, pointing to an elegant woman with porcelain skin. "That's Mistress Lo, she's one of the most famous Paper Girls. You must have heard of her. She runs a beauty parlor in Women's Court. We must ask Madam Himura if we can visit it...."

More pointing. "Oh, that's Madam Daya! She was married to a General straight after her time as a Paper Girl. Apparently the General saved the King's life in an assassination attempt and she was his reward...."

"Isn't that Mistress Ohura? She's still so beautiful...."

The voices of the girls float around me. My eyes keep sliding back to where Wren and the King are talking under a pagoda at the water's edge. They're too far to make out anything more than their outlines, but the closeness of their shadows, the King's huge bulk dwarfing Wren, sends something sharp down my veins.

"They've been there for ages," Aoki grumbles, her eyes following mine. There's jealousy in her gaze, too.

He makes me feel special.

Disgust quivers through me at the memory of her words. I tear my eyes away. "I'm going for a walk," I say, and get to my feet and start walking before she can follow.

I turn down a few of the floating walkways and head up onto the grassy bank of the river, picking a random direction to wander in. The noise of the party fades as I trudge into the dark grounds. Over my head, a flock of birds wheel noisily, wingtips kissing the sky. Their freedom pierces me. What would happen if I just took off right now? Chased after them, danced in the midnight shadow of their bodies so high above, and we could be mirrors, echoes, them in the air and me on the ground—

The thought cuts off. Because of course: the palace walls.

Somewhere in the distance, I sense their presence, their black embrace. The birds would fly right over them, and all I'd be able to do is watch, fingers pressed to the frozen rock.

Suddenly the darkness isn't so welcoming anymore. I've just started to head back to the river when I stop at the sound of something in the shadows. Is that…crying?

Scanning the grounds, I spot a woman sitting on the sloping grass a few feet away. Reflections on the river's surface outline her in shimmering silver. She's wearing a patterned sari, its pale-pink fabric light against her brown skin. I recognize her robes—she's one of the former Paper Girls, the one who was married to some General.

"Hello?" I call, taking a few steps toward her. "Madam Daya, is it?"

Hunched shoulders tighten. "Get away!" she hisses. It comes out strangled, the words strange and contorted.

"Is everything all right?"

The woman doesn't turn. "Who is that?" she replies, hoarse.

"I'm Lei. One of the Paper Girls—"

She whirls around in an instant, springing to her feet. I stagger back, but she catches me, nails pinching into my arms as she brings me close.

A scream catches in my throat. Madam Daya's face is shadowed, but that only seems to heighten what a mess it is, moonlight glinting off the raw peeling skin slipping from her face like melted wax; rotted teeth; the bulbous, veined eyes.

Words tumble from my lips. "I—I didn't mean—"

"Look at me!" she cries. "It's all his fault!"

"Wh-whose fault?"

"My stupid husband's! He made a mistake during the raid at Shomu Pass, and the King refused to grant him our annual magic allowance, and without my regular visits from the shaman..." She shakes me, crazed, tears leaking from those horrible red eyes. "I can't go back to the party looking like this!"

As she talks, skin drips from her cheeks and chin. A ragged scrap unpeels, falling on my own face, and I shriek, tossing my head to get it off me.

Madam Daya lets out a mad laugh. "That's it! Try to get away. But you'll look like this one day, too, you know. When you're forced to use endless enchantments just to keep yourself looking young and pretty for whatever worthless man the King gives you to like a prize show-tiger, you'll understand. You'll know."

And it suddenly clicks what's happened to her.

Qi draining.

Since magic is an element that comes from the closed circle of our world, it cannot be made, only exchanged through a shaman's chanted dao. Yin and yang, energy, lifeblood, qi—all of it is a balance. A flow. It's what the King was talking about earlier. Shamans must adhere to the equilibrium when drawing magic from the earth by offering gifts in return, whether it be burying money for spirits or scattering plant seeds, or carving tattoos in their skin, the pain serving as payment, the markings bindings of their loyalty. Even then, when too much magic is asked from the gods, their enchantments can start to fail, or even backfire.

"I'm—I'm so sorry," I stammer, though my words sound empty even to me.

The woman laughs. "You will be one day, little girl. You'll be sorry you ever came to this heavensforsaken place."

She lets me go and I jerk away, gasping, stumbling up the bank and back toward the party as fast as my dress allows me.

When I make it back to the floating teahouse where I left the others, it's empty, and at first I'm relieved that the party has ended. But then I notice movement ahead. Everyone seems to be gathered on one of the central platforms. The music that was playing earlier has stopped, and in its place is quiet—though not the good kind. The tense kind of quiet, when the air gets strange and taut, like elastic pulled too tightly. A few moments later, shouting rises up from the crowd.

"Hey!" A lone guard hurries along a gangplank toward me. "What're you—oh."

He falters. Rounded ears twitch as he recognizes me. It takes me a moment longer to recognize him as the bear-form guard outside the palace the night I arrived. The sweetness of his features doesn't seem to fit with his soldier's clothes, the sheathed sword at his waist.

"Mistress Lei-zhi," he amends with a bow. "My sincerest apologies. I didn't realize—"

"What's happening?" I interrupt.

He looks up. "The—the King wants to add a new part to the celebrations," he says, and I don't miss the slight stumble in his words.

Jeers erupt in the distance.

"What new part?" I ask as a cold wave of dread creeps over me.

The guard opens his mouth. Then he gives a small shake of his head. "The King requests the presence of all his guests," he says firmly, clearing his throat. He reasserts his grip on his sword. "Please come with me, Mistress."

I follow him along the walkways to the center of the flotilla. Discarded objects—bowls and plates, silk napkins, the wind-loosened petals of flowers—are scattered among the abandoned platforms, the water around them also bobbing with debris. As we get nearer, I catch some of the words being tossed into the air.

Rotten Paper. Worthless.

Keeda.

"Maybe this is close enough," the guard starts, holding out an arm. But I shove past him, elbowing my way through the crowd all the way to the front.

And freeze when I get there.

A memory, as vivid as the day it happened. A Paper caste woman with eyes full of hatred, and the swing of a club toward her skull.

The scene before me isn't similar in the details, but the shape of it is there. Demon guards herding a group of Paper castes in place with swords and spiked axes. The looks on the men's and women's, the *children's* faces, not anger this time, but fear. And the King, laughing as he paces back and forth to inspect them.

"...so I thought it only right that we give them a proper royal welcome!"

It's hard to hear him over the crowd. His grin is wide and sharp, more canine than bovine, and I can tell the energy of his audience is emboldening him. From the way he's swaggering, it's clear he's drunk. There's a frenzy on his face, the same crazed sheen I saw a glimmer of earlier, but alcohol has loosened it, and it sits vivid on his features.

Dread crests inside me. I look round for Wren or Aoki. Instead, I spot Chenna a few rows ahead and push my way toward her.

"What *is* this?" I ask breathlessly.

She doesn't turn. "The soldiers just got back from a raid in eastern Noei," she says, and beneath her usual composure is something troubled. There's hollowness to her voice, a constriction in her throat. Still staring ahead, she continues, "They've brought these Paper castes to the palace as slaves. The King is giving them away as presents to his guests."

I gape at her. *"What?"*

Just then, one of the captives pushes to the front of the group. A dog-form guard swings out an arm to stop him, and the man struggles to get free.

"Please!" he shouts. He's middle aged, dark hair fanning into grey. "Have mercy, Heavenly Master—"

"Ah," the King interrupts. "So you recognize your master, do you, and yet you dare ask for his mercy?" His deep voice is slurred from drink. "My mercy is for my peers, old man. Not some worthless keeda."

The word strikes me afresh coming from the King's lips.

"My wife and children are here!" the man tries again, his arms outstretched, face contorted. "Please, Heavenly Master. Have mercy. We have been nothing but obedient, all these years, giving away more than we could spare of our crops to your soldiers, never protesting when our taxes increase. Even now with the Sickness, we comply with every demand. All we ask is to be left alone. Please, Heavenly Master. Let us go home—"

The King roars. "I will not take orders from a human!"

With a thunder of hooves, he charges forward. It's unexpected, quicker than I'd thought him capable of. All of a sudden he seems more animal than human, driven by bovine instinct and rage. Swiping the guard aside, he seizes the man by the neck, lumbers to the edge of the platform and, with an effortless arc of his arm, flings the man into the river.

The crowd cheers, breaks into applause.

The balcony ringing the platform hides the man from view, but we hear him emerging in a splash of water, spluttering. A few of the other Paper castes try to break from the guards, but they are quickly forced back into place.

The King sweeps an arm toward the rest of the Paper caste slaves, a feral grin lighting his face. "Go ahead, friends. Choose as many slaves as you wish. The keeda should know now not to challenge their masters."

The demons move forward in a rush of excited chatter.

"Kunih save them," Chenna murmurs, making a quick motion across her brow that I've seen her make once or twice before. It must be a prayer ritual from where she's from.

I have learnt not to put my trust in the gods. Especially not Kunih, who—like all earth gods—is favored in the South, but my parents taught me to be wary of, for what God of Redemption would not one day turn upon you?

Instead, I yell at myself. *Go, Lei! Help!*

But I don't move.

A taloned hand lands on my shoulder. "Come, girls," Madam Himura orders in her croaky voice. "Time for us to leave."

My eyes flick back to the slaves, cowering as the King's guests inspect them. "But—"

"Do you wish to join them, Lei-zhi?"

I falter, and Madam Himura's smile is cutting, because she knows of course that I don't. She can guess the struggle inside me, and which instinct is winning. Because no matter how brave I might try to seem, really the heart that beats within my rib cage is weak and broken and scared, and I am just a human girl kneeling before her demon King.

Dzarja. Traitor.

I drop my chin as we turn away and head back to where our carriages are waiting at the top of the bank, my belly churning.

The slave-woman was right.

That's exactly what I am.

TWENTY-ONE

WHEN WE GET BACK FROM THE PARTY, sleep seems impossible. Even the concept of sleep: of rest, of peace, of—heavens forbid—*dreaming*. I'm on the verge of being sick. My mother's absence from the Night Houses list, Aoki telling me the King will call for me soon, the former Paper Girl's monstrous face, and the terror of the slaves as the demons circled in. Everything about this day has been horrible. And the worst part of it all is the hardest to ignore, because it is within me.

Is me.

I stare up at the ceiling, palms pressed to my forehead. The image of the Paper slaves won't leave my mind, burned onto my retinas like some ghostly afterimage. I cycle over the moment again and again, trying to find some hint, some opening that would allow for a different outcome, even though it's too late. I could have—*should* have—done something. Instead I let Madam Himura lead me away.

The pattering of rain fills my small room. It's a sound that always reminds me of home, of monsoon season in Xienzo, the earth turned to mud, Tien both happy because it means there would be plenty of mushrooms to forage and equally annoyed because of

Bao trailing paw prints across the floorboards. But home is the last thing I want to think about right now.

Punish those who disobey me. Rid the kingdom of those who are not faithful.

The King's words ring in my head, and I think of the birds I watched earlier, how easily they lifted into the air.

How impossible it is for me to follow them.

My parents taught me that if you have a problem or have made a mistake, you should be honest about it. "With us, of course," they said, "but more important, with *yourself*. That is the first step to finding a solution."

As a child I never would have believed that my parents could be wrong. Yet right now, aware of the problems, aware of all my mistakes, I'm still no clearer on how to address them. How to do the impossible? How to defy the King and help my kin? How to escape from the palace without the risk of Baba and Tien being punished?

"I don't know what to do," I say out loud. "Tell me what to do."

The room remains mute. There's only the soft, wordless whisper of rain.

Scrambling to my feet, I fling a fur shawl over my shoulders and head outside, suddenly needing air. I tiptoe down the corridor to the door where I saw Wren sneaking out all those weeks ago. I'm so wrapped up in my thoughts that when I open the door and find her behind it, I barely react. I just fall still, my mouth becoming a small O.

And it is particularly lucky I don't make a sound—because Wren is not alone.

I only have a few seconds to take in the scene. Wren, in her sleeping robe, standing close to a tall wolf demon, her head craned back to face him. The wolf: Moon caste, marbled ash-gray fur flowing silkily over angular features, a diamond-shaped patch of white on his long, muzzlelike jaw. He's dressed in soldier's clothes. One pawed hand is lifted to cup Wren's face, like the beginning of a kiss.

Then the two of them spring apart.

Shielding Wren behind him with an easy sweep of his arm, the wolf rounds on me. His eyes are a startlingly luminous amber, like honeyed marigold mixed with bronze—just a few shades darker than my own. There's something vaguely familiar about him, but before I can place it, he bends down until the wet tip of his nose almost touches mine.

"A word about this," he whispers, "and you die."

He spins around. In a few short bounds, he disappears into the night-tipped gardens.

Silence, and rainfall, and Wren watching me with uneasy eyes.

It's the first time I've seen her undone like this, so unsure. The collar of her nightdress has fallen low, exposing the swell of her breasts, and from under it her bare legs are long and glossy in the moonlight. I think of her and the wolf, what intimate moment I might have interrupted. My gut twists.

After everything today, now *this*.

"Lei," Wren starts, reaching for me.

I step back. "Don't touch me."

"I can explain—"

"No thanks. I can work it out just fine myself."

My voice has risen, and Wren's eyes cut to the open doorway behind me. Quickly, she slides it shut before grabbing my hand and pulling me down the steps of the veranda. Rain slicks my skin in an instant. She leads me across the gardens away from Paper House, to a large ginkgo tree whose long branches hide us from view.

"It's not what you're thinking," she says, and I snatch back my hand.

"How do you know what I'm thinking?"

"I mean, I know how it must have looked—"

"You were touching him. He was touching *you*."

Her lips tighten. "Not like that."

"Well," I say with a scowl, "your wolf certainly seemed to think what you'd been doing together was bad enough to *threaten to kill me*. Or did you miss that part?"

"He doesn't mean it," Wren replies. But there's a flicker of hesitation in her voice, and she rubs one hand at the base of her throat, a nervous movement I've never seen before. "Lei, he was scared. If anyone finds out he was here…"

I glare at her. "Don't worry. I won't tell."

"I know you won't."

She speaks the words with such purity that whatever retort I'd been planning drops away. "You…you trust me?" I say, clutching my wet shawl tighter at my neck.

Her eyes soften. "Of course I do," she answers, a whisper that I draw in like nectar.

I step forward, my feet sinking a little into the muddy ground. "Then tell me who he is."

"I can't." She reaches for my fingers again, but I jerk away. "Please, Lei," she pleads. "This is bigger than me. It's not my secret to give away."

I shove the wet hair from my face. "He's someone important in the palace, isn't he? The wolf."

Wren nods.

"How do you know him? What were you meeting about?"

She doesn't answer.

"Is he who you've been sneaking out all these times to see?"

"Not…every time."

I let out a bark of mad laughter. "There are *others*?"

"No!" Wren corrects hurriedly, shoving the wet tangles of hair from her face. "I mean, I don't always meet someone."

"What do you do, then?"

She looks at me tiredly, as if to say, *You know I can't tell you that.*

"You lied to me," I say into her silence.

It comes out childish and petty, and I hate the way my voice sounds. But the meaning of it, the feeling behind it, is anything but. I'm trembling, half from the rain and the cold, and half from something else, some wild, desperate sensation that's been snaking through me since the moment I stumbled upon Wren and the wolf.

Raindrops cling to my eyelashes, slick my lips. I lick them away. "I asked you if you were meeting someone. That night, when you brought me food. You promised me you weren't."

"Because I wasn't! Not in the way you were asking."

"I don't believe you."

This pulls a growl from her. "Lei," Wren sighs, almost angry, "there isn't anyone else."

I roll my eyes. "You've already said that," I say, but then I catch on to her turn of phrase.

Anyone *else.*

And I suddenly comprehend what she's trying to tell me.

That there *is* someone.

"Oh," I breathe, as a dizzying sensation wings through me. "You mean *me.*"

She comes closer, her stare so hot it's burning, scattering the raindrops away. Eyes fixed fiercely on mine, she lifts a hand toward my cheek.

I stagger back. "I—I have to go."

Even as Wren opens her mouth to retort, I'm already spinning on my heels, making for the house. I lurch blindly, soaked by the rain. The gardens are dark and the path is slick beneath my feet, and I skid on the wet cobbles, careening back, arms windmilling.

Wren is there in an instant. She catches me, fingers wrapping round my shoulders. "Please calm down."

I let out a choked laugh. "How can I? You know what would happen if someone found us! We—we can't, Wren. Me and you, *this*..." My eyes skitter away. "It's not right."

"Because we're both girls?" she asks, and there's hurt in her voice.

"No! I don't care about that." I pause, realizing only as I speak the words aloud how true they are. I've had time to think about it since understanding my feelings for Wren in Zelle's first lesson, and each time it comes back to what Zelle told me about love and lust. How natural they are. How simple it should be. That's just how my attraction toward Wren is: natural, and simple.

If you took away the minor issue of us being the King's concubines, of course.

Something breaks a little inside me as I tell her, "Not because we're girls. Because we're *Paper* Girls."

Wren shakes her head, still fixing me with that bold, defiant gaze. "Is it what you want?"

"That doesn't matter."

Her expression is fierce. "It's the *only* thing that matters."

The air between us vibrates, electric. Wren's hands are still circling my arms, and her touch sears me, sends my pulse racing.

She pulls me nearer.

Our lips are a heartbeat apart.

"We're Paper Girls," I say again, like this is explanation enough—and it is. It explains everything, because it defines everything. The one terrible, inescapable truth.

"So?"

"Madam Himura and Mistress Eira made it clear to us from the start." I'm whispering, even though the night is rain-locked and the garden is deserted. "What we want has nothing to do with it. We're only here for the King."

Under wet lashes, her dark eyes spark. "You fought him, Lei. You told him no, a man who is never told no. Even though you knew you'd be punished. You, more than anyone, understand that what we want *is* important." She takes a breath. "When the world denies you choices, you make your own." Her fingers skim to my wrists; she draws me even closer. "This is my choice."

Rain patters all around us. It traces tiny beads down Wren's temples and cheeks, clinging to the curve of her full lips. Her night slip is completely soaked through, revealing her to me, a cruel promise of what can never be mine.

Anyone could find us out here.

So what? part of me screams. Give them a show. They can sell tickets for all I care! But another part of me remembers the slaves at the party. Of what might happen if I humiliate the King again. Not just to me, but to my family.

Punish those who disobey me. Rid the kingdom of those who are not faithful.

I flinch, hearing the King's threat as if he were standing right behind us, bull eyes bright and raging, glinting like daggers in the dark.

I untangle our fingers. "I'm sorry," I whisper.

And then I'm running back to the house before Wren can stop me. Or rather, before I stop myself. Because the longing to kiss her, to lace my arms around her and bring our bodies together in the dark, is so strong it thrashes around inside me like something caged. And as I stagger back to my room, rain-soaked and defeated, a single word repeats in my head, shining darkly, slinking, serpentine.

Dzarja.

Never has it felt more true. Because it appears I have found a new person to betray, and it might be the worst one yet.

Myself.

TWENTY-TWO

OVER THE NEXT FEW DAYS, the memory of my almost-kiss with Wren hovers over everything I do. I barely follow a word our teachers say. In the evenings it takes all my effort to keep from staring at her in whatever beautiful outfit she's wearing, at how exquisite her face looks made up with paints and powders. How, even better, I have seen beneath that Paper Girl mask, the night when the rain washed away everything between us and left only the deep thrum of desire.

When dreaming of her isn't enough, I creep to her room. Hover outside her door, fingertips resting on the wood. But I can never bring myself to go inside. Always, there is fear at being caught. And—just as frightening—the fear that once I've kissed her, I won't be able to stop.

One morning a week later, Lill dresses me in a heavy, fur-trimmed overcoat. It's the coldest outside that it's been so far. It won't be long until winter arrives. I say good-bye to her and find Wren in the hallway, waiting for me.

"Hello." I greet her with our new awkward formality. She's still been accompanying me to lessons as per Madam Himura's request, but there's been a terse politeness in our interactions since that night. Then I notice the coat she's wearing.

White. Our kingdom's mourning color.

"Here." She hands me folded silver-white robes and a heavy brocade overcoat. "You should change."

"What...?" I start, but she talks quickly over me.

"It's a mourning day for both of us, remember?" She's speaking more loudly than usual. As Zhen and Zhin pass, giving me identical smiles, I realize it's for the other girls to hear. "Or have you forgotten about your own ancestors?"

I look blank.

"So kind of Madam Himura to give us permission to miss today's lessons to pray," she carries on, and finally I get it. Wren must have told Madam Himura that today is a day of mourning for the two of us, perhaps spinning some story about the funeral of an ancestor or a designated prayer day that both our families happen to observe at the same time. Spiritual commitments are one of the only things we're allowed to miss our lessons for. But what would she want to show me in Ghost Court?

Chenna comes out from her room a few doors away. She catches my eyes. "Everything all right, Lei?"

"Just great. I'll see you in a minute."

Her eyes glide to Wren, but she doesn't say anything, giving me a curt nod before turning away.

Once the corridor is empty, Wren steps in close. "You wanted to know where I've been going the nights I leave Paper House," she says under her breath. Her brown eyes glint. "I'm going to show you."

A short while later I'm back at Wren's side, this time dressed in the clothes she gave me. Wearing white feels strange. More than strange—*wrong*. The color is heavy with the implications of what it should mean to wear it, and I can't help but think of Mama. How even though she was lost to us, we never held a funeral, not even after the weeks turned into months, and the months into years.

It would have felt like an admission.

Wren and I take a carriage to Ghost Court, accompanied by Wren's maid, Chiho. Despite its eerie name, Ghost Court turns out to be a lush landscape filled with manicured rock gardens, ponds, and clusters of trees. Winding steps and arched bridges lead between temples of varying design. Some are small, hewn from rock, with wide, squat bases. Others are tall and multitiered, with delicate curving roofs and colored tiles. Bamboo parcels offering food and packets of ghost money burn in braziers outside the entrances, and from some of the temples drift the unearthly songs of shrine maidens.

We come to a stop in a secluded grove. The temple before us is small and unassuming, with a shingled roof and faded crimson paint peeling in long strips from its walls. Its stone base is shaggy with moss. Overhead, a great banyan tree towers, casting everything in murky green light.

"I'll wait for you here, Mistresses," Chiho says as we leave the carriage.

I shoot Wren a curious glance. She must have known chaperones wouldn't come into the temple with us.

The two of us make our way inside in silence. Immediately, the lingering smoke of incense tickles my throat. Something about temples always makes me feel as though I can't make any noise, but even if I wanted to, I sense Wren's energy, tense and coiled, and it keeps me quiet, too. We pass through a prayer room with gold idols set atop a shrine, both earth and sky gods staring down at us with in an array of smiles and grimaces. I rub my hands over my arms. I could swear their eyes were tracking us.

Unlike the other temples, this one is deserted. Our footsteps fall loudly in the quiet as we come to a courtyard at its center. The roof must have caved in long ago, dust motes dancing in the light slanting in between the hanging roots of the banyan. A shiver trickles down my back. I'm half expecting ghosts to peer out from lonely corners any second.

Wren leads me through more prayer rooms to an archway at the back of the temple. Just as we duck through, she slips her hand in mine. Pleasure bubbles through me—whipped aside the next instant by what we find beyond the arch, which is so unexpected and beautiful that it takes my breath away.

We're in a small, walled garden. The stone of the wall is crumbling, green with moss and winding vines, the paving beneath our feet cracked by weeds. This place seems even more forgotten than the rest of the temple, forlorn and lusterless.

Except for the tree.

In the middle of the courtyard is a tree unlike any I've seen before. Though its trunk is like that of a normal maple, with old, grooved bark of deep brown wrapped around knotted branches, the leaves that adorn it are paper. *Enchanted* paper. Despite the still air, the leaves flutter and rustle as if caught in a wind, humming with the golden light of magic, each one with something written across it.

I move closer and reach up for one. The leaf thrums gently under my fingers. A whir of air blows from the branches, ruffling my hair and clothes as I read the characters painted on it in delicate brush-strokes. "Minato." I glance at a few of the others. "Rose. Thira. Shun-li." I look over my shoulder at Wren. "They're girls' names."

She nods. Wordlessly, she leads me round the back of the tree. She stands on her tiptoes and draws down one of the branches, showing me a leaf near its tip, so small it looks like a teardrop.

"Leore," I read. My eyes flick up. "Who is she?"

"She was," Wren replies, "my sister."

There's a pulse of silence. The walls of the courtyard seem to take a step inward, and something inside me goes very still.

"I thought you were an only child."

"I am," Wren replies, "and...I am not. The Hannos aren't my real family."

My stomach gives a jolt. "Then who are?"

"The Xia," she answers simply.

Simply, as though she hadn't just spoken the name of the most infamous warrior clan in all of Ikhara.

A clan that was wiped out years ago.

"I was adopted by the Hannos when I was just a year old," Wren starts. "Before that, I lived with what was left of the Xia in the eastern mountains of Rain."

We're sitting under the boughs of the paper-leaf tree. The air is golden and warm from the glow of its magic, and it feels safe here with Wren, as if the tree's branches could protect us from the rest of the world. Our fingers are twined together. While she tells me her story, Wren's thumb skates across my palm, drawing hidden words upon my skin.

"I'm guessing you already know," she starts, "that the Xia were once the most prominent warrior clan in Ikhara. It's the unique form of martial arts they practiced, mixing physical movements with qi manipulation, that made them so famous. The Xia were warriors *and* shamans, both of the mortal world and the spiritual. Their skills were so legendary that many of the clan leaders sought to build relationships with them, enlist them to their causes. But the Xia lived by the strictest moral code. They only offered aid to those who they truly believed were deserving."

I nod. Tien told me stories of the Xia, how powerfully they shaped Ikharan history. "I wasn't sure whether to believe her," I say. "I thought the Xia might just be some legend she made up to frighten me."

"To a lot of people, that's all they are," Wren agrees. "A legend. Something talked about in whispers and rumor. Before, they could move freely without fear of persecution." Her voice cools. "But the Night War changed everything. Before the war, the Bull King of Han—the original Demon King—reached out to the Xia to aid him in his quest to conquer the kingdom. He'd always been a great admirer of their skill, though much of it was darkened by jealousy. He didn't just want them to help him. He wanted their abilities for himself. He'd already hired shamans to train him in using magic as a weapon, trying to mimic their fighting style. But the Xia trained their children starting from a young age. They made them understand how to call magic forth and use it in a way that respects the power of nature. They never asked for more than they could give. Unlike them, the Bull King was impatient. He tore at the earth's qi rather than nurture it. Tried to bully it to his will.

"Unable to master magic himself, the Bull King requested a meeting with the Xia to persuade them to join his army. They'd already heard of his violent way of rule, but out of respect, two of their warriors met with him. They listened to the King's plans but eventually declined to help. They knew better than to put their power into the hands of a ruler like him. But the King wouldn't accept it. Furious at their refusal, he captured the two warriors and took them prisoner, torturing them for information about their clan."

"Couldn't the Xia have fought him off?" I say. "They were the strongest warriors in all Ikhara."

Wren's lips are tight. "The King planned for that. He knew that a few guards were no match for the Xia, so before the meeting he readied a small army of both shamans and sword-masters. He used their combined strength to overpower the two warriors."

She falls silent, and I sense her anger. Her fingers grip mine a little tighter, her pulse racing against my own.

"Nobody had attempted to capture the Xia before," she goes on. "Just as with duels between clan lords, there was an unwritten code. An understanding that whatever the outcome, if it was fought fairly—either with words or swords—it should be honored. The Xia's decisions were to be respected. So to attack them outside of battle, to capture and torture them for information they would not freely give..." She rakes in a sharp inhale. "It was dishonorable. Something the gods would surely punish." A muscle tics in her neck. "But it seems the heavenly rulers had decided to stay out of mortal affairs. Week after week, month after month, the Bull King's armies tore through Ikhara, killing clan leaders and breaking apart alliances."

"What happened to the two captured Xia warriors?" I ask.

"No one knows. Maybe they never gave anything away under torture, so the King had them executed. That's what I believe, anyway. But some people think they managed to escape. Others that they turned and ended up fighting alongside the King in the Night War, and that's what enabled him to win."

A shudder runs down my spine at the thought. Might *and* magic. It would have been a bloodbath.

"Once he captured the eight provinces and established his court," Wren continues, anger still skating the edges of her words, "the

King turned his attention to destroying the Xia. He knew it was unlikely he could defeat them in battle. They'd fought against some of his armies during the Night War—those included some of the battles he lost. So he planned surprise attacks. Ambushes. He even had them attacked on prayer days, when he knew their warriors wouldn't fight back. The Xia were not a large clan. After years of these constant attacks, they were all but destroyed. The few Xia who were left went into hiding in the mountains of eastern Rain."

"And one of those survivors was you," I breathe.

Wren nods. "When I was born, I became the twenty-third member of the decimated Xia clan." She swallows. "And its last. I was just a baby, too young to remember much of that final attack. Ketai Hanno found me afterward, when the fires that had ripped through our home had burned themselves out. He managed to piece together a rough idea of what happened. Somehow, our location was betrayed to the Demon King, who sent an army in the middle of the night. My people put up a valiant fight. The snow was said to have been red with the blood of his soldiers. But there were just twenty-three of us, half of us children. We were hopelessly outnumbered. By the time the sun rose the following morning, the Xia had been destroyed." She turns away, lips pressed into a bloodless line, before drawing a faltering inhale. "My mother, my father, my five-year-old sister…all dead. I was the only one left."

The paper leaves of the tree rustle around us. Lacing my arms round her back, I pull Wren close, drawing her so tight I shift with every rise and drop of her shallow, shaky breaths. The day my mother was taken is so clear to me in this moment, so close, like a imprint burnt on my heart. I know what it's like to lose your family.

To lose your hope.

Wren draws back. "There's something I want to show you."

She pulls me to my feet. Reaching up into the boughs of the tree for the branch with her sister's name, she brushes aside a few of the other leaves to reveal another glowing paper leaf beside her sister's.

My throat closes when I see the name written across it.

Soraya.

My mother.

I turn to her, barely able to speak. "You did this?"

"This is the Temple of the Hidden," Wren explains. "It's for the dead we are unable to grieve for. For me, that's my Xia family. The family I'm not allowed to grieve for publicly, because I can't reveal they ever existed. I have a shrine for my parents in one of the other rooms, but this tree is for hidden women only, so I come here to pray for my sister's spirit." She hesitates. "After what you told me about your mother, I thought you might like a place to come to pray for her, too."

I'm silent for so long that her face drops. "I shouldn't have," she mumbles. "I overstepped—"

"No." I take her hands, our palms pressing together. "I needed this, Wren. You knew, even before I did."

Tears course down my face, but I ignore them, my breathing jagged. Because it's all so clear. Of course it is. I've been trying to convince myself, clinging onto the hope that my instincts are wrong. That the absence of my mother's name from the Night Houses lists was a mistake, or maybe she found a way to escape on her own, because she was my Mama and brilliant and of course she could find a way to escape from an inescapable fortress.

"She's dead, isn't she?" I choke out. "My mother is…dead."

The word is as ugly-tasting as it sounds, a solid slab of weight on my tongue.

It's the first time I have ever said it out loud. Ever admitted it to myself. I've thought it, felt the admission taking shape at the edges of my mind, but every time I wrestled it down. Now the truth hits me the way thunder strikes the earth—hard and fast, and with a flash that tears the sky apart.

It wrenches a rasping sound from my throat. Wren grabs me as I double over, holding me in silence as the gentle air of the temple courtyard fills with my cries.

You would think seven years would have dulled my wounds. But still they burn inside me, a fire too bright to extinguish.

TWENTY-THREE

A LONG WHILE LATER WE SETTLE back against the tree for Wren to finish her story. This time we sit closer, curled together like two puzzle pieces, her arms circling me from behind. Her breath is warm by my ear. The names of her sister and my mother flutter in the branches above our heads like protective charms, our own precious gods watching over us.

"I don't know how I survived the attack," Wren says, "let alone how I stayed alive for days afterward with no food or water, no shelter. Perhaps it was my Xia blood, or some last protective dao one of my family wove for me with the last of their breath. The mountainside was covered in bodies. I was hidden among them, the only living thing for miles. That's what my father says drew him to me—my adoptive father, that is, Ketai Hanno. He came to Rain after hearing about the massacre, hoping to find survivors. He's always believed the stories of the Xia. He wanted to learn from them, try to rebuild their presence in Ikhara."

My brow furrows. "But I thought the Hannos are one of the Demon King's biggest supporters."

"Yes," Wren says. "They are."

I wait for her to explain further. "Oh," I say eventually. "Another thing you can't tell me about."

She lowers her lips to my head, so I feel her warm breath mussing my hair. "I'm sorry, Lei. I want to tell you everything. The whole truth. But it would be too dangerous."

I'm stiff in her arms. "You still don't trust me," I murmur.

"Of course I do. I mean that it would be dangerous for *you*."

We sit in silence, the courtyard hushed with the rustle of the paper leaves, their faint chiming hum.

"So," I say, hugging her arms closer to me. "Ketai Hanno found you and took you back to Ang-Khen?"

"Exactly. Bhali—Ketai's wife, my adoptive mother—was sick. She hadn't been seen in public for two years, which fit perfectly with my arrival. They announced my birth late, saying that they were waiting for her recovery before sharing the news. No one questioned it. Maybe if I'd been a boy, it would have been different. But I was just a new daughter for the Demon King to eventually claim. My existence wouldn't have much consequence. And so I began my new life in the Hannos' palace, and grew up to love a new family."

"Do you?" I ask gently. "Love them?"

Wren replies after a beat. "As much as I can. I guess it's strange I should feel so connected to the Xia, seeing that I was just a baby when they were killed. But I can't help but think of them as my true family. Sometimes I'll catch scent of something that reminds me of them, of the mountains, and it strikes me so vividly then—the loss. The loneliness of being the only one left."

"I know," I say, tilting my head back to nestle my face into her neck. I breathe her crisp, blue-green scent in, so cleansing in my lungs. "I miss my family, too. Everyone keeps telling me to forget about them, but I can't just let them go."

Wren's voice is fierce. "Then don't. *I* haven't."

"Doesn't it make it harder?"

"Yes," she answers. "But I don't want an easy life. I want a meaningful one."

As we head back to Women's Court, and throughout the rest of the day, Wren's words play over and over in my head, building and strengthening, like a light growing brighter and fiercer the longer it burns, a candle-flame in reverse. Every time our eyes catch across a room—Wren's gaze soft with our secret but radiant with something else—or we stroll down a corridor, standing a fraction closer than before, the caged thing stirs inside me. Not just with desire, but for the kind of life Wren was talking about under the tree. The courage I heard in her words.

I don't want an easy life. I want a meaningful one.

The image of the old Paper Girl from the koyo party comes back to me: her melting face, her desperation. All this time I've been trying to adjust to my life here in the palace. To fit into the life expected of me. But am I losing sense of who *I* am, who I want to become?

Dzarja. The label is ugly, but only because I let it be. The realization strikes me with such force that I'm incredulous to have not thought of it before.

Perhaps being a traitor can be a good thing if you are betraying those who deserve it.

That night, I wait until the house is silent before going to Wren's room.

She is on her feet at once. "Lei? What are you doing?"

I cross the room. Push her up against the wall. "Telling the easy life where to go," I say, and lift my lips to hers.

"Wait," she murmurs against my mouth, stiffening.

My breathing is quick. "Haven't we done enough of that already?"

There's a moment's pause—and then her lips close on mine.

A sigh runs through me. Loosening a soft, sweet growl, Wren laces her arms round my neck, hands tangling in my hair, her mouth opening to move with mine. My world dissolves into heat and velvet touch. The two of us fall into rhythm, as natural and easy as if we'd done this a thousand times before. *Has* Wren done this before? The thought flares into my mind, almost taking me out of the moment. But I shove it away. Because maybe it's just like this because it's us, and it's right.

Desire charges through my bloodstream. Sighing, I draw Wren closer, our kiss growing fiercer. Urgent. Mouth wide, I brush the tip of her tongue with my own. She tastes like a monsoon, like storms and danger. In return, she nips my bottom lip, sending a sharp current of heat between my legs, where my pulse throbs, a fluid beat. My fingers skim over the silky fabric of her night robe. Her body is hard and muscled and so beautiful it hurts. I want to know every part of it at once. I want to melt into her. To disappear into the softness of her kisses, of her skin and smooth, liquid heat.

Sliding her hands down my back, Wren squeezes my waist, drawing a gasp from my lips. The flaring heat inside me swells. I have the wild notion that this must be what Master Tekoa's prediction was about: the fire, the red flames within me. But how would it bring down the palace? This is a secret fire that can only be kindled—and caught—by the girl whose lips are upon mine.

Eventually we pull apart, our breathing heavy.

Wren drops her forehead against mine, half panting. "All right," she says shakily, a trembling hand lifting to cup my cheek. "So maybe the hard life isn't so bad after all."

I laugh. "Was that a joke?"

"I am capable of them, you know."

"Prove it. Make another one."

She gives me a feline smile. "Can't I just kiss you again instead?"

My pulse flits as she dips her mouth toward mine. But just then, there's the sound of footsteps in the hallway.

We lurch apart. In the shadowy room, Wren's eyes are wide, moon-bright. We wait, breathless, the seconds ticking by slowly until finally the steps fade. There's the sound of a door closing a few rooms away.

"You should get back," Wren whispers once it's quiet again.

Our mouths find each other's one last time in the dark, and I sigh into her sweetness, her liquid warmth.

"Don't come tomorrow," Wren says when we pull apart. I freeze, but she continues with a smile, "I'll come to you instead."

"I'll hold you to that," I murmur.

Her expression sobers. "I keep my promises, Lei," she replies quietly. "Whatever they might cost me."

TWENTY-FOUR

WHEN I WAKE THE NEXT MORNING, I lift my fingertips to my mouth, still lying tangled in my sheets, eyes shut. My skin is warm and mussed from sleep. There's a tingle in my lips where I press them, but otherwise there's no hint of what happened just hours ago. At least, not physically. My mouth seems the same, my lips just as they were before: smooth, small, *lonely*. I brush my fingertips over them, hunting for Wren's presence. Honeyed shafts of sunlight fall across my sheets. I forgot to close my shutters last night, and the warmth of the rays seems to indicate that the gods are aware of what occurred between me and Wren.

And some of them approve.

Stretching, I roll over with a yawn. My gaze lands on the shrine in the corner of my room. A trickle of unease slithers through me.

I'm not in a rush to find out what happens to us if any of them *don't*.

When she comes to collect me for our morning lessons an hour later, Wren gives no outward indication of what passed between us last night. But once we're outside, the other girls chatting easily around us, she slows her steps just enough for us to fall out of earshot.

"I can't stop thinking about last night," she murmurs, her beautiful black-brown eyes shining.

Her words are as sweet as a song. I can't hide my grin. I chance a quick press of my shoulder against her arm, angling my face into her. As if on cue, Blue flicks her head round, and Wren and I spring apart, pretending to be very interested in the hems of our hanfu.

If I thought the day *before* our kiss was hard, the day after is a million times worse. It becomes a practice in patience, something Tien would no doubt say I have very little of. Time stretches out, infuriatingly slow. I'm longing for the night to come so we can get past whatever function we have that evening and I can once again be alone with Wren. But then Mistress Eira reminds us at dinner that we'll be seeing the King at the shadow play performance we're attending tonight.

Something dark and red hums through my veins at the mention of him.

Across the table, Aoki shoots me a concerned look. She must be remembering what I said to her at the koyo party about how I won't let the King have me. She cocks her head, questioning, and I wrest a half smile to my face.

"Are you all right?" Wren whispers once the other girls sink back into conversation. She's kneeling next to me, our thighs almost touching under the table.

"Yes," I answer, and though my throat is narrow, I mean it. As a maid reaches across us to tidy the plates away, hiding us from view, I catch her fingers in mine. It's just a moment—like all of our stolen touches. But it reminds me that I have the strength to defy the King, even in small, secret ways such as these.

After dinner, Lill picks a vivid orange cheongsam for me to wear to the performance, gold embroidery shimmering across the fabric.

She adds a slash of vermilion paint on my lips. Then she slicks my hair back into an intricate braid, twining it with flame-colored ribbons.

"Now you match the leaves," she grins, moving back to admire her work.

I lift a brow. "Isn't this is a bit…much?"

"Mistress," she says, serious, "the King still hasn't called you since that night. Don't you want him to notice you? To want you again?"

I quickly turn my cheek to hide my grimace. Sometimes I forget how young Lill is, but times like these remind me that she is just a girl. I recall how black and white the world seemed at eleven. How clear-cut life was, everything divided into good and bad, right and wrong, like two sides of a coin, and the edge between almost nonexistent, no bigger than a sliver. Lill believes I want the Demon King's attention. That my earlier slip was just a mistake, a moment that overwhelmed me. She thinks I want him because surely I must.

Because I am a Paper Girl and he is my King.

We make the now-familiar journey to the Inner Courts. Shadow play is a long-standing tradition in our kingdom. In Xienzo we had performances during certain festivals, with wooden cutout puppets on sticks moved by actors hidden beneath a makeshift stage. A small brazier created the fire that silhouetted the puppets against the rice-paper screen. As we arrive at the theater and enter a tall, stepped room with a wide stage and columns of billowing silks hanging from the ceiling at staggered intervals, it's clear that this will be a very different version of shadow play from the one I'm used to. Around the edges of the stage runs a deep recess, flames dancing from within.

"I'm a bit nervous to see the King again," Aoki admits as we take our seats toward the back of the theater, her voice almost swallowed by the noise as the audience streams in, snatches of conversations and bursts of laughter rising around us. She frowns. "He seemed different at the koyo party. Do you remember?"

Of course I remember. The King's drunken swagger. The human slaves he offered to the attending demons like a twisted kind of party favor.

"He hasn't asked for any of us since then," Aoki says. "He must be busy."

I shrug. "It's probably to do with the rebels. Or maybe the Sickness," I add, sending a mental thanks to both for keeping him away.

Wren leans in on my other side. "The King talked to you about that?" she asks sharply. "What did he say?"

"Not much. Just that it's getting worse. That nothing seems to be helping."

She turns away, a glazed look frosting her eyes.

"What?" I press as Aoki turns to talk to Zhin beside her.

"It's been going on for a while now," Wren murmurs, her nose pinched in thought. "All the clans are concerned. Just before I came to the palace, my father was arranging a meeting with the most powerful clans from every province to discuss how to manage it."

"Does he know what could be causing it?" I ask.

"Nothing for certain. One of his theories is that it's to do with qi-draining. Some overuse of magic that is putting Ikhara out of balance. But he has no idea who might be behind it."

"The King thinks the gods are punishing the kingdom."

The look she gives me is pointed. "For what?"

"I have no idea."

Wren turns back to the stage, the furrow in her brow deepening. "Me neither. But the reason doesn't really matter. The problem is that the King believes it. And I'm worried what it'll lead him to do."

To my other side, Aoki is still chatting with Zhin. "The King won't notice me in this at all," she mutters, picking at the draped sleeves of her beige ruqun, the fabric patterned with gold embroidery.

As Zhin starts to reply, Blue's voice sounds over her. "Of course he won't," she says crisply, glancing over her shoulder from the row in front of us with a toss of her hair. "That color makes you look ill. You should tell your maid to avoid it in the future."

"*I* think she looks beautiful," I say with a glare.

Blue's eyes flick to me, her chin tilted. "Looks like Master Tekoa was right about all that fire, Nine. You're practically a human lantern." The corners of her mouth tug up. "Such a shame how some girls have to be so *obvious* to attract the King's attention. At least little Aoki doesn't need to try so hard. You know, the King tells me her company is surprisingly pleasant."

To my surprise, Aoki beams at this. When Blue turns back round, she grabs my knee, leaning in. "Did you hear that? The King enjoys his time with me!"

I grimace. "And that's a good thing?"

Something darts across her face—hurt.

"I told you at the party, Lei," she says, shifting back. "He's kind to me."

"Only because he's getting what he wants!"

After my night with Wren—the softness, the fierceness, the tenderness of the hunger I felt in her lips, so different from how I felt under the King's touch—I can't imagine how Aoki could actually enjoy her time with him. And for the King to call her company pleasant. *Pleasant.* A word dull with mediocrity. Nothing like the dazzle and burn I felt at Wren's kiss. The way I hope for every girl to be thought of by her lover.

I open my mouth to say more, but just then the lanterns in the hall blow out. A hush falls over the crowd.

"I thought you'd be happy for me," Aoki whispers. Her face is shadowed in the now-dark hall, but I don't need light to know her expression. Even in the darkness, her eyes glimmer with tears.

My face twists. "Aoki—" I start, but she turns to face the stage, inching away.

Wren presses her shoulder gently to mine. "We of all people can't judge Aoki for what she feels," she says under her breath, chin tilted down. "Or for whom."

I go to retort, but the heavy beat of drums echoes through the room, silencing me. A lithe gazelle-form woman dances onto the stage. Unlike the typical shadow play performances I've seen, where the actors hold up puppets, this actress *is* the puppet. Her body is wrapped in a wooden cage mimicking her own form but making it twice as tall. A jewel-eyed gazelle mask perches at the top of the elongated wooden neck arching from the dancer's back. As she moves behind the rippling sheets of silk, her exaggerated horned shadow arcs and turns with every movement.

Murmurs rise among the crowd.

I shoot Wren a sideways look. "Where's the King? He should have been announced—"

A shout cuts me off.

At first I think it's part of the play, that the noise is coming from the stage. But then there's another shout, and another. In a handful of seconds, the whole theater erupts with cries, and I realize—this isn't a performance.

Something's wrong.

Panic floods the hall, a physical thing, buzzing and spilling over the edges with the rage of a monsoon tide. All around us, the crowd is scrambling to their feet, demons and humans, court members and their companions, stumbling over cushions and even one another in their rush to escape.

An object whirs over my head toward the stage. I catch a glimpse of it—a blazing arrow—before it strikes one of the hanging silks. The fabric bursts into flames, a waterfall of orange cascading to the floor. More fire leaps into life where the screen fell. A second volley of arrows whistles over our heads, so close it stirs the air.

Onstage, the gazelle-dancer runs through the blaze, her puppet silhouette elongated and ghostly, a horrible mimicry of the performance she was meant to be giving.

Wren seizes my hand. "We have to get out," she says, dragging me to my feet.

I barely hear her over the screams, the crackling burr of the flames. It's shocking how quickly the fire has spread; the hall is lit in flickering gold.

I stumble to keep up. "W-what's going on?"

"It's an attack. They must be after the King."

The stepped seats around us are deserted. Everyone has rushed to the exit at the back of the hall, causing a crush. Through the smoke, I spot Mistress Eira helping Zhen and Zhin, one of whom is limping. Ahead, Madam Himura marshals the rest of the girls.

There's a gleam of dark lapis hair. As Madam Himura pushes her forward, Blue looks around. Tears stream down her cheeks, her face white.

Aoki's fingers snap round my arm. "Lei!" she gasps. Her eyes are wide, the reflection of flames dancing within them.

"Don't worry," I say, gripping her hand. "I'm here."

I pull her along with me, following Wren to the end of the row. Just as we get there, there's a thundering crack. Dislodged from the roof, a burning beam of wood crashes down, landing right across our path. Flames lash out from it like fiery whips.

I stagger back, instinctively pushing Aoki behind me.

"We're not going to get out!" she sobs, squeezing my fingers tighter.

Wren whirls around. Without any explanation, she strides off again, picking her way easily down the cushion-strewn steps, in the direction of the stage.

"That's the wrong way!" I yell. But she doesn't change course.

Aoki and I take off after her into the smoke and fire-lit shadows. The roar of burning swells louder as we near the heart of the fire. And from under it, a new sound rises—the teeth-ringing clash of metal upon metal.

My stomach leaps. Swordfighting.

I'm just about to point this out to Wren when she comes to an abrupt stop. "It should be here," she says, so low I almost don't catch it. She drops to her knees, palming the floor.

"What should?" I shout back.

She doesn't answer. After a few more seconds, she lets out a little hiss of triumph and jumps back up. At first I can't see anything through the smoke, but she draws me into position at the edge of an opening in the floor. A trap door.

"It's a short drop," she says. "Move away when you're down."

I stare at her, blinking back the sweat stinging my eyes. "How did you know this was here?" I ask, but she turns to help Aoki, ignoring my question.

When she looks around to see if I've gone, she lets out an exasperated growl. "Just go!"

Jaw clenched, I move forward.

And drop into darkness.

The fall is short, as Wren promised. I land awkwardly. Pain shoots through my ankle, but I grit my teeth and roll out of the way as Aoki follows with a shout. I'm helping her to her feet when Wren lands, impossibly lightly, as graceful as a cat.

She strides down the tunnel, not even looking in the other direction. "This way," she orders.

We hurry after her. Seconds later, there's a fourth thud behind us. The growl of a male voice.

"Stop."

In one quick movement, Wren shoves us back. It's dark here under the theater, the air still clogged with smoke, but some light sparks down from the flames above, casting eerie flickers through the gloom. It illuminates the intense calmness on Wren's face as she strides past us toward the shadowy figure. Despite the heat, horrible shivers run across my skin as I see that her irises have turned white—pure, startlingly white—the whole of the eyes solid like ice. Fire reflects off them, sliding yellow flames on white.

"Leave us," she tells the figure. "The King isn't here."

And I flinch—because her voice is different, too. It has a deep echo to it, as though many Wrens were speaking through her, and in the space where her words hang in the air, there's a current of coldness.

The only answer is the screech of steel as the man draws his blade from its scabbard.

With a cry, he moves forward. Wren ducks as the sword slices through the air. The man raises it again, thrusting toward her.

She dances out of his way. Rolls to field a third blow. She dips, skating away from another parry, then with a whirl of her silk robes she jumps. Her left leg flies up and catches the man on the shoulder.

He staggers. Recovers. Loosening yet another battle cry, he lunges at her with a curving cut of his blade.

Wren is too quick for him; too quick for anyone. The way she moves is unnatural, her hair and robes flowing around her as if sifting through water, her movements fluid and precise. She leaps easily aside. While he's still propelled forward from the momentum of his strike, she moves behind him and hooks an arm around his neck. He lets out a startled cry as she knocks the sword from his hand and catches the blade, turning it toward him—

And sinks it into his chest.

It happens so quickly, so smoothly, that the man doesn't seem to comprehend at first what has occurred. His mouth is stuck in a surprised, almost comical O. Then he lets out a deep, awful groan. His face slackens. One hand grasps weakly at the sword, but his fingers slip on the handle, coming away slick with blood, and he rocks forward, limbs limp.

Wren lowers him to the floor. Her hands make the sky gods salute over his slumped body before she looks up at me, still with that eerie white stare.

In an instant, her eyes return to their normal black-brown. The focused expression drops from her face. She gets to her feet. "Lei," she starts, coming toward me with her hands held out.

If it's meant as a calming gesture, it has the opposite effect. Her palms are dark with blood, and I jerk away from them, a ragged shudder rippling down my spine.

"You're Xia," I say in a hollow voice that doesn't sound like my own.

She wipes her hands on her dress. "I already told you—"

"No. I mean, you're *Xia*."

Because I'm not talking about what she's already told me about being born to the warrior clan. She's not just Xia by heritage.

She's a *warrior*.

Not just by blood, but in practice.

We stare at each other through the shifting smoke. It stings my eyes, and I double over, coughing. The smoke is growing thicker, pooling the tunnel in dark, swirling coils.

"We have to get out of here," Wren says, turning. "Where's Aoki?"

I spin around. It takes me a few seconds to make out her slumped form on the floor. At once, I hurry to her side, pressing two fingertips under the curve of her jawbone.

"Is she all right?" Wren asks.

A pulse flutters against my touch, weak but steady. "I—I think so. She must have fainted."

Reaching past me, Wren threads an arm under Aoki's back and slings her over one shoulder in an easy movement. "Let's go."

Though Aoki is small, she isn't so light that Wren should be able to lift her this way. I follow her in silence, scared to get too close to this girl with the bloodstained hands.

The tunnel isn't long. At its end, we open the trap door overhead. Rain greets our upturned faces. Wren helps me out first—I cringe at the smell of blood on her—and then together we lift out Aoki. With another easy movement, Wren picks Aoki back up and we hurry around the side of the building, keeping a safe distance from the flames.

A crowd has gathered. As we join them, my eyes alert for the other girls, a number of carriages pull up to the front of the theater. I recognize the black handprint symbol on the sides of their carriages as the same as those on the robes of the shamans who purified me before seeing the King—and the one who fixed my bruises after.

The royal shamans.

Wren sets Aoki down. I kneel beside her to check she's breathing, shielding her face from the rain with my arm before turning my attention back to the carriages. Black-robed figures are filing out of them, orderly and calm. Even though their skin is hidden, I can picture the dark web of tattoos on their bodies, their skin a forest of ink, like some kind of dark map of sacrifice and pain. The shamans form a ring around the theater. In perfect synchrony, they raise their hands and begin to draw glowing characters in the air in front of them, chanting as they write.

The warm prickle of magic radiates from them, a growing thrum. When the air is so full of pressure it's like being in the midst of a thunderstorm, the shamans whip their hands upward. A gust of wind bursts from their circle. It blasts in both directions, billowing into us—making our eyes water and clothes fly out—and rushing toward the theater, swelling and rising to tower over the domed building, solidifying into a roiling pewter cloud.

It hangs there, dark and growling. Then it drops from the air, transforming as it falls into a plunging torrent of water.

Water gushes over the theater, swallowing the flames. Hitting the ground, we're soaked through in an instant as the wave barrels into us.

Aoki comes round with a gasp. I help her up, shoving the wet hair from her face. I'm gasping myself, numb from the chill night air on my wet skin, and we clutch each other, both shaking.

"What—what happened?" she cries, looking left and right. "Did you see them, Lei? I think someone followed us into the tunnel—" She cuts off, coughing.

I rub her back. "It was just something falling. A piece of wood. Don't worry."

"But—"

"You fainted, Aoki. Take it easy. I'm going to get you something warm to wear. Can you wait here?"

Still trembling, she nods. As I get to my feet, Wren puts a hand on my shoulder. "Lei—"

"Look after her. I won't be long." I take a sharp inhale, continuing in a low voice, "You knew the trap door was there, Wren. You knew how to fight. How to kill."

The crowd is moving around us, and someone bumps into me, knocking me into Wren. She lifts her arms to steady me, but I jerk back, the image of her in the tunnel reentering my mind.

"I thought I knew you," I say weakly.

She flinches. "You *do* know me."

"I'm going to get some robes or a blanket for Aoki," I go on, avoiding her eyes. "We can talk when you're ready to tell me the truth about what the gods just happened."

Wren catches me as I turn. "I haven't lied to you, Lei," she promises.

"Well, you haven't exactly told me the truth, either."

Her mouth parts, something pained pinching her face, and I force myself to walk away.

TWENTY-FIVE

WE SPEND A SLEEPLESS NIGHT BACK at Paper House, waiting in one of the parlors as a group of doctors and shamans check us over one by one. The hours slip by in shocked silence, all of us dazed. Madam Himura calls us to her suite early the next morning. We haven't even had a chance to bathe or eat breakfast, and our hair and clothes still reek of smoke. "The royal messenger just left," she tells us once we've all sat down. "Our guesses were right. The attack was an assassination attempt."

Wren shifts forward, her back rod-straight. "Who by?" she asks.

"All we know is that they were a group of ten Paper caste men. Three were taken alive. The other seven were killed at the theater by guards."

An image comes to me of Wren's white eyes as she turned the man's sword on himself. *Not just guards.* I sense her looking my way and stare ahead, my jaw set.

"But the King wasn't even at the theater," Chenna points out.

Madam Himura clacks her beak. "Thank the heavenly rulers! A messenger came to stop him just as he arrived. One of the royal fortune-tellers had a premonition of the attack. That's how they got the shamans to the theater so quickly."

Blue shifts forward, her fingers fidgeting with the hem of her skirt. "Was anyone hurt?" she asks, and though her voice is steady, there's an undercurrent of something nervous in it. The gray morning light picks out her cheekbones, carving dark hollows beneath them. "From the audience, I mean."

"Two court officials were killed. Twelve more injured."

"Because my father was there," Blue goes on, "and I haven't heard from him—"

Madam Himura holds up a hand to silence her. She looks around at us down the hook of her curved beak-nose, her yellow eyes unblinking. "The King has taken the assassins for questioning. For now, he has ordered your usual schedule to be on hold. You're to stay in Paper House until further notice."

As the rest of us go to leave, Blue makes a beeline for Madam Himura. "My father," she starts again, but the eagle-woman waves her away.

"Not now, girl."

"But—"

"How many times do I have to tell you?" Madam Himura squawks. "Just because your father is a member of the court does not mean it affords you any special privileges! Open your mouth once more today, and I will not hesitate to throw you out."

Blue's lips flatten into a bloodless line. Glowering, she strides past us, Mariko hurrying after her.

Aoki and I are the last to leave. We walk slowly down the corridor. "Two people dead," she mutters. She gives me a sideways glance. "Can you believe it? It could have been us, Lei. Thank the gods Wren found that trap door."

I make a noncommittal murmur—because I saw the look on her face, and it wasn't surprise. It was surety.

The two of us head to the bathing courtyard. I'm eager to get the stink of smoke out of my hair, the traces of darkened blood on my skin from where Wren lifted me out of the tunnel. We're just passing through the corridor where our bedrooms are when there's the sound of a door opening behind us. Zhen's head pokes out of her room.

"Oh," she says, looking relieved. "We thought it might be Mariko and Blue. Do you want to join us?"

I know what they're doing, and talking about last night is the last thing I feel like. Not least because since I confronted her outside the theater, Wren hasn't come to talk to me yet, and I'm starting to wonder whether maybe I was too hard on her. She was just protecting us, after all, like Aoki said. But Aoki nods, and I follow her into Zhen's bedroom, not wanting to be alone right now, either.

Chenna and the twins are inside. They look grim, Zhin sitting against the wall under the window with her legs pulled up to her chin while Zhen kneels on the bamboo mat floor, her dirt-stained robes ripped at one shoulder. Chenna gives me a humorless smile, shifting slightly to make room for us. As I kneel, I smooth down the rumpled fabric of my cheongsam. My fingers catch on a torn slash. Through it, the skin of my thigh shines palely. Even burnt and dirty, the dress is still almost the same hue as the flames that scorched it, making me think of what Blue said to me before the play began.

Looks like Master Tekoa was right about all that fire, Nine. You're practically a human lantern.

Was that what happened last night? Did I somehow, unknowingly, cause the attack?

"You were saying you think the assassins are from Noei?" Zhen directs at Chenna once we're settled. "The same region as those slaves at the koyo party?"

Chenna lifts a shoulder. "It's just a guess. But it seems too much of a coincidence that this happens a week after they were brought here, don't you think?"

"I'm not sure," Zhin replies. She rubs her arms where they're looped round her legs. "There are so many Paper families and clans with reasons to hate the King."

"And the raids have been going on all over Ikhara," her sister adds. "Our father told us before coming here that the King is blaming them on the rebels. That they're doing it to discredit him with the Paper castes."

Beside me, Aoki shifts, fluting her fingers over her skirt. "I don't think the King would do that...."

"I'm not sure what the King *wouldn't* do," Chenna says stonily, and though I agree with her, I don't say so.

Aoki's cheeks color. "He has a lot to deal with," she mutters.

"Yes," Chenna retorts. "It must be hard for him here in this luxurious palace, with all these beautiful things around him."

"You mean like us?"

The girls stare at me, an uncomfortable silence descending over the room. I haven't ever told them what I really think of being here—excluding Aoki and Wren, of course—though I suppose my actions have made it explicit enough. I've guessed at Chenna feeling a similar way; she wears her duty well, but grudgingly. But Zhen and Zhin have always seemed happy to be here.

"Don't you feel bad for the things we've seen happen to Paper castes here who aren't protected by the King in the same way we are?" I ask into the quiet. "Didn't you feel anything for those slaves the other night?"

"Of course I did," Chenna says, shooting me a stern, almost hurt look. I remember the disgust in her eyes as we watched the slaves, side by side in a crowd of demons. Her prayer to Kunih. She lifts her chin. "But what can we do about it? It's the same outside the palace. Even my father, as well respected as he is in Uazu, has had to suffer bullying from Steels and Moons. I've seen the way they look at us. The whispers behind our backs. Most of the time, they don't even bother to whisper."

"It was like that for us, too," Zhen says. "Sometimes the worst of it even came from other Paper castes. Like we were somehow betraying them by being involved in the court."

"That's what I mean," I press. "Here, we're not experiencing life the way most Paper castes do."

"Isn't that a good thing?" Aoki's flush deepens as all of us turn to her. "I mean," she continues, more tentatively, picking at the torn threads of her hem, "we're treated well here. We're looked after——"

"Oh, like how I was chained to the floor and starved for a week?"

"Well," she says, her cheeks pink, "it *could* have been worse."

Her words hit me with the shock of a slap. The twins stare as Aoki and I glare at each other.

"Look," Chenna says, raising her palms, her voice steady. "You both make good points. I hear what you're saying, Lei. I'm sure we all do. We're not denying the privilege our status has brought us. But I don't see how we can change anything. Aoki's right. It could have been a lot worse for you—and what you went through was already so bad. And that was for offending the King in a personal way. This is Ikharan politics we're talking about. This is bigger than us."

That's exactly what I'm trying to say! I want to shout. But I'm still reeling from Aoki's comment, and underneath their wariness, Chenna and the twins look exhausted. The same fatigue hits me afresh. After what we all just went through, we don't need to be fighting among ourselves as well.

The pleading look on Wren's face last night comes back to me. How she must be feeling even worse, given what she did to protect us.

I shift my legs uncomfortably. Now I'm *sure* I was too harsh on her.

Zhin clears her throat. "So. What do you think will happen to the assassins?"

I look across at her, grateful for the change of subject. "Well, we know they're being questioned."

She shakes her head, brow knitted. "I mean... after."

"Court law for treason of any kind is execution," Chenna states matter-of-factly.

Execution. The word is as sharp as its meaning.

"And in the palace," she goes on, "executions are public events."

My mouth twists. "We'll have to watch?"

Chenna nods. The twins share an apprehensive look. Aoki stares fixedly ahead, not meeting anyone's eyes.

"Maybe they'll just imprison them," Zhin suggests eventually.

"And I suppose," Zhen says, "they could always, maybe, find them *not* guilty?"

Chenna and I both raise our eyebrows at her.

"They would have killed him," Aoki says, quiet and a little shaky, looking down at her palms. "Are we forgetting that?" When no one replies, she scrambles to her feet, hands clutched into fists. "I'm tired of listening to this," she declares, her face red. "The King might be scared, too. Did any of you think about that? And we're not even allowed to see if he's all right. He's worried, and hurt, and all alone...."

"Aoki—" I start, getting to my feet.

"Not now, Lei," she mumbles thickly. Rubbing her face with the heels of her hands, she puffs out a loud breath before rushing out of the room.

"Maybe you should give her some time," Chenna suggests quietly when I move to follow her. "She's probably just in shock after what happened. She needs to rest."

Zhin's eyes click to me. "I think we all do."

The three of them decide to get some sleep, but when I leave, I pass the door to my bedroom. I continue to the bathing courtyard as originally planned, half hoping to find Aoki or Wren there. Still, when I find it empty, I'm suddenly grateful for a moment to myself.

Hidden in the steam, I undress by my usual tub, throwing my dirty clothes to the floor with slightly more force than necessary before climbing into the water. It takes a long time to scrub the dirt from my body. Even after I'm clean, last night's smoke clings to me, an invisible second skin. I stay in long after my fingertips grow wrinkly, unable to shake the unease that's been coursing through me all night. Every time I close my eyes the image of Wren and the assassin is waiting for me—the surprised look on his face, the calm, focused expression on hers.

She's a true Xia. A warrior.

A girl trained to kill, in the heart of the kingdom.

A girl who can get closer to the King than most.

I can think of an explanation as to why, but I'm not sure I want to believe it.

Just as I'm about to get out, the sound of approaching steps makes me start. I swirl round, splashing water over the side of the barrel. Through the clouds, I make out a tall figure coming toward me. My belly loops. It's her.

I duck lower, crossing my arms over my chest, suddenly hyper-aware of my nakedness.

Though Wren's face is composed, there's a tender look in her eyes. She stops a few feet away. "Can we talk?" she asks, and the tentativeness in her voice—the idea that she's even worried I could say no—strikes me with fresh guilt.

I nod, but she doesn't come any closer.

Even in last night's ruined dress she is beautiful. Though the jade-green silks of her hanfu robes are slashed and charred, the color still brings out the glossy tan of her skin, the definition of her long, muscled limbs. My instinct is to run to her, to hug her, kiss away her pain. But even if I understand why she did it, the memory of her stabbing the man in the tunnel holds me back.

That wasn't the girl I kissed two nights ago in a dark bedroom. The girl who held me as I cried under the whispering boughs of the paper-leaf tree, who made me feel so safe.

My eyes drop to the stain of blood on the collar of her robes. "You killed a man," I state, hollow.

"Only to protect you and Aoki."

"And that makes it right?"

"Of course not. But I had to do something, Lei. He would have tried to kill us all."

A bead of moisture slips down my temple, and I swipe it away, hurriedly crossing my arms again. "It wasn't us he wanted. They wanted the King. And he wasn't even there."

"Is that why you're angry?" Wren asks, an odd tilt to her voice. "Because you *wanted* them to kill him?"

I hesitate. "Maybe," I murmur, my cheek turned. Then I look back, forcing myself to meet her stare. "What do *you* think?"

Wren's expression is unreadable. She stands stiffly, arms rigid at her sides. "'Just as Zhokka and Ahla chase each other across the skies,' she recites, "does darkness not follow light, and light follow darkness, neither one truly ahead of the other?'" The saying is old, familiar with everyone in Ikhara. "I like to think there's some good behind even the darkest sins. That death can be warranted if it paves the way for hope."

I edge forward in the tub. "Is that why you are a warrior? Because you are, aren't you, Wren? You fight like the Xia."

Her neck flexes as she swallows. I sense her wanting to refuse to answer, but finally she gives a small jerk of her head that I take as a nod. "I've been trained in the Xia form since I was young."

A flashback to the glimpse of her feet that morning before the Unveiling Ceremony, when she held up her robe as she stepped into my room. So that's what turned them rough.

"Trained by who?" I press.

"My father, partly. And my shifu, Master Caen."

"They can fight like the Xia?"

Wren shakes her head. "My father is skilled at qi work, and Caen is one of Han's finest fighters. But I'm the only one who can bring the two together properly, the way the Xia did. It's in my blood," she finishes softly.

I remember her sadness at the temple in Ghost Court, her longing for her lost family. The same sense of loss rings in her voice now.

"Why were you even taught?" I go on, more gently now. "I'm guessing daughters of nobility don't usually get trained in martial arts."

"Actually," Wren says, "they often are. Especially in Ang-Khen and Han. Though it's seen as more of a ceremonial skill than one to be used in real battle."

"But yours isn't just an aesthetic practice."

"No."

"And it's a style that the original King himself outlawed."

"Yes."

"So why was it allowed?"

"It…wasn't. I was trained in secret."

Silence unfurls between us at this.

Wren remains still, not breaking eye contact. There's a defiance, a pride to the set of her shoulders and the way she lifts her spine tall, chin slightly tilted, that brings me back to the aloof girl I first met all those months ago. But despite her posture, that girl is looking at me with such tenderness in her eyes it makes my heart lurch, and all the intimacies we've shared shine within her warm irises, as luminous and sweet as stars.

Part of me is hurt by how much Wren has hidden from me—and I can tell she's holding back even more. But tightness knits my chest at the thought of losing her.

It hits me then how much trust she's putting in me by telling me this. I could ruin her with this information. Her entire *family*. The Hannos are some of the King's most trusted supporters, and here is Lord Hanno's daughter herself, a warrior trained in a forbidden language of fighting, within the palace of the demon whose ancestor massacred those who practiced it.

And I think I know why.

I take a breath, readying myself to ask her. But before I can say anything, Wren crosses the distance between us. Without a word, she reaches back and releases the sash round her waist.

I splash back, gaping at her. "What—what are you doing?"

"There are some things about myself I can't tell you," she interrupts, quiet and fierce, "but that doesn't mean I don't want to give myself *to* you. I'm always truthful to you in here, Lei." Her fingers hover over her heart. Then, holding the collar of her robes, she draws them off her shoulders and lets them drop to the floor in a cascade of silky fabric.

Wren's body is so different from the other girls. Lives of luxury have kept their figures soft, but hers is muscled and strong. Beautiful and dangerous. My eyes travel over her long, elegant neck; her wide shoulders; the deep shadow down the center of her chest, a line I long to follow with my tongue.

I return my gaze to her shining face. "Wren," I begin, but she shakes her head.

Slowly, not taking her eyes off mine, she climbs into the tub. As she slides down in front of me, water rolls over the edges and up to my neck in a warm wave that reminds me afresh that Wren isn't the only one who's naked.

I shrink back. "We—we can't do this. Not here. Someone could see."

"They're all sleeping." Her voice is husky. Low. Wet fingertips lift to my cheek. "Don't worry, no one can see through the steam. We'll hear them coming anyway." She moves closer, her breath hot against my face. Something more than desire shimmers in her eyes, some tender vulnerability that is betrayed in her voice as she goes on, "Last night I could have lost you."

The steam lifting from the water swirls around us, a soft cocoon.

"You saved me, Wren," I whisper. "Aoki, too. You got us out safely. I'm sorry I didn't thank you last night. It's just—"

"I know."

"I was shocked."

"I know."

"Scared."

Wren scoops her hand behind my head, dipping her forehead to mine. Her lashes flutter. "Me, too," she sighs.

"You didn't seem it."

"I'm trained not to. I'm trained to be strong. To not let anybody see my weaknesses. My fear. But I'm scared, too, Lei."

I lean back to look at her. Her face is grimy from ash and sweat, and her black hair is streaked with more dirt. She looks just how she sounds—tired. Broken. The circles under her eyes are deep, like bruised fruit. Tangling my fingers in her hair, I draw her close. I kiss each eye, as gently as I'm able. Then her lips.

Compared to our first kiss, this one is gentler, but no less deep.

Mouths, and softness, and the liquid heat of the steam. Our hands holding each other's faces in tight, as though we'd be lost without the press of the other's mouth to ours. There are words in our kiss. I feel them between our lips, unspoken but just as clear as if we had been talking. Or perhaps more clear *because* we're not. There's no hesitation or misunderstanding to block or diminish their meaning. Just the simplest, most instinctive language of forgiveness.

Forgiveness, and hope.

One of my hands moves down Wren's back, skimming her shoulder blades to nestle in the low curve of her spine as our bodies arc together under the water.

Footsteps. Entering the courtyard.

In an instant, we untangle. Wren jumps out of the tub. She slings on a bathrobe as a figure comes into view through the swirling mist.

Blue smirks at the sight of us—me, breathless and flushed, water shifting around me; Wren dripping water onto the wooden boards, the sash around her robe hastily tied. My lips feel swollen from the press of Wren's, and I resist the urge to cover them with my hands.

"This is intimate," Blue purrs.

"I was just leaving," Wren says smoothly, pushing her hair back over her shoulders.

Blue arches a brow. "Already? You haven't even washed your hair."

I glance at Wren, my breath hitching. Her hair is still matted with ash, and knotted now from my fingers. Giving Blue a cool, *I don't know what you're talking about* stare, Wren strides out of the courtyard, every bit as composed as usual. But I can tell by the way Blue's smile widens that she has noted my alarm. And while she may not know what just happened, she can certainly make a few guesses.

TWENTY-SIX

FOUR DAYS PASS. FOUR DAYS OF WAITING, holed up in the maze-like corridors of Paper House, speculating with the girls on the assassins and what must be happening outside the palace until there's nothing new to discuss. Then, at lunch on the fifth day, Madam Himura tells us that the court has finally finished its interrogation of the attackers.

Just as Chenna predicted, there will be an execution.

The room goes quiet at the announcement. Zhen and Zhin swap dark looks, and Chenna quickly lifts one hand, forming the same prayer motion across her brow that I saw her make at the koyo party. Next to me, Aoki lets out a long exhale.

"Serves them right," Blue says loudly. "Let the King show everyone what happens to those who oppose him."

Mariko nods, though she stays mute, picking at her nails, fingers spread on the tabletop.

"The execution will take place at sundown tonight," Madam Himura croaks. "Attendance is mandatory. You will return to your usual schedule the next day."

I meet Wren's warm-centered brown eyes across the table. I want to hear what she thinks, steal a moment of comfort from her words and her closeness. But Madam Himura sends us straight back to our rooms to begin yet another long sequence of preparations.

Usually, Lill has some freedom in what she dresses me in, provided she follows certain customs and expectations. But as she unfolds the robes I'm to wear to the execution, she tells me they were selected specifically by Madam Himura. "She was very strict about it," Lill says. "For all the Mistresses."

She doesn't have to explain why she's telling me this. As soon as I see the robes, I understand.

"It—it's too cruel," I say, almost whispering.

Lill avoids my eyes. "These are the King's orders, Mistress."

We don't speak as she dresses me in the plain black robes. Black—not white. The very opposite, the very *absence*, of our kingdom's mourning color.

It's clear what the King's message is. White is a color to be respected, and to be used for those we respect. Criminals don't fall into that category. Instead we dress in black to demonstrate our indifference to the assassins' suffering.

The thought that they'll die looking out to this, a sea of night, doesn't seem fair. Before leaving, I take an ivory ribbon from Lill's box of silks and tie it round my wrist, making sure it's hidden beneath my sleeve.

Our procession is somber as we make our way through the Outer Courts. There's a heaviness about the palace this afternoon. Even the sky and trees seem gray, as though the smoldering air from the attack on the theater has settled over the whole of the palace, a veil of smoke. The streets are packed, but the only sounds are the dull treading of foot- and hoof-steps and the rustle of fabric, the metal chime of spirit-warding talismans, snatches of whispered conversations that the wind whips away.

When we get to Ceremony Court, my eyes widen at the sea of people filling the vast square. Everyone who lives at the palace must be here—there are thousands of humans and demons of all three castes. At the center of the court are a stage and a separate viewing platform for court members, headed by the King's golden throne. The oryx carry us past the crowds, everything a whir of swirling ink-black robes. As soon as we arrive at the viewing platform, I go to Wren, pushing past jostling court officials craning for a better view.

She clasps my hand, low, so no one can see. Though she lets go a second later, she stays close. "Are you all right?"

I nod stiffly. "But I hate having to be here."

"Me, too." She takes something out of the fold of her robes just long enough to show it to me: a white flower, a tiny valley lily. Then she tucks it away. "It felt wrong," she explains. "Coming here without something to pay my respects. Especially considering what happened in the tunnel."

The sight of the flower sends a warm rush through my chest.

Carefully, I draw back my sleeve to reveal the ribbon at my wrist, and Wren's face softens. She gives my fingers another squeeze.

It takes half an hour for the entirety of the palace to arrive, the King turning up last in an extravagant palanquin carried by eight oryx-demons. I don't have a clear view of him through the thick crush of bodies as he settles on the throne, but even at this distance the sight of his curved horns makes the hairs on my arms lift. Somehow, I can tell he's smiling.

Soon after, the carriages with the assassins arrive to the thunder of drumbeats. Each is pulled by a pair of muscled black horses and marked with silks of deep obsidian. They stop before the stage, the horses stamping, clouds of steam blowing from their nostrils. An expectant hush ripples through the crowd.

First, the executioners step out. The assassins follow, stumbling from the carriages, gold circles shackled to their necks like dog collars.

The skin at my wrists tingles. Their chains look similar to the ones the shaman put around my ankles and wrists when I was in isolation.

All around us, the court erupts in a roar. The drummers beat harder, stirring the frenzy. I don't know whether the crowd is pretending to be excited for the King's benefit; unlike at the koyo party, there is a mix of castes and positions here. But my stomach lurches anyway. The whole thing is like a performance, with the crowd willing participants. I thread my fingers through Wren's. No one's paying attention to us, their focus all on the stage, and I need her right now, need the familiar warmth of her hands to ground me, to calm my already frantic heart from spiraling so far out of control that it breaks free—and me with it.

I want to scream. Thrash. Run at the King and tear that cruel smile off his face.

Blank, beige-colored masks have been strapped over the assassins' faces, curving creepily over their foreheads and noses to leave only the small lines of their mouths underneath. Another trick of this awful performance. Hide the faces of the people you're about to kill, so they don't seem human.

Then I think of the slaves at the koyo party. The woman on the bridge the night of the Unveiling Ceremony, her head caved in by a demon guard. Maybe it wouldn't make a difference even if the masks were off. It seems that to most demons, being Paper caste already makes you less than human.

The executioners are three Moon caste demons. There is a gray-coated wolf-man; a hulking crocodile demon with leathery, russet-scaled skin; and the white fox female who escorted me to the King's room that night. They must be the King's personal guards. Dull light glints off their long armored overcoats as they lead the assassins to the stage. While the other two drop to their knees to face the King in silence, the assassin being led by the wolf struggles against his bindings. He's shouting, lurching toward the throne. Even from here I can see the slash of red around the man's throat from where the golden collar digs in. It must be agony, but he keeps rearing forward, screaming words I can't make out over the braying crowd as the King regards him coolly.

The wolf soldier jerks the chain back. He slams his foot down on the man's back, forcing him to the floor, before dragging him onto the stage. I get a view of the wolf demon's face for the first time as he turns and my breath hitches.

It's Wren's wolf.

So that's why he seemed familiar—the Unveiling Ceremony. He stood at the King's side along with the fox and the crocodile demon.

I turn to Wren. "That's him, isn't it? The wolf you were with that night." When she hesitates, I say, "Please. No more lies."

Her lips part. Then she answers stiffly, "His name is Kenzo Ryu. Major Ryu. One of the King's personal guards. He oversees all the royal armies and advises the King on military tactics."

"And the other two?"

"The crocodile is General Ndeze. The white fox is General Naja. She's the highest-ranking female in the kingdom."

My brow furrows. "What about the Demon Queen?"

"Until she gives the King a male heir," Wren replies, "she's pretty much insignificant."

A thread of pity runs under her words.

"You don't think she will?"

"I'm not sure she *can*. There are rumors about the King's...

ability." She shoots me a sideways look. "No one would dare speak it here, but apparently some of the clans have given him a nickname. The Empty King."

It takes me a moment to understand. His fertility. Or rather, lack of it. A hazy memory returns of that first lunch in Mistress Eira's suites when Chenna asked whether the Demon Queen had produced any children for the King. Blue and Mariko had looked aghast. They must have heard the rumors before they arrived at the palace and couldn't believe Chenna would approach the subject so boldly.

Suddenly the King's anger makes even more sense. Not just anger—desperation. Because what is a King without an heir?

A warm, feather-light feeling rises in my belly.

Because what could Ikhara be without a Demon King?

Just then, the crowd falls silent as the King rises to his feet. He marches forward, his gold-plated hoof-fall punctuating the tense hush, a more controlled swagger in his gait than the last time I saw him. His gaze roams slowly over the crowd. I catch a glimpse of his arctic-blue eyes, the ugly smile on his handsome face.

"My loyal subjects, my fellow demons and humans." Magically amplified, his voice booms out, echoing off the walls. "It brings me no joy to stand before you today. Executions are ugly events— almost as ugly as the crimes from which they are born. As such, I could tell you that it would be better to close your eyes now. To turn away when the points of the blades pierce the black hearts of these criminals before us." The King rolls his shoulders back, chin tilting, voice gaining strength. "But that is the coward's way! Instead, we *must* watch. We *must* observe. To remind us of everything that has been built under the blessed rule of the Demon King. A rule that I share with each and every one of you. Because it is only together, demons and humans, good citizens of all eight provinces, working alongside one another in peace and alliance with all in their rightful place, that we can keep our kingdom strong!"

While the crowd cheers at this, I grind my jaw. *With all in their right-ful place.* I know exactly where he believes Paper castes' place to be.

"When an attack like the one masterminded by these anarchists occurs," the King continues, shouting to be heard over the noise, "it is an affront to our unity. To the world we have built so tirelessly over these past two centuries, with our blood and sweat and tears and hope. And we must come together in that very unity to bring down those who try to destroy us." He clasps two fists, raises them to the sky. "Today we demonstrate that ours is a power that cannot be broken!"

The noise of the crowd mounts, almost violent, a deep, wild roar. Wren and I don't join in, but I spot Aoki's shining face at the front of the viewing platform, her fists raised in the air with the others.

It hits me like a punch to the gut.

When the crowd has finally calmed down, the King strides up to the assassins. He bends down to face them. "You failed," he says simply.

They don't react. But just as he's about to turn away, the assassin who was giving the wolf trouble earlier pulls on his binds, neck arced upward, and spits in the King's face.

The crowd bellows. I brace myself, expecting the King to shout or strike the man. But his expression is composed. Calmly, he wipes his face with the back of one sleeve and smooths down his robes. Then he settles back onto the throne, his face cold.

His voice colder. "Executioners, prepare your weapons."

The crocodile, fox, and wolf soldiers pick up their swords, the crowd's braying growing louder. Each jian is long and thin with a jeweled hilt. The blades glint silver in the lowering light as the soldiers step behind the assassins to clear the view for the King.

It's almost dusk. As the sun dips beyond the palace walls, braziers around the stage burst suddenly into light, illuminating the scene in an eerie parallel of the attack on the theater.

Wind whips the flames sideways. I taste smoke in the air.

Shaking, I clutch Wren's hand tighter.

The soldiers draw back their swords—

The King raises his hand—

"Strike!"

I shut my eyes, but it's too late. The image of the blades disappearing into the men's torsos is there, a searing stain on the back of my eyelids. When I finally dare to look again, the assassins are slumped over, swords lanced through their chests.

Along with wearing black, the King sent out the order that we are not to make the sky gods salute to bless the assassins' souls as they rise to the Heavenly Kingdom. But the crowd is packed tight, so Wren and I make the sign with our free hands—her left, my right—our thumbs crossing together, palms turned out.

All around comes cheering and shouting. But though the King is talking, I don't hear a word. I can't tear my eyes away from the assassins, the jian sticking up from their backs like three broken spines and blood blooming across their clothes, winding down to paint the floor with ribbons of deep scarlet. The way they've collapsed is reminiscent of fallen dolls, discarded by their petulant owner.

Wren's heartbeat throbs against my palm, keeping time as anger rises within me. Hotter and fiercer than fear, stronger and surer than anything I've ever felt before, and as we stand hand in hand amidst the scream and bray of the crowd, there is no doubt when I promise myself that I will not give the King the chance to discard *us*.

One day, we will be the ones discarding *him*.

* * *

I go to Wren's room late that night, the house wrapped in postmidnight hush. She's awake when I come in, sitting up like she's been expecting me. She opens her arms and we lie under the blankets, limbs entwined, but it's not enough to stop the trembling, the wildness that's been rattling through me ever since the execution.

Wren is the one to break the silence. Her breath tickling my hair, she fans her hands across my shoulder blades and says, "I heard something about the assassins."

"What?" I murmur, face pressed into her neck.

"They were allied with the court. There are rumors that Steel and Moon officials were involved, too, and guards."

The news buoys me. "Why didn't the King say anything?"

"Because it would betray his weakness. It would be admitting he's vulnerable within his own palace. That there are those who defy him even in his own court."

"There are," I say, fingers threading with hers as I lift my face to kiss her. "Us."

The shadows are deep when I leave Wren's room. I head to the bathing courtyard to splash some water on my face—the memory of blood and gleaming blades still clings to my skin like dirt. But at the entrance to the courtyard, I stop.

A girl is sitting on the steps.

Moonlight catches on slender shoulders, the sheen of long, straight hair. The girl is hunched over, crying. It's barely audible, but I'd recognize the stifled sound of it anywhere. What I don't believe at first is *who* is doing the crying.

I pad forward tentatively. "Blue?"

She jerks at my voice, clambering to her feet at once. "Go away,

Nine," she hisses. Her usual scathing tone is dampened by tears. Her eyes are swollen, red-rimmed, but she doesn't wipe her tears away, as if ignoring them would make them disappear.

Gods. She's so obstinate she'll even defy *herself*.

"No," I say.

She looks as though I'd struck her.

"I know you hate me," I go on, standing my ground. "And I'm not really that keen on you, either. But you're hurting. You shouldn't have to go through this alone. No one should."

"I'm not alone," she sneers.

My eyes sweep the empty courtyard. "Sorry. Didn't realize you could see ghosts." Then I say, more gently, "Look, I'm sure Mariko would—"

"I don't want her seeing me like this," Blue blurts out, blinking rapidly as tears keep coursing down her cheeks.

"There's no shame in being upset," I tell her, and take a step closer. "What's wrong? Was it the execution?"

She turns away. Shakes her head. "The attack."

"At the theater?"

She nods jerkily.

"Is your father all right? Did something happen?"

A laugh spurts from her lips. The sound snaps through the quiet, a bitter bark that sends tingles down the backs of my arms. "Oh, he's *fine*. Not that he checked if *I* was. Not that he cares."

"I'm sure he cares, Blue. He's your father—"

Her voice pitches. "All that means is I'm a pawn to use in his game! He only cares about rising through the ranks of the court. Giving me to the King was just a step to secure his promotion." She lets out another mad laugh. "I'm the only one of us with parents in the palace, and they haven't visited me once."

"I'm so sorry," I say, reaching for her shoulder. But she shrugs my hand away.

"I don't need your pity, Nine!"

"It's not pity," I retort, my face hot. "It's understanding." I scrunch my hands. "Gods, why are you like this all the time? You're so adamant to put yourself apart from the rest of us when we're all going through exactly the same thing. The rest of us are trying to look after one another, but you keep trying to divide us."

Blue's top lip peels back. "We're not going through the same thing. It's nothing similar."

"Are you or are you not stuck here, forced to serve a man you don't care about?"

"You don't get it at all," she says in such a low hiss I barely catch it.

"What don't I get?"

"The difference is *you* aren't expected to like it." She clamps her lips together, jerking her head stiffly to one side. "I have a family here, a father who is important in the court. I can't go around refusing the King or speaking out against being a Paper Girl. And I keep thinking, maybe now I've been chosen, maybe now my father is one step closer to his promotion, he'll finally be happy with me." Her voice cracks. "I've done everything he asked. Been the perfect daughter. But from the way my parents act, most of the time you wouldn't even know they *have* one."

"Oh, Blue," I breathe. But she backs away, her wet cheeks shining in the moonlight.

"If you *dare*—if you tell anyone about this..."

"I won't," I promise, and I mean it.

But she pushes past me as though I were the one threatening her, leaving me alone with the eerie hush of the empty barrels and the rustle of wind through the swaying bamboo.

TWENTY-SEVEN

O N THE OUTSIDE, LIFE IN THE PALACE returns to normal in the weeks after the executions, the only main change for us being that we aren't allowed beyond Paper House without an escort of at least one guard. With the arrival of winter, the air grows icy, the wind hard and biting. Colors drain from the gardens like calligraphy paints being washed away. Since the executions, an air of unease has hung over the palace, and it seems a premonition somehow, all this gray and whiteness. A reminder that more death is to come. But while I continue to go dutifully with the other girls to classes and dinners, just as I had been doing all these months before, on the inside, everything is different.

With the increased security within the palace, everyone in Women's Court has been advised against leaving their rooms after nightfall. Even better, the King hasn't called for any of us in over a month, too busy with his hunt for the assassins' supporters and rumors of a dark new project that I suspect is just code for too much liquor. And as the days become shorter and the nights longer, this all gives Wren and me the cover we need to love each other in the dark.

As often as we can, we sink into the immediacy of our bodies moving together—our lips, fingertips, the hungry press of our thighs. Over the nights I learn how to lick the curving slopes of her skin, the way it makes her shudder when I run my tongue down the ridge of her spine. And even though I soon get used to Wren's body, I never lose any of the enjoyment. The wonder.

With every kiss, the pleasure is instant—a flood of heat, a fiery rush.

With every kiss, it consumes us.

In our first qi arts lesson, Master Tekoa told us that mastering control of our internal energy is about understanding the concept of "nowhere." Two words hidden inside the one: *now* and *here*. When we practice qi arts, he said, what we're really trying to do is to ground ourselves into the here and now. That being truly in the present means to disappear.

But with Wren it's the very opposite. Instead of disappearing, she makes me feel reappeared. Reimagined. Her touch shapes me, draws out the boldness that had been hiding in my core. Where the King's touch closed me, shut me down, Wren's opens me up. When I'm with her, every part of me is weightless and free, a soaring rush igniting my veins with desire as bright as sunlight.

Her kisses heal the parts of me that the King broke. They tell me: *You are strong, Lei. You are beautiful. You are mine.* And, always, most important: *You are* yours.

Because these kisses, these stolen nights with Wren, are the only thing I've had control of since coming to the palace, and it gives me satisfaction to know there are some things even the King does not have the power to stop. It builds my confidence that one day we'll be able to rebel with more than just our bodies and our love. That we will find a way to turn our growing hope and bravery into action.

Desire cannot be tamed, the King told me that night in his chambers. Well, he's got one thing right.

We might be Paper Girls, easily torn and written upon. The very title we're given suggests that we are blank, waiting to be filled. But what the Demon King and his court do not understand is that paper is flammable.

And there is a fire catching among us.

A month and a half after the executions, the King finally begins to summon us again.

Blue is first. After that night in the bathing courtyard, I can't help but feel sorry for her, knowing what I know about her now. But any pity I have is tempered by my relief at neither Wren nor me being called. These last few weeks have been a refuge, the two of us safe in the sanctuary of each other's arms, the spherical world of our small, secret geography. I always knew it was just an illusion of safety, a temporary reprieve. But I wasn't prepared for the fresh shot of fear at the moment the illusion is broken.

After that, the names click by, each bamboo chip delivered by royal messenger a countdown to the inevitable.

Chenna-zhi
Zhen-zhi
Aoki-zhi
Mariko-zhi
Zhin-zhi
Wren-zhi

As is custom, Wren has to stay behind after her name is announced for the preparations. We're in Mistress Eira's suite. Winter sunshine streams in through the open doors to her garden, glancing off the half empty plates and bowls on the table. I meet Wren's eyes, struggling to keep my expression level. While the world is bright around her, she has her back to the doorway, so her face is shadowed. The corners of her lips lift the tiniest fraction, more a grimace than a smile, and I get the strange idea that she's apologizing for something. Then she turns aside as Mistress Eira asks the rest of us to leave.

Numb, I get to my feet.

Someone nudges my shoulder. "Come on," Aoki says. "We have to go."

I've been staring. "Sure. Yes, sorry." With one last hopeful look to Wren—who doesn't return it—I follow Aoki out of the room.

"She seems a bit different, don't you think?" Aoki murmurs as we walk down the corridor, the other girls chatting ahead of us. "Wren, I mean."

I hardly hear her, too busy trying to breathe normally, to force thoughts of Wren and the King from my mind. "Oh? How so?"

"Just…she doesn't seem as focused anymore." Aoki throws me a sideways glance, slowing her pace. "You must have noticed. Has she said anything to you?"

"Not really. I guess it's just the stress of everything. Maybe she's homesick."

Aoki nods, though she's still watching me with an odd expression. "Some of the girls think she might be sneaking off at night to meet with a man."

I push out a laugh that I hope sounds disbelieving, but from the way Aoki doesn't react, I can tell she doesn't believe it. I tuck my hair behind my ears and carry on walking, a little faster now. "Which girls? And why would they even think that?"

"Zhin said she saw her the night she was coming back from the King. Wren was leaving her room. She didn't seem to be going to the toilet or to the maids' dormitory, because that's the direction Zhin was coming from."

"Maybe she couldn't sleep."

"Apparently she had shoes on, and an overcoat. Like she was going outside."

"So she just needed some air—"

"In the cold?" Aoki's nose wrinkles. "At three in the morning? With the guards outside?" She stops me with her arm. "I know you're close with her, Lei, but Wren is hiding something. I'm certain. I don't want you getting caught up in it."

If only she knew.

But I manage a nod. I palm my hands on the skirt of my robes and stride onward, wresting my face into an unfazed expression. "Thanks for telling me. I'll ask her about it tonight—*tomorrow*. I'm sure there's a simple explanation."

That night, as I wait for Wren to return, the hours crawl by. Every second is a slow, pulling agony. I pace my room so many times that my vision spins, the floor seeming to career sideways, and I eventually have to sit down before I faint. When footsteps finally sound in the corridor, I wait a few moments more before going to Wren's room. I don't mean to surprise her—I thought she'd have known I'd come. But I've only just slid the door shut behind me when she shoves me painfully against it, an arm across my neck, her eyes wide and alert.

She releases me immediately. "Lei! I'm so sorry." Blowing out an exhale, she circles her arms round my waist, dipping her forehead to mine. Her breath is sweet and warm on my skin. "I'm just on edge tonight. I didn't realize it was you."

"How was it?" I ask tentatively, shifting back.

She avoids my eyes. "He was…rough. More so than usual." I wince, and she carries on quickly, "But I expected he might be like this. The attack has exposed his vulnerability. He's angry. He's trying to reassert some of the power he's lost."

"So the rumors are true?" I say. "The assassins *were* helped from within the court?"

She nods. "I heard that he arrested eleven officials on suspicion of being involved with the attack just this morning. He's out for blood."

"Hasn't he had enough already?"

In the dark, Wren's eyes seem to flare as she answers huskily, "Not nearly."

Gently, I help her out of her clothes. She's wearing a tangerine-colored ruqun set with jewels, a slit running up the length of one side of the skirt. But as I pull her robes off, I discover that the slit isn't a part of the design; the skirt has been slashed clean in two. Only a makeshift knot at its waist was holding it up.

I swallow, a prickly sensation creeping across the back of my neck. The sky is clear tonight, a moonbeam slanting into the room. By its light, I make out the dark blossoms of bruises on Wren's skin. There's one on her shoulder. More along her hips. A huge handprint wrapped around her throat.

I stare at them, heart wild. Anger charges through me so forcefully I almost retch.

"How *dare* he," I snarl.

Wren grabs my hands. "Don't waste your thoughts on him," she says, lifting my fingertips to her lips.

"*But—*"

"Lei, please. At least not tonight. Not now. I can handle pain— it's only temporary. And Madam Himura will have a shaman heal me tomorrow."

I gape at her. "Do you realize how sick that sounds? 'Dear

shamans, won't you please give us some magic so we can go back to the King and get broken all over again?'"

Wren kisses my hands softly. "No one said anything about breaking."

We lie down and draw the blankets over us. Moonlight silvers Wren's face, draws a sharp outline along the line of her cheekbone and the hollow of her neck. My fingers trace it down to the upward roll of her shoulder.

"Some of the girls are suspicious of you." I say. "Aoki told me earlier. Zhin saw you leaving your room at night, and they think you might be going to meet someone. A lover. You have to be more careful, Wren."

Her brow wrinkles. "They don't know where I'm going."

"Neither do I."

"Lei—"

"I know," I say before she can finish. "You're trying to protect me."

"You say it like it's a bad thing."

I sigh. "It's just, I'd prefer it if you let me decide whether to be protected." My thumb skims her shoulder, sloping up into the warm dip of her neck. "Maybe I can handle it. Whatever you've got going on, maybe I could help."

Wren closes her eyelids. Tiredly, she takes my hand and moves it to cup her cheek, her palm on top of mine. She opens her eyes. In the moonlight they are bright—the opposite of her voice when she whispers, "You can't. Not with this. No one can."

I want to press her more. But remembering what she went through tonight—the thought of it makes bile fly up my throat—I stop myself. Pulling her close, I burrow my nose in her skin, drawing her cool, ocean scent into my lungs. She smells like home, like happiness and safety and hope and ... *love*.

I want so much in that moment to tell Wren how I feel. To offer her the words that come to my lips every time she kisses me now, every time she even looks my way. But I wait too long and my courage fades. Instead I murmur, "Can you imagine a world where we're free to be with each other?"

"Actually," she replies after a pause, "I can."

"Then take me there, Wren. Please."

She answers, so quiet I barely hear it.

"I will."

I leave her room shortly after, so full of the glowing thrum being with Wren brings, and the promise in her words, that a smile lifts my lips. So when I meet Aoki's eyes where she's watching from her own doorway, half wrapped in shadow, arms rigid at her sides, it takes a few seconds for the giddy look to drop from my face.

Perhaps if I'd not been smiling, I'd have been able to hide it. I could have said we were just talking, the same way Aoki and I still do some nights, though admittedly not as often recently. But I know that she realizes the truth the minute she sees my expression.

It's how she looks when she talks about the Demon King. Radiant. Lit from within.

Without a word, Aoki pivots on the spot and slams the screen door shut behind her. The sound has bite in the quiet of the hallway. I lurch after her, not caring in that moment who might hear. She backs away as I enter her room, and I falter, stung.

The look on her face. I never would have believed she could look at *me* that way.

"Please, Aoki," I say, my throat narrowing. "You—you can't tell anyone."

Her laugh is hollow. The scowl warping her mouth makes her look ugly, so unlike my sweet friend, the girl whose laughter lifts my soul like sunshine. She usually seems so young, full of lightness, her insides practically effervescent. But there's something about the way she's holding herself right now, as if she'd aged years in the blink of an eye.

"Is that how little you think of me?" she says, and there's hurt in her voice, too. "I thought we were friends. That we told each other everything."

"How could I have told you about this?" I cry, flinging my arms wide. "I know how close you are with the King! You wouldn't approve—"

"Of course I wouldn't! We're Paper Girls! We're not meant for anyone else."

My fingers tighten into fists. "*He* made that choice for us. How is that fair?"

"It's not about fairness. It's about duty."

"Gods, you sound just like Madam Himura."

"Good," Aoki flings back. "That means I'm doing my job well."

I scowl at her. "No. It means you're not thinking for yourself."

Aoki stiffens, anger rising from her like heat-shimmer on wet stones. Her eyes are fierce, and I realize what she's going to say a second before she speaks.

"I love him."

The sentence hits me with a physical weight. Silence stretches between us, a dark, pulsing thing.

I just about get the words out. "You hated him, once."

"I didn't know him then." Aoki softens, voice curling like a sleeping cat's tail, and she kneads her hands in front of her, wide eyes glowing in the dark. "He's good to me, Lei—kind and caring and fair. He's even said he'll consider making me his queen if I continue to please him."

I almost choke. "His *queen?*"

Her cheeks flush, and she shrinks back. "You don't think I'm good enough for the throne?"

"No! That's not it—"

"Because he could, if he wanted to. Instead of a Demon Queen, he could have a Paper Queen. *I* could be his wife."

My jaw slackens. Scenes from the past few months plow into me, one after the other: Aoki's eyes brightening when she talks about the King; what she told me that night at the koyo celebrations; her excitement at the executions; the look on her face every time the bamboo chip arrives and her name isn't the one on it. Like mine for Wren, Aoki's love for the King has been building over the months. I've just been so wrapped up in my own feelings that I didn't realize it.

I'm supposed to be her best friend, and I didn't even notice she was falling in love with a monster.

It takes me a while before I can speak. I lift my chin, looking her straight on. "You're too good for him. You deserve more."

"More?" Her irises are shiny. "What could be more than being his queen?"

After all the words we've thrown at each other, the silence that follows is horribly loud. It grows, stretches, spirals out, a physical distance, building feet and miles and whole countries and lifetimes between us, between me and the pure, beautiful girl who once blushed at the mention of just a kiss and worried that she wouldn't be enough for the King.

"I should go," I say eventually in a constricted voice. I wait in case she disagrees with me. But her expression is just as defiant as before.

I turn to the door, eyes prickling. As my hand lifts to slide it open, her voice sounds behind me.

"You really love her?"

There's a flash of the Aoki I know in her voice: tender, compassionate.

I spin round. "Yes," I reply eagerly, offering her a smile. I step forward. "Oh, Aoki, I'm so sorry—"

"You shouldn't."

The rest of my sentence tumbles away. In an instant, coldness returns between us, as jolting as a wave of ice water. Her look is so hard it's painful to hold, and I falter back toward the door, one arm wrapped across my chest, like a shield.

"At least *I* chose who I fell in love with," I say roughly.

As soon as it's out I want to take it back. But I can tell by the look on Aoki's face that it's too late, and I hurry from her room before I make it even worse, tears blurring my eyes as something splinters deep in my chest.

TWENTY-EIGHT

SCREAMING WAKES ME THE NEXT DAY. Instead of the usual gong, and too early, the dark still shivering with almost-burnt-out candles and traces of moonlight on the floor. A horrible raw sound that tears through the night on broken wings. Not even screaming. *Wailing*...wild and untamed.

The sound is close. It's accompanied by shouting, sharp words, and the rap of talons on the floor. Madam Himura.

Something is happening to one of the girls. That's my first thought. My second is—

Wren.

I lurch outside, sucking in a hiss at the coldness of the floor-boards on my bare soles. The other girls are already up, looking out from their doorways, faces tight with apprehension. From the room opposite, Aoki meets my eyes before quickly turning her cheek.

"Please!" a girl screams. "It won't happen again, I promise!"

Halfway down the corridor, Mariko is sprawled on the floor. The robe of her nightdress hangs open, revealing the heavy curves of her breasts, the pale flesh of her legs. She struggles, hanging on to where Madam Himura is gripping her hair to drag her down the hall.

"Let's just hear what she has to say," Mistress Eira pleads. She's crouching, trying to get between Mariko and Madam Himura.

The eagle-woman swings out with her cane. "You're too soft on them, Eira!" she snarls, and Mistress Eira doubles over as the cane cracks across her back. "I told you before, when Lei refused the King. You show them the slightest bit of leniency and this is how they repay you!"

"Blue!" Mariko cries. Her eyes are crazed as she seeks her out of the watching faces. "Blue, help me!"

Blue stiffens in her doorway. A glimmer of something passes across her face, but she doesn't move.

Wren steps forward instead. "Madam Himura," she asks steadily, "what is Mariko being punished for?"

Madam Himura's yellow eyes flare. "For being a slut! She was found by one of my maids last night, legs spread for a soldier."

I'm reminded suddenly of Wren's words that night in the isolation room. She said that the guard outside my room had slipped away to meet a girl. Was it Mariko?

"I'm sorry!" Mariko sobs, her face splotchy and red. "I won't do it again!"

"Of course you won't," Madam Himura retorts. "Because you're never coming back to the palace."

Mariko freezes. "Wh-what do you mean?"

A wheezing laugh escapes Madam Himura's throat. "You think you can defy the King in such a way and an apology is all that's needed to make up for it? Foolish girl!"

I wince, instinctively reeling back as she turns her attention to the rest of us. She glares around with her cutting eyes. The layered feathers on her humanlike arms ruffle open as they spread into the beginning of wings, making her seem twice her usual size.

"Come, the rest of you," she commands coolly. "You're about to discover what happens to paper that turns rotten."

Using her wings to steady herself against Mariko's struggles, she drags Mariko down the corridor. With no choice but to follow Madam Himura's orders, I pad behind them with the rest of the girls and our maids. Mariko's maid, a plump dog-form girl called Vee, is sobbing so hard she has to stuff her hands over her mouth to muffle the sound.

"It's all right," Lill whispers, helping her along. "It'll be all right."

She looks up, meeting my eyes where I'm watching over my shoulder, and it hits me that it's the first time I've ever heard her lie.

We trail Madam Himura to an empty room. She throws Mariko down the minute she gets inside. "Get Doctor Uo," she directs one of the maids as we file in with reluctant steps.

Mariko thrashes on the floor. "Please!" she begs. "I can't leave, not before I see Kareem! Where is he? Where did you take him?"

Madam Himura glares down her hooked beak-nose. "Your soldier is being dealt with by General Ndeze. He'll be stripped of his title and banished from the palace. That's *if* the King is feeling generous."

Mariko dissolves into wails.

"I can't watch this," I breathe to Wren next to me.

"We have no choice," she replies.

"I don't care." I take a step forward. Wren hisses at me, but I ignore her, rounding on Madam Himura. "Why can't we take lovers?" I ask her loudly, throwing out an arm. "The King has his pick every night, and when we leave, there'll just be a new set of girls for him to play with."

Her eyes widen. "*What* did you say?"

"Maybe if the King weren't such a cruel, disgusting excuse of a leader, we wouldn't look for comfort elsewhere—"

Though I knew it was coming, the crack of her cane still takes my breath away.

I double over, clutching my jaw. The metallic tang of blood fills my mouth. Wren pulls me back before Madam Himura can strike me again, but her attention is distracted just then by the doctor's arrival.

Doctor Uo looks as though he'd just woken up. His robes are mussed, his hair matted. "What's going on?" he asks, scratching at one curving boar tusk, blinking out from behind his round spectacles.

Madam Himura points to Mariko. "This girl has forfeited her place in the palace. She must be branded."

The doctor's expression is as blank as when he was inspecting me. "I see." Mariko scuttles away as he crouches down in front of her. "Someone hold her still," he commands, and I'm thrown back to the assessments shortly after I arrived, the helplessness I felt as the doctor stripped me.

I massage my jawbone, smearing blood across my sleeve.

Madam Himura waves at the waiting maids. "Help the doctor!"

They move forward reluctantly. Mariko lashes out when they get close, catching Lill in her ribs with an elbow. At once, Madam Himura whirls forward and slaps Mariko so hard it sends her cheek into the floor with a sickening crunch.

"Struggle all you want, girl," she spits. "You're just going to make the scarring worse."

It's not until the next moment, when Doctor Uo takes a knife from his bag, that I understand what is happening.

The doctor holds Mariko's face still. "Someone quiet her!" he orders as she starts to scream.

A maid brings over a wad of fabric. The doctor stuffs it into her mouth, muffling her cries. He raises the blade to her forehead.

The first incision heightens her shrieking. But by the last, her sobs are silent.

When he finally moves away, I see the bloody strokes of the character cut into Mariko's forehead: *Lan.*

Rotten.

"Now everyone will know what you did," Madam Himura hisses. She turns to us. "Remember this, any time you think you can defy the King." Her eyes land on me. "You will not get away with it." Then she flaps an arm, barking, "Back to your rooms! You have classes to get to. Don't think this has changed any of your duties."

I hesitate, and Wren draws me away. "Don't push it," she whispers.

"What'll happen to her?" I ask in a weak voice as we head down the corridor.

The rest of the girls are silent. As Blue shoves past her, practically running, Chenna stares down at the floor, her lips forming silent prayers. Zhen and Zhin walk hand in hand, shoulder to shoulder. I try to catch Aoki's eyes, but she's staring glassily ahead, absently picking at the sleeves of her robes.

"Mariko's marked now," Wren explains under her breath. "She won't ever be able to get a job, be married. She'll either starve to death or find work in the only places that'll take her."

"Prostitution houses?"

She nods, and I press my lips tight, battling the urge to retch.

When we get back to our rooms, I knock on Blue's door. She doesn't answer, but I go in anyway.

She's standing by the window, staring out. Morning light filtering through the half drawn shutters frames her outline in pale gold. There's something so painful about the stiff way she's holding her body, as though to keep herself together. As though she'd fall apart—literally, piece by piece, limb by limb, joints unraveling in an inelegant dismantlement—if she released herself even the tiniest fraction.

"Blue—" I start.

She interrupts, quiet. "Go away." Her voice breaks on the words. She repeats it, louder, with a jerk of her neck: "Go away!"

"I'm here," I say, moving closer. "I just wanted you to know. If you ever need to talk or anything, I'm here."

Blue spins round, her face streaked with tears, her eyes manic. "I said, go away!" she shrieks, and lurches toward me.

I stumble out, not stopping until I get back to my room. Inside, I stagger to the window and gulp in air, fingers shaking where they're twined around the latticed woodwork. It takes me a long time to get my breathing to slow, and even then I can still hear the ghost of Mariko's screams.

That night, I write home.

For months I've kept my letters positive, cracking jokes as if it were just another day in the herb shop. But tonight I can't do it. Outside, the wind howls, making the building creak and groan. There's the growl of thunder in the distance. Winters are even harder in Xienzo, and I picture my father and Tien in the garden, wrapped in furs as they brush frost off our dying plants with frozen fingers, their breath curling before them.

It's not right. *I* should be there. I should be with them, my own fingers chilled, my own exhalations making clouds in the air.

It takes me a while to come up with a way to express myself in the letter without giving too much away, but I get it right on the third attempt. I have no idea if my father and Tien will even read this. I've still not heard a thing back despite writing regularly all this time, and if I'm honest with myself, I know why. It's not hard to notice how Mistress Eira evades my questions whenever I ask her about the letters.

Still. Something keeps me writing.

Maybe it's the feeling of connecting with my father and Tien, even just in my imagination. Or the knowledge that this is my last link with home, and if I stop writing it's like acknowledging that I've given up hope of ever returning.

Tonight, my letter is short.

Dear Baba,

Do you remember that day we went to the stream where you found Bao and we stayed until sunset, our toes dipped in the water, the air so still and quiet, and there was just that one lonely bird singing?

Well, today's been just about as good as that day.

Missing you more than ever.

All my love,
Lei

Tears cloud my eyes as I roll the letter closed. That day was the first anniversary of the raid on our village that stole Mama away.

It was one of the worst days of my life.

I'm just about to lie down when I sense movement in the hallway—and somehow, I know it's Wren, leaving Paper House.

Anger hurtles down my veins, so sudden and strong it surprises even me. I jump to my feet. How dare she. How *dare* she, of all the days, when she knows exactly what could happen to her if she's found out.

What that would do to *me*.

I wait as long as I can bear before following her. Wind lashes my skin as I charge across the dark gardens. The air is frozen. Before I left, I threw a heavy brocade coat over my nightdress, but my feet are bare, the frosted ground numbing my toes. My hair whips around my raw cheeks.

It takes me longer than I anticipated to reach the pine forest where I've seen Wren disappear to before. I trudge through it, keeping to a straight line in the hopes that it's the right direction. After a few minutes I start to worry that I won't be able to find her, but as I pick my way over mossy roots and brambles of thorns, sounds rise from up ahead. Half hidden under the noise of the wind, I make out grunts, panting, the crush of leaves. Something dark and awful flares to life in my belly. It—it couldn't be.

Could it?

A few seconds later I emerge into a clearing. The long trunks of pines close in tight, a leafy canopy overhead. And in its center: Wren and the wolf. Not doing what I feared, but something else, something worse.

Fighting.

My heart bounces to my throat. I'm about to dash forward to tackle him off her, when I notice how none of their blows are followed through, just quick contact to indicate they've landed. Their movements seem practiced and familiar, dancelike almost. Wren's hair flies around her as she ducks a sweeping kick. She retaliates with a jab of her hands, the wolf's powerful haunches propelling him back. They're training.

Just then, Wren makes a leaping turn—and spots me.

Her eyes are the same icy white as that night under the theater. It takes a second for them to drain back to their usual fawn-brown. She lands messily but is upright at once, brushing down her clothes. "Lei," she says, breathless, starting forward.

The wolf looks around. His ears prick when he sees me, and with a whip of his gray-white tail he flies around, but Wren grabs him.

"Wait!" she shouts. "It's all right, Kenzo—"

"She shouldn't be here!" he growls.

"She won't tell—"

"How do you know?"

"I just know!"

"How is that—"

"Because I love her!"

Wren's shout is almost swallowed by the wind, but her words reach me as clearly as if she'd bent to whisper them in my ears. Everything seems to still—the growl of the incoming storm, the sway of the trees in the wind. Our eyes catch across the clearing. Wren's look, vividly fierce and beautifully soft at the same time, wrenches something inside me. I feel her heartbeat as if we were pressed together, chest to chest, cheek to cheek; I know its beat as surely as my own.

She expels a shaky breath, her face softening, "And," she says quietly, turning to Kenzo, "I think she loves me, too. So yes, I trust her. *We* can trust her."

Kenzo is still glaring at me. Wren tugs on his arm, half human, half furred, muscled wolf. His lips uncurl, hiding his fanged canines. But his ears are still pointed, the tendons in his neck corded.

"So that's how it is," he says, breath furling from his long, muzzle-like jaw.

"Yes."

"Well, she still shouldn't be out here."

Wren nods. "Give us a minute?"

With a last terse look my way, the wolf turns on his heels and bounds into the forest.

Wren crosses the clearing. In an instant, my anger fades. Tears are wetting my face before she's even reached me, and she frowns, thumbing them away.

"Lei?" she says, her gaze moving over my face. "What's wrong? Is it what happened to Mariko?"

I curl into her arms. "Everything," I say thickly.

She holds me close, waiting until my breaths finally calm. Then she draws back, palms cupping my face.

"What you said," I mutter, my cheeks warm under the heat of her palms and the sweet softness of her look. "Just then. To Kenzo. Did you—do you—"

"I do," she whispers.

My breath catches. "Me…me, too."

Her lips part, a sigh escaping them. Gently, she presses her mouth to mine. Then she steps back. "I'm sorry, Lei, but you have to get back to the house. It's not safe for you to be here."

I scrub my tears away with the back of my hands. "I'm not going anywhere," I tell her. "Not before you tell me what's going on." As she starts to protest, I shake my head and wind my fingers through hers, pulling her closer. "You're risking everything. Your life, *and* mine. Because if anything happens to you, I don't know how I'll cope. You're all I have, Wren. I need you."

"You *have* me, Lei."

"So tell me. No more lies."

Our gazes are fixed together. And for a moment this is all my world is: the feel of Wren's presence, closer than a heartbeat, and the brilliant, deep brown of her soft-centered eyes.

I squeeze her fingers. "It's time."

She regards me in silence. Then, finally, she nods.

"Everything I've told you so far is true," she begins, gripping my hands. "I promise. But I've never told you *why*. Why Ketai rescued me and brought me up as a Hanno. Why I'm here in the palace." She wets her lips. "Because when my father went to the mountains of Rain following the rumors of the Xia's massacre, he wasn't just searching for survivors. He *knew* there'd be survivors. Or rather, that there'd be one." She loosens a long breath. "Me.

"The night of the massacre, the Hannos' most trusted fortune-teller had a vision of a baby nestled in the snow. My father set out to find it with the intention of training it to continue the Xia bloodline. Not only would one of the Xia be skilled enough to assassinate the King, but, just as important, only this sole remaining Xia—who'd had their entire clan murdered before them—would have the hunger to do so."

Assassinate.

The word hangs in the air, sharp as a sword edge.

"The fortune-teller hadn't known the sex of the baby," Wren continues. "My father had been expecting a boy, but when he found me, he realized it was better this way. There are countless male assassins. The problem is getting them close enough to the King in the first place. A young girl dressed up in robes and elegant manners might be able to gain access where others could not."

"But what about Kenzo?" I interrupt. "Couldn't he...?"

She shakes her head. "My father and his allies have spent years getting him to the position he's in now. We need him there. Assassinating the King is one thing, but if the court remains loyal to him, what good would it do? Kenzo is our highest-ranking infiltrator. He's integral to seeing this change through. Once the King is dead, he can help steer the court to where we need it. It won't work if he's under any suspicion."

"So it's all down to you."

Wren nods, lips taut. "That's how I knew about the trap door in the theater. How I get around at night without being caught. I've studied the palace since I was young, learned every corner of it. And as a Paper Girl, I'm able to get close to the King without any guards around." Her eyes are fire. "I'm going to do it, Lei. I'm going to kill him."

Thunder rolls overhead, the wind still ice-cold and lashing. But the world seems far away, a space of stillness opening up around Wren and me, filled with my fear and her words and our love and the meaning, the incredible consequence, of what she's telling me.

"You've been alone with him so many times," I say, the words sticking in my throat. "Couldn't you have done it by now? The first time he called you?"

She shakes her head stiffly. "Other things have to align first. The timing is crucial. Trust me, Lei, if there were any way I could've avoided sleeping with the King, I would have found it." She pauses. "My father would have found it."

"So you don't know when it will happen?"

"Not yet. But it won't be long. Kenzo says things are almost ready."

As if he'd heard his name, there's the sound of leaves crunching underfoot. The wolf slinks back into the clearing. He keeps his distance but watches us, tail flicking, bronze eyes glinting in the moonlit clearing.

Wren circles her hands around my wrists. "You have to go, Lei. We've still got some training to do."

Training. Understanding rolls over me again. I'd had suspicions that this was what she was up to, but it's different knowing it. I get a flash of Wren in the tunnel under the theater, with her white eyes— but this time it is the King she is approaching, the King's heart she is driving a knife into.

For the first time, I question whether he truly deserves it.

It's only a passing thought. Because an instant later I remind myself of the Paper caste slaves at the koyo party. The way he coldly ordered the assassins' executions. Mariko's screams, just this morning, a few short hours ago. The King's hot mouth on my skin, how easily he tore my clothes apart; the pain and hunger of the week that followed.

I recall my promise at the executions. More than anything, I want to be free. Not just free of the palace, but free once I'm *outside* of it, too. How can that happen in a world where its King allows demons to do whatever they want to those they deem inferior? How can I live in happiness when I know now what happens to Paper castes all across Ikhara?

Can you imagine a world where we're free to be with each other?

Actually, I can.

Then take me there, Wren. Please.

I will.

So this is what she meant.

"Lei," Wren says again, after a glance over her shoulder at Kenzo. "You have to go. Now."

But I don't move. "Let me stay." The words are out of me before I've even realized they were there. "I want to help."

She pulls back. "What?"

"You're going to assassinate the King, and I can help."

Wren flinches, a deep furrow lining her forehead. "I don't mind risking my own life," she says sharply, "but I will *not* risk yours." She tugs on my arm. "Come on. I'll take you back to the house."

"But—"

She closes her eyes. "*Please, Lei,*" she begs, and there's so much tiredness in her voice that I can't bring myself to argue anymore. At least, not right now.

We trudge back to Paper House in silence. Wren plants a kiss to my crown when we reach the entrance. "I meant what I said," she murmurs.

"I love you. And you *are* helping me already, whatever you think. Just by loving me back. It makes me strong. It gives me more to fight for."

I bite back a reply, not trusting myself to speak as she hugs me tightly against her before she turns and jogs back to the forest with long, loping steps.

When I'm back in my room, I lie on my sleeping mat, trembling despite the furs wrapped around me. I stare up at the ceiling until the shadows seep from the room and the weak light of a winter morning settles in its place. Since that night at the theater, I'd somehow known about Wren, known that her fighting skills and Xia heritage were not just coincidence. But now it's finally become real.

Sometime soon she will try to kill the King.

And it's a fight she might not win.

I want to jump up, run back to the moonlit clearing, beg Wren to reconsider. Even if the King must die, there must be some way it can happen without *her* life being in danger, too. The icy focus in her eyes as she approached the assassin in the tunnel under the theater returns to me. How the grip of Xia magic overtook her, giving her more strength than a human girl should have. Maybe that's enough. Maybe years of training and her warrior heritage can protect her.

But this is the *King*.

The King, with his bull-driven power and lean, ironlike muscles. His deep, booming voice. I remember the savagery in his eyes that night at the koyo party, and before that, when he threw me down onto his bed and I felt more like a fragile human than ever before.

I shiver, cradling my knees to my chest. Because beneath her Xia heritage, and no matter how incredible she is to me, that's all Wren is in the end—a human girl. And we have all been taught what happens to Paper that tries to defy demons.

It gets torn apart.

TWENTY-NINE

THE NEXT MORNING, AOKI COMES TO my door just as I'm leaving to go to hers.

We say it at the same time. "I'm sorry."

I throw my arms around her, and she half laughs, half sobs, lacing her arms round my waist. "I thought it would be harder than that," she sighs against my chest.

"No," I reply, squeezing her tighter. "It should have been easier. I'm so sorry. Some of the things I said that night…"

She clears her throat. "Some of the things *I* said." We pull apart, and she gives me a wobbly smile, though her face is serious. "Just promise me, promise you'll be careful, Lei. I couldn't bear it if anything happened to you. After Mariko yesterday…"

The echo of her screams seems to reverberate down the corridor.

"I know," I say. "It's terrible. And it made me realize just how stupid our argument was. It could have been me in her place, and if that was the last conversation we had——"

Aoki's freckled nose wrinkles as she says firmly, "It will *not* be you." Her fingers loop around my wrist. "You still haven't promised that you'll be careful."

"I promise," I lie.

Aoki nods, seemingly satisfied. Then she hesitates. "Lei?" she says gently. "You do know you'll be called tonight, right?"

Her words lift the hairs on my arms. Of course I knew it had to happen. The only reason I wasn't summoned last night was because the King was too busy dealing with the fallout of Mariko's affair. But all the other girls have been called already, so it was only a matter of time.

It's clear to me now that he purposefully left me until last to torture me.

I remember Wren's declaration last night, her heartbeat tripping against mine. *I love you . . . It makes me strong. It gives me more to fight for.*

"I'm sorry," Aoki murmurs. "I wish there was something I could do."

"I'm just glad to have you back." I force a smile, and say in the lightest tone I can manage, "Anyway, we've got loads to catch up on. In your absence, Blue's become my best friend and we've started a Madam Himura fan club. We're calling ourselves the Beakies."

Aoki giggles. "How do I sign up?"

But as soon as we loop our arms together to head to the bathing courtyard, our smiles disappear. We walk on in silence, Aoki's words about the King calling me tonight slinking round my neck like an invisible noose slowly tightening.

Just as Aoki predicted, the royal messenger delivers my name at lunch later that day.

I take the bamboo chip from Madam Himura with trembling fingers, not hearing a word she's saying. It's all I can do not to look across the table at Wren. She's watching me—her gaze is like a call, a song I always want to answer. But I keep my eyes down as Madam Himura orders the girls out. It's taking everything in me just to sit here feigning calm and not throw the chip squarely at Madam Himura's smug face. I can't handle seeing Wren's expression as well.

The girls file out. Wren's footsteps slow as they pass.

"You too, Wren-zhi," the eagle-woman snaps.

I stare down, waiting for Wren to leave. A few moments later, there's the sound of the door sliding.

"So," Madam Himura says once we're alone.

I look up, gold eyes meeting yellow.

"You know what'll happen if you fail me again."

I grit my teeth. "Yes, Madam Himura."

She stamps her cane and gives me a dismissive wave with a feathered arm. "Rika! Take Lei for her ye lesson."

The journey to the Night Houses passes in a blur. When we get to Zelle's room, I'm a little nervous to see her after what happened last time, but she greets me warmly, with no trace of anger or suspicion.

"I didn't get a chance to thank you," I say, kneeling opposite her on the bamboo-mat floor. "For not telling Mistress Azami what I was doing in her office."

She lifts a shoulder, her dark hair falling past her ears in soft waves. "It would have caused more trouble than it was worth. And I can't blame you for wanting to find out what happened to your mother." She pauses. "I'm sorry it wasn't the outcome you were hoping for."

I drop my eyes to my lap. "Thanks."

"I lost my mother, too, you know," she says.

My head jerks up. "You did?"

"She was a courtesan," Zelle continues, a stiffness to the lift of her neck. She runs a hand over the viridian-green silks she's wrapped in today, her fingernails picking at the silver threads patterning it. "Like me, here for any demons in the palace with a Paper fetish. Mistress Azami gives all of us medicine to keep us from getting pregnant, but it doesn't always work, and once a courtesan has a baby, she's not allowed to work anymore."

I think of Mariko. "What happened to her?"

"Right after she had me, she was sent as a gift to one of the court representatives in Jana. I've never even met her."

"I'm so sorry."

Zelle gives a little shake of her head. "That's just life in the palace," she says with a bitter echo of her crooked grin.

"Have you...have you ever thought about escaping?" I ask quietly.

Her eyes glint. "Every second."

I have no idea how to respond to that, so we fall silent. Eventually, Zelle says, "I heard about Mariko. You know, it's not the first time that's happened. Some girls manage to keep their affairs hidden, but it's easy to get caught. I've had a few close shaves myself."

"You have a lover?" I say, gaping at her.

"Of course," she replies airily with a twirl of a wrist. "Hundreds, in fact. That *is* my job, isn't it?" She gives me a wink, but there's something pinched about her expression as she continues, "Yes, I did mean a lover of my own, not a client. Though it was a couple of years ago now."

I shift forward. "Can I ask what happened?"

"He died," Zelle says simply.

"Oh. I'm—I'm so sorry."

"It's all right," she replies with an odd little shrug. She casts her face to the window, and the muffled light glazes it into a white-gray mask. "I've come to terms with it. Anyway, if he were still here, we'd have been caught eventually. Then we'd both be dead."

Again, we fall quiet. Zelle must sense my mood, because she doesn't press to start the lesson. It's the coldest day so far this winter, the wind full of bite, but her room is warm, lantern light flickering off her glossy hair and making our shadows shiver.

As we sit in silence, something wild starts to wing through me.

A ragged, reckless feeling. I didn't sleep at all last night, thoughts about Wren and the assassination plans spinning on through the long, dark hours. Since finding out everything, my heart has been swinging between defiance and fear. Sometimes all I can think of is how powerful the King is, and how delicate Wren's human frame is. How futile it's been to believe we can defy him with just our love and hope. But seeing my name on the bamboo chip at lunch just made it even clearer how if we don't do anything, that's what the rest of our lives will be—waiting for someone to call us to do something we can hardly bear to do. Whether we become wives to generals after our year as Paper Girls, or stay on in the palace as courtesans, or artists, or teahouse owners, it will all be a performance. And all we'll ever be are actors in our own lives.

The first time I kissed Wren, I'd already decided that I wasn't going to let that life become my future. I might not have known at the time, but that's what that first kiss was—a promise. A seal. Not to Wren, but to myself.

I'm not spending the rest of my life a prisoner.

"*I* have one," I say suddenly. It comes out before I even know I'm about to speak. I risk a glance up, testing Zelle's reaction. "A…a lover."

She gives me a small smile. "I know," she says, and I can't help but laugh.

"Is it that obvious?"

"It was that obvious even in our *first* lesson." She tilts her head. "But it's progressed to something more now, hasn't it?"

I nod.

"You're in love."

My answer comes, bright and defiant. "Yes."

Zelle watches me, her face impassive. Then she lets out a sigh, folding her fingers in her lap. "I don't know what to tell you, Nine," she says, and her voice is weighted, a tightness to the cast of her shoulders. "I could say that I wish the two of you all the happiness in the world—and I do. Of course I do. But you're a Paper Girl. The King's concubine. That makes you his, and his alone."

Whatever reaction I'd been expecting, this wasn't it. Anger rattles through me. Out of everyone, I thought Zelle would understand.

"You told me that my thoughts and feelings are my power," I say, a ball in my throat.

"And they are. But I meant that you'd always have something the King could never take from you. Love will only make it harder."

"Did it? For you?"

"It still does." She cuts me a sharp look. "Falling in love is the most dangerous thing women like us can do."

"I don't agree."

"Oh? What do *you* think love is, then?"

"Necessary. Powerful. Maybe the most important thing women like us can do." I picture Wren's smile, the way her body fits with mine. My words shine with the truth of it, the truth of her, of *us*. "Love is what gives us hope. What gets us through each day."

Zelle lifts her chin, her brows arching. "And what about the nights? Will it get you through those?"

"I guess we'll find out soon enough."

For the first time, something almost angry flares across Zelle's features. "Don't deny him again, Nine. I'm sorry you have to go through this, I really am, but you have to find a way to endure it. To hold your true feelings back. Because if he finds out that you've given yourself to someone else, he won't just brand you—he will *kill* you."

"Let him try," I growl. My fingertips dig into my palms. "Maybe someone else will get to him first."

It's out before I can stop it.

Zelle blinks.

"I—I mean," I amend quickly, "maybe *I* won't take it anymore."

"And what do you plan to do instead? How are *you* going to stand up to the King? You aren't a warrior. I bet you've never even handled a weapon before. Didn't you used to work in an herb shop?"

Her words smart, even though she doesn't mean them cruelly.

Then I grin. Because yes, I used to work in an herb shop.

And it might just be what saves me.

My plan forms on the carriage ride back to Paper House.

When I knew the King would call me next, I thought that I'd just have to bear it. Wren told me last night that the assassination attempt will be soon. This might be the only time I have to go to his chambers before we get out of here. Just like Zelle asked me, I was prepared to endure it. That's why I avoided Wren's eyes earlier. Looking at her, seeing the hurt in them, would have made it a million times harder—when it's already impossible. But Zelle's throwaway comment about my herb-shop background reminds me that I might not be as helpless tonight as I believe.

I might not be able to kill the King, but I can at least stall him. And maybe this will prove to Wren that I can be counted on to help with the assassination.

"I need your help," I tell Lill the minute I get back to my room, my words coming fast. I crouch down and grip her shoulders. "There's something I need to do before going to the King tonight. Do you think you can distract Madam Himura and the maids for me? Just for a few minutes?"

She tenses. "But, Mistress, the maids are already here—"

"Tell them I'm not feeling very well. That I just need a bit of fresh air."

Her furred ears quiver. "Maybe we should call for a doctor if you're sick," she mumbles, teething her bottom lip.

"Remember how I grew up working in my parents' herb shop? I just want to make a quick remedy to calm my nerves." Lill still looks unconvinced, so I push on, "After what happened last time, I really need to impress the King. You understand that, don't you? Just a few herbs. That's all I need to calm myself. And then I'll be ready for him."

This last bit at least is true.

In an instant, Lill beams. "You should have said that's why, Mistress! Of course I'll help you with anything that'll win you favor with the King!"

I give her a hug, trying to ignore the squirm of guilt at lying to her.

Hours later: the sky strewn with stars, the palace streets flickering with lantern glow and the icy whip of the wind. This time, there are fifteen guards in my escort through the King's fortress. I bite down laughter at how ridiculous it is, all these armor-clad demons with weapons at the ready against a single human girl in flimsy robes, her only armament a handful of herbs hidden in the sash at her waist.

Major Kenzo Ryu—or Wren's wolf, as I have come to think of him, not without some jealousy—leads the group. He takes my arm when we near the King's door, shifting closer so I catch the musky, natural scent of him. It reminds me of long grass in the fields beyond our village, the smell of earth baking in the sun. Even though I only saw him last night, it's my first chance to get a proper look at him up close. He's young for a major, not more than ten years older than me, gray wolf fur poking between his armor and covering his handsome, long-jawed face. The sharp tips of canines are just visible under his top lip.

Over the last few months I've become used to being around Steel and Moon castes, but his predatory nature isn't lost on me.

He'd better not be in love with Wren. The thought comes to me in a burst of mad humor. Because I definitely won't be the one walking away from *that* fight.

The other soldiers drop back as the wolf leads me to the King's door, handling me with surprising gentleness despite his size. "I'm sorry," he says suddenly in a low voice.

My chin jerks up, and he squeezes my arm in warning.

"Eyes ahead." His voice is a deep, gravelly growl, yet somehow warm at the same time, like the comforting purr of a loved one's snore. "To have to deliver you to the King," he explains. "I'm sorry."

"Hopefully this will be the last time," I mutter.

His bronze eyes flick my way before he knocks on the door.

"Hopefully."

There is no shove this time. No hissed "whore." After the doors open, I take a deep inhale and step inside. Blackness swallows me. For a while I don't move, just trying to catch my breath, forcing down the liquid pull of nausea, the dizzying skip of my pulse.

"There's no point in hiding, Lei-zhi."

The boom of the King's voice startles me. Distance and the shape of the tunnel distorts it, giving it an almost physical presence, like a thunderclap in the dark. With a roll of my shoulders, I start slowly forward. While I'm still concealed in the shadowed tunnel, my footsteps echoing off the arched walls, I run my fingers along my sash. It's tied at my waist over the gathered silks of my ruqun robes, knotted firmly to keep all the material in place, and as I finger the comforting shape of the small leaf-wrapped parcel it's also holding, my heart skips faster.

Desire cannot be tamed. That's what the King told me the first time I was here.

Well, King. You should see how untamable *love* makes you.

His chambers are just as I remember. Candles fill the air, a ruby glow, and the overpowering scent hits the back of my throat. But there's something different this time as I pad across the cavernous room to where the King is watching my approach, sloped back in his massive throne.

Me.

The first time I crossed this room, my knees shook so badly I could barely walk. Fear seared every inch of me, like venom. Part of me even wanted to please him. I'd committed to being a Paper Girl, believing it was the only option I had to save my family.

Now I march toward him with the knowledge that that part of me is long gone.

"I was not hiding, my King," I say, my voice echoing off the high walls. I keep it steady. "I was just...readying myself for seeing you."

"You are still scared of me?"

His voice is gloating. He *wants* me to be scared.

"Yes," I answer, hating that it isn't entirely a lie.

The crooked grin he gives me is shot through with something tense, some raw, feral quality that reminds me of how he was that night at the koyo celebrations. His ebony robes hang open at the chest, revealing the hard swell of muscles.

My gaze slips to the vial of sake on the side table.

"Come here," he commands.

I do as the King says, the long skirt of my robes whispering across the stone floor. I've only just knelt at his feet when he grabs a fistful of my robes. He yanks me forward so hard I have to throw my hands out to stop from smashing my forehead into the marbled gold of his throne.

"No need to be so formal, Lei-zhi," he says with a cutting smile, leaning in close, frosted eyes leering. "I've seen you naked, don't you remember? Act coy, but I know all you Paper Girls are hungry for it. So hungry you'll even spread your legs for one of my soldiers. Imagine!" Flecks of spit hit my face as his voice rises. "A common soldier, when you have shared a bed with the *King!*"

His breath reeks of alcohol. I wince as he tears my robes open at the collar, baring my neck, the small swell of my breasts.

Panic flares through me. My eyes go again to the bottle of sake. I thought there'd be conversation like last time, time for me to carry out my plan.

"M-Mariko was thrown out by Madam Himura," I start, trying to keep him distracted. Twin currents of anger and fear twine through my voice, and they seem so much like the same thing now—hot, bright, defiant—that it's hard to imagine them unthreaded. "The doctor carved the word *rotten* into her forehead to make sure everyone knows what she did."

The King's laughter bounds around the room. "The girl got what she deserved. No one betrays me and gets away with it."

My jaw tightens. "Do many people betray you, my King?"

His nostrils flare. "A surprising number," he answers through peeled lips. "You would think my people would be grateful for what I have done for them. All the comforts and riches I've shared. The efforts I've made to stop the Sickness." He draws me closer, tracing a calloused fingertip along my chin, his hot breaths stirring the strands of hair around my cheeks that the maids earlier so carefully styled. "Tell me, Lei-zhi—are *you* grateful for what I've given you?"

"Of—of course."

"You ran from me last time."

I lick my lips. "I was scared—"

"I did everything I could to make you comfortable. I gave you a home. I made sure you had entertainment. And when you came to me that first time, I had your favorite foods prepared, I talked to you, shared things with you." One hand creeps round the back of my neck, and it's so big his fingers close at the front, pinching the base of my throat. His cold eyes bore into mine. "And still you ran. Still you humiliated me. So I ask you again, Lei-zhi. Are you grateful for what I've given you?"

I push the words past my lips. "Yes, my King."

He lets me go, and I gulp in a deep breath, lifting my fingertips to my neck.

"Then show me," he commands. "Show me how grateful you are."

The intent in his words makes my skin crawl. Out of the corner of my eye, I focus on the vial of sake, imagining releasing the crushed herbs in my palm, the poison drifting into the liquid.

"L-let me dance for you," I start, my voice pitching. Holding back my draped sleeve, I reach for the vial. "Madam Chu taught us a new routine I think you'd enjoy. I'll pour a drink for you while you watch—"

"Enough!"

The King's roar snaps me to attention. Knocking my hand away, he snatches the vial with such force the glasses beside it tip over, shattering on the floor. Scarlet candlelight glints off the broken shards.

"It's you who needs a drink if you think I brought you here to watch you dance!"

Seizing my face, he grips my cheeks to force my lips open, and pours the sake straight into my mouth. I splutter. The alcohol stings my throat. I gag, but the King laughs, holding me until my clothes are soaked and I'm coughing and spluttering, eyes squeezed shut, skin sticky with the liquid.

When the vial is empty, he flings me aside. I double over, retching. Wet drops splatter the floor around my hands.

"You think I don't understand what you're up to?" he roars, arms wide, fists curled. "You cannot hide from me forever, Lei-zhi. This is my palace. My *kingdom!*"

The boom of his voice shakes the room, sending a ripple through the floating candles. I sway to my feet. Cast a desperate look over the scatter of glass around me, the splashes of ruined rice wine. There's no more drink left to poison with the herbs I took from the kitchen gardens earlier; the ones that would have cramped the King's gut and made him too sick to move for the rest of the evening, sparing me at least one more night.

It would only have been a temporary reprieve. But maybe it would have been enough. Maybe after tonight, Wren would have managed to get to the King before he got to me.

As the King makes a lurch, I spin round, clutching up the layers of my skirt and stumbling into a run. But I've only taken a few steps when his hands seize me. Lift me into the air. With a bellow, he throws me to the floor.

My cheekbone cracks.

Pain splinters through me, fissures my skull.

The next instant, I'm swallowed by the King's shadow as he bears down on top of me. He brings his mouth to my ear and whispers, crooning almost, like some kind of sick, twisted lullaby, "*I ordered the raid on your village, Lei-zhi. My soldiers told me they killed all the women they took that day—including your beloved mother.*" And then he grabs a fistful of the silks at my waist and tears them open as I let out a cry no one else can hear.

THIRTY

EVEN THE SOLDIERS ARE UNABLE TO hide their shock when I finally stagger from the King's chambers.

I have no idea how long I've been in there. Only minutes could have passed. Or an entire lifetime. How long does it take to break a person? To take their will and fire and spirit and love and crush them beneath your fists?

As the doors swing shut behind me, my legs give way. Wren's wolf strides forward to catch me. He lifts me gently, the other guards watching in silence as he lopes past, cradling me to his chest. The torn robe I've wrapped around me is bloodied. Dully, I notice the servants as we go by, the way they avert their eyes. Even the Paper caste ones.

Shame flows through me, a constant, unforgiving ebb.

I look up at Kenzo. My voice is a croak. "They'll suspect you."

"No," he says, staring ahead. "They won't. This is not the first time a Paper Girl has had to be taken from the King's rooms in such a condition."

Underneath the pain and horror: a shot of rage.

"I hate him," I whisper with the last bit of strength I have.

Kenzo doesn't answer, but he holds me a little closer, and before I pass out I understand this to mean that he agrees.

When consciousness returns, the comforting scent of Wren's wolf is gone. There's the whisper of voices around me. The soft pressure of a warm hand on mine. I must be back in my room at Paper House. I try to move, but currents of pain snap and fizz through my body, forcing me to fall still. The pain wasn't so strong earlier. My mind must have blocked it out as the King took from me what I have denied him for so long.

That's what it felt like. A taking. A robbery.

I inch my eyes open, and even this hurts.

"She's awake!"

Aoki's face is the first I see. Her hand is the one wrapped round mine, and she leans over me, eyes so wide that my entire vision is an ocean of deep green. Then she draws away and is replaced by Wren.

The expression on her face. I can barely look at her.

"Oh, gods, Lei," she whispers, dipping her forehead to mine. "I'm so, so sorry."

I lick my cracked lips. "The wolf. He—"

She shoots me a warning look. "You mean Major Ryu? Yes, he brought you back. He escorted you all the way here."

My eyes drift shut.

"How kind of him," Aoki murmurs.

There's the sound of the door opening.

"The doctor's on his way, Mistresses. He won't be long."

My heart gives a little leap at the sound of Lill's voice. Even though my plan failed, she'd been the one who made it possible in the first place.

And then I remember. My plan. The herbs.

The *poisonous* herbs.

I jerk upright. Pain erupts, a starburst all over me. Aoki and Wren try to draw me back down, shushing, but I struggle against them, eyes wild.

"Where are my clothes?" I cry.

"Lei," Aoki pleads, "you need to rest—"

But I'm almost screaming now. *"Where are my clothes?"*

Lill snatches up a torn bundle of fabric, lantern light illuminating the layered pattern of my robes—wildflowers and vines, twisted in a kaleidoscope of deep magenta and lapis. "This is all you had with you," she says sorrowfully, holding them out for me.

I riffle through the flimsy material. A sob racks through me and I slump back as if winded.

"Lei?" Wren asks, fingers light on my wrist. "What's wrong?"

I close my eyes. "The sash," I whisper. "It's gone."

I have to wait until much later, until the doctor and shaman have checked on me and magicked away my wounds, and Aoki and Lill have gone to bed, to tell Wren about my plan to poison the King.

She lets go of my hand when I've finished, and the gesture loosens something in me. "So the herbs are still there?" she asks sharply. "In his chambers?"

"Yes."

"If he finds them—if *anyone* finds them…"

My teeth are gritted. "I know."

"What were you thinking? You shouldn't have taken such a risk."

I edge slightly away. "I was thinking," I say thickly, "that I couldn't bear having to sleep with him."

Wren's face drops. "Lei—"

"And I was *thinking* you'd understand."

"I do. Oh, love, of course I do. I'm so sorry." Warm fingertips trace my cheek, winding round to cup my head as she leans down and brings her lips to my hairline, holding me close. "You know how much this hurts me, too. But if you had managed to poison him, don't you think the royal doctors would have been able to figure out how it happened? It could ruin everything we've been working toward. They could increase the King's security. Stop us from seeing him. Even cancel the Moon Ball. Not to mention what the King would do to punish you."

Tears sting my eyes. "I—I didn't think about any of that. I just... I couldn't bear the idea of having to go through with it. Even once."

Sighing, Wren laces her arms around me, hugging me tighter. "Oh, Lei. Of course not. I'm so sorry. If there was anything, *anything* I could have done, any way to save you tonight..." Pulling back, she scans my face. "Do you want to talk about it?"

It.

Such a tiny word for everything contained within.

I squeeze my eyelids, trying to expel the images from them. But I know that no matter how hard I try, what happened tonight is going to stay with me forever. The shamans might have healed my bruises, but the King's brutality is still all over me. It lives in my skin.

It breathes in my bones.

More than anyone, I know how some wounds can stay hidden and yet still be felt so keenly, day after day, year after year.

"Not yet," I tell Wren eventually.

She takes my hands. "Well, when and if you need to, I'll be here."

I nod. Then, eager to change the subject, I ask, "What are we going to do about the herbs? Maybe I can get them back. I'll go back to the King's chambers, make up some excuse—"

"No." Wren stops me. "It'll only make them suspicious. And I'm not letting you go anywhere near that monster." She looks away, forehead puckered, then nods. "I'll get word to Kenzo. He should be able to get to them before the King."

"You think so?"

Her lips curve into a half smile. "It's Kenzo. He'll find a way."

I try to return her smile, but the tuck of my lips is wrong and all I can do is grimace. Then her words just a couple of minutes ago echo back to me.

"The Moon Ball," I say. "Isn't that the party the King is hosting to celebrate the New Year?"

Wren nods. "What about it?"

"You said you're worried they might cancel it." Her expression stiffens, and suddenly I understand. All this while we've been sitting on my sleeping mat, close enough to whisper, but now I shift back, my voice hollow. "That's when it's to happen, isn't it? You've been given the order."

She looks down, long lashes hiding her eyes. "Kenzo told me when he brought you back earlier. Everything's in place."

"The New Year is less than four weeks away," I choke out. I let out a dull, humorless laugh. "Did you know it's my birthday then, too? Some present you're giving me, Wren. You'd better not die, too, or it'll all be too much."

I mean it as a joke, even if it is a twisted one. But her jaw sets and her eyes flick away, and in that moment I know.

"Oh, gods." I scramble to my feet, something wild racking through me. Wren reaches out, but I back into the wall, shaking my head, my ears rushing with the whoosh of blood, the deep pulsation of my heartbeat. "Tell me there's an escape plan, Wren. Tell me they're going to get you out."

She falters. "They'll do their best."

Neither of us moves as the morning gong rings. Footsteps and voices began to spill into the corridor. The normalcy of it seems absurd, obscene even. How can the world still tick simply by when this beautiful girl is admitting her fate to me, when I can still feel the pain of the King's fury imprinted upon my body?

How can we just go back to that life, knowing what we know now? *Feeling* the way we do now?

"You think you're going to get caught," I say, not taking my eyes from Wren's.

"Lei—"

"Tell me the truth! You think there's no hope of you getting out. That they'll capture you once you've killed him."

Something in her face slackens. After a beat, she whispers, "Yes."

The word cleaves me, splits me straight in two.

"That's why you didn't want to tell me. You knew what was going to…you didn't…didn't want to hurt me.…"

She gives a tiny nod.

My breath rattles through me, almost painful, but I force myself to draw another. Then another. And with each new inhale the fire returns to me—the red flames that burned through my bloodstream when I walked into the King's chambers last night, the boldness of my love for Wren that sings in our veins every time we're pressed skin to skin, our hearts racing each other.

I recall Mama's saying: *Light in, darkness out.*

Perhaps it works another way, too.

Fire in, *fear* out.

"Let me help," I say steadily. I take a step forward. "You're going to kill the King, and I'm going to help you do it."

Wren tenses. "I told you the other night. No."

"Yes." I close the distance between us, my fingers sliding between

hers. "When the world denies you choices," I say, echoing her words to me that night in the rain-filled garden all those weeks ago, "you make your own." I keep my eyes fixed on hers. "This is *my* choice. The King hasn't just harmed me and you. Think of all the Paper castes he has his soldiers capture as slaves and kill as easily, as if we weren't even human. All the families and lives they tear apart. Just like they did with ours." I grip her tighter. "I don't know how much longer I can bear it. So I'm going to help you, and then we're getting out of here—alive."

Her lips press. "Lei—"

"He gave the orders, Wren." My voice catches. "He told me. It was him who ordered the soldiers to raid my village." The wet kiss of a tear tracks my cheek. "How many others has he ordered? How many more families have been broken the way mine was? I can't take it anymore. I can't just keep sitting here doing nothing."

More tears flow. Releasing my hands, Wren cups my face to thumb my tears away, her dark eyes soft. Then she draws me to her. We kiss slow and deep, a kiss I feel from the very tips of my toes to the core of my being. A kiss I feel in my *soul*. And for a few moments we get a glimpse of what the future could be like for us—to be with each other, free, with no fear that our love might get us killed.

When I was young, my parents used to kneel by my sleeping mat at bedtime and tell me stories from the Ikharan *Mae Scripts*, the myths about how our world was born. According to the *Scripts*, the sky began as a sea of light. There were no distinctions between stars or moon or clouds. Everything was white.

Then Zhokka, Harbinger of Night, came.

He was jealous of the sky's brightness. Zhokka was originally an earth god, and he hated how he could see the sky gods dancing high up above, bathed in light. He wanted that light for himself, but also to take it *away* from them. So he gathered an army of creatures from the darkest parts of the earth and brought them to the sky.

The battle is supposed to have lasted over a hundred years. The sky gods fought valiantly, but Zhokka and his dark army finally defeated them, and as a victory prize Zhokka swallowed all the light of the sky. Now there was only darkness.

But Zhokka had been careless. With no light left, he didn't see Ahla, the Moon Goddess, creeping up on him. She'd fled when she saw he would win the battle, and had been waiting for the right moment to return. Taking her powerful crescent-form, she lanced herself through the darkness at Zhokka and split a huge, grinning gash through his face, blinding him in the process.

Some of the light he'd swallowed managed to escape through this tear, and these returned to their beloved sky as the stars. And for the rest of eternity, Zhokka is doomed to roam the galaxies, searching blindly for Ahla to take his revenge.

The story comes back to me now as Wren and I hold each other. I always wondered what that night-filled abyss looked like before Ahla cut Zhokka open. I could never quite picture it. But tonight I finally understand how it would have felt.

The King is Zhokka, swallowing everything. And Wren is Ahla—the moon, the light, the only one who knows how to bring the stars back to my sky.

"I'm going to help," I tell her when we finally draw apart. "I'm going to help you kill him."

And this time she agrees.

THIRTY-ONE

THERE IS AN OLD PROVERB IN our kingdom: "He who seeks revenge should dig two graves." I've already prepared to dig the Demon King's. The other is for the girl I used to be. The girl who was sleepwalking through her time here until she fell in love, until she had her eyes opened to the world beyond her walls. The girl who accused Aoki of falling for the King, for being seduced by palace life, when she, too, was embracing it.

Well, no more embracing.

No more sleepwalking.

I don't want an easy life. I want a meaningful one.

Now that I know what they're planning, Wren involves me in her secret meetings with Kenzo. It takes some convincing on Wren's part, especially because Kenzo narrowly missed getting caught when he went to the King's chambers to retrieve the poisonous herbs I'd left there. But the wolf eventually concedes, deciding that my role as a Paper Girl can be useful as a distraction while Wren gets the King alone. While it's not much, I'm pleased to be able to do anything to help. The smoother everything goes at the ball, the better Wren's chance to come away safely will be.

Every few nights, we wrap up in furs and overcoats and head into the forest, listening to news Kenzo has brought from the court—changes to the guest list for the Moon Ball, more signs that the Sickness is worsening, outbursts of rebellion in more of the provinces. Anything that could affect the plan. And though our everyday routine as Paper Girls continues as normal, I float through it with a kind of absent focus, tired from our midnight excursions but also too fixed on the approaching New Year to concentrate on much else. It's taken the form of a color in my mind—the brightest, sharpest white, like light catching the edge of a blade.

In a few weeks' time, I'll be at the Moon Ball, distracting the King's guards as best as I can while Wren steals him away to bury a knife in his heart.

One morning Lill says, "Not long now, Mistress."

She's in the middle of fixing my hair into its usual bun. I start, causing her fingers to tangle.

"What—what do you mean?"

"Your Birth-blessing pendant," she clarifies with a frown. "Isn't it your birthday on the New Year?"

I follow her gaze to the shrine in the corner of my room. Because we're not allowed to wear jewelry during our lessons, ever since coming to the palace I've kept my Birth-blessing pendant there, hanging from an unlit stack of joss sticks. It seems like another thing from the life of the girl I used to be. Something else to bury with her.

"Is there something you're hoping for?" Lill asks.

"Anything involving cake," I reply, and she laughs.

But the truth is I know exactly what sort of fate I hope to find within my pendant, and it's one that life within the palace walls could never offer me.

Freedom.

*   *   *

When there's less than two weeks to go, Wren and I sneak out to the clearing in the woods. I'm expecting for us to meet Kenzo as usual, but he isn't here.

"He's not coming tonight," she tells me. "This is something for just you and me to work on."

It's a still winter's night. The forest is wrapped in silence, the trees towering around us, shifting drops of moonlight filtering in through the canopy overhead. The air is cool with the promise of snow. The screech of some night bird cuts suddenly through the quiet, and I start, grabbing my fur shawl tighter around me.

"*That*," Wren says with a smile, "is what we're going to try to deal with."

"What do you mean?"

"You need to be prepared in case there's any trouble on the night. Kenzo's going to get a weapon to you—something small, easy to conceal. But in case you lose it, or for whatever reason he can't get it to you, you're going to have to know how to defend yourself without it. Have you ever had any martial arts training?"

I arch a brow. "What do you think?"

"Well, we only have a couple of weeks. We're just going to have to dive in."

Wren shifts into position, knees bent, arms raised, palms open. I'm just about to copy her because it seems that's what I'm supposed to do, when she lunges forward and strikes her right hand at my head.

I clamp my eyes shut, expecting a flare of pain. When it doesn't come, I inch my eyes open to find her hand hovering by my head. She draws back.

"How—how did you do that?" I gulp.

The corner of her lips tuck up, but her face is serious. "I'm one of the Xia, remember? I won't hurt you, Lei. I promise. But you have to act like this is a real battle."

"Sure," I mutter. "Let me just recollect the last time I was at war."

"It's a bit like what Master Tekoa teaches us," Wren continues, ignoring my quip. "You want to access your most natural instincts and allow them to control you without you having to think about it too much."

"If someone is coming at my head with their fist, my natural instinct is to run as fast as I can in the opposite direction."

After a moment, she asks, quiet, "Is it?"

The stillness of the forest seems to draw in. Wren moves closer, boots crunching on the frosted grass. Our breaths form clouds in the air.

"Think about all the times you've fought against what's been happening to you. I told you that night when the King had you locked up. You're brave, Lei. Braver than you think. You fought him then, and you've fought him since, and I know you are strong enough for whatever is coming next."

I drop my eyes, bunching my hands at my sides. "It wasn't enough. Not that night."

Even though Wren has made it clear she's willing to listen, I still haven't spoken to her about what happened in the King's chambers. I'd been close a few times, lying in her arms in one of our rooms, wrapped safely in the velvet darkness. But my thoughts never seemed to form into a language I could share. The only time we touched on it was the first time I was to see the King after that night, at a dinner a week later. She'd asked me how I felt; if maybe I wanted to feign sickness to try to get out of it. That she'd help me do the same if he called for me again. But somehow I know he won't.

At least, not for a while.

The King likes to prove his power, yes. But he's shown me his insecurities enough times for me to know that he also wants to be adored and admired. And he knows that those are two things he can never force from me.

Wren twines her fingers through mine, my numb skin tingling at their warmth. "You're stronger now," she says. "You're prepared. And you're not in this alone." She squeezes my hand. "Do you remember the day of the Unveiling Ceremony? Our maids got us ready together, and afterward you asked me—"

"How I looked," I interrupt dully. "I remember."

She loosens a long exhale, wrapping us in a cloud of hazy white. "I'm sorry for what I said then. I was so adamant when I first got here to not let any of you in. To not let any of you *want* to." She pulls me closer. "But when I saw you later in your dress, I couldn't help it. I had to tell you what I thought, because I understood then."

My brow furrows. "Understood what?"

Wren smiles. "You. The dresses were made to represent us based on the results of our assessments," she explains. "Mine was everything I've been trained to be. Strong, without compromise. Unforgiving. I knew what yours meant the minute I saw you. Your dress showed me that you had strength, but softness, too. A sense of loyalty, but not without fairness. Fight, *and* mercy. Things I wasn't allowed to feel. Things I didn't know how badly I needed." She brings her fingertips to my cheeks, lacing them through the tangles of my hair. "I knew from that moment that I would fall in love with you. And for a long time, I did everything I could to resist it. But you made it impossible."

With a sigh, I tuck my chin, nestling into her. Her heart thuds strong and steady against my cheek.

"Lei," she says softly into my hair, "we can do this another night if you're not up to it...."

"No," I say, drawing back. "Now."

Gathering a long inhale, I picture all the memories associated with that night with the King turning into little knives in my veins. *Fire in, fear out.*

My hands bunch into fists. "All right—come at me."

The words are barely out of my mouth when she leaps back. With a spin, she slices the side of her hand toward my middle. This time, I'm a little better prepared. I manage to jolt out of the way, though she comes for me again a beat later and has to hold back, her open palm seconds away from cuffing my shoulder.

"Give me a chance!" I say, panting, but Wren moves again, this time lashing out for me with her leg.

She arcs it in a low sweep along the floor, catching my feet, and I fall back, letting out a puff of air as I land heavily on the mossy ground.

She rolls on top of me.

"I thought you weren't going to hurt me!" I groan.

She flashes a smile. "I only did that so I could do this."

Her mouth lowers to mine. A familiar heat fizzes along my veins as we kiss, tongue to tongue, lips to lips, our arms laced around each other. I slowly forget about the frozen ground beneath me, the eerie sounds of the forest replaced by the rustle of our clothes and bodies as we cling to each other, our kiss deepening.

Though flashes of that night still come to me every time Wren and I have touched since, and she's been careful to only take it further when I've made it clear that's what I want, there's something slightly different about our intimacy now. Still, each time it gets a little easier to stay in the moment, and right now I allow myself to let go. To lose myself in lips and sensation and heat and love.

We're both panting when we finally draw apart.

"Does every shifu do this with their students?" I say, breathless. "If so, then sign me up."

Wren gets to her feet, holding out a hand to help me up. "I can give you as many lessons as you like when we're out of here. But for now, we need to concentrate. I did that to get you fired up. To remind you how naturally you can move your body. You need to home in on that same passion when fighting." Then she's lashing at me again, spinning round with a high arc of her leg.

I flail back a split-second before impact. "Aiyah! At least go easy on me."

She doesn't smile. "I am."

Forty minutes later—though it feels like hundreds—I'm doubled over, gasping for air, a stitch winding up one side. I've just managed to counter one of Wren's attacks properly for the first time, ducking out of the way of her right leg as it kicked high toward my head, and knocking into her with my shoulder. It barely shifts her, and she lands easily. But still. It's a hit.

"That was great!" she says. "Really good!"

"Thanks," I mutter between gulps of air.

Wren closes the gap between us. She tugs my face up, smiling. "I mean it, Lei. You're so much stronger than I could ever be."

I roll my eyes. "What are you talking about? *You're* the warrior."

"Only because it's all I've known. I've grown up learning this, how to fight and be brave. You've had to find it within yourself, all on your own. That's *real* courage." She looks away, her voice growing quiet. "You know, it's not too late to back out. I'd understand."

I slide my arms around her waist. "Well, *I* wouldn't. I'm in this now, Wren. I'm all in."

Her eyes flick back to me, widening—warming—with the double meaning behind my words. *I love you.* The phrase hovers on my lips then, three words, three simple trips of the tongue. But ever since that night when we first admitted how we felt, I still haven't spoken them to her. However brave Wren believes me to be, I'm not yet brave enough for that. So instead I press my mouth against hers, hoping she can sense the words in my kiss and know that I mean them, that I love her and need her, and that I'm terrified for these weeks to end because our lives are about to change forever. And some part of me can't shake the premonition that it's not going to be in the way we're hoping.

THIRTY-TWO

PREPARATIONS FOR THE NEW YEAR begin the day before the Moon Ball.

As soon as we wake, we're herded into carriages and taken to a bathhouse in Royal Court. It's an impressive four stories, a large central room divided into various areas, the upper tiers circled with balconies decorated with colored silks. I pick up familiar scents in the clouds of steam—calendula, mulberry, passionflower. Homesickness tugs so firmly on my soul that it actually hurts. I could close my eyes and I'd be back there, working in the shop with Baba and Tien, Bao barking and the mixing pots bubbling away.

By some unwritten rule, Wren and I haven't discussed what will happen after we escape. It would be too much like tempting fate, and from the way the gods have played with me so far, that's not a bet I'm willing to make. But alongside being with Wren, the only thing I really want is to go back to Xienzo and reunite with my family. Maybe we could even make a life there with them. Our little unit has been shattered so many times, but we've proven we have the strength to heal. To make something new and beautiful from the sum of our broken parts.

We're led to an enormous tub in the middle of the bathhouse.

Water pours in from a waterfall-like feature, filling the air with its rich bubbling. Three black-robed royal shamans bless the water. Then, one by one, we step inside as they chant a dao, settling a soft, golden magic on our skin. The ceremony is to symbolize purification, helping us shed this year's sins before we enter the new one.

I stifle a grim laugh when it's my turn. If only they knew what Wren and I are planning. The only thing this bath is helping me shed is the ache in my muscles from our midnight training sessions.

Back at Paper House, we spend the next few hours having meetings with the court's most trusted fortune-tellers, qi doctors, and diviners. The New Year marks the halfway point in our year as Paper Girls. The results of these assessments will shape our training next year as we prepare to move from being the King's concubines to our next roles in the palace. Or in Wren's case and mine, they *would* have, were we staying in the palace.

I cross Wren in the corridor as our maids lead us between rooms for the final assessment of the day. She gives me a knowing smile that lights my heart up in an instant. As we pass she turns her hand so it brushes against mine, almost like a kiss.

By the time our assessments are over, night has fallen. The grounds are cloaked in darkness, the stars hidden. As Lill changes me for dinner, I gaze out the window, an uneasy feeling rippling through me.

Tomorrow.

That's it. Just one more day.

"Are you all right, Mistress?" Lill asks, fixing an ornament in my hair with deft fingers.

I shrug. "Just nervous for tomorrow's ball, I guess."

"Well, don't be. I heard the King has arranged a surprise for you!"

Despite her grin, her words make me cold. It's the worst possible time for surprises. Whatever the King's organized, I'm sure I won't like it. The only thing we have in common is that we both defend what's ours, and tomorrow night I'm going to prove it to him.

When I arrive at Madam Himura's suite twenty minutes later, one of her maids leads me out into the courtyard. A canopy of twinkling lights stretches overhead. At the center of the garden, the pavilion has been hung with heavy velvet curtains to keep out the cold. As I step inside, my eyes sweep the group for Wren. She isn't here yet. Instead, Aoki catches my eyes. She looks a bit panicked, and she opens her lips to mouth something at me, but before she's able to, Madam Himura waves me to a seat next to Blue.

"Now that we're all here," the eagle-woman says in her usual croak, "I want to go over tomorrow's proceedings. In the morning—"

"Aren't we waiting for Wren?" I interrupt.

The table falls quiet.

Madam Himura's head swivels in my direction. *"We,"* she responds sharply with a flash of her bright yellow eyes, "are not waiting for anyone."

I blink. "What do you mean?"

"Wren-zhi has had to leave the palace."

My stomach gives a dull kick. The ground seems to take a careening slope underneath me. A high-pitched ringing enters my brain.

"Her mother has been killed," Madam Himura continues. "The King has ordered her to return to her family. It's uncertain when she'll be returning."

I gape at her. *"What?"*

Just then, Aoki jerks forward, knocking a glass of plum wine to the floor. Half of it splashes onto Chenna, who jolts back with a cry. A maid rushes over to clean the mess as Madam Himura shrieks at Aoki and Zhen, who was next to Chenna, who yanks the hem of her dress away from the spreading amber puddle. Amid the chaos, I breathe raggedly. My heart hammers painfully against my ribs. I know Aoki was trying to stop me before I said something that would have given me away or Madam Himura punished me for insolence, but though the rest of the girls are focused on the fuss at the table, next to me, Blue is still.

She watches me from the corner of her ink-black eyes. There's a knowing twist to her lips, and after a few moments she leans in close, cheek grazing mine, and hisses, just for me to hear, "So *that's* your dirty little secret. Won't the King be shocked to learn what you've been up to all this time?"

I don't know how I make it through dinner. Somehow I manage it, though I almost throw up a few times, and not from the raw fish we're served as part of more tiring New Year purification symbolism. As soon as Madam Himura permits us to leave, I get up from the table without meeting any of the girls' questioning looks and stagger back to my room.

"What's wrong?" Lill asks as I burst through the doorway, shaking.

I don't answer her. I lurch to the window and collapse against it, gulping in breaths, but the air is clotted, like curdled milk, and no matter how much I gasp I can't seem to fill my lungs. Lill tries her best to calm me. When nothing she says or does works, she even brings me a cup of sweet, milky teh tarik from the kitchens, but the sugar just spikes my nerves.

When she finally manages to get me to lie down, I'm shivering all over. "Please try to rest, Mistress," she pleads. "There's nothing to be nervous about. It's just a ball."

I close my eyes, feigning tiredness. But the minute she's gone, I shove back the blankets and get to my feet, pacing the short length of my room.

One more day. That's all that was left. One more day to keep our secrets. One more day and we were out of here.

We were going to be free.

Now Wren is gone, and all the years of careful planning and preparation have been ruined in just a handful of hours. And Blue—*Blue*—knows about the two of us. She could tell the King any moment now and that would be it. All my actions with him would confirm it. He'd know. He'd know, and my beautiful, ferocious-eyed assassin won't be around to take him down before he can punish us for it.

A thought comes to me, so painful I actually gag.

The next time I see Wren could be at our own execution.

I recall the last time I saw her. The brush of our hands in the corridor, just a second of contact. How can that go down as our last moment together? How can that be our last touch?

My room is too suffocating to stay in any longer. Without Wren here, I go to the room of the only other person in the palace I fully trust.

Aoki rubs her eyes as I shake her awake. "Lei?" she mumbles, her voice thick with sleep. "What's happening? What's wrong?"

"I can't sleep," I say.

Yawning, she sits up and opens her fur blanket. She drapes it around my shoulders as I nestle in beside her. She smells like sleep, like softness and safety, and I release a long exhale, leaning against her in silence. It reminds me of when I used to snuggle in with my parents when I had a nightmare. The thought that just a few hours ago I was so hopeful that I'd make it home lances me afresh, and I grind my teeth together to stop the tears.

Aoki wraps her arms round her legs, propping her cheek on her knees to look sideways at me. "I'm so sorry about Wren's mother. Do you know if they were close?"

It takes me a moment to untangle her question from Wren's original Xia family. She's talking about the Hannos, of course.

"I'm not sure," I admit. Wren has always spoken far more about Ketai Hanno than his wife. "I don't think so."

"Still, it must be awful." After a beat, she goes on carefully, "The King is close with the Hannos. I'm sure he'll do everything to look after Wren and her family."

"They're Paper castes, Aoki."

"And still one of his most trusted clans. You know, he even gave them a special guard made up of his own soldiers?"

"Maybe one of those guards *was* the killer," I snap before I can stop it.

Aoki winces. "I know you're upset, but what you're saying is—"

"Possible? Likely?"

"The King and the Hannos have always supported each other, Lei. Why would they turn on each other now?"

Because maybe the King suspects what the Hannos are planning. Maybe Wren's mother was murdered by the King's men to send a message to them. Or maybe, if he believes Wren to be involved, he had her mother killed as a way of getting her out of the palace. A death in the family is one of the only reasons a Paper Girl is allowed to take leave.

But I keep my thoughts to myself.

I walk out of Aoki's room half an hour later, feeling even worse than before. My mind is reeling, and I'm so distracted I don't notice the figure in my room until it's too late.

A fur-covered hand clamps across my mouth.

"Not a word," growls a low, husky voice.

THIRTY-THREE

K ENZO DOESN'T LET ME GO until we're outside, cloaked in the darkness of the gardens. His bronze eyes fix on my own as he glares down at me, waiting as I gulp in air, recovering. Our breaths spiral in the frozen air. It takes me a moment to notice that he's wearing silk robes, his marbled wolf's coat combed and slick. He must have come straight from the King's pre–Moon Ball banquet.

"You scared me!" I hiss at him once I'm able to speak.

"I'm sorry," he says, though his expression remains hard. "It was the only way I could get you alone. I was meant to meet Wren to finalize the plans for tomorrow. Then I heard the news. I waited as long as I could before coming to find you."

I blink. "Find…me?"

"The plan has to go ahead, Lei. Wren won't be able to return in time, but everything else is ready. You are going to have to kill the King in her place."

There's a pause.

Then I laugh. "You can't be serious."

"I am deadly serious," he replies, a growl deep in his throat.

"Look," I say, lifting my hands and taking a step back, "I want to help, but—"

"You didn't expect to have to get your hands dirty?"

My mouth snaps shut. "I didn't *expect* to be the one to do it. Last time I checked I wasn't a lost member of the Xia trained since birth to be a secret warrior-assassin-goddess."

Wind catches my hair, making it dance. I clutch my night robe tighter around me. The air is as frosted as the ground, and the flimsy material of my nightdress isn't much protection from the cold. But Kenzo doesn't seem to notice. I suppose having fur makes you forget how vulnerable bare skin can be.

He regards me impassively with his bright wolf eyes. "We can adapt the plan," he suggests eventually.

I goggle at him. *"Adapt the..."*

"All the elements are in place. You'll be taking over Wren's role, which you're already familiar with. Being able to get the King alone, for him to let his guard down—that's the important part. That's why Wren had to spend this time cultivating a relationship with him. Only a Paper Girl can kill him without us risking our position in the court or exposing our involvement." He pauses, something gentler in his look when he adds, "You have motive enough. It will look like a passion crime."

"But Wren will be coming back, won't she? She'll come back and then we can try again."

Kenzo shakes his head. "There's no time." Even with his voice lowered, it still has bite. He moves nearer to grip me by the shoulders and I brace at the sensation of demon hands on me. They're so large they easily span the space from my neck to where my arms start to slope down. Memories jolt through me from that night with the King. Noticing my discomfort, Kenzo lets me go, but he stays close. "Listen to me, Lei. It has taken us years—Wren's entire lifetime—to reach this point. You know how much we've sacrificed for this. We're so close. If we don't act now, we might not get another chance."

I hug my arms across my chest, shivering. "What—what do you mean?"

"The King has been growing suspicious. I fear the Hannos are losing influence over him. Since the assassination attempt, he's been hungry for retribution, to catch the court members who helped them. He knows there are those in the palace who'd betray him. I believe he's starting to look at me as one of them."

"But I thought you're one of his most trusted advisers."

"I am." Kenzo's lip curls, a wolfish gesture, his ears flicking forward. "And it's been many hard years to get there. But recently, the King hasn't been so receptive to what I've been advising. The Sickness is getting worse, and he's convinced it's because of the gods. That they're punishing him for being a weak ruler. He's been pushing ever more aggressive tactics to try to demonstrate his might."

I nod. "He told me the same."

"It hasn't been easy," Kenzo continues, rubbing a hand at the side of his neck, mussing his smoothed-down fur. "I've been trying to advise him differently, but I need to maintain my cover. It sickens me to think of all the deaths I'm aiding." He turns his face away jerkily and lets out a cold laugh. "You know, there are official royal executioners. By ordering me, Naja, and Ndeze to do their work that day, the King was sending a clear message—do not cross me. Look at what happens to those who do."

I squeeze myself tighter. "If he's suspicious of your loyalty, why hasn't he confronted you yet?"

"Because he understands the benefit in keeping his enemies close. Do you know how the Hannos even came to be aligned with him?"

I shake my head.

"They were one of the strongest clans in Ikhara before the Bull King's ascension two hundred years ago," Kenzo explains. "They occupied the entire Han territory. That's where they get their name—from the two ancient families in the region, the Hans and the Nos. The Bull King was originally from Jana, from a tiny trading post village in the southern deserts. He had no influence over Han. He was only able to take control because the Hannos were supporters of equality between demons and humans. They welcomed immigrant clans and were keen to develop bonds between all castes. By all accounts, the Bull King impressed them with his intelligence and ambition, and he rose quickly through their ranks. And what were the Hannos rewarded with?" Kenzo's nostrils flare as he lets out a hard puff of air. "Betrayal. The Bull King used his influence on the Hannos' rule to empower the demon castes, manipulating them, making them hungry for control, then used their power to overtake their court."

My eyes go wide. "And the Hannos *still* made an alliance with him after all that?"

"The Night War was devastating for Paper castes, Lei. We've all heard the stories passed down by our ancestors. Years of cooperation and partnership with demons, eradicated in an instant. Of course, there has always been conflict between clans. But now there was a force uniting the demon clans, giving them reason to forge alliances and maintain peace between their groups in order to hold power over Paper castes. You yourself have experienced this force firsthand. I am sure that the last thing the Hannos wanted was to pledge their allegiance to the very demon who betrayed them. But the clan needed time to recover, and Ketai's forbears understood that they needed the King's support in this new world. That they could later use his power as their own. So they went to him, groveling." A growl rises in Kenzo's throat. "How could the King resist the sight of his enemies, made to kneel at his feet like beggars?"

"But he knew what he'd done to them," I say, absently pushing aside the windblown hair from my face. "Didn't he worry they'd end up betraying him, too?"

Kenzo releases a rough laugh. "An arrogant warlord like him? I bet he didn't think of it once. All he saw was a chance to use their connections among the human clans. Look at the trouble the King is facing now. Winning a war is the easy part. All it takes is brawn. Maintaining your rule afterward is the real test."

I stare. "So the Hannos have been planning their revenge for *two hundred years?*"

"How many years would *you* wait for revenge against those who stole your kingdom from you?" Kenzo's bronze eyes fix me to the spot. "Who tore down what you had so patiently been building? Who slaughtered hundreds of thousands of your kind, and laughed while doing it?" The hatred in his voice is as powerful as thunder; it rolls through the air between us and into my bloodstream, an electric vibration that charges my whole body. He adds, quieter, but just as fiercely, "I'd wait a lifetime to gain my revenge against someone who hurt just one person I love. For an entire kingdom of them?"

I think of Mama.

Of Wren.

Kenzo watches me. "Two hundred years doesn't seem so long now, does it?"

"But…what happens after? Once they've had their revenge? If that's what it's all about—"

"Of course it's not. By all accounts, the Hannos were genuinely open to seeing how this King's rule developed. Along with needing to recover their military strength, I'm sure that was another factor in their waiting so long. But the Demon King's regime only proved to them the importance of claiming back the throne. Now, with the Sickness and greater rebel activity than ever before, the King's rule has grown even harsher. And not just for Paper castes."

He turns jerkily away, staring into the darkness. When Kenzo looks back, there's something sad and almost broken in his eyes, which makes me wonder if there's a story behind his words, what memories might be haunting him.

"Is that why you're helping the Hannos?" I ask. "Something happened to make you turn against the King?"

"Yes," he answers simply. He looks down at me through narrowed eyes. "Wren told me you're from a rural village in Xienzo. Maybe it's hard for you to understand, coming from somewhere so peaceful."

I take a shaky inhale, harden my gaze. "We were attacked by the King's men seven years ago. They took my mother."

"So you know what it's like to have a loved one stolen from you," the wolf says. With surprising tenderness, he reaches for my hands. His huge, pawlike hands easily swallow mine, but unlike his touch earlier, it's comforting this time, almost brotherly. The way he is with Wren. He comes closer, the earthy scent of him unfurling from his ash-gray coat, ruffled now from the wintry wind. "Wren trusts you, Lei. She believes in you, and that means we all do. Will you do this for us? Will you kill the King?"

And even though it terrifies me—even though all I want is for a laughing Wren to come out behind a bush to tell me this is all some crazy, horrid joke—there's no hesitation when I answer.

"Yes. I will."

Kenzo blows out a forceful exhale. Lowering his head, he brings the backs of my hands to his forehead in a light press and murmurs huskily, "Thank you, Lei. Eighty times, thank you."

"On one condition."

He looks up.

"My father and Tien are protected from any punishment should..." I swallow. "Should it go wrong."

"Of course. We'll look after them, whatever happens. You have my word."

I nod. Then I take a ragged breath. "Well. I guess it's settled, then."

In an instant, Kenzo's furred fingers wrap around my own, as though closing the promise into my skin. "Come," he says, and tugs me in the direction of the forest. Though I stumble to keep up with his long, loping gait, he doesn't slow. "Time to show me what you've learned from Wren."

The clearing is hushed, the heaviness of the cloudless night pressing down on us like one of the sky gods' mighty hands. Kenzo draws me into the center, and I think he's going to say something—I've just agreed to murdering the King, after all. But just like that first time with Wren, the swing of his fist takes me entirely by surprise.

I yelp, scooting back just in time. "Wait—"

He cuts me off with a spinning kick, the whir of his foot as it passes overhead making me flinch.

"The King will not wait," he growls.

"Don't you think I *know* that? At least give me a moment to prepa—"

He interrupts me with a thrusting punch to the gut. His pointed fingers catch me right in the middle, the contact throwing me off balance. I fall over, more out of shock than anything, a sharp exhale escaping my lips as I land painfully on my tailbone.

"Wren never hit me!" I shout up at him, rubbing my spine.

Kenzo's lips pull back in a wolfish snarl. "But the King will." Still, he holds out a hand, helping me to my feet. "This time tomorrow, you'll be alone with him. And unlike us, the King will not go easy on you. He will not hold back. You have to be prepared for what that will be like. The minute he realizes what you are doing, he'll retaliate. It'll take everything you have to stay alive."

I jut my chin, glowering. "Why did you even ask me, then, if you think I don't stand a chance?"

"I don't think that. It's just that your chance is *slim*. But this is how the earth and heavens work. How they have always worked. All that is needed for anything to happen is for someone—god or mortal, demon or man—to see that slim chance, and take it."

He fiddles with the tie at his waist, pulling up the hem of his shirt to reveal a leather band slung above his hips. Fixed to the belt is a short sword. I get a glimpse of a delicately engraved jade hilt before Kenzo's fingers close around it. The metallic song of the blade as he pulls it free from the scabbard sets my teeth on edge, reminding me of that night under the theater, the moment the assassin drew his blade on Wren.

The moment so many things changed.

"All court members carry a dagger like this one," Kenzo says. He holds it out for me to examine. "Including the King."

I finger the edge of the blade. The thought of it piercing the King's skin—digging in through muscle and tendon, spilling blood—seems unreal, something out of a dream.

Stowing the dagger, Kenzo steps back. "Take it from me," he says, and splays his arms.

My first few attempts are pitiful. I comprehend now just how easy Wren was being on me. Kenzo offers no such exemptions. He bats me roughly away every time I get close and attacks back at a relentless pace. In just a few minutes I'm sweating despite the cold, my panting breaths fogging the air. I can feel bruises beginning to flower under my skin.

"Maybe you were right," he says after my latest attempt has me sprawled on the ground where he threw me—and not lightly.

I clamber to my feet, massaging the cramp in my side. "What do you mean?"

"Maybe it *is* hopeless. We should have asked one of the other girls. Any of them would do a better job than you."

"I know what you're doing," I shoot back.

He cocks his head. "Whatever do you mean?"

"Wren got me fired up, too. But at least she did it with kisses."

Something twitches across his lips. "Would that work?"

I grin, half manic with exhaustion, and he returns it, his wolfish mouth widening, until both of us break into laughter, Kenzo with his head thrown back and me doubled over, clutching my belly. The noise is jagged and wild in the wintry hush of the forest. We laugh harder than his joke warrants. Tears fill my eyes, and suddenly I'm not laughing anymore. When Kenzo sees this, he hesitates, a tender look crossing his eyes, and it's this that reminds me so strongly of Wren—of the way she looks at me right before a kiss, or right after, open and vulnerable and full of hope—that before I even realize what I'm doing I'm lurching forward.

Kenzo reacts a second too slow. For the first time, my hands make contact. I push him back, clinging onto his rough fur as he grabs my collar to prize me off. With a grimace, I butt the heel of my right hand into his neck. At the same time, I bring my knee between his legs, and as he slackens, I tug aside his robes and wrap my fingers round the hilt of the knife.

I tumble off him, laughing again now, holding the blade up to the sky. "I did it!" I shout. My voice breaks. I swipe a sleeve across my face, and though the tears don't stop, I keep laughing anyway, the knife lifted high in my shaking fist. "I—I did it."

Kenzo gives me a half smile just as humorless as my laughter. "Yes. You did." His furred hand wrapping around my own, he brings the point of the blade to rest at the soft underbelly of his neck. "But do not forget the last part. Right here, Lei. This is where you aim tomorrow." He squeezes my fingers, the engraved edges of the jade hilt digging into my skin. "Push the blade deep, and do not stop."

THIRTY-FOUR

THE EVE OF THE NEW YEAR, the palace is transformed. Decorations have been going up in all the courts. I'm kept busy as a small army of maids prepare me for the ball, but Lill manages to sneak me outside for a few minutes to see what's been going on. A tidal wave of scarlet and gold appears to have stormed through the palace. Women's Court is on fire, vibrant ribbons and streamers adorning every building. Lanterns of all shapes and sizes hang from the eaves, along with strings of copper coins, glinting as they turn in the breeze. Bowls of offerings filled with kumquats and stacks of succulent peaches and clementines sit on porches. Cracked mirrors to ward off evil spirits have been set beside every doorway, a New Year's superstition that we also followed back in Xienzo.

Lill tells me the King lent royal shamans to each court to infuse magic into some of the decorations. She points out a giant paper crane, symbolic of good fortune and longevity, that has been erected in a courtyard across the street. The bird is at least fifteen feet tall. Its garnet beak glitters in the winter sun. As we watch, it stretches its great wings, paper feathers rustling.

I lace my arm round her shoulders and smile down at her. My eyes sting. I blink quickly to keep the tears away. "Thank you, Lill," I say thickly. "For everything."

The smile she returns me is so wide and trusting I have to look away.

Over the next few hours, I, like the palace, am also transformed. My body is polished and oiled with an amberlike liquid containing flecks of gold that catch the light with every movement. Kohl rims my eyes, artfully smudged with bronze shadow; shimmering pearl-powder embellishes my cheeks. A pale paint is swept over my lips, enhancing the brightness of my irises. It's like putting on a mask, each dab of color, each stroke of a brush, and I imagine the paint as armor. My battle gear.

As they work, I visualize adding other, hidden layers onto my armor—all the reasons I am doing this.

What happened to Mama. What has happened to *other* mothers, other women and men and children of raids just like the one on my village. My love for Wren. My love for Aoki and even the other girls, and the hope that this can bring all of us freedom, along with every Paper caste slave. The executed assassins. On my second night in the palace, the woman who screamed at me a word I've been unable to forget since.

Dzarja.

It's not my own kin who I'll be betraying tonight.

And then, of course, the final reason: a night, just a few weeks ago. A night I will *never* allow to be repeated.

Once my makeup is complete, the maids arrange my hair into a plaited bun at the nape of my neck, twined through with beads and tiny yellow chrysanthemums, before dressing me in a vivid red cheongsam with long lace sleeves. It's so tight-fitting it pins my rib-cage in place.

I repress a mad laugh. Well, at least I'm dressed the part. Because what reputable assassin *doesn't* wear perfume and a slinky dress?

By the time the maids leave, night is falling. They file out slowly. I'm about to turn away when the last girl pauses in the doorway, fiddling with the hem of her dress. I go forward to help her—it must have caught on something—but as I bend down she pushes something into my palm.

"Good luck, Lei," she whispers, pewter eyes meeting mine. She bows and hurries away.

As soon as I'm alone, I open the silk-wrapped package. Lantern light catches on a thin blade, barely longer than a needle. Its lacquered bone has been made to look like a hair ornament. Carefully, I tuck it into the top of my thick braid with trembling fingers.

This is it, the last piece of my battle gear.

My weapon.

Before I leave, I go to the little shrine in the corner of my room and take my Birth-blessing pendant from where it's been hanging. I loop it around my neck. It's heavier than I remember. Just like I used to, I cup it in my palm, wondering what future it holds for me. But this time there is an additional question I've never had to ask myself before.

Will I even live to find out?

Aoki meets me outside Paper House. She's also dressed in red, as is tradition for New Year celebrations, delicate robes, as thin as moth wings. Her lips look sensual painted in a dark ruby color, and she seems so far from the nervous sixteen-year-old girl I met on that first night in the palace that I have to blink back a sudden rush of tears.

"The King won't be able to take his eyes off you," I tell her, and from her smile I can tell that for the first time, she truly believes it.

The journey to the Inner Courts flies by in a whirl of color and noise. Every street overflows with decorations. Music sifts through the air, dancers performing in twirling dresses, the bells on their anklets chiming. Children scream with laughter as they chase each other down the streets, scarily realistic origami masks of the heavenly rulers strapped across their faces. One of them dashes so close to my carriage the oryx veer quickly aside to avoid her. The little girl laughs, long hair streaming behind the angry red face of Nizri, Goddess of Chaos. She waves as she watches us go, but there's something creepy about the contrast of that light, high-pitched laugh with the furrowed leer of one of the most dangerous gods, and I shrink away from the window.

By the time we arrive at the Moon Ball my heart is beating so hard it physically shakes me. The tree-lined avenue is busy. As my palanquin waits in a long line of others, I check again that the pin is still in place. My fingers tremble so much that I almost unravel the whole fancy hairstyle my maids spent so long creating.

Outside, I join the rest of the guests as we're led toward a large round building made entirely of glass. Its domed roof sparkles with streams of tiny lights. A ring of enchanted gardens surrounds it, fireflies shimmering over the treetops. Mistress Eira told us earlier that the building is called the Floating Hall, and I see now why— because of the way it perches over a lake, held up by thin crystal columns rooted in the water, it looks like it's hovering in midair. The aquamarine glow from the lake below sends shifting ripples of color across the glass.

Inside, the hall is packed. For the New Year, all the guests are wearing red, but instead of looking celebratory it's like being swallowed by a sea of blood. Bodies press from every side. Music fills the domed space, rising over the buzz of voices.

I try to stay close to Aoki, but the wave of the crowd separates us. I end up getting shifted toward Blue and the twins.

"Beautiful dress, Lei," Zhin remarks, her sister nodding in agreement.

"Yours too," I say, distracted, barely glancing at what they're wearing. "Both of you."

Smiling, they turn away to greet someone else. As soon as their backs are turned, Blue wraps her hand round my wrist, pulling me close. Her fingers dig into my skin. "I know what you've been up to, Nine," she whispers. "You and Wren."

I wrench my arm away. "Please, Blue. Please don't tell anyone."

She laughs, her eyes wild. It takes me a few moments to realize what it is I'm seeing in them.

Triumph.

"You've already told him," I croak. The words stick in my throat. "After what happened to Mariko—"

"You don't understand at all, do you?" Blue cuts in, scowling. "It's *because* it happened to her that I told! It wasn't fair, Nine. She was cast out to heavens know what kind of life and we're still here, living in luxury, and all this time, you and Wren, *loving* each other..." Her voice spits with venom. "Being *happy*."

"He'll kill us," I say.

Something broken crosses her face, making her look strange, not quite right, like the echo of a person. "So? You don't even want this life."

Just then, someone bumps into me, knocking me off balance. By the time I look back around, Blue is gone.

I make my way into the crowd, ice unspooling in my veins. The King knows.

As if what I have to do already weren't hard enough.

Laughter and the cascading song of strings whirl round me. I shoulder my way past gossiping court members and servants carrying trays of tiny cakes nestled on crystallized sakura leaves. Overhead, strings of lights drape from the dome like scattered stars. The sapphire glow of the lake shimmers up through the glass, giant koi and sea horses swimming in its depths. The ball is a dizzying kaleidoscope, but my focus is honed, and I whip my head left and right, hunting for the King. I can't act until Kenzo's signal, but I need to keep an eye on him.

And then.

There.

Thick, pointed horns. Mahogany-brown hair. That familiar smile, all teeth. The red of the King's robes is dark, almost purple, the color of plums or old blood.

Naja's with him. Her snow-white fur sparkles with silver powder, a long-tailed sari clinging to her lean, foxlike figure. She scans the crowd as the King gazes down the length of his smooth bovine nose, talking to a couple dressed in red baju sets, surprisingly plain for the occasion, their backs to me. As if sensing me watching, the King lifts his eyes.

His grin sharpens. He leans aside, whispering something to Naja.

The white fox glides over to me, slinking sinuously through the crowd. "Hello, whore," she remarks casually.

"Hello, jealous bitch," I shoot back.

No point acting polite anymore. One way or another, I'll be out of here tonight.

I can tell my comment catches Naja off guard. She stiffens, cool eyes gleaming. "I would be offended," she purrs, composing herself, "if I actually cared what Paper trash thought."

"Well, let me try harder, then—"

She holds up a hand to silence me. "Enough games. The King has a message for you. He's kindly invited a couple of people he thought you'd be pleased to see. He wants you to know that if you try anything tonight—run away, disrupt the ball—they *will* be killed." She leans in, her voice smooth, like the gleam of stones on a riverbed, and just as hard. "Don't they look happy? Such a shame they won't be that way for long." And with a flick of her tail, she stalks off.

I frown, peering ahead through the shifting crowd. The couple glance around as the King gestures to something on the other side of the hall, and I glimpse their faces.

My heart stutters. It's some trick of the light. A waking dream. Because surely it can't be real, the two of them here, so far from where they should be, safe and hidden on the opposite side of the kingdom.

But it *is* them.

Baba. Tien.

My eyes take in their pressed clothes, the self-conscious way they're holding themselves. And worse: the way they seem distracted despite the fact that they're talking to the King, because they are looking with hopeful, eager eyes for *me*.

"You bastard," I snarl.

Because now I understand what the King's plan is. *This* was the surprise Lill was talking about yesterday. Thanks to Blue, he knows I have betrayed him. That I've been betraying him night after night, with no less than one of my fellow Paper Girls. And as with the assassins, he's going to teach everyone what it means to betray the King.

Tonight he is going to kill me.

And he has brought my family here to watch.

I'm striding forward before I know what I'm doing, my hands curling in fists, a shout readying on my lips—

Someone grabs me by the arm.

"No!" I cry as they drag me away. I struggle, but their grip is strong. They lead me out of the hall and onto a balcony. A glimpse of night-cloaked gardens, fireflies dancing over the treetops, and then I'm whirling round, my voice rising to a shout. "How dare you!"

Zelle gazes back at me, the ghost of a smile on her lips. "I just saved you from doing something exceptionally stupid, Nine," she says calmly. "A thank-you would be preferable."

I fall still. "What—what are you doing here?"

She gives a little sigh. "I'm part of the plan, aren't I? Anyway, Mistress Azami always sends a few of the Night House girls to events like this. Good for trade." At my confused look, she says, "Oh. Kenzo didn't tell you."

I gape at her. "You're working for them, too?"

"Well," she replies with a sniff, "I prefer to think of it as working *with* them. But yes. I am."

Her words from the other week come back to me: *Love will only make it harder.*

"That's why you were like that in our last lesson," I say slowly, finally understanding. "You knew about Wren and me. And you knew I'd get hurt when Wren left the palace, or she—" I cut off. With a lick of my lips, I go on, "Was that why you covered for me when you found me in Mistress Azami's rooms?"

Zelle shakes her head. "I didn't know then. But I could tell you were telling the truth about looking for your mother, and I felt sorry for you. You have a good heart, Lei." Her voice hardens. "But you wear your emotions on your sleeve. You've got to keep yourself together, at least for a few more hours."

"He was talking to my father!" I burst out, splaying my arms. "And Tien! Blue told him about Wren and me, and he's going to use me as an example tonight. Punish me in front of everyone." My breath hitches. "He wants my family to see me die."

Zelle grips my shoulders. "We won't let that happen, I promise. Anyway, you'll get to him first, right?" She winks, shifting back, but her voice is serious and I look away.

"I wish Wren were here," I murmur.

"We all do."

"Do you think the King had her mother murdered to get her out of the palace because he suspects the Hannos?"

"I'm not sure about that," Zelle says with a frown. "The King is definitely suspicious of them—but he's suspicious of everyone right now after what happened at the theater. I don't think he'd attack some of his most prominent supporters without being certain they're working against him. It's different from acting out against the Cat Clan, for example. They've always been enemies. He'll want to maintain a good relationship with the Hannos. I think it's more likely that what happened to Wren's mother was a bad stroke of luck on our part." Gaze fixed on me, she asks, softer, "So. Are you ready?"

I swallow. "Yes."

"You have to be confident, Nine. Do it cleanly and quietly. This way, we take control from within, with the least amount of bloodshed."

"And if I fail? If the King discovers the Hannos' plans?"

"There will be another war."

War. It's a word in our kingdom that carries power, even though none of us have lived through one. The memories have been handed down to us, heavy handfuls of violence and slaughter, and the decades of rebuilding afterward, which, directed by the Demon King, inscribed prejudice into the landscape as deeply as if it were grooves of water in bedrock.

A group of female demons stroll by in a cloud of perfume and giggles. Once they've passed, Zelle moves to my side, elbows hooked over the top of the railing as she leans against it, gazing over the gardens. Something about the expression on her face makes me sure of who she's thinking about.

"Your lover," I ask. "Did the King…?"

She jerks her chin. "Not himself. But…on his orders. There was a rift in the court a few years ago after the way the King handled an uprising in Noei. The soldiers who spoke out against him were executed. Mistress Azami told Kenzo what happened—yes, she's working with us, too," she adds at my sideways glance. "He'd been looking to recruit one of us for a while. Courtesans have access to the court's most powerful members. With a glass of plum wine and the slip of a dress they can be easily persuaded to give their secrets away."

"It seems everyone's had someone they love taken from them by the King," I say bitterly.

Zelle's fingers lift to the base of her neck. "Well, not after tonight."

The cerise ruqun she's wearing is slung low, collar wide and hanging off her shoulders to expose the shadow of her cleavage and the gold choker sitting above it. The choker is emblazoned with the character *ye*, marking her as one of the palace's concubines. Her fist tightens around it, as though she wants nothing more than to rip it off and fling it out over the treetops. Then, pushing back from the railing, she shoots me a crooked smile.

"We're all behind you, Nine." Her fingers brush my arm before she glides back into the party.

I wait a bit more on the balcony, taking in the cool night air. I'm just about to leave when the tread of approaching hooves makes me freeze.

"My, my. Can this really be the same shopkeeper's daughter I met in Xienzo six months ago?"

Lights hanging overhead catch on the scar that snakes down the left side of General Yu's face, that familiar, scar-wrenched grin. Our paths haven't crossed, even after all this time in the palace, but I've felt him with me every step of the way; in the memory of his threat to Baba and Tien, everything he represents as the beginning of all this, the demon who tore me from my home.

But General Yu is right. I *have* changed.

When he reaches for my cheek, I step back before he can touch me.

"General," I say smoothly. I flash him a sweet smile, though my tone is acid. "You should be careful. I doubt the King would take kindly to seeing you touching one of his Paper Girls." My smile sharpens. "Actually, *I* don't take kindly to it, either. Touch me again, and I will cut your fingers off."

Biting back a grim laugh at the look on his face, I head back into the ball.

My heart beats quickly as I locate the King, this time keeping my distance as I wait for Kenzo's cue. The informal style of the Moon Ball is one of the reasons why they chose tonight for the assassination—chaos provides cover. But it's also the only time in the whole year when the royal shamans stop working. At the turn of the New Year, for one hour only, their protective enchantment on the palace lifts as they perform the customary rites of giving thanks to the heavens. This magic-free hour is our only chance at escape.

As the minutes tick by, the King keeps Baba and Tien close to his side. A few times I catch a glimpse of their faces, and the happiness that lights them—the *hope*—aches deep in my gut. It's all I can do not to run across the hall and throw my arms around them. To distract myself from my nerves, I plot ways in which to get them alone.

So when a chance actually opens up, it takes me a while to realize it's more than just a fanciful daydream.

The King has stepped aside to discuss something with a group of intimidating-looking demons I take to be clan lords. Naja has joined General Ndeze to attend to some important business outside the hall. Before she goes, she leaves a couple of guards with my father and Tien, but I don't pay them any attention as I push my way across.

I stride right up to Baba and throw my arms around him. He bursts into tears at the same moment I do. Our bodies shudder against each other. Then Tien is joining us, her bony arms clutching me so tightly I'm amazed they don't snap.

"What happened to politeness and decorum?" I mumble through tears.

She squeezes me tighter. "Oh, be quiet, you little nuisance."

It's almost like being back in Xienzo. I'm wrapped in everything I've been missing so badly, the smell and feel and *love* of my lost home, and none of us needs to say anything because everything we could say is contained here, within the press of our bodies.

Then the guards wrestle us apart.

"No!" I yell, thrashing.

Around us, the guests are stopping to look. The guards don't hold my father and Tien once we're separated, just reaching out arms to keep them back, but the gorilla-form guard who's got me restrains me a bit too tightly, his huge furred hands easily spanning my shoulder blades.

"We were instructed to keep you apart," he tells me, pulling me away.

"Wait!" I cry. Baba and Tien look horrified, and I want just one more moment with them—even half a minute, a few seconds, just enough to tell them everything will be all right. But the guard is twice my size, and gods know how many times stronger, and soon I'm on the far side of the hall.

When he lets me go, I jerk away, puffing aside a loose lock of hair.

"I will wait with you," he says, the leathery skin of his face impassive.

Glowering, I turn away. There's no point in trying to get to Baba and Tien again, but I still look into the crowd, standing on my toes to try to catch another glimpse. Instead, I spot the sloping gait of Kenzo stalking toward me.

In an instant, everything stills.

Kenzo gives the guard a glance, but keeps his expression neutral as he strides past me, just close enough for me to feel the brush of his fur—and to slip something into my hand. Keeping it low so the guard won't see, I open my fingers. Inside: an origami bird.

A wren.

It's time.

With a deep inhale, I tuck the paper bird into my sleeve. But as I'm about to move, the music stops. Raised voices are suddenly loud in the quiet, and there is the clink of glasses being set down, murmurs of surprise, the trailing ends of laughter.

"Heavenly Master and honorable court members," announces an invisible voice, magically magnified. "Our esteemed guests. Please make your way to the stage for a special performance by this year's Paper Girls."

Fingers pinch my shoulders. "Come on, girl," snaps Madam Himura's hoarse voice. "The others are already dressed."

My stomach drops. The dance Madam Chu's been teaching us to perform tonight. I'd forgotten all about it.

Ignoring my objections, Madam Himura drags me across the hall and out onto the balcony, broader here at the back of the building, where a curved, weblike cage arcs overhead. A stage is set up beneath it, polished floor shining.

She pushes me into a curtained-off area where the other girls are waiting. "Get her into her costume," she orders the maids.

I try to object, but they crowd me, peeling my cheongsam off. They re-dress me in the multilayered gold robes of our dance costume. One of the maids picks at my hairstyle and the braid loosens. I clutch at my hair, swirling round just in time to see the blade fall. Light catches on its edge. Then it's hidden by the skirts of the maids as they usher me toward the other girls.

Panic unfurls, fast and hot.

"Please!" I say, batting them off me. "I can't do the dance! I need to go!"

Holding up the hem of her long skirt, Mistress Eira hurries to my side. "Lei? What's wrong?"

From behind the curtain, the musicians start playing. The murmuring of the crowd mutes as a melody rises.

Mistress Eira smiles. "There's no need to be nervous. Your dancing has improved so much over the past few months. You should be proud."

I crane my head to look past her, hardly hearing what she's saying. The blade glitters on the crystal floor, picked out by the aquamarine glow of the lake. "I—I dropped something," I say.

"There'll be plenty of time to get it after the performance."

"It can't wait. Mistress, please..."

And finally, she follows my gaze.

There's a long pause. She asks, sharp, "Is that yours?"

"Yes," I whisper.

In one quick movement, Mistress Eira goes over and snatches

the blade from the floor, swiftly hiding it in the folds of her robes. Her mouth is set so tightly her lips have almost disappeared. "I am going to dispose of this, and you are going to go out onto the stage and perform as though this never happened. Do you understand me, Lei-zhi?"

That first night I arrived at the palace, Mistress Eira's use of the Paper Girls' honorific with my name was given with pride. Now it stings.

Know your place, she is telling me. *Remember who it is you are.*

I flex my fingers. Because I know exactly who I am, and it is *not* the perfect Paper Girl she wants me to be.

My gaze hardens. "Did you even *try* to send my letters?" I ask icily.

She just blinks.

"I thought as much." Then I turn my back on her, taking my place in the line of girls.

A moment later, the music swirls into a new chord. Our cue. One by one, we pad onto the stage, our arms raised high, the trailing sleeves of our costumes hiding our faces, and one of us hiding something more—a sinking heart, a pang in her chest, and the feeling that everything she has been fighting for has been lost.

THIRTY-FIVE

MADAM CHU EXPLAINED THAT THE DANCE we're performing tonight is another symbolism of purification for the new year, though it seems to me more a way for the Demon King to show us off to his guests.

Over the course of the dance, each layer of our costumes is shed. Every robe we remove has to be cast off in the careful way we were taught, the fabric rippling through the air, a shining arc of gold in the lantern glow. Beneath the last layer is a thin slip that barely hides our modesty. As the best dancer of our group, Wren was chosen to have center stage during this final act to offer her last layer to the King, but in her absence Chenna was given the role. She moves gracefully across the stage, dark skin luminous under the lights. The mesmerized faces of the crowd follow her. But as she flutes out her wrist, angling her throw just right so her discarded robe settles in the lap of the King, it isn't her he's watching. It's me.

Me his eyes are fixed upon, bright and dangerous.

Me he coils his lips back at in a smile that shows every one of his teeth.

Hatred pulses inside me, a dark heartbeat. I might not have a weapon anymore, but I still have my fists. During our midnight lessons, Wren's shown me just how effective a properly angled kick to the groin can be. It won't be enough to take down the King. But it'll give me enough time to find the blade he always carries and turn it against him.

We leave the stage to the applause of the crowd. As soon as we're behind the curtain, I hurry past the swarm of maids, ignoring the curious looks of the other girls as I head back into the ball, still just wearing the tiny gold slip. At least it'll be easier to run in than that ridiculous cheongsam.

I haven't gone far when the sound of my name makes me look round.

Aoki's followed me. "What's wrong?" she asks, her breath catching. "Why haven't you changed back into your dress?" Her face is flushed from dancing, a gloss to her vivid emerald eyes. She looks radiant. Queenly.

I gather her into my arms. "I love you, Aoki," I whisper into her ear.

She jerks back, scanning my face. "Lei? What's going on?"

"I just want to wish the King a happy new year."

"But—"

I kiss her forehead. While she's still blinking in surprise, I hurry away before she spots the tears welling in my eyes.

How painful it is to say good-bye to someone who has no idea you are leaving.

The King is still on the balcony, servants fussing around him. I slow as I approach, trying to arrange my features into a calmer expression than what I'm feeling, but a jolt shoots down my spine as he sees me coming. His stare hardens. He waves the servants away. Behind him, Naja's lip curls. General Ndeze is nearby but too busy entertaining a giggling group of courtesans to take any notice. A flash of long, glossy hair, a revealing ruqun—Zelle is a member of his doting audience. As she swings her head round midlaugh, she catches my gaze and gives an almost imperceptible nod.

"Lei-zhi," the King greets me. Sparkling lights catch on his gilded horns.

I bow. "My King." I force my voice steady, though it sounds strange to me, too hard and low. "I hope you enjoyed the performance, even if you have seen us undressed before you so many times already."

Something stills in him. His smile sharpens. "Perhaps even more so," he answers coolly. "It's especially pleasurable to know that none of those watching have had the same privilege. Because, of course," he adds, leaning in, "your lover isn't here tonight, is she?"

Though my pulse skips, I furrow my brow, feigning confusion. "Forgive me, my King, but I don't know what you mean. My only lover is right here." And even though it sickens me to do it, I inch closer. My fingers quiver as I rest them against his chest.

Behind him, Naja starts forward. But she stops at the King's raised hand.

"I haven't been honest with you the nights we've been together, my King," I go on quickly, keeping my eyes on his. "I've—I've been scared. I admit that I didn't want this life at first. But after our first proper night together, my emotions have changed. My...desires." One hand still on his chest, I bring the other to my neck and trail it down the front of my slip, lingering at my navel.

The King regards me in silence.

"Please," I say. "May we go somewhere private? These feelings are overpowering me. I need to explore them with you, my King. Alone."

His expression remains unmoved for a few long, torturous seconds. Finally a lazy grin stretches across his face. "I knew you'd come around, Lei-zhi." Straightening, he circles his fingers round my arm, a fraction too tight. "We'll go to the gardens. They will be private enough."

He turns us toward the staircase winding down from the balcony. A few of his servants and guards hurry forward, but he waves them away.

Naja strides over, ears pricked. "My King—"

"Leave us," he orders.

As we start down the steps, I look around and find the white fox watching us with her cool silver eyes. Even when we're out of sight, I shiver, sensing her gaze still on me, like the hidden eyes of the moon.

The King leads me deep into the enchanted gardens. They're wilder, more wooded than the typical Han style, knotted banyan and katsura trees forming a leafy ceiling overhead. Light from the receding hall speckles the ground. A stone path cuts through the undergrowth, the shadows all around spotted with color: the pink leaves of hibiscus flowers, cobalt-blue orchids, yellow frangipani. We follow the path to a pond crowded with water lilies. Sweet fragrance honeys the air. Each lily sparkles, a tiny star nestled at the center of its petals, and I sense the warm brush of magic like a kiss in the air.

The King looks at me. "What do you think?"

"It's beautiful," I say.

He hasn't let go of me all this time. As we draw up to the water's edge, he pulls me close, one hand cupping my chin. "It is, isn't it?" he murmurs. He smiles, and it seems like he's about to kiss me.

Then his lips twist into a sneer.

"A beautiful lie."

Panic snaps through me.

I try to shift back, but his grip tethers me to the spot. "What—what do you mean?"

The words have barely left my mouth when his hands clamp around my neck. With a roar, he lifts me into the air, holding me out over the water. A group of nearby birds scatter into the night sky—and with them, my composure. With horrible choking sounds, I claw at his hand, gasp for air.

"That is what *you* are, Lei-zhi," he snarls. "What did you think? That you could fool me? I am the *King!*"

I dig my fingernails into his hide-wrapped wrist, but it's thicker than human skin and I can't get purchase. Distantly, I register music drifting from the party. The scattering of notes and lilting strings is half lost under the pounding in my ears, the King's heavy breathing.

The corded muscles in his neck tense as he squeezes my neck tighter. "What is it with you women, always spreading your legs for lesser lovers? Does it make you feel wanted? Loved? Never mind. The reason does not interest me. Only the punishment."

"You...*bastard*," I choke out.

He roars, slamming my head into the trunk of a nearby tree. The pain is instant, a crack so fierce it splits my vision.

When the King's face appears again, spit clings to his lips, a vein throbbing in his forehead. "I brought your father and that old lynx-woman here to watch you die. You know that, yes? But a public execution would have to be at the hands of someone else." A grin, all teeth. "This is better. Here, I can take my time. I can break every bone in your body, until the pain is so consuming you won't even know your own name."

He swings me round, smashing me into the tree a second time.

The force makes me bite down on my tongue. Blood fills my mouth. Tears stream down my cheeks. But the pain helps sharpen my focus. Reminds me why I'm here.

Takes my hate and turns it into a blade.

I spit a wad of bloody saliva into his face. "You can kill me," I hiss, forcing each word past his tightening grip, "but it won't stop them. They are coming for you."

It's fleeting, but I see it spark across his eyes then—fear. And I comprehend now that it's not a new emotion to him. It's just been in hiding. All it needed was something to call it forth, to trip his mind into panic.

He stills. "You know." A pause, then his voice rises. "Who? Tell me! Tell me who dares plot against me!"

Blood trickles down my forehead. I blink it away. "Go ahead. Kill me. I'll never tell you."

With a deafening bellow, he rears down and plunges me headfirst into the pond.

Choking—

Spluttering—

So cold it's burning—

Water plugs my mouth and throat, clamps around me like a fist. I kick out, but the King holds me down. Lights burst in front of my eyes. There's rushing in my ears and my stomach is churning and my heart is pounding, pounding, *pounding*—

He pulls me from the pool, and I hang from his arm, retching and coughing, teeth chattering in the iced winter air.

"Who?" he demands again. "Is it the Cat Clan? The Hannos? What are they planning?"

I sneer at him. "You'll be dead before you know."

This time I'm expecting it, but that doesn't make it easier. Water rushes up my nose as the King pushes my head down. Something slimy brushes my face as it swims past. He holds me under for longer, until blackness creeps across my brain, a tempting dizziness that tries to spin me to sleep. Part of me is ready to let it take me. But the other part—the stronger part—rallies desperately against it.

This time when the King drags me out, he casts me to the ground. I skid along the grass. The earth is hard, frosted over. My fingers scrabble at the soil, trying to find purchase. Just as I push myself up, he kicks me in my middle.

I collapse, mouth wide in a silent scream. Something cracked; I felt the snap. A rib.

One more stomp and he'll crush my heart.

Rearing over me, the King pins my arms overhead. "I'll ask one more time, Lei-zhi." He speaks slowly, almost calm, though his eyes are wild with fury and something else, that mad look I first saw in him the night of the koyo party and worse each time since, like he's unraveling from within. His breaths steam in the frozen air. "If you still refuse to answer, I will go back to the ball and drag your father and lynx-woman here and kill them in front of you. Will *that* be enough incentive for you to speak?"

I growl, jerking underneath him, but he presses his full weight on me and it's useless, *I'm* useless, I can't win. How could I ever have thought I could win, a Paper Girl against her King? And then—

Shouting. The crunch and snap of plants underfoot.

Someone's coming.

The King looks up.

Just in time for the knife that is whirring through the air to embed itself hilt-deep into his right eye.

THIRTY-SIX

ZELLE CHARGES INTO THE CLEARING AS the King pitches off me, blood streaming down his face.

"Finish it!" she screams.

Behind her—Naja.

The white fox is astonishingly fast. She catches up to Zelle in two bounds, her sari loosened at the front and flaring behind her, and in one swift movement she reaches out, clasping Zelle in her long, clawlike fingernails, and snaps her neck in two.

The sound is awful, a clean, high crunch.

I stagger to my feet. Naja looks up, Zelle discarded in front of her. There are noises in the distance—clashing weapons, screams, something like the deep churn of fire—and I see flames reaching into the sky, lighting the night with streaks of orange and vermilion.

The Floating Hall is on fire. Which means the palace must be under attack.

The knowledge hits me hard.

We failed.

Then I lock eyes with Naja and everything else is whipped from my mind, leaving only the burn of anger, hatred, darkest, deepest pain, and Zelle's last words to me, so simple, so terrible.

Finish it.

I lurch toward the King. The grass is wet with his blood and my feet skid, but the fall helps me, propels me forward. He sees me coming a second too late. His face contorts. Hands shaking, he reaches for the hilt of the knife embedded in his eye—but I get there first. Letting out a cry, I wrench it out of his blood-drenched socket.

And drive it into his throat.

Surprise. That's his first expression.

The second is fury.

He jerks under me, but I cling to the hilt, fingers slick with the blood gushing around it. I throw my whole body forward, using my weight to embed the knife deeper. Together we fall. I'm flung forward, sprawled over his chest, but I keep pushing the blade into his neck. The sounds he's making are horrible—gurgling, babylike. He thrashes. Lashes out. Even though they're sloppy, there is still power in his blows, and the pain of my broken rib flares with each one. But I grit my teeth against it and hang on.

One of the King's eyes is blue and piercing. The other is a vivid red mess.

I snarl like a wild thing and jerk the knife side to side. It barely moves, wedged into bone and cartilage, but I force it, feeling things breaking, the snap of living tissue. Over the King's choked noises, there is an awful keening sound, high-pitched and raw, and I think at first it's Naja, but of course it's not.

It's me.

Then I remember—Naja.

My fight with the King could have only lasted seconds. The fox female is upon me just as I turn to look for her, curved claws breaking skin, drawing blood as they dig into my shoulders. She tosses me to the ground. Kicks me again and again. The blows come too fast for me to escape. I can't even catch my breath, can barely see. The pain is agonizing, unbearable, the hottest heat and fiercest white, a widening sky opening to swallow me whole. I'm going to die, and the knowledge of it, the searing certainty, is the worst feeling I've ever known.

"Get off her, you bitch!"

Wren's voice rings out, as bright as a dream.

I don't see her until she tears Naja off me, and even then it takes me a moment to recognize her. She's wearing battle clothes, leather armor over a midnight-blue tunic and trousers, and her eyes blaze with the white of a Xia warrior, the same as that night under the theater. She draws two swords from the sheaths crossed at her back. Some unfelt wind moves the hair around her face, making her seem eerie, like some dark goddess, and even I get an instinctive lurch of awe.

Naja falters, just for a moment. Then she shakes herself. Draws tall. "I told the King it was you," she snarls, and lunges.

They fight viciously. Instinct overpowering form. Naja's all animal, the wildness of her demon form taking over. Gone is the composed court guard standing always at the King's side. The cool, still gaze. She doesn't even have a weapon because her body *is* the weapon. Hunched over in a crouchlike stance, she fights with spins and jabs, slashes and bites.

They move so quickly it's hard to follow. The clearing is a whir of limbs and blood sprays, the thud of bone on flesh.

"He defended you," Naja spits. Her mouth is foaming, blood turning it pink where it runs from a gash in her cheek. She blocks a parry from Wren and swipes a leg in a low sweep, which Wren jumps to avoid. "Even though you betrayed him by sleeping with that little golden-eyed slut, he said he couldn't punish you yet because the Hannos have done so much for him. He had his suspicions, but he still hoped. That's why he sent you home when he heard of your mother's death. He was showing your clan the loyalty *he* deserved."

Wren's knuckles are white where they grip her swords. "Loyalty?" she says with a disbelieving laugh. She lurches forward, arms arc overhead as she leaps, bringing down the two blades together as one.

Naja dances back just in time.

"He doesn't know the meaning of the word," Wren spits.

"And your people do?"

"They thought they did. They learned the hard way that it's a rare thing in this world."

"Ironic, isn't it? How now *they're* the ones teaching others that same truth. Tell me, how does it feel to betray the demon who has been unfailingly dedicated to your worthless keeda clan all these years?"

Wren ducks a blow. Naja recovers quickly, and this time her elbow catches Wren in the side, causing her to stumble.

"Bitch," Wren pants.

Naja laughs. "Manners, Paper whore." But I catch her barely veiled awed look again as she appraises Wren's unnatural appearance.

In the time it takes for the fox to hesitate, Wren strikes out. One of her swords catches Naja's shoulder. Blood spurts in an arc, staining her snow-white fur. Hissing, she lashes out, her heel cracking across Wren's jaw, making her head snap round and drawing a spurt of red, the crunch of bone.

The two of them drop back into defensive stances, chests heaving. Wren swipes a sleeve across her mouth.

Then Naja looks to me. Her eyes widen. "Watch out!" she yells.

Wren pivots to look, lowering her swords a fraction—and opening up space for Naja to attack.

But I saw what the fox was planning a second before she acts.

As Naja kicks off her back feet, I lunge to intercept. We collide with a crunch. Pain screams through me as my broken rib is crushed even more, the gashes in my shoulders ripping open. I throw a punch, but it's weak and she overpowers me in a second. Tosses me aside. She swings an arm back, clawlike fingers aiming for my throat—

"Wren! Lei!"

Naja falters as Kenzo bounds into view.

He moves fast on his muscled wolf haunches. He's gripping a bamboo stick sideways in both hands. Its ends drip with blood.

"Go!" he roars. "There's no time!"

Naja's face is wild. "Keeda-lover!" she spits.

She starts upon him in a whir of kicks and claw swipes. Kenzo holds her off with his staff, his powerful wolf haunches digging into the earth as she pushes him back.

"Go!" he shouts at us again.

Wren hesitates, her eyes slipping back to their normal brown. "But—"

"Now!"

She stows her swords and grabs my hand. As she pulls me away, I look back over my shoulder and catch one last glimpse of the King's body sprawled upon the bloody grass. He looks strangely small. His limbs are thrown out at his sides, as if he'd fallen over from too much sake. At his neck, the knife juts, sticking up where I left it, and a ragged exhale escapes my lips.

It's over. It is done.

I did it.

The King is dead.

Wren leads me in the direction of the Floating Hall, the growls and thuds of Naja and Kenzo's fight fading behind us. As the trees start to thin, the hall comes into full view. It's utterly consumed by flames, a glowing dome of gold. Heat blazes off it. The noise is a living thing, full with electric crackling. From under it come the sounds of battle; metallic clash and hoof thunder, screams and yelling. Flecks of burning ash drift through the air, like the opposite of snow.

This is it, then. Master Takeo's prediction. A night of smoke and flames, the palace destroyed from the inside out by a girl with fire in her veins.

"What happened?" I call out to Wren as we run.

"Our cover was blown," she shouts back. Her hair whips behind her. "Someone must have given us away. You got to the King just in time." She squeezes my hand. "You did it, Lei. You killed him."

I almost trip. "But now the court knows who was involved! Everything you were working for, the care you all took to keep it secret—"

"We'll worry about that later."

"And why are you even *here?* You shouldn't have come back, Wren. You shouldn't have risked it."

"Of course I came back. I had to make sure you were safe."

When we reach the edge of the gardens, the ground shifts from loamy earth to a hard stone path. We're right by the hall now. Underneath, the lake glows from the blaze above. Its surface fissures with ripples—the fish are jumping, stirred by the heat. There are bodies in the water, and I cast a terrified eye over them, praying that none of them belong to Baba or Tien.

My stomach jolts. Kenzo promised to keep them safe. But how can he protect them when he's fighting with Naja?

"My father," I choke. "Tien—"

"They're being looked after," Wren promises.

Slowing, she leads us around to the east side of the lake. I'm finally able to breathe somewhat normally, though now that the shock is wearing off, pain replaces it. My wounds from the King's and Naja's attacks burn and throb. They're hurting more with every step, but I grind my teeth together, determined not to show it.

"How are we getting away?" I ask.

Wren looks round, firelight sliding across her face. "The same way I got here so quickly. Wings."

With a tug on my arm, she pulls me off the path and into the undergrowth. We swipe away the tangled branches. The ground is uneven, clumped with roots. I focus on my steps, trying not to trip.

I hear the demon before I see him: the deep rumble of giant lungs. Wren calls out, and a croaky voice answers.

"Did you find her?"

"Yes," she replies as we emerge into a dappled grove. "Merrin—meet Lei."

Wind tugs the furled petals of flowers from the magnolia trees lining the clearing, a whirling flurry of pink and white. Some of the leaves catch on the dusky pewter feathers of the huge bird demon rising to greet us. He is an owl-form, far larger than any demon I have seen, with an intelligent face—beaked owl features molded with human—and keen orange eyes. Like Madam Himura's, his arms are long and humanoid, rippling feathers wound over them and fluting out at the edges in the weird hybrid wings that all bird-forms share. He has his elbows cocked, his wings only extending halfway in the small grove, but still their span is impressive. Each feather is tipped with black. Power thrums from him, and as we approach he stands a little taller, the pierce of his eyes making me falter.

"Merrin?" I say.

He gives me a mock bow. "At your service, lovely. But I'm afraid we have to hurry the introductions." His head tilts, listening. "Someone's coming, and I doubt it's a welcoming committee."

He dips a wing to the ground. Wren leads me up along it and onto his back. I try to move lightly; his feathers are soft, downy-light.

Merrin laughs, a rattling sound at the back of his throat. "No need to be so gentle, sweetheart. I've caught mice for dinner heavier than you."

Behind me, Wren tucks her legs alongside mine and leans forward, gripping the back of Merrin's feathered neck. "Ready?"

Before I can answer, we jerk back.

There are shouts, thudding footsteps.

A blaze of arrows cut through the air.

"Hold on!" Wren yells, pinning me down as Merrin kicks off the ground so powerfully the shudder in his muscles ripples through my own.

We lift into the air, the forest rushing past. A second volley of arrows fly our way and Merrin careens sharply to the side to avoid them. An arrow tip grazes my cheek. He banks. One wingtip brushes the treetops. He rolls a tight corner, then beats hard to gain height. In just a few seconds we are soaring high, the clouds just above our heads, a dark, silver-glazed belly.

I've always wanted to fly, to know what it's like to dance on the wind currents.

The reality is nothing like I imagined. Merrin cuts fast through the air, the pounding of his winged arms rocking Wren and me, and I cling to his feathers, convinced I'm about to slide off his back at any second.

Far below, the palace is a blaze of lights and fire. Relief washes over me, as fierce and radiant as a sunburst.

We're free.

Then Wren cries out, "To the right!"

My head whips round and I spot them—a group of Moon caste bird demons. There must be more than twenty. I make out the shape of hawk, crow, vulture, eagle. Of all the demon forms, bird castes are the most foreign-looking, with their unsettling blend of feathers and beaks with humanoid form, and to see so many now, winged arms spread wide, racks fear through me.

They're approaching fast, not weighed down by passengers. Though they aren't as large as Merrin, everything about these birds screams predator. Glowing yellow eyes. Beaked, hook-tipped maws. Armor is strapped to their bodies, their taloned feet fitted with blades.

Merrin lets out a hiss. "Not these assholes."

"The Tsume!" Wren shouts in my ear. "The King's elite bird warriors."

"And of course," Merrin says, "they keep badgering me to join. How many times must an owl say no?" There's a pause. "Sorry about this, girls," he says, then tucks in his wings.

We flip upside down—

And plummet through the air.

I scream as we hurtle toward the earth, wind lashing my face, my gut lurching. Tears stream down my frozen skin. The drop is so fast that one of my hands slips from where I'm clutching at Merrin's feathers, and the wind tugs at me, trying to yank me away. With a twist of her arm, Wren grabs me. She digs her heels into Merrin's sides, holding us down. The caws of the Tsume follow us.

Ahead, the rooftops of the palace are getting closer, but Merrin doesn't slow.

"We'll crash!" I yell.

Neither Wren nor Merrin answers. I squeeze my eyelids shut; the last thing I see is the curved eaves of a temple roof hurtling toward us.

Merrin pulls out of the dive without a second to spare.

The movement is so sudden it almost jerks us from his back. Pain flares through my rib cage and shoulders. Wren and I grunt, our arms almost wrenched from their sockets, but we manage to cling on.

Thuds, shrieks, the sound of wood shattering behind us. Some of the Tsume didn't pull back in time.

I risk a glance round and my pulse stutters.

Some of them *did*.

They speed toward us. The hawk at the head of the group lets out an ear-splitting caw. He gains on us in seconds and slashes out with a metal-tipped talon, the blade catching Merrin's flank. He cries, dropping suddenly, but then he rights himself and takes a sharp turn, weaving between the rooftops.

The hawk follows. Smaller and lighter than Merrin and the rest of the birds, he gains on us quickly again, this time drawing up beside us. Garnet eyes glitter from under a hooded bronze battle helmet that wraps his upper face and covers the top of his short beak-nose, tapering to a sharp hook.

"Shame on you, brother," he says, his voice a high-pitched croak. "Letting Papers ride you."

Merrin shoots a quick look over his shoulder as Wren reaches back to draw one of her swords. "At least I'm not wearing that ridiculous hat."

The hawk hisses. With a flap of his wings, he swerves towards us, lashing out with his metal-hooked beak. Wren is ready for him. Still clinging on to Merrin's feathers with one hand, she arcs her other arm toward him, blade flashing. The sword catches the hawk across his helmet with a metallic crash. He squawks in surprise, faltering, just as we take a sharp turn.

There's a sickening crunch. I look round to see the hawk tumbling down the side of the tall temple pillar we managed to avoid.

Merrin flies between the rooftops, the palace a blur of shapes and colors. The perimeter wall rears up ahead. We fly straight for it. Again, Merrin turns at the last second. The bird demons following us hit the black rock at full speed, the sound of their necks snapping loud as a whip crack. Twisting round to look, I see the huge crow pull up just in time—though judging by the way he lands sprawling on the top of the wall, clutching a winged arm across his torso, he damaged one of his shoulders.

He lets out a furious shriek as he watches us fly on.

Below, the landscape changes to the shadowed stretch of bamboo forest. Darkness falls as the lights of the palace recede. Merrin keeps close to the treetops, but as time passes and no more of the Tsume come for us, he spreads his wings wide and takes us up into the clouds.

"Oh, dear," he says when there's nothing around us but white mist and eerie silence. "They'll only want me even *more* after that."

I let out a shaky laugh. My skin feels raw, lashed by the wind. The air is wet up here in the clouds. Beads of water cling to my body, making me suddenly aware that I'm still just in my thin dancing slip, though the gold fabric is soaked through with red: my own blood, and the King's.

"Is this a good time to wish you a happy birthday?" Wren asks, and I laugh again. She lowers her lips close to my ear. "You have it with you, right?" she asks, serious this time.

I know immediately what she's referring to. "Yes," I reply.

She plants a kiss on my cheek. Her breath is hot on my frozen skin. "You can open it when we land."

I sense the pull of my necklace, suddenly heavy where it's hanging, exposed, over my collarbones and swinging with Merrin's wing beats. All these years waiting for this day, waiting to discover the word—the future, the *world*—my Birth-blessing pendant contains for me. But now, flying through a sky that tastes like ash and endings, I'm not sure I want to know anymore.

We were meant to escape the palace quietly. Instead, the Hannos and their alliances have been exposed.

There is no doubt about it. A war is coming.

THIRTY-SEVEN

ERRIN FLIES ON UNTIL WE ARE far from the palace. The night is starless, snow clouds thick above. The air tastes like ice. Below: a carpet of darkness. There are no settlements here, or at least any that I can see. Wren tells me we're to the northeast of the palace, in the foothills of the mountains bordering Han and Rain—the infamous Kono Pass, impassable even by flight because of the turbulent currents and jagged peaks. We'll stay at a hideout tonight before leaving for the Hannos' fort in Ang-Khen tomorrow.

Or at least, that was the plan.

"We'll send a message to my father as soon as we can," Wren says as Merrin begins to lose altitude. "Ask him what we should do. I doubt our home is safe anymore, or any of our holdings. The ones the court knows about, anyway."

"Could you ask him about my father and Tien, too?"

"Of course. I'll make it one of his priorities. I'm sure they are safe, Lei."

My stomach is hollow. "The court know Kenzo is working with your father now. That he's been plotting against the King. He won't be able to take over the council."

Wren's voice is hard. "Not if he killed Naja."

I picture the fox female's wild eyes, her relentless energy. Somehow I can't imagine her allowing herself to lose. At the same time, I can't imagine Kenzo losing, either. The warmth of his fur as he carried me from the King's chambers comes back to me, the safe feel of his muscled arms and his smell, deep and almost sweet, like wind-stirred grass.

He'd better win. Not just for us, but for what Naja did to Zelle.

"She killed her." The words choke in my mouth and I have to clear my throat before I continue, "Naja. She killed Zelle."

"I know," Wren replies quietly. "I saw her body."

"She was kind to me," I murmur, my eyes blurring. "When I was scared, that first time before going to the King. And when I snuck into Mistress Azami's room. And at the end. The King was about to kill me. She saved me. But I couldn't save her."

I push my face into Merrin's feathered neck, tears sliding down my frozen cheeks.

The screeches of animal calls rise as we approach the forest. Merrin flies low. It's difficult to make out much in the blackness, but soon he shifts course, wings canted back to catch the air, and after a few wide, slow circles he brings us down through the treetops into a clearing, where we land with surprising lightness. He lets out a caw. As if in answer, lights spark into flame in the near distance. Through the matted vegetation, they illuminate the hulking silhouette of an abandoned temple, half of it seeming to be carved out of the very mountain itself. There's the glimmer of water from a lake stretching out to one side.

Wren and I climb down from Merrin's back. I stagger sideways as my feet hit land. It still feels like I'm listing from side to side, and every part of my body aches from clinging so tightly to his feathers. More of me is hurting than not, but I hold myself upright, forcing a grim smile when Wren tries to help me.

"I'm all right," I say. "Honestly."

With a throaty purr, Merrin shakes himself, stretching his arms wide. The feathers wrapping them flutter before half of them fold back down, lying flat over his arms so his wings are only half the size they were before.

"I take it back, lovelies. You're definitely heavier than mice. Palace food has spoiled you. I hope you brought some with you?" he adds hopefully.

"Actually," Wren says, "we should have. I'm not sure how long we'll have to hide out here."

"I think you're forgetting we're an elite pack of warriors," Merrin replies. "Hunting won't be a problem."

"*I'm* not a warrior," I say.

"Sweet girl," he replies, head swiveling in my direction, "you killed the King. You're the most *warrior* of us all." His beaked mouth lifts in a grin. "Besides, are you sure you aren't part demon? I guess you haven't had time to look in a mirror, what with all the assassinating and mortal danger and whatnot, but whatever those fools at the palace put on your eyes earlier has smudged." He flaps an arm. "You're looking a little...panda-form."

Before I can thank him for his kind assessment, the sound of footsteps makes us look round. Three figures emerge from the shadows of the foliage. Their lanterns cast an amber glow on their faces. One is a human boy, Paper caste, with a narrow face, a worried slant to his soot-black eyes. The other two are wiry Moon caste leopard demons—siblings even, judging from their appearance, and not much older than Wren and me. They approach in a feline prowl, tails flicking behind them. Their spotted heads are similar, with short, black-lined snouts and round ears beaded with piercings.

"Wren! Merrin!" shouts the female leopard, breaking into a loping run. She squeezes Wren before looping her arms round Merrin's neck. "You're late! We were so worried."

"I hope your lateness isn't a sign that things didn't go smoothly?" asks her brother.

Wren's gaze meets his. "I'm afraid it is." She pulls me forward. "But our main goal has been achieved, and we have Lei to thank for that."

The leopard-boy looks at me, his eyes wide. "The King is dead?"

I take a shaky inhale before replying, the answer still unimaginable even to me, with his blood smeared all over my skin.

"Yes."

The first flakes of snow are beginning to fall as I step out under the temple's eaves. The moss-trimmed lake spreads before me, dark and glossy in the starless night. I set the lantern down and take a seat on the wide stone stairs, clutching the fur cloak the leopard-girl, Willow, lent me. The temple looks like it's been abandoned for centuries. Weeds and wildflowers grow in thick sprouts from cracks in the rock. Birds have made their nests in the minarets and peaked rooftop. A great banyan tree towers from one of the temple's walls, roots as large as the rooms it has grown through, its vines dangling in netted curtains and littering the ground with leaves the size of Merrin's hands.

I pull my necklace over my head and sharply inhale at the fresh pain it flares in my shoulders. The gold shell of my pendant is still unbroken, perfectly seamless. Carefully, I cup it in my palm, looking for a way in, when its casing cracks neatly open in two. And, years after it was made, its secret is finally offered to me.

For a moment, I stare in silence. Then a laugh escapes my lips. Tears blur my vision. Because the word that floats inside, a single character in brushstrokes of softest black, is so perfect it's a wonder I never guessed it.

Flight.

I look a moment longer. Then I snap the pendant shut and run back into the temple, shouting Wren's name over and over, half laughing, half crying, heart bursting with the awe and sun-bright surety of it. Because that is what Wren is to me—my wings. And with her love, she's taught me how to use my own. To fight against what oppresses me. To lift and launch and soar into the air, just as we did tonight, just as we will have to do every day if we are to make the kingdom safe, just as we will continue doing for the rest of our lives, flying, dancing through the brilliant skies, reaching new heights together, always together.

A war might be coming.

But we have the wings to fight it.

IN THE FLAME AND SHADOW OF the burning night garden, the white fox crouches beside her King. The motionless form of the wolf is sprawled on the bloody earth behind her.

She doesn't care about him. She doesn't care that the two keeda girls have escaped. Let them run. Let them believe they have won.

She knows better.

Careful to avoid his wounds, she touches her hand to the King's wrist—and feels it. A pulse. Faint, but unmistakable.

He lives.

The fox caresses her King's face. "I knew a mere human girl couldn't kill you," she whispers. Then she stands and calls for one of the waiting soldiers to fetch a shaman.

AUTHOR'S NOTE

THE STORY WITHIN THESE PAGES IS a work of fiction, but also a work of love. The world of Ikhara has been heavily inspired by growing up in Malaysia, a country with a dense mix of cultures, and also by my identity as a person of mixed ethnicity. As such, it's a bit of a hybrid—like me. I feel extremely lucky to come from a multicultural home. It has shaped my influences and perspectives—and will forever continue to do so.

The conception of *Girls of Paper and Fire* also comes from a personal, deep yearning for more diverse novels, particularly in YA. I believe it's important for everyone, but especially young people, to see themselves in the stories they consume—to feel acceptance and kinship. To be inspired for their *own* stories, real and imagined. Even magical worlds have their roots in our own. I would love to see more books reflecting the rich variety of our individual realities.

The story of the Paper Girls is one that is, sadly, representative of many women's experiences. My own included. While I realize these are hard discussions, especially for teens, it is of vital importance we have them. Books can be safe places to explore difficult topics. While we cannot shelter young people from being exposed to sexual violence, whether through lived experience or indirectly, we *can* give them a way to safely engage with and reflect upon these issues. I hope *Girls* provides such a space.

For any readers who have experienced sexual assault: I am so, so sorry for what you have been through. My wish is that, like me, you were able to find some form of kinship and empowerment in Lei's journey. Despite the darkness of the story, there are many positive messages that I wanted to convey to readers going through their own traumas: supportive relationships and friendships. The ability to find hope even in the hardest times. The power of female strength. The knowledge that you can go through horrible things and not just survive, but *live*.

This is a story close to my heart. I hope you enjoyed it.

If you are the victim of sexual, emotional, or physical abuse, please consider speaking to a trusted adult, or contacting one of the following resources if you need to seek help anonymously.

RAINN (Rape, Abuse & Incest National Network)
Call: I-800-656-HOPE
Chat: online.rainn.org
Info: rainn.org

Love Is Respect—National Dating Abuse Hotline for Teens
Call: I-866-331-9474
Info and chat: LoveIsRespect.org
Text: LoveIs to 22522

National Domestic Violence/Abuse Hotline
Call: I-800-799-SAFE
Info and chat: thehotline.org

ACKNOWLEDGMENTS

THIS BOOK AND I HAVE BEEN through a lot. If I do the math, it's something like three relationships, five homes (across two countries), one change of agent, one change of career, eleven rounds of editing, two disastrous haircuts, what must be fifty million cups of tea, and countless emotional crises, quite a few of which the book itself caused. But despite our difficult journey together—or perhaps, because of it—*Girls* has become a sort of friend to me. Seeing it now so beautifully made up and having its own life out in the world independent of me is a proud, proud moment.

I owe a hundred *thank yous* to everyone who helped get us to this point:

To my yoga teacher, Matt Gluck, whose class I was in when the first line of *Girls* came to me and led me into the story. Also for inspiring me to set out on my own yoga teaching career! My classes have become the perfect antidote to lonely writing days.

To author friends who read early versions of *Girls* and gave much-needed feedback and encouragement: Kendra Leighton, Katy Moran, Emma Pass, Kerry Drewery, Sangu Mandanna, and Lana Popovic. Your enthusiasm for *Girls* kept me going. Thank you also to Brian Geffen for early notes that helped shape the world of Ikhara into what it is now.

To the Mad Hatters—Sarwat Chadda, James Noble, Alex Bell, Louie Stowell, Jane Hardstaff, Rohan Gavin, and Ali Starr—for celebrating the highs and commiserating about the lows with me, and providing the best kind of response to both: cocktails and laughter.

Our London nights are some of my favorites. Sarwat, thank you especially for your early insight and never-ending encouragement.

James, you are my rock. Thank you for always believing in me and knowing how to pick me up. I'm endlessly grateful to have you in my life.

To Taylor Haggerty, for being *Girls'* tireless champion and always being ready with insight and positivity whenever I'm lacking in either. When I was querying this time around, a friend told me to choose the agent I feel like I could write the best books under, and so that's what I did. I look forward to many more books together. And to Holly Root, thank you for playing matchmaker!

To my amazing Jimmy team—Jenny Bak, Sasha Henriques, Sabrina Benun, Erinn McGrath, Julie Guacci, Aubrey Poole, James Patterson—for taking a chance on *Girls* and working so hard to make that chance count. Jenny, you're a dream to work with. Thank you for your patience, understanding, impeccable editorial insight, endless bounds of enthusiasm, and always knowing the right thing to do for our book. You made *Girls* into what it is today. I feel like the luckiest author in the world to call you my editor.

To so many of my amazing friends who have spent hours listening to me talk about imaginary worlds—Alex, Peter, Claudia, Tom North and Tom Latimer, Luke, Amber, Polly, Rich Galbraith and Rich Lyus, and to many more I haven't named—I blame sequel brain. Thank you so much for your support and inspiration throughout this process.

To my parents, for being the perfect blend of crazy and caring. Dad: I have no doubt that I wouldn't have become a writer were it not for your bedtime stories and quiet, unwavering support. Mum: you brought me up to be both knowledgeable and proud of my Chinese-Malaysian heritage. This book is a testimony to that.

To Callum, for championing me always, anywhere, and through anything. You still know me better than anyone. You also frustrate me more than anyone, but I love you even so.

To Fab, for giving me a new home and a life filled with so much happiness I can hardly stop smiling. You've made writing a lot more difficult because of that, but I forgive you. It's worth it a million times over.

Pour la vie.

Finally, to everyone who picks up a copy of *Girls*—it means a lot to me that you've given your time to this little book. It's not perfect, but I did my best to write it with sensitivity, passion, honesty, and care, and I hope you can feel that through the words. Thank you for reading.

THE GIRLS OF PAPER AND FIRE
DID THE IMPOSSIBLE.

THEY *ESCAPED*.

But out in the unforgiving wild, hunted like prey,
Lei and Wren learn that the most terrifying prisons have
no walls. To be truly free, they must resurrect
their impossible plan to destroy the king who refuses to die.
And this time, they won't be alone.

A STORM IS COMING.

Read on for a sneak peek of

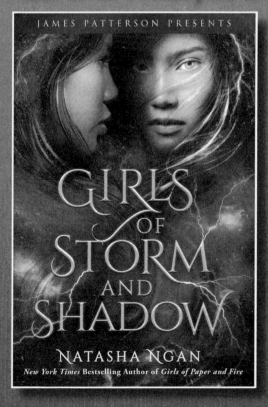

DEEP IN THE DARK HEART OF the royal palace, the King was hiding.

He'd been there for weeks, eschewing all visitors save for the shamans who worked on his injuries, and his two closest confidants who nursed wounds both of the body and the ego. He would never have admitted this was what he was doing, of course. And if anyone were to dare even *suggest* he was struggling, he'd swiftly have them executed. None of it was painful. None of it was too much for the great Demon King of Ikhara to handle.

Yet, like most lies people tell themselves, it came apart in the shadow and quiet of the night. The King, however much he expressed otherwise, *was* shaken. His wounds had penetrated deeper than flesh and bone. They had burrowed, insidiously, down each vein and cell and pore, until he could feel the fear echoing alongside every beat of his heart. And this fear took a shape. A name.

Lei-zhi.

He refused to speak it out loud, but his body betrayed him. It whispered her name to him in the rhythm of his pulse. Showed him her face when he was asleep: blood-splattered porcelain skin;

furled lips; wild eyes, those bright golden eyes honed with so much rage it pierced right to his soul, right down to places within him he thought he'd long since stamped out of life.

When it got too much—when her name and face would mock him so that he felt he couldn't breathe and the walls of his rooms were closing in—the King called for a girl.

None of *those* girls, of course. Those girls he had yet to properly deal with.

Though he would.

But another girl. A pretty Steel-caste lynx-form from the Night Houses, with softly furred hips, perhaps, or a young Paper slave fresh from a raid. He didn't care. They would bring him a girl, and he would ruin her, just to prove he could. To feel once again that he was all-powerful. One human girl would not get the better of him—even if the constant sting and ache of his scars reminded him how close she had come.

Each day, royal shamans came to heal the injuries to the King's throat and face. Naja had done well. The shamans had arrived after the girl's attack just in time to save much of his vocal cords, though it hurt to speak and his voice was hoarser than before: rough, a guttural grunt. His right eye, however, was beyond repair. The socket had been a mess of severed nerves and pulpy flesh, too damaged even to fit a glass eye. In the weeks since the attack, it had gotten a little less horrifying under the magic of the shamans. While it would be many months more until the rest of his face was back to normal, even shamans couldn't bring back life from the dead, and his missing right eye would forever be a reminder of that night.

The King recalled one of his generals, also a bull-form, who'd once come to him about using the royal shamans to remove an ugly slash across half his face. "Battle scars are a badge of honor, General

Yu," he'd told the soldier. "They are marks of power. To rid oneself of them would be to show weakness. Wear your scars with pride."

Wear your scars with pride.

What godsdamned crap. He always knew it, of course, but some part of him had believed in the sentiment once.

Not anymore. The King knew now exactly what scars were: reminders of your own failings. And so were those who dealt them.

The girl was still out there. But the King had faith. Naja had not failed him yet. She would find her, just as she promised she would, along with the traitor Ketai Hanno's daughter, and she would bring both of them back to the palace for him.

Because this was something else the King had learned about scars—they were a brilliant furnace of hate. And if rage like this could give a weak human girl the power to attack *him*... well. They would see what it could do to a Demon King with a ferocious hunger for revenge.

ONE

FROM THE NIGHT WE ESCAPE THE palace, what was at first a light scattering of flakes grows into a snowstorm.

It takes less than twenty-four hours for the first layer to settle, and just over a day until it builds into a thick blanket of glittering white. One more day and the snow has covered everything, a carpet of muffling powder that stings your eyes in the daylight and casts eerie shapes at night from the shadows. After two weeks, it's as though we've lived in this frosted world forever.

I trudge through the deep drifts beyond the temple, my boots breaking the pack with heavy crunches. The cold has numbed my entire body. I flex my stiff fingertips in my gloves. Melting shucks of ice keep sluicing over the tops of my borrowed leather boots no matter how tightly I lace them. But at least my hands and feet have some sort of protection from the weather. My face battles directly with the elements—and this is a war it is losing.

Wind stings my exposed cheeks as I peer through the whirling flakes, trying to see where the leopard demons have gone. We've been trekking through the mountains for almost an hour now. The steep forested hills are packed with snow, each leaf-stripped tree encased in ice. The afternoon is eerily silent: just rustling snow crystals and boot-crunch and my own heavy breathing.

"How you doing back there, little Princess?"

I sigh. Not *quite* so silent.

"My *name*," I shout back, "as I've told you a million times, Bo, is *Lei*."

No sooner are the words out of my mouth, than they are whipped away by the wind. Ice flakes dance around my nose, land cold, wet kisses on my raw cheeks.

"Princess?"

Bo's voice sounds again, this time clearer. The siblings must be just a few yards ahead.

My breath billows around me as I hurry to catch up. Their tall forms materialize through the snow-blurred wind, as long-limbed and willowy as the trunks of the trees around them, and almost human in appearance. As I get closer, their demon details reveal themselves: snubbed leopard ears; athletic haunches; long tails flicking from side to side, sheathed in the same beige-black spotted fur that covers the rest of their bodies. Green eyes glint from dark-rimmed lids. Their round faces are so similar it's hard to tell them apart at a glance.

One of the two sets of eyes is soft and kind. Nitta.

The other pair—her brother Bo's—dances with amusement.

Nitta rushes to me with a relieved cry, brushing the wet straggles of hair back from my brow. "Thank Samsi! We were scared for a moment we'd lost you. I'm sorry, Lei, we're moving too fast. We were trying to go slowly, but—"

"Any slower, and we'd be traveling back in time," Bo quips. "You Papers," he adds with an impatient cluck, scratching the underside of his chin as he regards me down the length of his flat, feline nose.

Nitta shoots him a frown. "Bo."

"What? Anybody born without built-in weather protection is missing out, I say."

"Maybe we should turn back." Snowflakes dust Nitta's spotted fur, and she brushes a hand over her brow absentmindedly, looking worried. "We haven't found anything yet, and Lei looks frozen half to death. Merrin was right. This was a bad idea."

Bo rests a hand on his bony hip. "You're going to trust Feathers now? Come on, Sis, what does that bird-brain know?"

"*You'll* defy Merrin's orders just to annoy him," Nitta retorts.

"Why else do you think I agreed to let Lei come along on our little hunting trip?" The leopard-boy grins. "No offense, little one," he tells me, "but it wasn't exactly for your expert tracking skills."

"A lot of good *your* tracking skills are doing us," I point out. "Found anything yet, hmm?"

While Bo cocks his head in amusement, I straighten, shoving my shoulders back. I'm still barely half the height of the leopard siblings, but it makes me feel stronger all the same. "I asked you to let me come today because I'm sick of hiding away in that temple. It's been over two weeks now. If I have to spend another day listening to Hiro's chanting and the rest of you sparring or talking war tactics while refusing to let me do *anything*, my brain will burst." I reshuffle my scarf, bunch my gloved hands into fists. "Now, can we please go catch something good to eat? I'm sick of roasted taro for every meal."

Nitta hesitates, but Bo tosses up his hands. "You know what? Princess is right. If I have to eat one more piece of taro I'm going to *become* a taro." With a dramatic huff, he throws himself onto his back. "Look," he croaks in mock-horror, blinking up at us from a distinctly Bo-shaped hole in the snow. "It's already starting. I am one with the taro. And it feels...taro-ble." He flounces back up, his heavy coat covered in ice, and beams his wide, snaggle-toothed smile. "Get it? *Taro-ble?*"

"Oh, little bro," Nitta sighs. "Your jokes are just so *taro-iffic.*"

All three of us laugh at this, the sound breaking the eerie quiet of the forest, until a loud *crack* to our left cuts us off. We whip around, my heart lurching into my throat, only to see a pack of snow that had been balanced on a banyan's crooked branches crash to the floor with a heavy *flumpf.*

Nitta and Bo straighten from the defensive stances they'd instinctively adopted.

Bo snorts, releasing hold of the knife at his belt. "Scared of snow, big sis? Afraid it'll turn your pretty hair wet and scraggly?"

Nitta's eyes cut to him. "Don't think I didn't see you react exactly the same way." But there's a touch of something cautious as she turns around, lifting her nose to test the air. Her ears twitch, listening. Then she starts forward. "Come on," she says. "Something's definitely out there. And Lei, stay close this time."

We continue into the swirling white. It's all I can do to keep up with the siblings, their lithe Moon caste bodies slinking easily between columns of ice-wreathed trees. While Nitta and Bo cut the layers of snow cleanly, stepping lightly with neat lifts of their lean leopard haunches, I slog clumsily through the thick drifts. The snowpack is as deep as my knees. Hidden tree roots tangle with my boots. Each drag of frigid air cuts my throat, but despite the chill, sweat beads inside my coat and under the fur scarf wrapped around my neck and chin.

The demons don't let up their pace. We stop only to take quick swigs of the water flask at Nitta's waist or to check for signs of the animal she and Bo are tracking, the siblings dipping their heads together to discuss its markings in low voices.

After one hour of focused trekking, Bo breaks the silence. "We're closing in," he announces, half-hidden by the sheets of driving white where he's walking a couple of feet ahead.

Nitta cants her nose higher. "You're right. I've got something too. Sharp, musky . . . what do you think it could be?"

"Your delightful natural scent?" her brother suggests.

Nitta rolls her eyes. "See these?" she asks, pointing to a nearby tree.

Bo and I move closer. Two deep grooves are etched into its bark, just below my head height. They look freshly made: only a light dusting of snow covers them.

Bo traces his fingers along the marks. "Could be a large mountain goat."

"Wait," I say, backing up to take in the tree's low, twisting branches. "This is a mango tree. A *mango* tree," I repeat, awed. "Does it usually snow here? We can't be that high up in the mountains if there are banyans and fruit trees."

Neither of them shares my surprise.

"The Sickness has caused all sorts of weird climate changes," Nitta says with a shrug, then turns back to her brother, forehead wrinkled. "That would be one big goat. I'm thinking more along the lines of yak."

"Ugh, I hope not. Yak meat is gross."

"Do you want taro for dinner again?"

"Better than yak butt."

Nitta peers ahead into the glittering drifts, her rounded ears twitching. Like her brother, her ears are peppered with studs and hoops in a variety of tarnished silvers and gold, and dim wintry light winks off them as she looks left and right. "This way," she says, already moving.

Bo winks at me. "Ready to play your part in the hunt, Princess?"

"What part is that?"

"Bait," he replies with a grin.

I glower as he stalks off. It takes a few moments for a retort to come to me. I stomp through the snow, ready to deliver it, when movement to the left snags my attention.

I freeze. My heart beats loud in the hush of the ice-limned forest.

The still, empty forest.

Under my scarf, gooseflesh plucks at my skin. "Are you—are you sure there's only *one* animal around?" I call ahead.

Nitta and Bo both spin around, silencing me with identical green-eyed glares.

"We need to be quiet—" Nitta starts.

There's the sound of snow crunching ahead. She whips back around, lowering into a defensive stance. Bo points into the swirls. Smoothly, he loosens his knife while Nitta swings her bow from her shoulder. She holds it with her left hand, her right plucking an arrow from the quiver strapped to her back. In one swift movement, she fits the feather-tailed arrow in place and draws her right arm back to extend the bowstring, resting the tip of the arrow on her left knuckles. Lean muscles under her cotton shirt shift as she aims into the iced air, but Nitta doesn't loose her arrow.

Not yet.

Ears pricked, face focused, she slinks forward between the trees. Bo crouches slightly as he moves after her, his fingers clamped around his throwing knife.

I fumble at my waist for my own knife with clumsy glove-clad hands. It's a short, plain blade; one of the others' spares. Gripping it tightly, I follow the siblings, doing my best to keep to the path they create with their precise steps. My skin prickles with unease. A few times I think I catch movement—not ahead where Nitta and Bo are advancing up the wintry slope, but at the corners of my vision. The shadowy shape of something large and…not human. But when I look, there's nothing there. Only thick swirls of glittering flakes. Wind-chill and billowing breaths and deep, blizzard-muffled silence.

Nitta and Bo move faster now. Though I do my best to follow them, the gap between us begins to widen. Ahead, Nitta turns abruptly, leading us up a steep incline, the glimmer of a frozen waterfall to our right. My breath comes out in thick clouds as I try to keep up—and then my toes catch on a rocky outcrop beneath the drifts.

With a yelp, I fall face-first into the snow. Clumps of ice latch to my skin; melt trickles down the sides of my scarf. Grimacing, I push myself to my knees, shaking the snow from my face and hair, when I sense movement behind me.

A voice—light as a feather, yet deep, deep as gods' bones and earthshakes—uncurls on the wind.

I've found you.

Something cold trickles down my spine that has nothing to do with the snow. In an instant, *his* face comes to my mind.

Grooved horns, etched with gold, tips as sharp as knife-points.

A slim, handsome face, bovine features melded immaculately with human form.

A smug, satisfied smile.

And those eyes—irises such a clean, clear, arctic blue I can recall the feel of them piercing me even now. Over two weeks on from that night, the very moment I drove a blade deep into his throat and cut the life free from him.

The King.

I've found you.

Crouched in the snow, I swirl around with my knife brandished in trembling fingers, heart thumping against my ribcage. But the forest is empty. The trees stand tall, silent sentinels armored in frost.

Blood rushes in my ears. I look once more in all directions, shivers still rippling up my arms and the back of my neck from the voice. It had felt so real. So *close.*

When I get to my feet to carry on after Nitta and Bo, there's no sign of them. I'm alone.

Then my breath hitches.

Because maybe I'm not. Though I couldn't have heard the King's words—of course I couldn't, only those in the Heavenly Kingdom can hear them now—the movement I've been sensing and the feeling that someone's watching us could be because we *are* being followed. Not by the ghost of the dead King, but by one of his soldiers or elite guards.

That's why Wren and the others haven't let me out of the temple all this time. We know it's only a matter of time until they find us, if they haven't done so already. It's been more than two weeks since the attack on the palace the night of the Moon Ball. Plenty of time for them to have tracked us down, even to our remote location here in the northern mountains. Plenty of time to wait outside the temple, where we've hidden ourselves with protective magic. To wait until we leave to our next location, or until *I* get stupid and reckless enough to disobey my orders to stay hidden.

Exactly as I've done today.

An alarm screeches in my head, at the same moment more

movement—real, this time, paired with panting breaths and the crunch of breaking snow—comes from higher up the slope.

"Lei!" Nitta's yell cuts through the blizzard, pitched in panic. "Run!"

Just as a hulking shape leaps across my path and loosens a bone-shattering roar.

Complete the story in

GIRLS OF STORM AND SHADOW

ABOUT THE AUTHOR

NATASHA NGAN is a writer and yoga teacher. She grew up between Malaysia, where the Chinese side of her family is from, and the UK. This multicultural upbringing continues to influence her writing, and she is passionate about bringing diverse stories to teens. Natasha studied geography at the University of Cambridge before working as a social media consultant and fashion blogger. She recently moved to Paris, where she likes to imagine she drifts stylishly from brasserie to brasserie, notepad in one hand, wineglass in the other. In reality, she spends most of her time getting lost on the metro and confusing locals with her French. Her novel *Girls of Paper and Fire* was a *New York Times* bestseller.

JIMMY Patterson Books for Young Adult Readers

James Patterson Presents
Stalking Jack the Ripper by Kerri Maniscalco
Hunting Price Dracula by Kerri Maniscalco
Escaping from Houdini by Kerri Maniscalco
Capturing the Devil by Kerri Maniscalco
Gunslinger Girl by Lyndsay Ely
Twelve Steps to Normal by Farrah Penn
Campfire by Shawn Sarles
When We Were Lost by Kevin Wignall
Swipe Right for Murder by Derek Milman
Once & Future by Amy Rose Capetta and Cori McCarthy
Sword in the Stars by Amy Rose Capetta and Cori McCarthy
Girls of Paper and Fire by Natasha Ngan
Girls of Storm and Shadow by Natasha Ngan

The Maximum Ride Series by James Patterson
The Angel Experiment
School's Out—Forever
Saving the World and Other Extreme Sports
The Final Warning
MAX
FANG
ANGEL
Nevermore
Maximum Ride Forever

The Confessions Series by James Patterson
Confessions of a Murder Suspect
Confessions: The Private School Murders
Confessions: The Paris Mysteries
Confessions: The Murder of an Angel

The Witch & Wizard Series by James Patterson
Witch & Wizard
The Gift
The Fire
The Kiss
The Lost

For exclusives, trailers, and other information, visit jimmypatterson.org.